Born to a Glaswegian father and a Geordie mother, Alison Brodie left home at eighteen to live in Athens as an artist before moving to India. On her return to Britain, she was talentscouted by a London modelling agency, soon appearing on magazine covers and television commercials throughout Europe. She was adopted by a Scottish regiment as their mascot. Alison now lives in Shawnee, Kansas, with racoons up her chimney and chipmunks in the yard.

Praise for Alison Brodie's first novel, *Face to Face*:

'Classic bathtime reading . . . very well done' *Minx*
'Wildly funny leading lady' *Scottish Daily Mail*
'Fun reading for urban Sassenach lassies' *Ms London*
'Clever and funny first novel, told by someone who obviously knows their subject very well' *Wigan Evening Post*

Also by Alison Brodie

Face to Face

Sweet Talk

Alison Brodie

CORONET BOOKS
Hodder & Stoughton

Copyright © 2000 Alison Cutts

The right of Alison Cutts to be identified as the Author of the Work
has been asserted by her in accordance with the Copyright,
Designs and Patents Act 1988.

First published in Great Britain in paperback in 2000
by Hodder and Stoughton
A division of Hodder Headline

A Coronet Paperback

10 9 8 7 6 5 4 3 2 1

All rights reserved. No part of this publication may be reproduced,
stored in a retrieval system, or transmitted, in any form or by any
means without the prior written permission of the publisher, nor
be otherwise circulated in any form of binding or cover other than
that in which it is published and without a similar condition
being imposed on the subsequent purchaser.

All characters in this publication are fictitious
and any resemblance to real persons, living or dead,
is purely coincidental.

A CIP catalogue record for this title
is available from the British Library

ISBN 0 340 71830 7

Typeset by Hewer Text Ltd, Edinburgh
Printed and bound in Great Britain by Brodard & Taupin

Hodder and Stoughton
A division of Hodder Headline
338 Euston Road
London NW1 3BH

To David and William

I am indebted to my editor, Kirsty Fowkes. For her intelligence, patience and guidance I would like to express my deepest appreciation.

To Georgina Moore, my publicist, and all at Hodder.

To Dinah Wiener, my agent, as always.

A big hug for Peter Oakes at Dillons, Guildford, England, for his enthusiasm and support.

In America, I would like to thank Debby Perry, Eric James Dahl and Teresa 'Te' Holmes.

As always, I want to give 'BJC' a long, lingering kiss.

Prologue

Castlemaine House, Corwyn, Welsh borders

Distractedly, Beatrix passed the piccalilli to the Reverend Beardsley and carried on eating, her thoughts firmly focused on the man to her left: John Chadwick, village butcher and lifelong friend. Marriage to you would be so convenient, she thought. You would save on petrol and I would no longer be labelled a spinster.

With John's attention taken by Grandmother, she was able to study him, noting the greasy strands of flaxen hair over a balding forehead, the pale humourless eyes. Although the spring sunshine was bright as it slanted into the room, it held little warmth; yet there were beads of perspiration on his upper lip.

'Beatrix, dear, where are your manners?' Her grandmother flapped a hand at the plate of cold meats. 'Do give Mr Chadwick some tongue.'

Daphne snorted. She was now carrying the empty soup bowls to the door, her face crimson with suppressed laughter. What is it this time? Beatrix thought irritably, picking up the plate. Life with Daphne was a minefield of sexual innuendos. At the thought of this one, she shuddered.

Blithely unaware of this, Grandmother continued to smile at John. 'I'm sure if we ask Beatrix nicely she will volunteer to help, won't you, dear?'

'Pardon?'

'In the shop. He's having such a wretched time with the staff.' The old lady turned back to John as if the matter were settled. 'Beatrix is such a sensible girl, you know. I was not at all surprised when the WI voted her Treasurer. An excellent choice.'

Gritting her teeth, Beatrix stared down at her plate. *Sensible.* She hated the word.

'Hear, hear, Mrs Bayley,' the Reverend Beardsley piped up, agreeing with Grandmother, as always. 'Such a *sensible* girl.'

London

Lara peered drunkenly down the dimly lit alley that they were about to enter. 'Jeez,' Kelsey exclaimed, coming to stand beside her. 'This is like southside Chicago. Are you sure this is the right place?'

Lara hiccuped. 'Absolutely.' Standing under the street-light, she held the serviette up to her eyes. '35, Abbey Road, NW10,' she read. 'And this is Abbey Road.' She paused and frowned suspiciously at the back of Clarissa's head. Earlier they had stuffed her into an abandoned supermarket trolley, giggling uproariously. Now she lay motionless. Lara jerked the handle, startling her friend awake. 'This is your hen night,' she berated. 'You can't just go to sleep!' They had started out with twelve girls but one by one they had gone home, complaining that they had work in the morning. Wimps! Now they were down to three – and it was only midnight!

At No. 35, they heaved Clarissa out of the trolley and stood her upright. 'I'm going to miss you two,' she said in a maudlin voice. 'And I'm going to miss London and the gallery. And Timothy.' She flung her arm wide, a finger clipping Lara's nose. 'Oh God,' she wailed. 'I'm so, so sorry.'

'It's OK.'

But Clarissa insisted on pawing her in drunken melancholy. 'I don't know why you don't go and work for him. He would love you.'

'Work!' Lara muttered derisively, kicking a crumpled beer can off the pavement. 'No way.'

Kelsey considered her. 'I think you'd look cute. At least you'd have some place to wear all those power suits you keep buying.'

Of course! Lara swayed back on her heels, trying to keep her friend in focus. An art gallery would be the perfect accessory. 'I'll do it!' Satisfied with this decision, she turned, saw the number 35 on the basement wall and lurched down the steps. Groping blindly for a handrail, she felt her knees buckle beneath her, and, with the clattering of stilettos, landed in a heap at the bottom.

As the serviette fluttered to the ground, Kelsey caught it and glanced at the address. 'Abbey Road, *NW6!*' Her voice rose to a shout. 'Can't you read? For Christ's sake, Lara, you're *hopeless!*'

Manor Farm, Harnet, Dorset

'This is the first I've heard of it!' Jack Havers stared down at his eldest son.

'But I told you last week,' Jamie insisted, pushing the mop of brown hair out of his eyes. 'Football practice has been changed to Saturday afternoons.'

'So, what about the barber's appointment?'

Jamie shrugged.

'Well, you still need your hair cut. We all do.' Jack sighed. 'I'm just going to have to use the electric clippers.'

Sam looked up from the kitchen table, a yellow crayon in his chubby hand. 'I don't mind,' he said eagerly.

'No, I know you don't.' Jack chuckled. As a typical five-year-old, Sam much preferred the shaved 'Action Man' look. But still, Jack was annoyed with himself. He prided himself on his efficiency in taking care of his little family, writing down party dates, activities and school outings, yet he couldn't remember anything about football practice being changed.

He glanced down at his son's crayoning. 'What's that you're doing?'

'I'm drawing God.'

'But, sweetheart, no one knows what God looks like.'

'They will in a minute.'

'Right.' Grinning, Jack took out the mirror and shaver and headed for the door. Being a single parent was hard work but it was worth every second. Outside, he hooked the mirror on the nail in the farmhouse wall and began to run the clippers back over his scalp.

Sam appeared beside him, shielding his eyes from the sun. 'Daddy, can you push us on the ropeswing afterwards?'

'I'm sorry, soldier, I haven't got time today. I've got to drive Jamie to his football and then take Nero over to *Tankards.*' He saw the big blue eyes cloud with disappointment and felt a stab of guilt. He was so busy putting food on the table that he hardly had time to have fun with them anymore. Once again, the Colonel's words echoed in his brain. 'You're a great father, Jack. We all know that. But, whether you like it or not, those boys are going to need a *mother.*'

Friday Morning

Beatrix

Her little potting shed. It stood in the bright April sunshine, the old felt roof steaming damply in the heat, the timbers worn and buckled.

Inside, the smell of winter lingered in the chilly air, the rafters festooned with last year's cobwebs, now limp and dusty. Humming 'Edelweiss', she put on her gardening gloves, selected a trowel, a spade and her favourite secateurs and carried them outside to load in the wheelbarrow. On impulse she stopped and closed her eyes to the sun, savouring the warmth on her face. This was the first dry day of the year, a day for mulching the rose beds and dead-heading the daffodils; and, knowing the work that needed to be done, she roused herself briskly, took the handles of the wheelbarrow and started along the path.

She was content, she decided, utterly content. For lunch she would have cheese on crackers whilst listening to *The*

Archers. At five o'clock there would be *Gardener's World,* after which there would be plenty of time for a scrub-up before John Chadwick arrived to take her to the barn dance. Yes, this was going to be a perfect day. Humming softly, she let her gaze wander over the sweep of green lawn, the herbaceous borders bright with spring flowers. This was her garden, her creation.

Ahead stood Castlemaine House, its slate-grey roof peppered with lichen, its white-painted woodwork smart against the grey stone walls. Although her grandmother, Mrs Constance Bailey, owned the house and grounds, it was she, Beatrix, who took full responsibility for them, acting as both housekeeper and gardener. Daphne, their weekly cleaner, disapproved of this arrangement, though, insisting that Mrs Bailey was too miserly to pay for full-time staff, which would prompt Beatrix, once again, to explain that her grandmother simply didn't want strangers around the place. At this, Daphne would change tack: 'All right, but you tell me why someone *that* rich does all those competitions, eh? Because she wants something for nothing, that's why.'

Beatrix considered this now. Her grandmother was not miserly, she was simply competitive. It was a hobby . . . no, it was more than that; it was an obsession. Mrs Bayley had an obsession to win.

Smiling ruefully, Beatrix looked towards the French

windows on the corner terrace, knowing that the old woman would be inside sitting in a patch of sunshine at the study table, surrounded as usual by cereal boxes, magazine clippings and a pile of *Competitor's Journals* whilst busily filling out a free-prize-draw. And she was often successful, greeting each prize with equal triumph, be it an egg cup or a year's supply of Lapsang Souchong. Or another T-shirt. Beatrix sighed in mild exasperation. Although her grandmother detested lager, she had, nevertheless, won countless lager promotions: T-shirts, baseball caps and an American football. There again, she had suffered from fungal infections and yet, only last month, she had won a bumper pack of Mycil foot towels. No, Grandmother was not miserly – merely eccentric.

At the rose bushes, Beatrix stopped, lowered the wheelbarrow and parted the branches to check for green fly. At the same moment the French window opened and her grandmother appeared waving vigorously. 'Beatrix,' she shouted. 'I've won! I've won!'

'Coming.' Beatrix took off her gardening gloves, threw them into the barrow and headed for the house. What would it be this time? she wondered, watching the thin, white-haired figure disappear inside. Well, the old lady would be in a good mood today – unlike that grim afternoon last September.

She thought about it now, remembering how her

grandmother had arrived at the Corwyn Produce Fête expecting, as always, to win first prize for her giant marrow but the judges that year thought otherwise and declared Edith Dobbs to be the winner. Edith Dobbs – Grandmother's sworn enemy! From that moment, the rivalry between the two old ladies had accelerated out of all proportion. Grandmother could neither forgive nor forget, and her plans for revenge were well underway; with hand-picked marrow seeds planted in rotted manure and deliveries of plant food arriving daily. It was only the third of May but the battle had begun.

At the French windows, Beatrix slipped out of her Wellingtons and went in. As usual there was the pungent smell of Lapsang Souchong and when she looked she saw a teapot and two cups laid out on a tray on the table.

'Look what I've won,' her grandmother declared, triumphantly holding a large white T-shirt up against her chest. Across it were printed the words I'VE PULLED. 'What do you think it means?'

'What was the promotion?'

'Beer.'

'It's obvious then. Must mean *pulling* a pint of beer. It's a term used in pubs for pouring beer from the pumps.'

'O-h-h, I see.' The old lady slipped the T-shirt on over her head. 'I've got three of them. They're nice and large. Perfect for gardening. Try one.'

Beatrix pulled it down over her dungarees, noting the contrast between the dazzling white cotton and the faded, muddy denim.

'It really suits you,' her grandmother insisted. 'Oh, I nearly forgot. There's a letter for you.'

'A letter?' Beatrix received statements, circulars and bills but never letters. Curiously, she took it and glanced at the unfamiliar handwriting before tearing it open.

'Tea?' her grandmother asked, picking up the teapot and beginning to pour.

'No, thanks.' Up until a few weeks ago, Beatrix had rather enjoyed the odd cup of Lapsang Souchong but after having to drink gallons of the stuff, she was beginning to get heartily sick of it. Now she spread out the letter and glanced at the signature: John Chadwick. Why was he writing? He only lived at the end of the road. She began to read.

Dear Beatrix . . .

'But you must,' a voice protested.

Beatrix looked up. 'What?'

'You must drink this tea. We have a year's supply. Who else is going to drink it?'

'I don't know.' Abstractedly, Beatrix turned back to the letter and continued to read.

I will not be taking you to the barn dance tonight. I will be taking Susan Dobbs instead. This might come as a bit sudden but I've been seeing her for a while now and so we've decided to get engaged. I'm sorry, but there's no other way to tell you.

John C.

Beatrix could only stare at the words, stunned. John Chadwick to get engaged to Susan Dobbs. But why? How? She looked up from the letter and gazed into space. Of course, she didn't love him, but everyone in the village knew them as a couple. They went to the cinema together, the local quiz nights, and, sometimes, they would serve side by side behind the counter of his butcher's shop. Now that was all finished. But Susan Dobbs was so much older. And a snob! As the library manager she always dressed impeccably with never a hair out of place, her powdered face set like a mask, contemptuous and unsmiling.

Beatrix looked back at the letter in her hand. This was humiliating, but it was more than that; she had lost a companion – the only man within a twenty-mile radius with his own hair and teeth.

'What's the matter, dear?'

Beatrix looked up. 'It's John Chadwick. He's getting engaged.'

'No!'

'Yes.'

'But what about our delivery of free meat?'

Beatrix was stung by this insensitivity. 'Well, that's finished now, isn't it,' she answered coldly.

The lines and crevices on the old face converged into a scowl. 'So what are you going to do about it?'

'Nothing.'

The reply came swift and sharp. 'You must fight for him!'

Beatrix shook her head.

'Where's your Dunkirk spirit?' her grandmother demanded.

'I don't want to fight. If he wants Susan Dobbs, he can have her.'

Her grandmother stiffened. 'Did you say . . . *Dobbs*?'

Beatrix nodded, still too stunned to realise the significance of the question.

'You don't mean Edith Dobbs's girl, do you?'

Beatrix gazed beyond the French windows, down to her potting shed at the foot of the lawn. Only minutes ago her life had been so . . . content.

'Pay attention, Beatrix! Are you telling me that Edith Dobbs's girl has stolen John Chadwick?'

'Yes.'

'That's it!' The old lady banged her fist on the table. 'I've had enough of that woman. First she thinks she can steal my marrow title and now this!'

'Oh, Grandmother,' Beatrix murmured in annoyance. 'You can't compare me to a prize marrow.'

'I most certainly can!' The old lady folded her arms

tightly and sat down heavily on her chair. 'It's the principle of the thing. For thirty years that woman has been a thorn in my side.'

And you've been a thorn in hers. Despite her mood Beatrix had to marvel at the energy that hatred could produce. Suddenly her grandmother was looking her up and down with accusatory eyes. 'You know why he's gone off with her, don't you?'

Beatrix sighed. 'No, actually I don't.'

'Because she dresses like a lady. She shows her legs. I bet he's never seen your legs, has he?'

Beatrix thought about this. 'Um . . . no, I don't think he has.'

'That's it then. I'm throwing your dungarees on the compost, along with that ghastly headscarf. And tell me, has he ever seen you without your spectacles?'

'I can't remember.' As Mrs Bayley raised her eyes to heaven, Beatrix protested, 'But I have to wear spectacles, otherwise I walk into doors.'

Her grandmother was staring hard at her hair, her face. 'How old are you now?' she asked.

'Twenty-five.'

'Twenty-five!' The old lady sat back in alarm. 'Goodness gracious! You don't look it. You look positively *middle-aged!*'

Beatrix flushed angrily. 'It's only because I'm wearing my gardening clothes.'

'But you're *always* wearing your gardening clothes.'

'Not always!'

'Well, I can't remember the last time I saw you in a dress.'

'That's because I don't wear them.'

'And that's why you've lost the only eligible man in the county.' The voice changed to a wail. 'Oh Beatrix, what have you been doing with him all this time?'

Beatrix turned away, remembering the feverish kiss of cold wet lips, the clumsy hand pummelling her breast as if kneading bread dough. She had tried to love him but it had been impossible. Perhaps she had set her expectations too high? She moved towards the window and gazed out onto the sunny lawn. Suddenly she felt melancholic. Once John Chadwick had gone, there would be no one else to take his place.

Her grandmother persisted. 'We must also consider that he will one day inherit the family business. A chain of butcher shops is not something to be sniffed at. Tell me, do you really want to lose him to someone like Susan Dobbs?'

Beatrix was silent. In that moment, she saw herself entering the library, putting her books on the counter and Susan pulling them towards her, her face unsmiling, the hard eyes avoiding her as if she were something distasteful. Inferior. 'No, no, I don't.'

'Right, then.' Her grandmother stood up with new energy. 'Lipstick – that's what we need. I will take you to the shops tomorrow. We will buy dresses, fashionable dresses – something feminine.' She narrowed her eyes thoughtfully. 'Then we will address your personality. There will be no more *Gardener's World*. Instead, you will concentrate on learning some womanly wiles.'

Womanly wiles! If Beatrix hadn't felt so miserable, she would have laughed. 'And who's going to teach me?' she asked. '*You?*'

As if conceding this, Mrs Bayley fell silent, sat down once more and stared at the wall. After a moment, she slammed the flat of her hand down on the table. 'That's it! I have the answer. You will go to London – stay with you Cousin Lara.'

Lara? Beatrix hadn't seen her in fifteen years. In fact, she hadn't seen any of her relations in that time, her inherent shyness preventing her from attending the usual engagement parties and christenings.

'Normally, I would not approve of such a companion,' her grandmother continued, 'but we have no alternative. She is young, single and worldly-wise – the perfect candidate to teach you all you should know.'

'But Grandmother . . .'

'Money is no object. Spend, spend, spend. But you must

buy dresses that show your knees, and a brassière and rouge and shoes. Shoes with *heels.*'

'But—'

'Then I want you to come back and show Edith – I mean *Susan* Dobbs – that you mean business. Ha! We'll show them!'

Beatrix spoke quickly, fearfully. 'But you can't simply foist me on to my cousin. We're complete strangers. In fact, she probably doesn't even know I exist.'

'Of course she does! She was at Jonathan's wedding last year and I told her all about you.'

'But that doesn't mean she would want to be bothered with me.'

At this, the fierce light in those old eyes slowly dulled, the thin body seeming to sag in defeat. 'Yes, perhaps you are right. And there is no point in offering her money because she doesn't need it.'

'I just want to forget the whole thing.' Beatrix moved towards the French windows and shoved a foot into a Wellington boot. Her grandmother had certainly shown kindness and generosity in wanting to help her, but *going to live in London!* It was just another one of her eccentric ideas.

As she crossed the lawn once more, Beatrix allowed herself to imagine what it would be like to take the train to London, to see the sights, to be with a girl of the same age, to giggle, to share secrets. She sighed wistfully, knowing that it could never happen. After all, why should her pretty, sophisticated cousin want to be lumbered with a country bumpkin like her?

Lara

Lara was late. Yawning widely, she strolled along Bond Street, glancing desultorily into shop windows as she passed. She was discontented with life, bored with the same old parties, the same recycled faces night after night. Suddenly, she stopped short. There, displayed in the window of Manolo Blahnik stood a pair of gold stilettos. They were identical to the ones she had bought yesterday in Harvey Nicks except these had prettier buckles and higher heels. She peered into the interior of the shop. It was empty. Should she go in and buy them? No! If she were tempted in, it could be hours before she re-emerged, and she was already late enough as it was. With a sigh of resignation, she turned away and carried on walking.

Gallery assistant! I should never have let myself be talked into it, she thought. Thankfully, though, it wouldn't last much longer now that Timothy was advertising for a full-time assistant. Of course, she would miss him and she would miss Meryl, but the reality of it was that, for three hours on a Monday and a Friday she was an absolute *slave* to the place.

In the beginning, she had been thrilled by the novelty of it all, viewing the gallery as the perfect accessory to all her darling little suits whilst smugly anticipating the moment when she would meet some stupidly rich collector. In the event, she had met Justin at the frozen fish counter of Budgens.

Justin. She groaned inwardly. Whyever had she fallen for someone like him? All right, he was sexy in a tired, crumpled sort of way and he was certainly different from the usual guys she dated, but just like her job, the novelty was rapidly wearing off. He was simply a corporate man who lived and breathed mergers and balance sheets. He would regularly cancel dates because of some business meeting and then, when he finally managed to slot her into his schedule, he would arrive late, take her to a party and, by one o'clock, would be fast asleep. How many times had she had to apologise to their hostess while peeling him off the sofa?

She frowned. Daddy would be furious if he could see her like this. Sebastian Bayley wanted his princess to be happy, and even though he lived on the other side of the Atlantic, he had bought her an apartment in Kensington and made sure she received a generous allowance that left her free from worries. He would be furious if he knew that some workaholic boyfriend was giving her stress.

Crossing the road towards the gallery, she quickened her pace, so that when she reached the door she was almost running. 'Sorry I'm late,' she exclaimed, falling into the room, panting.

As usual, Meryl sat behind a pile of ledgers on the back table. 'Morning, Lara,' she said, her eyes flickering to the clock on the wall.

Lara put a hand to her heaving chest, ready with her usual sick-Rottweiler routine but the other woman forestalled her. 'Chardonnay been ill again?'

Hearing the weary tone in Meryl's voice, Lara felt uneasy. 'No, he's fine,' she answered breezily, walking over to her desk and dropping her briefcase on the floor. 'I broke a heel and had to go home to change.' With a cursory glance, she was relieved to see that Meryl was nodding. She didn't look happy but she was nodding. Good. Owning an imaginary dog had come in useful over the past two months but perhaps she had overdone it. At first it had been a brainwave of an alibi – considering Meryl's love of dogs and the fact that a Rottweiler was far too big an animal to bring into the West End tucked under one's arm – but now she would have to think of some other excuse. An elderly bedridden neighbour, perhaps?

Taking off her jacket, Lara casually inspected Meryl's outfit from the corner of her eye. Not the maroon cardigan again! Meryl was a pretty Cockney woman in her forties who came in to do the bookkeeping. She had black hair, fiercely lacquered into stiff waves, and wore hand-knitted scarves and cardigans. Although extremely efficient, she had the dress sense of a Soviet munitions worker, which drove Lara crazy.

Meryl bent to her work once more. 'Your dad's just phoned,' she said.

'Oh, what did he want?'

'He didn't say.' Meryl screwed up a piece of paper and threw it in the bin. 'Did you get the stamps?'

Lara clamped a hand to her mouth. 'Oh gosh, I completely forgot!' This was not an act – she was genuinely shocked, having told herself last night that she would definitely remember to buy them.

'Oh Lara,' Meryl moaned. Then she stiffened. 'You did remember to post those letters on Monday, didn't you?'

This triggered something in Lara's brain, prompting her to grab her briefcase and look inside. 'Oh God, Meryl,' she wailed. 'I forgot.'

'What am I going to do with you?' Tight-lipped, Meryl stood up and marched over. 'Give them here. I'll have to post them on my way out.'

Guiltily, Lara handed them over. Sometimes responsibility just seemed to swamp her, making her feel inadequate and frustrated. 'You won't tell Timothy, will you?' she pleaded.

'When do I ever?'

'Thanks, Meryl.' As Lara went to close her bag, she saw the package and remembered. 'Oh, I've got a present for you.'

'But it's not my birthday.'

'That doesn't matter.' Lara looked stern. 'But I want you to wear it *regularly* and not just when you go to the dog track.'

Meryl held up the Georgina von Exdorf scarf in admiration, fingering the silky velvet fabric. 'It's lovely.'

'It's just your colour, don't you think?'

'Yes, but . . .' Meryl looked up in consternation. 'It's far too expensive.'

'Don't worry – I can afford it.' Lara draped it around her friend's shoulders. 'As long as you promise to keep your old scarf at home.' She held up a hand, ready to ward off a protest. 'And I don't care if it was hand-knitted by your Richelle or Bruce Willis – it's hideous.'

Meryl laughed. 'Is it that bad?'

Lara nodded solemnly and then broke into a grin.

'Well, it's ever so kind of you.'

'It's my pleasure.' Lara adjusted her jacket on the back of the chair. 'I've decided that I'm going to finish with Justin,' she declared, preparing herself for a nice long chat.

'Oh, why? He sounded really nice.'

'Well, yes, he is – but all he can think about is *work!*'

'I'm not surprised,' Meryl answered, returning to her table. 'Isn't he striking some multi-million-pound deal with the Japanese?'

'Yes, I know all that,' Lara said impatiently, irritated that Meryl was taking his side. 'I just want to see what he looks like in *daylight hours,* that's all.' She picked up a pile of envelopes and put them down again. 'I phoned him at his office yesterday and suggested we go to the zoo after lunch, and do you know what he did? He laughed!'

'He's building a career. Support him now and it'll cement your relationship.'

'I don't care about his career. Either I come first, or we're finished!'

'I think you should give him a chance – after all, you've only been going out together two months. Wait until he's done his deal and then see what he's like. Sacrifice is the cornerstone to a lasting love.'

Lara grinned. 'Cornerstone to a lasting love?' she queried, raising her eyebrows. 'Cement a relationship? Where do you get your romantic ideas? A builder's manual?'

Meryl chuckled. 'No, I'm serious. Give the bloke a chance.'

Lara shook her head. 'I'm not right for him. What he

needs is a corporate wife – a hostess to clients and colleagues, a showcase of efficiency who can effortlessly produce elaborate dinner parties for forty. Me? I can't produce a TV dinner-for-one, without turning the kitchen into Armageddon.' She turned away, the matter closed. 'Do you want another coffee?'

'No, thanks.'

Lara found the coffee still hot. If it hadn't been for me, she reflected, picking up the cafetière, Timothy and Meryl would still be drinking that awful instant stuff. Now the cupboard was stocked with the finest organic Puerto Rican beans, expensive but essential. She might forget to post a letter, but Lara Bayley could always be relied upon to add that touch of sophistication.

Lara returned with a cup of coffee and a chocolate-coated Bath Oliver and, seeing that Meryl had resumed her work, went over and sat on the edge of the table to look down at what she was doing. It was all numbers. Boring. She let her gaze wander around the room, over the beechwood flooring, the potted palms, the black leather chairs, the chrome accessories. Two years ago, this would have been the height of fashion. Now it looked safe, unimaginative and completely out of touch with the modern works that lined the walls.

Feeling, yet again, that strange sense of discontent, Lara went back to her desk and sat down, twirling around and around in her chair for a minute before stopping to peer at a painting on the wall. 'Is this one new?' she asked.

'Yes, it came in yesterday. Ten thousand quid.' Meryl shook her head in disbelief and carried on working.

Lara stared at it for a moment longer. A white canvas with a few black dots – how ridiculous. If it had been up to her, she would refuse to promote this minimalist art; instead, she would go for something with *life* in it, something with richly textured colours, earthy rather than bright. Losing interest in the painting, she swivelled in her chair to view the street. It was beginning to rain. She swivelled again and came to a stop, mesmerised by the speed of Meryl's finger moving over the keys on the calculator. Lara was bored and wanted to chat. 'How's Terry's prostate?' she asked.

Without a pause, Meryl answered, 'Much better. He's gone over to Walthamstow with Trudi today.'

'That's nice.' What a life, Lara mused, watching your greyhound running around all day, chasing a piece of shredded fur. Meryl had taken her to 'the dogs' a couple of weeks ago – an evening of sweet tea in styrofoam cups and jellied eels – but she would never go again. The smell of the place had simply clung to her for days. No wonder Meryl was so addicted to romantic fiction – her only means of escape from a humdrum existence.

As Meryl started on another file, Lara tried once more

to keep her attention. 'Has Timothy found my replacement yet?'

'Not yet. He only put the advertisement in on Thursday.'

Lara took on a wistful expression. 'I'll miss this place,' she lied. 'But I've got so many other things to do.'

Meryl looked up sharply. 'Yeah? Like what?'

Lara rotated a limp hand. 'You know, the usual sort of things, taking clothes to the dry cleaners, shopping . . .' She trailed off, unable to think of anything else.

'And taking Chardonnay to the vet's,' Meryl added helpfully.

'What?' Lara was quick to cover her confusion. 'Oh yes, absolutely. Sick pets can take up an awful lot of time.'

'I can imagine. So, what else will you do?'

Lara had not expected to be interrogated like this. 'Um, sorting out my stockings into pairs and throwing away the ones with holes.'

'Is that all?' Meryl exclaimed. 'Don't you ever get bored?'

Lara thought about this for a moment. 'I never used to but now . . . now I feel sort of . . .' How could she explain it to Meryl when she couldn't even explain it to herself? But she wanted to put her feelings into words and to understand what was wrong. 'It's as if someone has taken away my script.' Seeing Meryl's blank face, she tried again.

'It's as if I'm on stage and I don't know what I'm expected to do next.'

Meryl studied her for a moment. 'Do you know what I think? I think it's time you thought about other people besides yourself.'

'But I do!' Lara exclaimed in protest. 'I give tons of clothes to the Oxfam shop and I donate money to the RSPCA and I buy the *Big Issue.*' She tried to think what else she did for others. 'I think about Kelsey. I'm always helping her when she's loaded down with carrier bags. And whenever I'm at a party, I'm always telling people about the gallery. To be honest, I'm better than any advertisement in the *Tatler.*'

Meryl smiled at this.

'In fact,' Lara continued, 'only last night I was talking to one of Kelsey's friends from the States and he said he would definitely come in today.'

'Well done.'

'And I think about *you,*' Lara added, now buoyed up on a wave of self-congratulation. 'I bought you that scarf, don't forget.'

'I know and that's kind of you. But I don't mean that. How old are you now – twenty-nine?'

Lara nodded.

'When I was your age I had a husband and two young children to look after. It was hard work but when I look back on it now they were the best years of my life.'

Lara guffawed. 'I would rather gouge my eyes out!'

Meryl remained serious. 'You don't mean that. You just haven't met the right bloke yet, but when you do, you'll soon change your mind. You'll realise it was just what you wanted all along.'

Yeah, like a hole in the head. 'I'll think about it,' Lara lied, not wanting to continue the conversation. As Meryl returned to her work, Lara swivelled back to her desk, placed an elbow on either side of the mail and gazed out of the window. I'm bored with my life, she admitted. For the past year all her efforts had gone into organising the redecoration of her apartment but now that it was finished, she didn't know what to do with herself.

A country cottage. She sat bolt upright. Of course! It would be her weekend retreat. She would do it up in calico curtains from Heals, antique milking stools and bunches of dried lavender in copper jugs. Then she would invite her closest friends to join her for wild parties on the lawn, sleeping off their hangovers in hammocks strapped to conveniently placed apple trees. Now the picture inside her head began rapidly to expand and fill with colour. There were rolling green fields, a wishing well in the garden, roses around the door and white doves cooing on the thatched roof. There was blue sky, lots of it and the baker wheeling his bicycle up the garden path, his basket full of hot crusty loaves. She grinned, gleefully spinning around and around in her chair. She didn't care what Meryl said – money *did* buy happiness.

Keen to share her ideas, she skidded to a halt and turned back. 'Meryl, guess what? I've had the most marvel—' But she was interrupted by the sound of the door opening. Timothy had arrived. Now she would have to wait before revealing all her wonderful plans.

Timothy Ashley-Smith backed in, shaking raindrops from his umbrella. 'Good morning, ladies,' he said over his shoulder. As usual he was immaculately dressed; that morning he was wearing a scarlet Paisley cravat and a khaki-coloured suit, the jacket well-padded at the shoulders. Although his hair was thinning on top, it was fluffy baby-soft, a pale unnatural yellow. 'How are we this morning?' he asked, hanging his umbrella on the coat-stand.

'Great,' Lara bubbled, her thoughts full of strawberries and cream.

'Splendid, splendid.' He came into the room, straightening his cravat. 'Any response to the advertisement?'

'Lara's just sorting the mail now,' Meryl answered.

At the mention of this, Lara promptly picked up an envelope and made a show of opening it.

'I'm sorry to nag you, Timothy,' Meryl continued, 'but I

will need the Drummond receipts and February's bank statement, if I'm going to finish the tax returns.'

Knowing that she could not compete with this efficiency, Lara stood up and started for the kitchen. 'Coffee, Timothy?' she asked sweetly.

He beamed. 'Good idea, Lara.'

When she returned, she found Timothy sifting through envelopes whilst chatting to Meryl who now stood beside him with a notepad. '. . . and *such* an Italian name: Vittorio de Fiorelli. Has a wonderful gallery in Milan. In the via Montenapoleone.' He let the words roll off his tongue. Seeing the cup of coffee, he took it from her. 'Thank you, Lara. Just saying to Meryl that I've found myself a partner.'

'How exciting.' She looked suitably interested but all the while her thoughts were bounding through a buttercup-spangled meadow. The ringing of the telephone snapped her back to reality and she picked it up. 'Good morning,' she gushed. 'Smith's Galleries.'

'Princess!' It was her father, his voice cracked. 'Oh, Princess.'

Hearing the note of distress, she tensed. 'Daddy?'

'Darling, I don't know how to tell you this . . .' His voice faltered and died.

She felt a tightening in her chest. If Daddy ever had a problem he would never worry her with it, so this had to be bad. 'What is it?'

'It's a lawsuit – a big one. I thought I was covered, I really did.'

'I don't understand.'

'The company . . . I'm ruined. I'm . . . Oh God, I'm *bankrupt.*'

'Oh.' She was stunned into silence. Bankrupt? That sounded bad.

'I'm sorry,' he murmured. 'So sorry.'

Sorry? What was he sorry about? 'What do you mean?'

'Your allowance . . .' His voice trailed away.

Lara went cold. Her allowance! No! Her allowance was sacred. This couldn't be happening, not to her. Daddy was rich – he had one of the biggest shipping companies in Latin America. 'Does that mean . . . ?' She swallowed.

'I'm afraid so. In a year or two things will be different but until then, I am unable to support you.'

Although her heart pounded, she stayed calm, trying to assimilate the facts. 'I see,' she said softly. 'Um . . .' She kept her voice casual, but her brain darted in all directions, like Meryl's fingers skimming across the calculator. *How was she going to pay all of her astronomical bills – her credit-card bills, her Harrods store card, her phone bill?* 'And this month,' she queried nervously, 'Will you be sending me—?'

'No, darling. It's impossible. I know this must be a dreadful shock for you, but you'll be OK – for a little while, anyway. I'm so thankful that you took my advice and opened that high-interest account.'

She felt sick. She had not taken his advice. Why save money when there was always a ready supply of it? Now all that had changed: she was penniless. 'Isn't there anybody who could help?' she suggested lightly, trying to keep the panic from her voice. 'What about Mummy?'

'Even if I knew where she was, do you really think she would help me?'

There was no answer to this. Suddenly, she had a vision of a white-haired old lady sipping champagne, her cheap dress faded and worn, her neck and wrists loaded with priceless family jewels. 'What about Grandmother Bayley?'

He snorted contemptuously. 'I've just spoken to her. This might sound harsh but I've got to say it, even though she is my mother. Your Grandmother Bayley is the most miserly, hard-hearted creature on Planet Earth.'

'Oh.'

'Listen, Princess, don't worry about me. I'll be fine. I just want to know that you'll be OK.'

'Of course I will,' she exclaimed. Lara had always found it easy to lie.

'Good. Unfortunately I have to leave the estate tomorrow, but as soon as I've got myself sorted out I'll give you a call. OK, sweetheart?'

'Yes, Daddy.'

'Good girl. Well, I'd better say goodbye for now. I love you.'

'Goodbye, Daddy. I love you too.'

As if in a dream, Lara put the phone down and gazed at it. Her allowance, gone – just like that! But she couldn't be left penniless – she wouldn't know how to survive. All her life she had been taken care of, so how could she be expected to look after herself now? She glanced up to see that Timothy and Meryl were looking at her with worried frowns.

'Is there a problem?' Timothy asked.

'It's nothing,' she said blithely. 'Just Daddy's house, that's all. Nothing to worry about.'

Timothy opened the envelope in his hand. 'He lives in Buenos Aires, doesn't he?'

Lara nodded.

'Ah, Buenos Aires.' Timothy sighed, gazing dreamily into space. 'A world of tango and gaiety!' At this, he cocked his elbows and swayed his hips as if moving to some imaginary music.

Lara stared through him. Who could she turn to? Mummy would be useless. Even if she were to be found, she would probably be in some Buddhist commune chanting a mantra or hugging a tree with a tribe of American Indians.

Timothy had come to a halt and now opened out a sheet of paper. 'An applicant,' he murmured, scanning the letter. 'Swedish. Bilingual. Worked in Galleri Nordenhake, Malmö and the Neuman Gallery, New York.' He handed the letter to Lara. 'Would you give her a call and arrange an appointment for next Tuesday, please.'

Automatically, Lara picked up the telephone. *She was penniless!* Reading the telephone number on the letter, she began to dial. She needed money, but how would she get it? How did *anybody* get it? On the last number, she stopped and thought hard. A job? A full-time job. She banged the phone down. 'I'll take it,' she cried.

Timothy peered at her. 'Take what?'

'The job.'

'What job?'

'The assistant's job.' She was puzzled to see his eyebrows lift in alarm. Then he shot Meryl a quick, anxious look. Now they were both staring at her in consternation. 'What's the matter?' Lara asked. 'I can do it. I've been here for two months. I know the ropes.'

Timothy shook his head. 'I'm afraid that the position requires commitment.'

'I've got commitment,' she cried, feeling a growing panic. She had to have this job – it was the only thing she knew how to do.

Timothy stared at her, opened his mouth and closed it again. There was a moment's silence before he spoke again. 'I need someone who is punctual, conscientious.'

'I can do all that,' she insisted. Frantically she looked from Timothy to Meryl and then back to Timothy. *They don't want me to have it!* Was she that bad? But she had a nice voice. She wore beautiful suits. She was pretty. She had introduced decent coffee into their lives. Didn't that count for anything? 'Please,' she begged. 'Give me a chance.'

Meryl looked at her sadly. 'Timothy is right,' she said. 'It would be too demanding for you. I don't think you'll be able to cope.'

'But I will.' She took a deep breath. 'OK,' she conceded, 'I *have* been late a couple of times and I've forgotten to write down messages, but I've just been *acting*. This time, I'm going to do it properly.' She thought swiftly. 'I'm always telling people about the gallery,' she added. 'And I've got the right connections.'

Timothy shook his head. 'I know that, but I really need someone I can depend on, someone who can accept responsibility.'

Silence. Beseechingly, she looked from Timothy to Meryl but they would not even meet her eyes. Was she such a failure? Yes, it seemed that she was. Timothy continued to open the mail while Meryl moved back towards her desk. The matter was closed.

Gazing miserably out of the window, she saw a long black limousine slide to a halt outside the gallery. The chauffeur jumped out and opened the rear door. A customer. It took Lara a second to realise who it was. Bob Schneider! He was the guy she was speaking to last night. She had told him about the gallery and now he was coming in to see it for himself. She jumped up. 'Timothy, listen,' she said urgently. 'If I sell a painting, will you give me the chance to prove myself?'

Timothy hesitated.

'Please.' The man was heading for the door.

Her boss answered hesitantly. 'Perhaps, but only if you sell a painting.' He put a hand on her arm as she rushed past. 'And please, Lara, stop calling it a job. It's a *position*.'

'Of course, of course. Sorry.' With her sights levelled on the American, she headed for the door, mustering every ounce of charm. Time to sweet talk! The man was rich – and he wanted to impress her. Selling this painting would be like stealing candy from a baby!

Jack

A warm breeze heralded a fine day, the early-morning sky tinted with the palest shade of yellow. On Buckthorn Hill, Jack Havers shovelled the last of the pig manure into the cart and straightened up, steadying himself against a wave of giddiness. 'Wine tasting,' he muttered bitterly. 'Huh! That stuff could strip an engine.'

Year after year it was the same. Colonel Archibald Stirling would commandeer the Black Lion for the evening, setting charity boxes along the bar before proceeding to serve up Patsy's homemade wine; wine with wholesome names like elderflower, parsnip, dandelion, accompanied as always by small pieces of cheese on small pieces of bread. All very civilised, but by closing time even the toughest of the hill farmers could barely stand up. Jack had a vague recollection of stumbling back to the farm but there was something else he ought to remember – something that concerned him.

An advertisement came into it somehow. He frowned in concentration, his head throbbing. Suddenly, a muffled grunt interrupted his thoughts. At the far end of the pen, half-buried in straw, lay a heavily pregnant sow, her small eyes watching him belligerently. 'Oh, Cleopatra,' he crooned. 'Have I disturbed your beauty sleep?' The effort of holding up her head proved too much for her and she flopped back in the straw, snorting a blast of air. Jack smiled ruefully; this was his prized possession, an aristocrat among pigs, a pure-bred Tamworth, pregnant for the first time, foul-tempered and lazy.

Turning, Jack looked out across the valley. At the foot of the hill, his farmhouse lay in shadow and beyond, half-hidden by trees, stood the Black Lion, curtains drawn. What was it Ernest had said? In the soup-like consistency of Jack's brain, two words surfaced. *Lonely* and *Hearts.* The pain intensified behind his eyeballs. He would speak to the fellow today. Discover what was going on.

With the mucking-out finished, Jack whistled to Rosie his sheepdog and turned for home. As he walked, he took a roll-up from his pocket and lit it, glancing at the fertile pastures beyond his boundary wall: Old Matthew's land. He had always assumed that when the land eventually came up for auction he would buy it, but now that time was fast approaching and – unless a miracle happened – he would not have the money. What made it worse were the rumours circulating in the village, rumours that some company was on the lookout for a local landfill site. A landfill site! The thought of it made him grow cold.

With a heavy heart, he stopped and let his eyes follow the line of the undulating hills, softly folded and curved like the shape of a sleeping woman. On the slopes stood trees of rowan and wych-elm leading down to chalk streams, their banks dressed with bluebells and lilac-coloured rampion. He could almost see his Tamworths rooting through the green grass, see the fields of feathered barley ready for harvest. 'How am I going to get the money?' he whispered.

Slowly, his gaze swept over his own land, over fields that had lain unprofitable for two years while the chemicals within the soil leached away. He only had to wait seven more weeks before the Soil Association gave him their stamp of approval, and then he would be back in business, set to become one of the most successful organic farmers in the south of England. But had all the hardship and sacrifice been worth it?

From reading recent newspaper reports and talking to supermarket buyers, he knew that the public's demand for organic food was rapidly on the increase. They wanted food that was free from fungicides and pesticides, they demanded that livestock be humanely reared and slaughtered. The twelve-month forecast looked good. Sainsbury's would be holding its premium price for organic milk for the next five years while Somerfields had placed orders for pork, carrots and spring onions.

But that was in the future. He needed money – *now!*

Never once had he doubted his ideals, but the truth was, if he had not allowed his fields to lie fallow, he would now have a hefty bank balance, enough to buy Old Matthew's land and so prevent it from falling into the wrong hands.

There was only one thing he could do, he decided. He would heed the Colonel's advice and attempt to sell his paintings in London. Suddenly, this ray of hope vanished. Even if he were able to persuade a gallery to show his work, how much would he get? A hundred pounds per painting? That would not be enough.

As he came into the yard, he saw Sam dressed in his school shirt and underparts standing at the kitchen door. 'Daddy,' he called. 'I can't find my shorts.'

Jack hurried in. 'Where did you take them off last night?'

'I can't remember.'

Jack groaned. 'Sam, I keep telling you. When you take your school uniform off, you leave it in a neat pile on the bench then we don't have this panic in the morning.'

'I'm sorry, Daddy.'

Jack went on his knees to look under the furniture and

then stopped. 'Well, give me a hand!' he exclaimed, seeing that his son was standing by, content to watch him.

Jamie stood at the sink, drying the last of the porridge bowls. 'We can't be late today,' he fretted. 'I'm taking assembly.'

Jack looked up sharply. *Assembly!*

Jamie's face crumpled. 'Oh Dad, you forgot!'

Jack nodded guiltily. 'I'm sorry, Jamie, but I've been asked to help out on the Wyatts' farm. And I've got to do it because we need the money.'

Jamie fell silent, rubbing hard at a plate, his face set in hurt and resentment. Jack went over and put his arms around his shoulders. 'I'm sorry I forgot, Jamie, but I've got so much on my mind at the moment. How about I come for the first ten minutes?'

His eldest son nodded reluctantly. 'OK.'

'I'll make it up to you, I promise.' He straightened. 'Now, where are these shorts?'

'Here they are, Daddy,' Sam cried, waving them above his head.

'Put them on quickly or we're going to be late.' Jack gathered up the school bags, buttoned Sam's coat and led the way out to the pickup truck. As the boys settled beside him in the cab, he gazed proudly at their shiny hair and polished shoes, their satchels holding their neatly written homework. Jamie was a handsome lad of nine, sweet-natured and protective of his younger brother and, although shy and awkward with the girls, he would doubtless be a heart-throb in the not-too-distant future. Beside him sat Sam, turning six at the end of the month, his face still chubby with baby fat, his eyes bright with mischief. He had his mother's eyes. For a moment Jack felt an ache of loss. Four years ago he would have crumpled up in anger and grief but the years had tempered his pain, leaving him with only moments of fleeting sadness.

'OK, boys,' he said cheerfully, starting the engine. 'Let's get the Havers gang on the road.'

He smiled down at their grinning faces, feeling as if his chest would burst with love and pride. His little gang. It was tough keeping everything together, but most of the time he managed. He didn't know how, but he managed. Now, as he turned the truck onto the road, he thought back over the years. At first, he'd had brief help from his sister-in-law and then his aunt, but after that he'd been on his own. Sam had been too young to understand what was going on, Jamie old enough to be bewildered, crying out for his mummy in the night. It had taken time but they'd got through it; and now they were happy.

Jack changed gear as the truck gathered speed. Being a single parent was like continually juggling balls, knowing that if one ball fell, they would all fall. Up until now, he had coped, but what would happen in six weeks' time, when the farm was up and running to full capacity? He would definitely need help with the boys then. But where would he get the money to pay for a housekeeper? His land would not yield him a penny for at least seven months.

Rounding the bend, he saw Ernest backing his tractor into the bottom field. As he slowed to greet him, he remembered the question that had been plaguing him that morning. 'Hello, Ernest,' he called. 'There's something I've been wanting to ask you.'

The other man turned in his seat and touched his cap. There was egg yolk on the front of his knitted waistcoat. 'Mornin', Jack,' he said solemnly. 'Mornin', boys.'

'Good morning, Ernest!' they trilled.

It was always a surprise to Jack that his sons readily showed such enthusiasm for this dour, ill-humoured man. 'It's about last night,' Jack said hesitantly. 'What was it you said about an advertisement?' He was surprised to see a shifty expression pass over the fellow's face.

'I'm having nothing to do with it,' Ernest muttered, turning back to release the trailer catch.

Jack frowned. 'So it *has* got something to do with an advertisement. Is it about me?'

'I'm not saying. All I know is that you'll be asked up to the Black Lion s'afternoon. Then you'll find out for yourself.'

As Jack opened his mouth to question him further, he

felt Jamie nudge his arm. 'Dad,' he whispered. 'Hurry up or we're going to be late for assembly.'

'Oh, right, yes.' Jack put his foot on the accelerator, threw Ernest a fierce look and headed for the village.

'Are you going to the Black Lion then?' Jamie asked eagerly.

Jack nodded, those two words shining like neon in his brain: *Lonely Hearts*. 'Yes, Jamie, I certainly am.'

'Oh, goodie,' Sam cried. 'Can we come?'

His father nodded distractedly, his thoughts unsettled by the look on Ernest's face. Something was going on behind his back and whatever it was, he had a feeling that he wasn't going to like it.

Friday Afternoon

Beatrix

Beatrix tossed the bundle of rose cuttings onto the bonfire and stood back to watch them burn. John Chadwick was a coward, she decided grimly. Why had he sent a letter? Didn't he have the common decency to tell her to her face? Hot and irritable, she reached for the plastic bottle of water and drained the last mouthful. Now she squeezed the empty bottle between her palms, feeling it buckle and pop under the pressure. She was angry with John Chadwick but more than that, she was angry with her grandmother. I'm not middle-aged! she thought furiously.

Looking back towards the house, she saw that Daphne had arrived and was now placing the tea tray in front of Grandmother on the terrace. Although she was thirsty, Beatrix did not want the old woman's company. Not today. She turned back to the fire, kicking a burning stick into the flames. When she heard her name called, she turned to see Daphne beckoning from the top of the path. 'Your grandmother needs to speak to you,' she called, her soft Welsh accent making the words almost melodic.

Beatrix sighed, knowing that she would need to go back for water anyway. 'I'm coming.' Pulling the wheelbarrow away from the flames, she turned and headed for the house. Up ahead, Daphne was walking along the terrace towards the kitchen, her plait of dark hair bouncing against her spine, her short skirt fluttering around narrow hips, her ballerina slippers treading lightly. She looked cool . . . unfettered.

Mrs Bayley sat at the white wrought-iron table, her T-shirt and curlers replaced with twinset and pearls. 'Wonderful news,' she trilled, waving a silver teaspoon. 'I've solved our little problem.'

Beatrix was both curious and cautious. 'What do you mean?'

'Sit down, sit down.' The old woman jabbed the spoon at a chair. 'We will have to be quick. Reverend Beardsley will be here any minute.'

Beatrix sat down, hugging the empty plastic bottle to her chest.

'Tea?' her grandmother offered, picking up the teapot.

'I don't want any of that, thanks.'

The teapot continued to pour. 'Yes, you do.'

'No, I don't.' Beatrix spoke sharply, surprising herself.

Maybe it was the heat. She put the plastic bottle on the table and got up. 'I'm going to make myself something else.' She walked along the terrace and into the kitchen, curious to see Daphne backing in from the hallway, bent double as she dragged a cardboard box along the floor. 'Hi Daphne,' she said, switching on the kettle. 'Do you want a hand?'

'No, it's OK, thanks. I just want to move it out of the hall so that Reverend Beardsley doesn't fall over it.' With the box inside the kitchen, she straightened up and began to push it with the sole of her shoe.

Taking two mugs from the shelf, Beatrix glanced at the box. 'What's in it?'

'I don't think you really want to know,' Daphne muttered, bending forward to read the label. 'It says: *High-Concentrate Miracle Feed.*' With one final shove of her foot, she had the box up against the wall and then turned, flicking her plait back over one shoulder. 'What's she trying to grow, anyway? Triffids?'

Beatrix chuckled, opening cupboard door after cupboard door in her search for the PG Tips.

'You're wasting your time,' Daphne said, slipping into her housecoat. 'She's hidden them.'

'The tea bags?'

'Yes. Here, have one of mine.' Daphne produced a small plastic bag from the pocket of her housecoat and put it on the counter. 'I smuggled them in.'

Beatrix shook her head in exasperation. 'This is getting ridiculous,' she said, taking out a teabag. 'Do you want a cup?'

'Please.'

As Beatrix turned to get the milk from the fridge, she was startled to hear a shout of laughter. Daphne was pointing a finger at the words on her T-shirt.

'*I've pulled!*' she chortled. 'I haven't seen that one before.'

Beatrix looked down at her chest and then back at Daphne's grinning face. It wasn't that funny, surely.

The cleaner's grin changed to a hovering smile, her eyes gleaming in sharp curiosity. 'You don't know what it means, do you?' she said.

Beatrix thrust a mug at her. 'What does it mean then?'

'It doesn't just mean pulling a pint of beer, it also means *pulling* a bloke.'

Mystified, Beatrix could only gaze at her.

Daphne tried again. 'Look, it's like me saying: "I went down the Legion last night and I picked up a man".'

As the meaning sank in, Beatrix pressed the flat of her hand against her chest, horrified. 'You're joking?' Then, suddenly she was laughing. 'Heavens,' she cried. 'And Grandmother's been wearing one, too!'

Daphne's eyes nearly popped from her head. 'Has she? Oh, I wish I'd seen it.' She sat up on the stool and began to sip her tea. 'By the way, she's just told me about . . . John.'

Beatrix shrugged, leaning against the kitchen cabinet.

'She also asked me to live-in while you're in London.'

Beatrix looked up sharply. *London!* Daphne was watching her, her head tipped to one side, her small brown eyes inquisitive, looking very much like the robin who often shared her lunchtime sandwiches. 'So, what's that all about?' Daphne prompted.

'It's just another one of her pie-in-the-sky ideas,' Beatrix muttered.

'I wouldn't be so sure, if I were you. From the way she was talking, I got the impression it had all been arranged.'

Beatrix frowned. Was this the wonderful news that her grandmother had referred to?

Daphne leant closer. 'So, tell me.'

'Well, as you know, she's had a running battle with Edith Dobbs for the past thirty years, and she just can't bear to lose to that woman – yet again!'

'Hang on – this has got nothing to do with Edith Dobbs.'

'Yes, it has, because it's her daughter who's taken my boyfriend.'

'Oh, right – Susie Dobbs, of course.'

'So, naturally, Grandmother wants me to get him back, and in order to do that, I've got to turn myself into a more attractive proposition, which means going to London to buy lipstick and dresses.' Despite her mood, Beatrix couldn't help but be amused at the astonishment on Daphne's face. 'In fact, she told me to *spend, spend, spend.*'

Daphne whistled. 'I don't believe that for one moment. She wants you to spend money? *Her* money?'

Beatrix nodded, enjoying herself.

Daphne continued to shake her head. 'There's got to be something in it for her. But, for the life of me, I can think what.'

'I've told you. She doesn't want a member of her family losing out to Edith Dobbs.'

'Mm . . .' Daphne's thin, freckled face had screwed up in thought. Then she opened her eyes wide and stared. 'Free meat!' she exclaimed, jabbing the air with a finger. 'That's what it is. Think about it! Since you've been going out with John Chadwick, he's been delivering free meat every week, but that's all going to change, isn't it? Who's going to get it now, eh? *Edith Dobbs!*'

Knowing her grandmother so well, Beatrix could only nod her agreement. 'I suppose that's it,' she said lamely.

'There's no supposing about it,' Daphne said darkly. 'Your grandmother is prepared to spend a fortune for the sake of a five pound of mince and ten lamb chops!' This revelation caused them both to fall silent. 'Still, it's worked out lucky for you,' Daphne enthused. 'It means you get to go to London.'

Beatrix had peeled a sheet of clingfilm from its roll and

now stretched it neatly over a bowl of cherries. 'I can't really see it happening,' she said quietly.

'Why not? Make it happen! Go to London. Have fun for once in your life. Who will you stay with?'

'She said something about my Cousin Lara.'

'And how old is this cousin?'

'She's about my age.'

'Thank God for that. It's about time you mixed with your own age-group, instead of old women, Cub Scouts and John Chadwick. God, I don't know how you do it. I would've been tearing my hair out by now.'

'It's not that bad,' Beatrix murmured, getting up to go out and rejoin her grandmother on the terrace. It would be rude to keep her waiting any longer. 'Thanks for the tea, Daphne.'

Mrs Bayley turned on her approach. 'You've certainly taken your time.' She peered into Beatrix's cup as it passed by, sniffing. 'What are you drinking?' she demanded.

'PG Tips.'

The old woman opened her mouth as if to remark on this, but in an instant, her face cleared and she smiled brightly. 'I've had the most wonderful news,' she began. 'Your Uncle Sebastian telephoned earlier.'

Beatrix sat down, surprised to feel a dart of disappointment. Uncle Sebastian owned a shipping company in South America. Obviously this had nothing to do with her visit to London as she had supposed.

'He's been made bankrupt,' the old lady continued, 'and was calling to ask for money. Of course I said no.'

'But Grandmother, he's your son. Surely you want to help him?'

'I'm helping him by *not* baling him out. That's why he's been so successful all his life – he has never had to depend on me.' The old woman waved this off. 'Anyway, we're here to discuss Lara, not her father.'

Beatrix paused, mid-sip. So this *did* have something to do with London.

'From the age of eighteen, Lara has received a substantial allowance from her father, an allowance which has given her a life of complete idleness.' Mrs Bayley shook her head scornfully. 'Such a mistake. Now, of course, she is penniless.'

Beatrix interjected, 'She could get a job.'

'A job! Lara Bayley?' Her grandmother snorted. 'Never. She's like some pampered Poodle. Can you imagine a Poodle being let loose into the wild – to hunt, to forage, to defend itself? It wouldn't know how to survive. It would yap itself senseless, and that – no doubt – is exactly what Lara is doing at this very moment.'

Beatrix was beginning to feel sorry for her cousin. After all, it wasn't her fault that she had been pampered. But her grandmother was in full flow.

'The blame lies with the parents, of course. They were simply too busy for her and so, out of guilt, they capitulated to all her demands. I can still remember her tantrums.' The old lady tutted. 'My goodness! I used to think she was weak in the head. If that girl didn't get what she wanted – immediately – she would throw herself to the ground, kicking and screaming. Of course it worked every time, everyone scurrying around like headless chickens doing anything to stop the noise.'

Picturing the scene, Beatrix smiled.

'And the perfume! The lipstick! She was in high-heeled shoes when she was *twelve*. Can you imagine it?'

Beatrix leant closer, fascination replacing pity.

'And for her sixteenth birthday her parents allowed her to have a party – unchaperoned – and by midnight the police had to be called in.'

At this, something sparked in Beatrix. It was a sense of admiration and excitement, fizzing through her veins. Oh, how she would love to meet her! 'Grandmother,' she began hesitantly, 'I understand Lara's situation, but what has it got to do with me?' She realised the answer as soon as the last word left her lips.

Seeing this, her grandmother nodded. 'That's right. She will be in desperate need of funds. I will therefore telephone her – the minute Reverend Beardsley has gone – and suggest that I will pay all expenses if she would be kind enough to take you under her wing.'

Beatrix bit her lip. 'But what if she doesn't like me?'

'Of course she will like you. There is nothing about you that she could possibly *dis*like. Indeed, with your influence, she may learn to be a bit more sensible.' The old lady sighed heavily. 'Don't look like that, my dear. It's a compliment.'

But Beatrix didn't want to be *sensible*. She didn't know what she wanted to be, but it certainly wasn't Miss Beatrix Metcalfe, Treasurer of the Women's Institute, Cub Scout leader, organiser of the church cleaning roster, Sunday School teacher and buffer between two cranky old women.

'So that's settled,' her grandmother stated briskly.

Beatrix felt her rebellion beginning to waver. 'How long will I be away?'

'For as long as it takes for you to become elegant and sophisticated. For once in your life, Beatrix, I want you to cultivate a *personality* – not a cabbage patch!' Suddenly, she cocked her head to listen. From the far side of the house came the sound of a car engine. 'That will be Reverend Beardsley,' she said briskly.

Beatrix rose to leave.

'Stay. You will need to inform him of your decision so that he can begin to hunt for a temporary replacement.'

With this sudden revelation, joy and relief swept through Beatrix. No more WI meetings! No more Cub Scout jumble sales. She was going to be free!

London – here I come!

Lara

It was six o'clock by the time Lara reached home. Dazed and bedraggled, she unlocked her apartment door and staggered in, dropping her briefcase and a carrier bag of groceries on the floor. 'Bloody hell,' she muttered, kicking the hot sweaty shoes from her feet. Accustomed to the luxury of travelling by taxi at civilised times of the day, it had come as a shock to be herded onto a tightly packed underground train in the rush-hour, hanging from a strap with her nose buried in some man's armpit. The fact that she had saved fifteen pounds was of little consolation.

'I don't want to be poor,' she whined, stripping off her jacket. 'I can't bear it.' At the sight of the orange light flashing on her answer-machine, her hopes immediately soared. This would be Daddy leaving a message to say that it had all been a ghastly mistake. She pressed the rewind button and waited for that familiar voice, but it was Justin.

'Hi darling,' he said. 'I just want to warn you that I may be late in picking you up tonight.'

Lara raised her eyes to heaven. 'Surprise, surprise,' she muttered heavily.

Next came Kelsey. 'Are you going to Amelia's tonight? I'm wearing my scarlet Versus pants so don't wear yours. Bye.'

The next caller did not speak; instead, there was a moment of shallow breathing before the phone was abruptly disconnected. The next call was exactly the same. How strange.

With no more messages, Lara picked up her bag of shopping and plodded into the kitchen, noting how clean the place looked. It was always a source of wonder how a room could look twice as big when it was tidy. The kitchen smelt of pine disinfectant, the dishcloth neatly folded over the tap, evidence of Heidi's thoroughness. With a jolt, Lara realised that she would no longer be able to afford her. 'Oh no,' she cried. 'I can't bear it. I can't bear it.'

Sighing miserably, she dumped her groceries on the side and began to unpack, taking out tins of sardines and tomato soup, storing them in the cupboard alongside jars of asparagus tips, truffles and almond-stuffed olives. These were her favourite treats . . . but no more. She was poor now, too poor to shop in Harrods food hall. Instead, she would be forced to drink wine from a box and eat bulk-standard pizzas. 'Damn!' she exclaimed. 'I've forgotten the bread.'

Opening the fridge, she saw the bottle of champagne and paused. This was her last one. Should she open it? No, she was too miserable to enjoy it. And yet she had every reason to celebrate; after all, Timothy had given her the job. Wasn't that cause for celebration? But he had only given it to her reluctantly, repeatedly telling her that it would be for a trial period only. She put her elbows on the worktop and dropped her head into her hands, thinking back over the day.

With the triumph of selling the painting to Mr Schneider, all her problems had been momentarily swept away, leaving her eager to astound Timothy and Meryl with her commitment and responsibility. Nodding wisely, she had listened to Timothy's explanation of her duties but after fifteen minutes of this, her eagerness had dissolved rapidly, leaving her with a feeling of helpless panic. How could they expect her to remember so many things? She could never do what was asked of her. When her salary was mentioned, she had dropped into a chair and gazed at the carpet. What was the point of working when her wage would barely cover her taxi fares?

Lara headed for the bathroom, her mind repeating her father's words over and over again; '*I'm ruined. I'm bankrupt.*

In a year or two things will change, but until then I cannot support you.' How could this have happened? It was all so sudden. So terrifying. Could she hold out for a year or two? She didn't know.

At the sound of the telephone she scowled, believing it to be Justin, calling back to cancel their date – yet again. She marched into the sitting room and yanked up the receiver ready to finish with him, once and for all. '*Yes?*' she demanded.

'Lara? Is that you?'

At the sound of the cut-glass voice, she frowned. 'Who is this?'

'Your grandmother. Thank goodness it's you and not that infernal machine. So, how are you?'

Lara took a moment to gather her thoughts. 'Fine, fine,' she replied. Why on earth was Grandmother Bayley phoning?

'Excellent,' the old woman exclaimed. 'I presume you are still single?'

'Yes, that's right.'

'And you still live alone?'

Lara frowned. 'Yes.'

'And how many bedrooms do you have?'

'Two,' Lara said cautiously. Why was her grandmother asking these questions?

'Splendid. I want to ask a favour of you. Actually, it's a favour for Beatrix.'

'Who?'

'Your Cousin Beatrix.'

Lara's mind went back over the years, picturing a small timid girl peering up from under a thick fringe of coarse brown hair. 'Oh, yes.'

'She would like to come and stay with you.'

Lara bristled. There was no way she was going to allow it. She didn't want a stranger sharing her life.

'In exchange for this favour,' the old woman continued, 'I will, naturally, pay all living expenses for both of you.'

Lara paused, speculating on this. In the circumstances, it sounded an excellent proposition but there had to be a catch. 'I see,' she said slowly. 'And how long does she want to stay?'

'You will be the judge of that. Allow me to explain.' The old lady paused and began again. 'Beatrix has been jilted. Her suitor – let us call him Mr X – has gone off with another woman, who is very much older, I might add.' She sniffed indignantly. 'I want Beatrix to win him back. And I want *you* to help her.'

Lara pulled up a chair and sat down. 'I see.'

Mrs Bayley continued briskly: 'The woman in question is the elegant sort, always well-groomed, unlike your Cousin Beatrix who insists on looking like Alan Titchmarsh! Now this is where *you* come in. In order to retaliate, we need to fight fire with fire.'

Lara balked at this rousing speech.

'I want you to prepare her for battle – help her select the right dresses, the right shoes, the right lipstick. Spend, spend, spend. Can you do that?'

Lara wanted to leap to her feet and yell: 'Yes, yes, yes!' But she remained cautious. 'Buy dresses and shoes,' she repeated. That sounded easy enough. 'No limit?'

'I don't care how much it costs. I want Beatrix to win. I will go one step further,' her grandmother continued. 'If I am pleased with your efforts, I will naturally wish to bestow a gift upon you to show my appreciation.'

Lara's brain went into top gear. What would it be? A priceless family heirloom? A mention in her will? A cheque for £30,000? 'I'll do it,' she said firmly.

'Good girl. But remember, Beatrix has no femininity, no sophistication. I want you to teach her how to flirt with a man, to make the right sort of noises. And none of this talk of propagation units and cabbage rot. No more hammering nails and behaving like some backwoodsman.'

Lara considered this. It was obvious that she would have to meet her cousin for herself before understanding what was needed. 'So when does she want to come?'

'Thursday.'

'This Thursday?'

'Yes. Is that inconvenient?'

'Um . . .' Lara thought wildly. 'No.'

'Capital. The sooner we tackle this problem the better because, should Mr X begin to make wedding arrangements, Beatrix will need to be whisked back here *immediately*, ready or not. So, as you will appreciate, time is of the essence.'

'I must say, to go to all this bother, this Mr X must be quite some catch.'

'Oh yes, he certainly is. Right, I think that's all settled. She will arrive at your address on Thursday evening at about seven o'clock. In the meantime, you may send me a list of your expenses, on receipt of which I will send you a cheque. Is that acceptable to you?'

You bet! 'Yes, Grandmother,' Lara said evenly. 'That is perfectly acceptable.'

'Now don't forget, my dear. When you send Beatrix back to me, I want to see *changes*.'

Lara could feel herself bubbling with excitement, eager to face the challenge. Yep! Whatever happened, Grandmother was definitely going to see changes. 'You can depend on me.'

'Good. I would like you to know that I will not interfere in your endeavours. I give you a free hand.'

'Fair enough.'

'Well, goodbye, Lara and – good luck.'

'Goodbye, Grandmother.' At the sound of the line disconnecting, Lara slowly replaced the receiver and stared at it. This was amazing! She jumped to her feet in glee. All living expenses paid! She would make a list immediately. Of course, she couldn't put champagne on it, nor Moroccan black, nor condoms, but her salary would pay for those sorts of things. She skipped into the kitchen, dragged the bottle of champagne from the fridge and popped it open, pouring the fizzing liquid into a crystal flute. Now she had something to celebrate.

'Cheers, Grandma,' she trilled, raising her glass briefly before tipping the contents down her throat.

With glass and bottle, she returned to the bathroom. What could the mysterious gift be? She couldn't wait to find out. Humming gaily, she shook lavender oil into the foaming bath, undressed, pulled on a shower cap and lowered herself into the water, topping up her glass with champagne before lying back.

Grandmother is going to be thrilled, she thought complacently, relishing the challenge of turning a country bumpkin into a woman of elegance. Obviously, the old bat was not too gaga to realise that it was Lara – *and Lara alone* – who would get results!

Suddenly, she went cold, the glass of champagne poised halfway to her lips. Suppose Cousin Beatrix was too awful to transform? As a child, she had been pale and insipid, with that thatch of brittle brown hair, her eyes magnified behind thick lenses. Lara resolutely knocked back her champagne, feeling supremely confident. This was the twenty-first century, for heaven's sake. There were enough beauty aids out there to transform an orang-utang. Anyway, Beatrix couldn't be that awful if she had managed to attract a man – a man who was a real 'catch'.

She smoothed a mud pack over her cheeks and forehead.

She would dress her in Prada, Chloë, Escada, Lara decided dreamily. It would be just like having a Barbie doll again. Then she would teach her to be feminine, flirtatious . . . capricious. By the time this was over, Cousin Beatrix would have the sophistication of a French countess and the dress sense of Jackie O. It might take time and more than a little effort, but she would do it.

Time? Suddenly she sat bolt upright, causing a tidal wave in her bath. Now that she was working, she wouldn't have time. She had completely forgotten! How could she take Beatrix shopping when she had a nine-to-five job? Well, she would just have to enlist help . . .

Kelsey?

As a rich American divorcée, Kelsey had plenty of time on her hands and, with a low boredom threshold, she would probably be keen to muscle in on the act. But – and this was a big 'but' – she had none of the finesse of her European sisters. If Kelsey took charge, Beatrix would end up with all the sophistication of a clam bake and the dress sense of Lily Savage. According to Kelsey's rules, the way to a man's heart was taking the short cut: Spandex and black leather and forget the knickers. No, she must not be allowed to take charge. She could help, but would need to be closely supervised.

With this decision made, Lara cleansed her face, stepped out of the bath and slipped into a towelling robe before padding through to the bedroom. Her grandmother's proposition would not be a permanent solution, she knew, but at least it was a start.

Sitting at her dressing table, she opened up her jewellery box and dipped her hands into the jumble of sparkling diamond necklaces, the lustre of ruby earrings, the shimmer of a gold bracelet. Whatever happened, she could never sell her jewellery. It meant too much to her: a symbol of all the love and adoration heaped upon her through the years, a reflection of her worth. 'Life will treat me right,' she whispered. 'It always has done.'

Turning back to the mirror, she pulled off her shower cap and began to brush out her hair, drawing pleasure from the sight of the thick auburn waves falling against her pale creamy complexion. A distant uncle had once made a comment that she had a face like a pansy, a comment she had never forgotten. True enough, she had a small, heart-shaped face, a tiny turned-up nose and big brown eyes. She would never be beautiful but she was little-girl cute. She smiled to herself, knowing the effect those eyes could have on a man when she gazed up with an air of vulnerability.

Feeling happier, she began to apply her make-up for the party, determined to boost her spirits by looking extremely wonderful. By eight o'clock she was dressed and ready to go. By eight-thirty she was glancing at the clock. By nine she was standing at the window looking down on the street. By ten she was slumped over the table with her head on her arms, surrounded by two empty jars of truffles, an empty bottle of champagne and a list of expenses scribbled on the back of a brown envelope. She could imagine everyone at the party laughing, dancing, having fun, while she was stuck here waiting for Justin as the evening gradually slipped away. What right had he to keep treating her like this? If only she had the money, she would take a taxi to the party and leave him to wonder where she was. When the intercom buzzed, the force of her anger threw her back in her chair. 'About time!' she fumed, grabbing her coat and purse.

As she marched down the stairs, her head was a jumble of violent accusations. Ten o'clock! He had done it again! She threw open the door to see him standing on the doorstep, his shirt collar open, his tie loose, his arm resting on the doorjamb as if for support. 'Well,' she exclaimed, appraising him with a cool, haughty sneer. 'They finally let you out of your cage.' With this she banged the door shut and headed down the steps to his silver Mercedes.

'Hey!' he called after her. There was the sound of hurrying footsteps. 'Didn't you get my message?' He turned her to face him.

'That's not the point!' A burp exploded from her lips, startling her wide-eyed, but she ignored it and carried on. 'How dare you expect me to hang around waiting for you all night?'

'I'm sorry, darling.' He went to take her hand but she stiffened, holding her hands behind her back. 'It's the Kanasaki merger,' he explained. 'It's taking up a lot of my time at the moment. Once it's finished, things will be different.'

In the glow of the streetlights she could see his pale narrow face, the dark shadows under his eyes, the lick of black hair falling over his forehead. He looked crumpled and tired, handsomely careworn. For a moment she almost softened.

'Do you want to go somewhere quiet and talk about this?' he asked.

'No!' she exploded. 'I want to go to the party.'

With a sigh, he zapped the central locking control of the Mercedes and, before he had a chance to open the door for her, she had got in and slammed it shut.

'I'm really sorry,' he said, slipping into the driver's seat beside her and turning on the ignition.

'Phff!' Further recriminations were a waste of time.

Their relationship was definitely over but she was in no mood to tell him now, and then have to listen to him weeping and wailing.

The Mercedes purred throatily as it swung away from the kerb. 'We can't spend an evening together like this,' he said reasonably.

'Then we won't! You go off with your friends and talk about mergers and I'll got off with mine and have *fun*.'

'I think I might just do that,' he muttered gruffly.

She looked up at him in surprise. He had never spoken like this before. He's working too hard, she thought, studying the harsh lines of exhaustion on his face. Why does he do it? Tense and silent, he drove unusually fast, weaving in and out of the evening traffic and braking sharply at a bend. Once into Park Lane, he accelerated hard.

She, too, remained silent, hiccuping gently, her mouth tasting of bile and truffles. She was tired and drunk and depressed; her brief flight of optimistic fantasy had crashed-landed long since, leaving her with a feeling of dread. Whatever happened, she had to survive until her father could once again support her. But what if she couldn't survive? Would she end up moving to a bedsit in Balham? Living hand to mouth, day to day? Would Harrods become a thing of the past? And Prada and Fendi? And hair by Geno Ventti?

Justin glanced at her as they slowed to a halt at a red traffic-light. 'I do not intend to stay until the early hours,' he stated. 'Unlike you, I have work in the morning.'

'So have I!' she retorted.

'Yeah,' he murmured derisively. 'Twirling around in that chair of yours for five hours a week. Phew! I bet that gives you a few headaches!'

She sat bolt upright to confront him. 'Well, let me tell you something. Today, Timothy gave me the position of his assistant. Full-time!'

He shot her a look. 'You're joking!'

His astonishment infuriated her. 'Why do you say it like that?' she stormed. 'Don't you think I can do it?'

'Um . . .'

'Well, I can!' she cried. 'I know all about responsibility *and* I've got commitment. Timothy needs a right-hand man and that's why he chose me! You might think I'm just some air-head, but I'm not.' They had turned into a wide gravel driveway, the garden illuminated by the soft glow of spotlights.

Why did everyone have such a low opinion of her capabilities? Never once in her life had she been trusted with anything! When she had become pregnant . . . No! She didn't want to think about it. But she *would* think about it. She had been sixteen and pregnant and determined to keep the baby. But her parents had thought otherwise. 'It's such a responsibility, dear,' her mother had said. 'Life is for having fun. Just be more careful next time.' The termination had been fitted in between the Grosvenor Ball on the Monday and the Oxford and Cambridge Boat Race on the Saturday. Mummy had been right of course, but . . .

'I'm sorry to sound surprised.' Justin swung the car to a halt and turned off the ignition. 'But you don't even like the paintings. How are you going to sell them when you don't even like them?'

'You just watch me!' Ignoring the car valet, she swung open her door and got out, staring balefully up at Amelia Harcourt's mansion. There was the sound of laughter and music coming from within, but for once it did not stir her blood. Instead, she felt angry and humiliated.

As Justin took her arm to lead her up the steps, she snatched it away.

'Hey!' he exclaimed. 'Let's at least be civilised.'

She snarled in her throat. She would show him. *Twirling around in her chair all day* – what a cheek! She would have business cards printed, she decided furiously. Then he would see her handing them out at parties while talking at length on Sherman and Devoroc, saying things like: 'Sherman has successfully invaded contemporary art and taken it over. Devoroc's work is less angst-ridden, less conceptual. Neurotic realism will make history.'

As soon as Justin had handed in their tickets and the maid had taken her coat and purse, Lara walked off, immediately swallowed up in a noisy throng of glittering guests. Above the staircase hung a banner proclaiming *Save the Corinthian Mosaics.* She didn't give a damn about the Corinthian Mosaics!

Justin caught up with her. 'Listen. Congratulations—'

'Sweeties, sweeties!' The charity organiser, Amelia Harcourt, bore down on them, her fat body rippling with vivid pink chiffon, her fat wrists choked with pearls. A pink hovercraft at full throttle, Lara thought belligerently.

'Where have you two been?' the woman demanded.

'It was my fault,' Justin replied, bending down to kiss the powdered cheek. 'I got caught up in the office.'

'Again?' Amelia playfully slapped the back of his hand. 'What am I going to do with you?' She encompassed them both in a wide pink smile. 'I want to say a big thank you for coming along tonight to support us. Sir Patrick Ludlow will be hosting the raffle later on.' She smiled, snuggling close to Justin, but speaking to Lara. 'But first, darling, would you mind awfully if I stole this handsome man away? I have discovered the most exciting investment and I do need his advice.'

'Help yourself,' Lara said off-handedly, glancing away.

Amelia had already taken Justin's arm. 'Shall we slip off to the library?' she suggested coyly.

Conscious of a tantrum threatening, Lara scooped up a glass of champagne from a waiter's tray, wanting all the bubbles to zing through her body and make her feel gay once more. Instead, it lay on her stomach, flat and acidic.

When she caught sight of Oliver Marchant, she was surprised and thankful. If anyone could cheer her up, it would be him. He must have just arrived back from one of his trips, she reasoned, noting the tanned skin, the brown hair bleached by some tropical sun. What daredevil stunt had he survived this time? Bungee jumping? Canyoning? Or simply hurling himself off a cliff? Threading through the crowd towards him, she saw who he was talking to and groaned. Bella, the candyfloss redhead with a squeaky giggle and a brain bi-pass who kept a wire coat hanger on the back seat in case she locked her keys in the car.

'Hi, Ollie,' Lara exclaimed, tilting her cheek for him to kiss. 'Still in one piece then?'

He laughed, his vivid blue eyes sparkling. 'Just about.'

'What was it this time?'

Bella answered for him. 'He's been clearing mines in Angola. I think he's so-o-o brave.'

Lara gave her a weak smile, knowing that the girl was wasting her time. Oliver was a love 'em and leave 'em sort. Life to him was one big, irresponsible adventure and if a girl couldn't accept it – well, that was her decision. She smiled tightly and moved away.

At that moment Kelsey appeared in the doorway, her white-blonde curls rising above the crowd, her red lips parted in a wide dimpled smile, a cigarette held at shoulder-height, the smoke of it streaming back like a banner. 'What's wrong with your face?' she exclaimed, bending forward to touch cheeks with Lara. There was a heady scent of Organza. 'You're frowning!'

'I've just had the worst day of my life,' Lara wailed softly, thankful to have a shoulder to cry on – although Kelsey's silken, shoulder-padded Armani jacket was the last place she could rest her head. 'Daddy's gone bankrupt,' she stated, holding back tears. 'And he's had to stop my allowance.'

'Hell.' Kelsey flicked her cigarette into a nearby ashtray. 'So, what are you gonna do?'

'I've decided to work full-time at the gallery.'

Kelsey looked perplexed. 'And Timothy's OK with that?'

Lara stiffened. 'Yes, actually he is.'

Kelsey was still doubtful.

'I know you and the rest of the universe think I'm hopeless, but you just wait. I'm like a teabag,' Lara boasted. 'You don't see my strength until I'm in hot water.' She nodded to emphasise this. 'I've got it all planned out. I'm going to make myself so indispensable to Timothy, he'll start to pay me these huge commissions. He might even make me a partner!'

Kelsey's eyes had opened wide. 'Before you start buying

a ticket on another one of your fantasy rides, can I just say something here? Sure, you look good in the window but it's going to need more than that. Now, I've known you for what – eight years? And in all that time, I've never seen you focus on anything more than a stain on your dress.'

'I can do it!'

'Are you kidding me? You've got as much substance as a scatter cushion.'

Lara gasped, recoiling in shock.

'You're high maintenance,' Kelsey went on relentlessly. 'A wage isn't going to keep you in lipstick. You should do what I do – marry some rich guy.'

'Is that all you can say. Thanks for your support!'

'Jeez, I'm just being a realist. A job won't even pay your cab account.'

'I don't take cabs anymore.'

'You don't? So what do you do?'

'*Fly*.' Hurt and angry, Lara was ready to burst into tears.

Seeing this, Kelsey pulled a chequebook from her Pollini clutch bag and opened it. 'Let me give you something to help you out.'

'I don't need your money,' Lara hissed, but, watching the chequebook sliding back into the folds of black leather, she began to change her mind. No, she told herself firmly. I will not be spoken to like that. I will show her. I'll show everybody! As she flung back her head, ready to flounce off and never speak to Kelsey again, a thought struck her: But who would help with Beatrix?

Kelsey was now elaborating on her rich-husband theme. 'Kelsey?' Lara said, interrupting the flow of chatter.

'Yeah?'

'I need your help.'

'You just name it, honey.'

'My grandmother phoned this evening. Said that if I let my cousin stay, she would pay all my living expenses.' At this, Kelsey's eyebrows shot up alarmingly but Lara ignored her and carried on to explain the plan.

When she had finished, Kelsey nodded. 'I get it. So you've got to turn her into a foxy lady.'

Lara hesitated, feeling the first strings of unease. 'Something like that. And, if I succeed, my grandmother promises to give me a gift.'

'What sort of gift?'

'I don't know, but she's wealthy, so it could mean a big cheque or some valuable heirloom. I'm not sure.'

'And you need my help.' The American girl gave a broad grin. 'Honey, you've come to the right lady. First we'll make her a peroxide blonde. Then—'

'Hang on!' Lara put up a restraining hand. 'Our brief is to mould her into a sophisticated and elegant woman. We have to make her eligible for marriage – not for the centrefold of *Playboy*.'

'But men don't want sophistication; they want black leather and suspenders.'

'I don't care what men want,' Lara retorted. 'If Grandmother wants sophistication, that's what she's going to get.'

Kelsey made a face, her lips pressed tightly together, her eyes rolling heavenwards. 'So what's the budget for her clothes and stuff?'

'There isn't one, which is completely out of character for my grandmother. Although she's wealthy, she's some kind of miser, never known to part with money.'

'Perhaps this guy is someone special. What do you know about him?'

'Nothing much. She simply referred to him as Mr X and said he was a real catch. Apparently, the woman he's gone off with is not only beautiful but also sophisticated. The good news is, she's much older than him.'

Gravely, Kelsey shook her head. 'Don't underestimate the older woman. They've got something we haven't. I don't know what it is, but it's potent.' She folded her arms. 'And this cousin of yours – what's her name?'

'Beatrix.'

'This Beatrix. What's she like?'

'Quite ordinary, really, but she could have changed.' Lara sipped her champagne pensively. 'I haven't seen her since we were children. Her parents died in a car crash when she was about eight; that was when she went to live with Grandmother.'

'Poor girl.' Kelsey's brow furrowed thoughtfully. Suddenly, she stood straight, eyes bright and hard. 'Right. When does she arrive?'

'Thursday evening.'

'Heck – that doesn't give us much time to arrange stylists and stuff. I know for a fact that Gavin's booked up solid for two months.'

'I wouldn't want Gavin to do her hair – he's too extreme. I'd prefer Anabelle Walters, if we can get an appointment.'

'I think we should just take the first slot that comes along, don't you?'

Lara nodded. 'I suppose so, yes.'

'OK, I'll be at your place Thursday evening to meet her and discuss our plan of action.'

'Thanks, Kelsey. I knew I could rely on you.'

'My pleasure. But as far as you're concerned, you're going to have to look to the future, long-term.'

'I don't want to think of the long-term,' Lara muttered. With the heat, the smell of perfume and the cigarette smoke, she was beginning to feel nauseous. 'I need some air,' she moaned, starting for the French windows.

Kelsey came with her. 'Yeah, you do look a bit pale.'

As they settled side by side on a garden bench, Lara flopped forward, elbows on her knees and thought back over the day. Bitterly, she laughed. 'Do you know what I was going to buy this morning? A country cottage!' At that moment, the music inside the house stopped and in the sudden silence, the roar of traffic could be heard. Then the music started again.

'I'm telling you,' Kelsey said softly, 'the only way you're going to get the life you want is to marry rich. Forget a country cottage; get yourself a country mansion with a lord to go with it. Sophie Parker-Johnson did it, so why can't you?'

'He isn't a lord.'

'I thought she said he was. So what is he?'

'A gentleman farmer.'

Kelsey laughed delightedly. 'So she's ended up milking cows?'

Lara shook her head. 'No, no. A gentleman farmer is usually very wealthy and although he's got lots of land, he doesn't actually *farm* it. Normally, he just walks around with a cap on his head and a gun under his arm.'

'So what's the big deal?' Kelsey asked dubiously. 'They do that in the Bronx.'

Lara forced a smile, knowing that her friend was trying to cheer her up, but this time, it wasn't going to work. She felt too depressed. Maybe tomorrow, things would seem better. 'Listen, Kelsey, I don't feel too good. I'm going to ask Justin to take me home.'

Kelsey stood up with her. 'Do you want me to help you look?'

'It's OK – I know where he is.' As they entered the building, Lara veered off in the direction that Justin had taken earlier. It was quieter in this part of the house, the long corridor lined with oil paintings of country life, the smell of stale cigars lingering in the still air. Pushing open a door, she found herself in a library. It was empty. Without warning, her stomach heaved and she staggered to an armchair by the open window and sat down, breathing deeply. After a moment, she looked up, staring sightlessly at a magazine in the wastepaper bin. As her eyes began to focus she found herself reading the words *Gentleman Farmer.* What a coincidence; she and Kelsey had just been talking about that. Sickness forgotten, Lara picked up the magazine and opened it out.

Gentleman farmer, 33. Handsome polo champion. Would like to meet a vivacious brunette to share a life of country pursuits and weekend house-parties. PO Box 2126

Her eyes scanned the page. This was a dating column. She turned to the cover to see a bluebell wood and the title *Country Living.* Swiftly, she flipped back to the advertisement: *Gentleman Farmer.* Feeling strangely breathless, she read through the advertisement again before dropping her gaze to the one below it. *Pig farmer, 34. Hard worker. 6′ 3″ Strong. Looking for a wife. PO Box 2176*

She gave this a patronising smile. Pig farmer – how unglamorous. The advertisement might as well be selling an ox for all the charm and excitement in it. Eagerly, she looked back to *handsome polo champion.* It was very tempting . . . 'No!' she said, throwing the magazine to the floor. The guy could be some nutter. It was too risky. All she wanted to do was to get away from this smell of stale cigars, go home, go to bed.

Abruptly, she stood up, overwhelmed with nausea once more. What if she were sick in front of all those people? Yanking out the potted palm, she carried the copper bowl to the door. At least if she was going to throw up, it would be in this and not on Amelia's carpet.

Moving to the door, she let her gaze sweep over a painting of a Victorian girl in a meadow. She stopped and stared at it, imagining herself standing there, smelling the fresh fragrance of meadow flowers, feeling a sense of space . . . and silence. She sighed. *A life of country pursuits.* The words on the advertisement came back to her.

Suddenly, she stiffened. Why not? Swiftly, she put the copper bowl to one side, snatched up a pen, found the advertisement and scribbled down the address of the magazine on a scrap of paper. At that moment she was disturbed by the sound of men's voices out in the corridor. Quickly now, she added the PO Box number to the paper, shoved it up under the elastic of her knickers, picked up her bowl once more and made for the door.

Out in the corridor, she exchanged a nod with two elderly men as she headed back to the party. She would find Justin and tell him to take her home. Then she would write the letter . . .

Disco music reverberated in the main room, now a mass of gyrating bodies. As she pushed her way through, Lara became aware of a hand shoving something into her bowl. Ignoring this, she carried on, her polite words of, 'Excuse me,' drowned out by the music. Again, she noticed a hand putting something into her bowl. Then another. Abstractedly, she looked down. There was a crumpled mass of twenty-pound notes! People were giving her money! Why? 'Well done!' boomed a voice in her ear as another note went in. Of course, she realised – they think I'm collecting for the charity. 'But,' she turned to explain to the man but was met by a wall of floundering bodies. Oh, to hell with it, she thought, pressing on. She could always keep the money, After all, she was a charity now and certainly far more deserving than a heap of Corinthian ruddy floor-tiles!

She didn't bother to search this room, knowing that Justin was not the type to throw his arms about in gay abandon. No, he would be in some quiet corner talking *mergers*. She came out into the hallway, relieved to be free of that heat and noise.

'Lara.' It was Kelsey, grabbing her arm. 'I was just looking for you.' She paused to look with curiosity into Lara's bowl. 'What's that?'

Lara hugged it to her chest. 'Money.'

'I can see that. Where did you get it?'

'I was collecting it.'

'Oh, right.' Kelsey looked mystified for a moment but then carried on quickly: 'I saw Justin and he says he'll take you home, but he's still talking to Lord Harcourt, so can you wait for about twenty minutes?'

'*Wait*!' Lara snarled.

'Hey, what's the matter?'

'Justin, that's what's the matter. Go back and tell him that I never want to see him again. He can find some other mug to wait for him. I'm going home. Alone!' As soon as she had said this, she realised she had no money for a taxi. Then she looked down into her bowl. Oh yes, she had money. Plenty of it.

'You've had a rough day,' Kelsey said gently, stretching out a hand to take the bowl. 'Don't worry about this. I'll give it to Amelia.'

Lara clung on.

'Hey!' Kelsey's eyes widened in horror. 'You're not planning on keeping it, are you?'

'Why not? I'm a charity, too.'

'But you can't. That's stealing! You do this and you don't know where it might lead. Have you no morals?'

'No.'

Furiously, Kelsey wrestled the bowl from Lara's grasp. 'Stop it!' she cried.

Lara gave in, and then stared mulishly down at the carpet, her arms hanging limply by her sides. It's OK for her, she thought nastily. She's rich. She's got no idea what this is like. Suddenly, she stood erect, gave Kelsey a fierce look and promptly snatched up a twenty-pound note. 'Call it commission,' she said defiantly and turned on her heel.

Arriving home, Lara threw open her apartment door, marched straight to the table, pushed the jars of truffles to one side, and snatched pen and paper from the drawer. Then she stopped. It would be too risky to give her own address. Looking towards the window, she saw the neon sign across the road. *Mario's Wine Bar.*

She scribbled that address at the top of the page and underneath added, *Dear Box No 2176.* She stopped again, trying to construct a sentence in her champagne-befuddled brain.

Then she began to write.

Jack

The air was thick with the smell of stale beer and cigarette smoke, and the late-afternoon sunshine slanted through the window of the Black Lion public house, illuminating the corner of the bar with a bright copper-coloured light.

'I don't believe it!' Jack read it through again. *Pig Farmer, 34. Hard worker. 6' 3". Strong. Looking for a wife. PO Box 2176*

There was a whiff of potato and onion pie as Trevor leant over to point a soil-encrusted finger at the ad. 'The "hard worker" bit was my idea,' he said proudly.

'It makes him sound boring,' Patsy complained, poking the lemon in her gin and tonic.

'No, it doesn't,' Trevor retorted. 'That's what a woman is looking for, a hard worker, not a malingerer.'

Patsy looked unconvinced. 'I still think we should have put "handsome" in it,' she added reproachfully, leaning back to take a packet of crisps from the counter behind her.

Trevor shook his head. 'No, that'll attract the wrong sort of lady. Anyways, he's not handsome.'

With her head to one side, Patsy studied Jack. 'I think he is. Well, he was until he got his front tooth kicked out.'

'I agree with Trevor,' the Colonel began, pushing himself back in his chair importantly. 'I think—'

This was too much for Jack. 'Hang on!' he ordered, holding up a hand for silence. He had been listening to them all with growing astonishment but now he'd heard enough. 'Can I say something here?' He looked down at the advertisement and back to his friends, not knowing how to begin. They meant well but he couldn't allow them to map out his life. For months now they had been encouraging him to find a wife, and now, evidently impatient with his lack of progress, they had taken the matter into their own hands.

'This is a kind thought but,' all eyes were pinned on him, 'but,' he laughed suddenly, 'I can't advertise myself as if I were a stud bull, can I?' He looked down at the magazine once more. 'What is this anyway?' He turned to the cover and saw a bluebell wood and the title. '*Country Living!*' he exclaimed. 'This is a bit out of my league, isn't it?'

'It might have escaped your notice,' Patsy said sourly, 'but *Farmers Weekly* does not have a dating column in it.'

Apart from the crackling of a crisp packet, there was

silence in the bar. From the adjoining room there came a clicking sound as Jamie and Sam rolled balls along the snooker table. The Colonel solemnly picked up his tankard of beer while Trevor folded his arms and stared out of the window.

'I had a bad feeling about this all along,' Ernest muttered, darting a knowing look around the table. No one else spoke.

'I'm sorry,' Jack said, 'but I can't go along with this. You'll have to cancel it.'

Patsy spluttered through a mouthful of crisps, 'Cancel it? How can we cancel it? At this very moment, this magazine is on sale in millions of newsagents all around the country. Maybe the world.' She leaned forward and spoke gently. 'Jack, my love, you've got to be realistic. Your sons need a mother; you need a wife. You've said it yourself – come June, you're not going to have time to look after the house, let alone the boys.'

'But I don't want to find a wife in this way.' He flicked the tips of his fingers against the page.

The rising of Patsy's voice heralded the rising of her anger. 'So how else are you going to do it, eh?' Glancing towards the snooker room, she lowered her voice once more. 'I think you're going to have to forget your high ideals for once, and be practical.'

Jack could not meet her eyes. She was right, but, at the

same time, he didn't want some stranger coming into their lives and taking over. He could only share his bed with a woman he loved and not for some practical reason. And as far as love went, he didn't know if he could ever feel that way again.

'Yes, I had a bad feeling about this all along,' Ernest repeated. He sounded pleased.

'Oh shut up,' Patsy snapped.

'Give it a try, lad,' the Colonel urged. 'There's nothing to fear. No one will know where you live. Simply wait for the replies, and if there's nothing you like, just chuck them in the bin. It's as simple as that.' He wiped his hand across his moustache. 'Of course, you may not receive any replies. Must consider that.'

Thoughtfully, Jack gazed down at the advertisement. It would be humiliating not to receive a single reply. He read through the advertisement again. Patsy was right; they should have put 'handsome' in it. The advertisement above his own had the words: *handsome polo champion*. How could he compete with that?

'Oh, let's forget the whole thing,' Patsy declared irritably, whipping the magazine out of his hand.

Jack whipped it straight back, startling her. 'The Colonel's right,' he admitted. 'I'll just see what happens.' The faces around him broke into grins, apart from Ernest who was now looking alarmed.

'Jolly good show,' the Colonel declared. 'Let's get organised, shall we? As I will be taking photographs of your paintings for those London galleries, I might as well get a couple of you at the same time. In front of my Wolseley, mm? Put you in a shooting jacket with a gun under your arm, perhaps?' He cast jaundiced eyes over Jack's recently shaved head. 'And a flat cap,' he added.

'Have Rosie sit beside you,' Patsy suggested.

'No, no,' the Colonel remonstrated. 'She's a cross-breed. Lower the tone and all that. Have my Persephone instead. A pure-bred flat-coat retriever always gives the right impression.'

'But what about his tooth?' Patsy enquired.

'He can smile,' the Colonel suggested, 'as long as he keeps his mouth closed.'

Self-consciously, Jack put a hand to his mouth. Nero had kicked out the tooth last Saturday but being too busy, Jack had not bothered to do anything about it.

Suddenly, it was all too much for Ernest. 'You'll regret this, mark my words,' he said heavily.

'Ernest!' Patsy hissed. Silenced, he shook his head as if denouncing all involvement and began to pick the scab of dried egg yolk from the front of his woollen waistcoat.

Thursday Morning

Beatrix

Once again, Grandmother's hand flapped vigorously. 'Slow down, slow down!' she exclaimed, keeping her gaze fixed firmly on the road ahead.

With a sigh of annoyance, Daphne braked gently. 'We're going to miss the train at this rate,' she muttered.

'No, we are not.' The hand withdrew. 'I would only ask not to be hurled off the road and down the hillside.'

Watching the backs of their heads, Beatrix smiled ruefully. These two were about to live under the same roof – a recipe for disaster unless Daphne learnt to succumb to the old lady's authority. But that would never happen, for she was too much like Grandmother – obstinate, outspoken and very, very determined. There are going to be fireworks, Beatrix predicted, but there's nothing I can do about it, because I will be miles away. In London!

At the thought of it, she felt a surge of trembling excitement. She had only ever been to London once and that was when she had been a young girl. Now she was going back. There would be Trafalgar Square, Big Ben and Buckingham Palace. And, in the evening, the lights of Piccadilly and street vendors selling roast chestnuts from barrels of burning embers. Her Cousin Lara would be her guide and, with cameras flung over their shoulders and sturdy shoes on their feet, they would walk the whole day, returning to Lara's flat footsore but exhilarated and ready to inspect their trophies of the day – bus ticket, postcards, a miniature Union Jack.

Thoughtfully, Beatrix folded her hands together on her lap. Admittedly, she was not going to London solely to see the sights; there would also be dress shops, shoe shops, perfume counters. She gazed down at her neat beige raincoat, buttoned and buckled, her new beige handbag and court shoes. If she felt odd and uncomfortable in these smart clothes, how was she going to feel in short elegant dresses and high-heeled shoes? She bit her lip nervously, studying her grandmother's profile. Was this all just a waste of time and money? Obviously, Grandmother didn't think so. Now, with her battle plans set in motion, she had taken on a jaunty, confident bearing, her eyes bright with the gleam of war. In fact, she looked years younger.

Beatrix gazed out at the passing landscape. Along the

Marcher crest were turf tracks and bold rock formations. Beyond would be the Welsh peaks, their valleys dotted with white half-timbered farmhouses. She and John Chadwick had spent many a Sunday walking single-file along those tracks, their kagouls and woolly hats protecting them from the bitter westerly winds. She would miss their walks – or would she? What would she miss about them? The cold chapping her lips? John, moody and silent as he trudged on ahead? Did she really want to win him back? To marry him? But she had never seen him in a romantic light; perhaps that had been the problem. She had treated him as a companion and nothing more, content simply to watch him oil his cricket bat out in the sunshine and to trudge behind him along the Marcher crest.

Blocking out the bickering voices coming from the front, Beatrix recalled how, that morning, Grandmother had issued her with a credit card, telling her to purchase whatever was necessary. 'I want to see changes,' she had said sternly.

Beatrix took the mirror out of her handbag and studied her reflection. At Daphne's insistence, she had put on mascara and pink lipstick. The effect of the mascara was lost behind the thick rim of her spectacles, while the pink of the lipstick only served to accentuate the dark downy hair above her upper lip.

In her mind's eye, she could see Susan Dobbs with her

flawless skin, her sleek bob of grey-streaked hair, her elegant fingernails. Beatrix looked down at her own fingernails, broken and cracked with years of gardening and mixing cement. How could she compete? Admittedly, she could bleach the hair on her upper lip and wear short skirts, but she could never develop that air of confidence. As a sophisticated Londoner, Lara would be the first to spot this. Would she become annoyed, knowing that the whole idea was futile? Like a dark wave, Beatrix's doubts washed over her.

Up until now, she had presumed that she and her cousin would become friends, but how could they? One was pretty and vivacious, the other plain and boring. Searching her memory, she could vaguely remember her cousin as a loud, quick-moving child, always shouting and demanding. Spoilt. Selfish.

By the time Daphne had backed the car into a parking spot outside the station, Beatrix was anxiously twisting the strap of her handbag. Swiftly she got out and went to stand beside Daphne, who was now opening the boot. 'Daphne, I don't think this is such a good idea,' she whispered urgently.

'It's a brilliant idea.' Daphne pulled out a suitcase and gave it to her. 'You've just got cold feet that's all. You'll be fine once you get there.'

'What are you two whispering about?' Grandmother

had eased herself out of the car and now came forward, poking the air with her walking stick.

'It's nothing,' Daphne answered.

The old woman was not to be placated. 'I hate whispering,' she complained as they made for the entrance. Then: 'Careful with that suitcase, girl! It's not a haversack.'

Daphne groaned, rolling her eyes, but Beatrix was unable to smile.

In silence they waited on the platform as the crowd of commuters gradually thickened. Beatrix felt the sweat on her palms, heard the buzzing in her ears, her gaze drifting towards a young office worker, her legs encased in sheer stockings, her dress moulded to her figure. Making a comparison, Beatrix looked down at herself, seeing the bulge of raincoat above the belt, her thick beige tights and flat shoes. She stared at the woman once more. Everyone in London is going to look like her, she thought frantically. I'm going to be the odd one out – a frump! As she turned, her words came out in a rush. 'I can't do this!'

Two pairs of hard, intractable eyes stared at her. As Beatrix gazed fearfully from Daphne to Grandmother, the realisation dawned on her. These two, who couldn't even agree on the time of day, were united on one thing: Beatrix Metcalfe was going to London.

Lara

With a bottle of vodka in one hand and a bottle of cassis in the other, Kelsey tiptoed in, stretching her neck to peep round the door. 'Is she here?' she mouthed.

'No, not yet.'

The American girl strode forward, pulling off a wet mackintosh. 'Boy, is it raining. I thought I'd never catch a cab.'

Lara closed the door and headed back to the kitchen, her thoughts once again revolving around the bills that needed to be paid, the country cousin who needed to be 'mothered' and the impossible task of selling the work produced by Timothy's bunch of angst-ridden artists.

'My God.' Kelsey was staring around the room in alarm. 'What's happened in here? You look as if you've been burgled.'

'I haven't had time to tidy up,' Lara muttered, irritated

by Kelsey's dramatic outburst. Hadn't she seen a dishevelled room before?

'What about your cleaner?' Kelsey stopped, embarrassed.

Lara said it for her. Heidi? Well, I can't afford her now, can I?'

'Yeah. Sorry, I forgot.'

Back at the chopping board, Lara picked up the knife and began to cut a green pepper into thin slices, feeling resentful. Kelsey had it all: a top-of-the-range BMW that she never drove, a private trainer with the biceps of Arnold Schwarzenegger and a house in Belgravia from her first divorce, while her second divorce held the promise of an apartment in New York.

In a cloud of Hervé Léger perfume, Kelsey had followed her in and now planted the two bottles on the work surface, pausing to glance at the cookery book which lay open on its stand. '*Boeuf carbonnade à la Flamande,*' she exclaimed in admiration. 'I'm impressed – didn't know you could cook.'

'I can't. You've got the wrong page.' Lara pointed a finger at the small photograph of lettuce leaves on the opposite page. 'I'm doing a green salad followed by Kentucky Fried Chicken take-away, followed by Haägan Dazs ice cream.'

'Nice.' Kelsey sounded unsure. 'I suppose that's what you call eclectic.'

What does she want, Lara thought. A baked Alaska? 'I've only been back for twenty minutes,' she muttered, feeling tired and tense. 'I haven't even had time to change.'

'You poor kid.' Kelsey opened a cupboard and took out the cocktail shaker. 'Hey, I've been able to book Gavin for next week. So, do we have him or wait for your guy?'

'We might as well have Gavin,' Lara said wearily. 'I just haven't got the time to keep phoning for cancellations.'

'Sounds as if you've had a lousy day.'

'I can't seem to cope with the early mornings,' Lara complained. 'And rush-hour on the Tube is just a nightmare.'

'Mm.' Kelsey's sympathetic murmur was almost absent-minded. With a bottle in each hand, she sloshed the vodka and cassis into the shaker. 'I hope you've got enough ice,' she said, turning for the fridge. 'I can't understand you British. You can throw the wildest parties in the Western Hemisphere and yet there's always ten cubes of ice in your freezer.'

Lara frowned at this. Kelsey seemed more concerned with making a cocktail than listening to the problems of her best friend. The shaker was now being deployed like a maracas, Kelsey's wide carefree smile evidence of the fact that she had absolutely no comprehension of Lara's anxieties.

'I got the recipe from Moretons,' Kelsey trilled.

Saddened, Lara turned back to the chopping board. She and Kelsey had always been on the same wavelength, with the same lifestyles, the same carefree existence, but that was all changing. It was as if a hand was now slowly turning a dial, tuning them out of frequency.

'Wine glasses?' Kelsey was searching the overhead cupboards.

'I haven't got any clean ones. You'll have to use those water tumblers.'

Kelsey poured the foaming pink liquid into two glass tumblers and then handed one to Lara. It looked like a strawberry milkshake. 'New York Slammer,' Kelsey declared gaily. 'Cheers!'

'Cheers.' Lara drank deeply, feeling the sweet, potent liquid warming her veins, relaxing the tension in her muscles, softening her mood. Perhaps she was being too harsh on her friend.

Kelsey leant back on the stool. 'So – did you sell any paintings today?'

'I wish. Do you remember me telling you about Nick Thornham?'

'Yeah, isn't he that new stylist?'

Lara sighed. Surely her friend could make an effort to see beyond her life of self-maintenance. 'No,' she replied tartly. 'He's an *artist.* Timothy took him on but can't sell his work, so I've suggested I would try and come up with some publicity ideas – press releases, reviews, an intimate gathering between artist and client – that sort of thing.'

Her friend was now licking a thumb, concentrating hard as she wiped a mark off her leather skirt. Lara pressed on. 'Do you want to see my ideas?' she asked.

'Sure.'

Lara went to her briefcase on the chair, took out two new notepads and put them to one side before lifting out a folder of A4 paper and proudly handing it over. Kelsey fanned through the pages swiftly and with little interest. 'Wow! This stuff could sendya to sleep.'

This was too much! Lara grabbed the folder from her and banged it down on the work surface. Kelsey's grin went from her face. 'No, no, I don't mean it like that. It's, like, not everybody's into this stuff.'

'Can you stop calling it "stuff". It's *art!*'

'Sure.' Kelsey looked around as if lost, helpless. 'Sorry.'

Lara scattered the slices of green pepper into a bowl. 'I admit that I don't share Timothy's tastes but I believe that, if I can win his confidence, he will allow me scope to find an artist who I can believe in.'

This remark was greeted with a lascivious wink. 'When you do, just make sure he's tall, dark and handsome.'

Lara groaned. For the first time in their relationship, she was trying to talk to Kelsey on a serious level, but she might as well be trying to communicate with a Furby.

'Lighten up!' Kelsey chided. 'Where's your sense of humour?'

'I'm trying to discuss my work, my career. This is serious.'

'But I don't like you being serious. It doesn't suit you.'

'You're just going to have to get used to it.' Using her teeth, Lara ripped open a packet of lettuce leaves and tipped them into the bowl. 'My life's changed, whether you like it or not. I've got responsibilities now.' She looked up resentfully. 'But that's something you can't understand, isn't it?'

Kelsey folded her arms. 'It's not fair that you're taking this out on me.'

'I just want you to understand what I'm going through, that's all.'

Silence. For the first time in their friendship, there was friction between them. Day by day, the gap between them was growing wider. The gap between idle rich and busy poor. Now, they were no longer able to discuss the latest Versace show or complain about the newest beauty therapies. Soon they would have nothing in common; their conversation would become stilted until finally there would be . . . silence.

Kelsey uncrossed her arms. 'Actually, I wouldn't mind having another look at your ideas,' she murmured, picking up the folder once more. At the sight of that peroxide-blonde head bent over her work, Lara felt a surge of affection. Kelsey was trying. Perhaps she, too, had sensed their growing differences but refused to let their friendship die.

'This launch party,' Kelsey remarked. 'You should get Oliver Marchant to organise it.'

'Yeah, good idea. That's if I can catch him in between trips.'

'Yeah.' Kelsey looked at her watch. 'She's late. Jeez, I'm nervous, are you?'

'A little.'

'We're going to have a ball,' Kelsey assured her. 'You just keep focused on that gift!' She topped up Lara's glass. 'And as you said, it's gonna be like having a Barbie doll again. Except it'll be a *live* one.'

'Mm.' Lara could not share her friend's optimism. Would Beatrix still be that pale, bespectacled girl with thick wiry hair? 'Look, we may not be able to change her,' she added cautiously.

'Of course we will. Trust me. We're going to make her *hot, hot, hot*. I tell you, this Mr X – his tongue is gonna hit the floor.'

'And Grandmother's temper is going to hit the roof,' Lara muttered, but she could feel herself being swept up on Kelsey's enthusiasm.

'Hey! We're—' Kelsey was interrupted by the buzzing of the door bell.

Immediately, Lara hurried past her and into the sitting room. 'Beatrix?' she called, pressing the intercom button.

There came a small, muffled response.

'Come on in.' Lara pressed the door release but it took three attempts before there was the sound of the door clicking open. Breathless now, she hurried out of the apartment and descended the stairs. At a downward glance, she saw a figure in a shapeless beige raincoat, a suitcase held in each hand. That coat's for the bin, she decided immediately.

'Hi, Beatrix,' she called. Reaching the foot of the stairs, she saw a sallow-faced girl in spectacles, the eyes a blur behind the steamed-up lenses. A downy moustache framed the top lip and a fringe of coarse brown hair stuck out from under a rain-soaked headscarf. Lara's shock was so great, she nearly missed the bottom step. With an effort, she kept the smile fixed to her face as she stepped forward to kiss her cousin's cheek. This was much worse than she had anticipated. 'I'm Lara,' she said cheerfully. 'Did you have a good journey?'

'Yes, thank you.'

Stepping back, Lara noticed the cluster of pimples around the girl's nostrils. Heavens! What would Kelsey think? Would she refuse to help? Lara had taken the suitcases from Beatrix's hands and now led the way up the stairs. 'Is Grandmother well?' she asked. Maybe the girl had a great personality.

The reply came in a flat monotone. 'She's very well, thank you.'

Lara's thoughts spun. Oh no! What a disaster. She entered the apartment to see Kelsey putting her cocktail on the table as she advanced eagerly, craning to get a look at their visitor. This was it! Lara swung the suitcases up against the wall, turned back to Beatrix and led her forward. 'Beatrix, this is Kelsey,' she said, keeping her voice light and breezy. 'She's been dying to meet you.'

Kelsey shook hands with the girl, her eyes intent, a small frown puckering her pencilled brows. What was she thinking? Lara wondered. Would she storm out in a childish tantrum, furious that her new doll was not what she had expected? Suddenly, she gave an exclamation. 'You're drenched,' she cried, tugging at Beatrix's coat sleeve. 'Come sit by the fire and we'll get you dry.'

Exhaling with relief, Lara picked up the suitcases and headed for the spare room. 'I'll just put your cases in your room,' she offered. Kelsey, who never thought of anyone's comfort but her own, was now clucking around Beatrix like a mother hen.

When Lara returned, she saw that the gas-fire had been lit, the flames roaring up from the fake logs. To one side of it, Beatrix sat rigidly on the edge of the armchair, knees together, hands balled tightly on her lap.

'You OK?' Lara asked cheerfuly.

'Yes, thank you.' Beatrix nervously slipped her spectacles down the bridge of her nose in order to circle a fingertip inside each lens. Now, when she looked up, there were two pinpoints of black peering out of the fog. The raincoat and headscarf had gone, to reveal a flower-trimmed cardigan, a tweed skirt and a twisted bun of brown hair. She looked like a church visitor.

And Kelsey was smiling! It looked like a real one, too; not the ceramic one she used in unpleasant situations. With the wet raincoat draped over one arm, she dropped a small cushion behind the girl's back and turned to the table, fitting the coat over the back of a chair. 'Now, Beatrix, honey, what would you like to drink?'

The spectacles turned to the glass tumbler on the table. 'I don't mind. I'll just have what you're having.'

'Alrightee.' Kelsey swept off to the kitchen.

Lara followed quickly, closing the door behind her. 'You can't give her that,' she hissed.

With the cocktail-shaker poised over an empty glass, Kelsey looked at her in enquiry. 'Why not?'

'Because – unlike you – I doubt whether she's developed the drinking constitution of a Polish docker.'

Kelsey considered this. 'Yeah, you're probably right. I'll make it weaker.'

Lara watched her carefully, doubtful about the trickle of lemonade now being added to the pink mixture. But she was not really in a position to make a fuss. 'I'm sorry about . . . about . . .' She jabbed a thumb back over her shoulder. 'I'll understand if you don't want to go through with this.'

Kelsey turned with a drink in her hand, her face expressionless. 'You don't think we can do it, do you?'

Lara regretfully shook her head. 'We'll be able to make *some* changes, but it's not going to be like we thought.' She laughed nervously, trying to make light of it. 'I can't see Mr X's tongue hitting the floor now, can you?'

With her head to one side, Kelsey studied her. 'So you think it's hopeless?'

'Well . . . yes . . . don't you?'

'No. It's just going to be more of a challenge, that's all. You can give up on her, but I'm not.' She walked to the door. 'You think it can't be done – but you just watch.'

Lara followed, curious to find out what would happen next. Kelsey handed Beatrix her drink and now settled herself on the couch, facing her. 'Are you comfortable?' she asked.

Beatrix nodded.

'Now we all know why you're here,' Kelsey began. 'Is that right?'

Hunched over, Beatrix nodded again, those two pin-points staring myopically through the clearing fog.

Kelsey continued. 'Lara has asked me to take charge of this assignment and—' She stopped, interrupted by the sound of Lara's cough. 'Well, not quite take charge,' she amended. 'Let's just say that I've been brought in as a *consultant.*'

Kelsey spoke with such gravity that Lara had to suppress a smile. Now Kelsey lifted a hand as if to a waiter. 'I need to make notes,' she said loftily. 'Lara, go and get me one of your notepads. And a pen.'

Lara promptly stood up, went to the kitchen and brought them back.

Kelsey took them with brisk efficiency. Now she was beginning to behave like a New York cop. Sitting back, she rested the notepad on her knee, flicked it open and held the pen poised, ready to write. 'OK, Beatrix. How would you like to see yourself? What changes do you think are necessary?'

Beatrix had taken a sip of her drink and now coughed. 'I need to buy dresses that will show my knees,' she whispered hoarsely, pressing a hand to her chest.

Kelsey nodded encouragement.

'. . . and I need to buy a pair of high-heeled shoes.'

Silence.

Eventually realising that there was nothing more forthcoming, Kelsey nodded again. 'If we're gonna make changes, honey, we're gonna have to be more adventurous – yeah? Go for the whole enchilada.'

'That means "everything",' Lara chipped in helpfully.

Beatrix nodded. She dipped into her handbag and brought out a Mastercard. 'Grandmother said this would help, but I really don't know how to use it.'

'You don't?' Kelsey stared in astonishment.

'No. I'm sorry.'

Kelsey's shock was swiftly replaced by a smile of indulgence. 'Well, sugar, don't you worry. Kelsey's here and she'll show you how.'

Lara shot her a nervous look. *Oh great!*

Kelsey steamed on. 'OK, Beatrix baby, we can't get you fixed up with a hair stylist until next week, but until then we can study fashion journals and find out what suits you.' Once again, she had her pen poised ready to write. 'Let's get some background information. This Mr X – he's *hot,* right?'

The eyes behind those thick lenses blinked. Beatrix was obviously perplexed by the question.

Kelsey tried again. 'He's awesome?'

Lara stepped in. 'Kelsey is referring to your boyfriend. She wants to know what he's like. Is he nice?'

Beatrix looked at them in turn before nodding.

Kelsey scribbled industriously. 'And the competition? She's the sophisticated type – right?'

Beatrix nodded again.

'Now, let's get a picture of this guy in our heads, so we know what we're aiming for. What sort of things turns him on?' She stopped and started again. 'I mean, what does he like doing?'

There was a moment's silence. 'He likes walking.'

The pen had almost made contact with the paper; now it stopped. 'Walking?' Kelsey queried. It was her turn to look perplexed.

'That's right.' There was a growing confidence in the girl's voice, her glass almost empty in her hand.

Kelsey paused, obviously trying to work this one out. Once again, Lara intervened. 'People in England like walking. You have it in America. What do you call it? Hiking.'

Kelsey seemed dubious about this, but she carried on. 'What else?'

'He likes stamp-collecting,' Beatrix added. 'And oiling his cricket bat.'

Kelsey looked up sharply. Then she swung to Lara. 'This is a joke – right?'

Lara could only shrug helplessly, desperately trying to keep her twitching lips from breaking into a grin.

Beatrix had made a murmur of protest and now spoke. 'I am not joking.'

Kelsey studied her for a moment and then sighed.

'I'm sorry, but I have to say this,' she muttered, beginning to doodle impatiently. 'Your English guys are . . . *wacko!*'

To Lara's utter astonishment, she saw Beatrix break into a wide smile. There was a flash of perfect white teeth, the lips drawn back and tilted up in each corner. The transformation was astonishing. Suddenly, Lara's hopes soared. Maybe there was a chance . . .

Kelsey had seen it too. 'Hey!' she exclaimed. 'What a smile!' Eagerly, she turned to Lara for confirmation, and Lara nodded in agreement. 'Can I just ask you something?' Kelsey indicated with her pen. 'Could you remove your glasses, so we can see your eyes?'

Beatrix lowered her head to slip them off, then lifted her chin to gaze at them in turn. Lara could only stare in wonder. Beatrix's eyes were beautiful. They were hazel-coloured, almond-shaped and fringed with thick black lashes.

'Wow!' Kelsey breathed.

'Absolutely,' Lara whispered. Without those heavy black-framed glasses, Beatrix's face had suddenly taken shape; she had high cheekbones, the outline of her face sloping round to a small pointed chin. It was hard to imagine what she could look like without those eyebrows, that moustache, the thatch of coarse brown hair, those pimples . . . but maybe, just maybe . . .

Evidently, Kelsey had had the same thought. She swept them both with a wide grin. 'Boy, oh boy – are we gonna have fun!'

Jack

'Glad you could make it, old chap.' The Colonel opened the door wide. 'This won't take long.'

With one hand resting on the doorpost, Jack slipped out of his Wellingtons and crossed the threshold in well-worn socks. The Colonel looked beyond him to the front lawn. 'Do the boys want to come in?'

'No, they're fine. They've every intention of trying to teach Persephone to play like a dog.'

The Colonel chuckled. 'They'll have a job.' He led the way across the hall. 'Any replies yet from those London galleries?' he asked.

'Afraid not.'

'Still early days.' The Colonel took him into the dining room, gesturing expansively at the neat piles of photographs and letters that covered the long oak table. 'I must say, we had a damned good result.'

With growing curiosity, Jack approached the table. There were ten, maybe fifteen photographs. Swiftly his eyes moved across the table but he knew almost immediately that he would not find a wife among these plump and grinning faces. It had all been a waste of time. He felt sorry for the Colonel, he felt sorry for the others. They had tried.

'So, what do you think?' The Colonel was looking at him for an answer.

'Wow,' he murmured, picking up a photograph and perusing the letter attached. He had to make some show of interest.

'I've highlighted the pertinent points,' the Colonel explained, pointing to a line of words scored with a band of fluorescent pink. 'Marker pens are a marvellous invention,' he added. 'Would you like a cup of tea?'

Jack shook his head. 'No thanks.'

'Beer?'

'No thanks.' Jack didn't have time for this. He still had to get the boys home for supper and homework. Inexorably the band of fluorescent pink drew his eyes to the words on the letter. *I lived on a farm until I was fifteen . . . I have experience in animal husbandry and modern farming practices. I like to bake my own bread and bottle fruit preserves.*

'She looks the wholesome sort,' the Colonel said heartily. 'Just the type you need.'

Jack put the letter down and picked up another. *I was married to a poultry farmer up until two years ago. Now we're divorced but I'd still like to work on a farm.* He returned the letter to the table and picked up another.

'Have a good look at them,' the Colonel encouraged. 'There's a couple of gems in among that lot.'

I've lived with my parents on a sheep farm all my life and I'm proud to boast that I hold the title of top sheep breeder of Hereford. Quite an achievement! Suddenly, a shout from outside caught Jack's attention. With a tight hold on Persephone's collar, Sam was attempting to drag her across the lawn towards the ball, which was held invitingly in Jamie's hand. 'What are they doing now?' he grumbled, going to the window and opening it. 'Leave her,' he shouted. 'If she doesn't want to play, just leave her.'

'OK, Dad.'

Jack closed the window and turned back to the table. It was then that he caught sight of a photograph in the wastepaper basket. It was the face of a woman, a beautiful woman. Curiously, he picked it up and gazed at it. She was laughing, her dark brown hair like a cloud around her kittenish face. He could almost feel the softness of that hair, hear the laughter in her voice.

'She's not what we want,' the Colonel muttered grumpity, taking the photograph and tearing it in two.

Jack was appalled. He reached out a hand, wanting to

put the pieces together so that he could gaze upon that face once more.

'No, old boy, completely unsuitable.'

'But why? What's wrong with her?'

'See for yourself.' The Colonel pointed to a crumpled ball of paper in the wastepaper basket. 'That's the accompanying letter.'

Swiftly, Jack took it out and smoothed it flat, eager to know more. The address was *Mario's Wine Bar, Kensington Avenue, London SW6*. Evidently, she was a barmaid in London. He read on:

Dear PO Box 2176,

I'm rather drunk so I hope you'll excuse the writing. I saw your advertisement at a party tonight and I just had to answer it. The country life really appeals to me. I want meadows of wild flowers, a harvest moon (is there such a thing?). I want to see lambs gambling (or is that gambolling?) in the fields.

Jack laughed at this, eagerly reading on.

I want cool cider in the summer with picnics on top of a haystack. I want a real log fire in the winter with a jug of mulled wine (I'm not an alcoholic – honestly!)

I'd be great company. I can't cook, I can't even change the dust bag in the Hoover and I don't know one end of a cow from the other – but I do know how to party. So what do you say? Do you want to give me a call?

Best wishes

Lara Bayley.

Jack realised he was grinning. He made to read through the letter once more, but it was snatched from his hand. He looked up in surprise to see the Colonel frowning heavily. 'Don't even *think* about it, Jack.' With one hand, the older man crushed the letter into a tight ball. 'You need a wife, you need a mother for your children. Do you think someone like *this*–' he held up the ball of paper and shook it – 'would want to take on the responsibility of two small boys?'

Defeated, Jack could only hang his head and stare at the carpet. 'No, I suppose not.' Suddenly, he was filled with a strange melancholy. It was as if a beam of bright light had entered his life but just as quickly, it had gone.

'Come on, laddie,' the Colonel coaxed. 'Let's have a look at these other letters, eh?'

Jack shook his head. 'There's no point.' From deep within him, he felt determination, growing and strengthening by the second. 'I'm sorry, Colonel,' he said firmly, 'but I want to meet her.'

'She's totally unsuitable, man!'

Jack stood his ground. 'At least, give her a chance. Let

me meet her. I'll explain everything to her and then if she doesn't want to continue, I'll understand perfectly.'

The Colonel's brow had furrowed, his shoulders hunched, his mouth set in a stubborn line. He looked like Nero the bull – all he needed was a ring through his nose and a great hoof pawing the ground. 'She's nothing more than a good-time girl. For heaven's sake – she can't even *cook!*'

'I know she's unsuitable,' Jack agreed humbly, changing tactics, 'but as you well know, I haven't had a woman's company for a while now, and this just might be the right opportunity for me to get back into the *swing of things.*'

The Colonel narrowed his eyes suspiciously. After a moment, he sighed, glanced down at the crumpled letter in his hand and then looked back up at Jack. 'I think you're making a big mistake,' he said unhappily. 'I really do.'

Friday

Beatrix

The blare of a car horn roused Beatrix from sleep. With bleary eyes, she peered at the unfamiliar curtains, conscious of the muted hum of traffic coming from far below. Where was she? London! She was in London! This sudden realisation jolted her upright, causing a stab of pain to shoot through her head. Accustomed to Daphne's frequent displays of head clutching, she knew exactly what she had: her first hangover!

Groping for her spectacles, she swung out of bed and hurried to the window to pull back the curtains to see rooftops and chimney pots stretch away into a pearly sky of pink and grey. Directly below, pedestrians crowded the pavements, cars and motorbikes filled the road. And there was a red double-decker bus!

Last night she had been too drunk to notice her surroundings, but now she let her gaze travel over every detail of her bedroom. She marvelled at the pink wallpaper stamped with tiny roses, the old mahogany wardrobe, the green velvet-covered armchair, the pile of furry toy animals stacked upon the chest of drawers and along the shelves. This was like a child's room; there were teddy bears of all sizes, pink pigs, gorillas and koala bears. Moving into the centre of the room, she was alarmed to see her clothes strewn across the floor. Hastily, she began to pick them up. She had not even removed the grips from her hairbun. Strangely, she didn't feel guilty. After all, she was a single girl now and this was how she was meant to behave.

She smiled, remembering back to the previous evening. There had been giggling and chatter, a delicious meal of fried chicken and ice cream and glasses of pink foaming alcohol. Contrary to all expectations, Lara had been kind and considerate, not at all how Beatrix had remembered her. In fact, thinking about it now, Grandmother's description of her cousin had been quite inaccurate. Not only was she fully employed but she was also very sensible, at pains to curb the American girl's outrageous plans. Beatrix chuckled now, recalling Kelsey's flamboyant gestures and American pronunciations and her references to John Chadwick as 'Mr X' – as if he were some glamorous being. There had been talk of make-overs, fashion victims, style surfing, accessorising, toe cleavage and pulling power.

At midnight, Lara had gone to bed, saying that she had work in the morning but Kelsey had stayed on until the early hours, planning and scheming. Although bemused by her new friend's high expectations, Beatrix had determined to put herself in her hands – completely – and to do whatever was asked of her.

Now she cocked her head to listen. There was the sound of movement out in the sitting room. Putting on her dressing gown and slippers, she emerged from her bedroom to see Lara in a white slip tossing cushions aside as if searching for something, a corkscrew of hair bobbing over one eye as she glanced up. 'Oh, sorry Beatrix, did I wake you?'

'No, no, I was awake already.' Beatrix felt no lingering shyness towards her cousin. Last night, the New York Slammers had successfully wiped away her timidity and, warmed by their show of concern and exuberance, she had fallen into their arms like a homeless puppy welcomed by a pair of loving owners.

Lara continued her frantic search. 'I'm running late so I won't be able to make breakfast but you just help yourself, OK?'

'Please, don't worry about me.' Beatrix advanced into the room. 'Would you like me to make you a cup of tea?'

'You're a sweetheart, but I haven't got time.' Lara grabbed a hairbrush that lay half-hidden under a magazine and began to pull it back through her hair in firm, quick strokes, the waves of deep chestnut bouncing back with each stroke. 'I'm sorry to have to leave you like this, but Kelsey will look after you. She might've said she'd be here by ten but, knowing her, she won't appear until after lunch. Or maybe not at all.'

'I'll be fine. Don't worry about me.'

Lara threw her brush back on the sofa and hurried into her bedroom. 'As you've probably gathered, Kelsey can be a bit mad,' she called out. 'So, if she does turn up, take everything she says with a pinch of salt.'

Beatrix smiled at this, remembering last night and her panic when Kelsey had begun to lecture her on the art of flirting.

'Oh, fuck!' Lara exclaimed suddenly. 'My zip's stuck. Beatrix, could you help me, please?'

Immediately, Beatrix went into the bedroom, freeing the material that had snagged in her cousin's zip. Finished, she stepped back to stare in awe at the mess around her. Drawers lay open, spewing out stockings and satin slips, the wardrobe doors stood ajar, disgorging shoes and shoe boxes, wine glasses littered the dressing table and the floor was covered in clothes and balls of cotton wool.

'Now don't forget,' Lara said, slipping her feet into powder-blue shoes whilst clipping on a pearl earring. 'We've got everything organised to give you a full make-over next week. I've taken time off Monday and Thursday mornings. In the meantime, I've put some magazines out on the coffee table. They'll give you some ideas.'

'Thank you.'

'I'm not sure what Kelsey intends to do today but if you do go out, don't forget to take your key.' Lara was now in the sitting room, buttoning up a short, powder-blue jacket, which matched her slim-fitting dress. Lara was astonished that someone could emerge from that chaos looking so elegant. 'And if there's anywhere you want to go,' Lara continued, fitting a cardboard folder into a briefcase, 'you just tell her and she'll take you.'

'Actually, I wouldn't mind going sightseeing.'

Lara paused. 'Sightseeing?'

Beatrix nodded. 'I'd love to see Big Ben. I've brought my walking shoes.'

A slow smile spread across Lara's face. 'Yeah,' she agreed enthusiastically. 'Kelsey would love that.' Remembering her urgency, she grabbed her case. 'Make sure you ask her.' In a wave of perfume, Lara kissed her cheek and was gone.

After the frantic activity, her departure left a stillness, and suddenly Beatrix felt very alone. Would Kelsey forget her promise to come and keep her company? Why should someone so extrovert and glamorous want to waste their time on her? Even now, Beatrix glowed warmly with the welcoming reception she had received last night, but at the same time, she couldn't help but worry that her two new friends would soon lose interest in her.

She crossed the sitting room and opened the curtains wide on London. 'Whatever happens,' she whispered, 'I am going to make the most of every minute.' On the other side of the road stood Mario's Wine Bar, shuttered and dark, and beside it a patisserie, bright and colourful, with a queue trailing out onto the pavement. So much was happening out there and she couldn't wait to be part of it.

Remembering her camera and guidebook, she went into her bedroom and took them out of the suitcase, returning to place them on the dining table ready for use. Then she looked around her new home and her chest expanded with happiness.

Above the marble mantelpiece hung an enormous gilt-framed mirror and on either side of the hearth were two deep soft sofas in pastel pink. Between them sat an oval glass-topped coffee table littered with magazines. Her research material! It was a big room with a high coved ceiling, and a vast window lined with heavy flowered curtains.

She loved this room, she loved the bathroom with all its curious boxes, bottles, tubes and lotions, she loved the kitchen with its stark modern design and under-cupboard lighting. Everything was so new and exciting. The noise of the traffic outside. The smell of roasted coffee beans and cigarette smoke mingled with perfume and nail varnish. All the smells of a single girl's pad in London! She felt a deep gratitude to Grandmother for making this happen and to Daphne for her stern, but encouraging, insistence.

Humming 'Edelweiss', she got dressed, brushing out her hair and twisting it neatly back into a bun at the base of her neck. Then she began to tidy up, folding Lara's clothes, watering the jade plant by the window, putting the magazines in a neat pile. Then she stopped and picked up the top copy. Accustomed to *Gardener's Weekly*, she was curious to discover what other girls read. There was an article headed *R&R: A User's Guide to Rehab Clinics. Catwalk Report: From Techno Peasant to Miami Princess. Design: The Art of Bikini-line styling.* Bikini-line styling? What did that mean? She turned to the relevant page to be met by a trim shape of pubic hair peeping over a pair of leopard-skin underpants. Goodness! Was this what was fashionable?

She flipped through the pages to see an evening gown of shimmering copper threads that looked like tinsel Christmas decorations, and a short dress of green interwoven plastic that reminded her of the polypropylene ground cover she used to suppress weeds. Was this what she was expected to wear? Having spent her teenage years with the village butcher and a gaggle of old women who discussed doodlebugs and rationing, she was completely out of touch with the modern world.

Preoccupied, she carried on her work, collecting the glass tumblers and carrying them into the kitchen. As she emptied the wastepaper basket into the fliptop bin, she saw a piece of torn photograph caught up in the wickerwork. It was part of a man's head. She found the other piece. Now, she was looking down on a grave, handsome face, a lick of black hair falling over a high forehead. On the back had been scribbled *To darling Lara. I will love you always. Justin, xx.* What had happened to make Lara want to destroy this photograph? Knowing that it was none of her business, Beatrix dropped it into the bin. After everything that Lara had done for her, she could not betray her trust by snooping into her life.

She carried on, stacking the plates in the dishwasher before slipping on an apron and a pair of Marigold gloves ready to wash the kitchen floor. She was doing exactly what she would have been doing at Castlemaine, but there was a big difference; this was all new and exciting and she was more than happy to keep her new home spruce and tidy. Suddenly, the intercom buzzed and she looked towards the sound. Kelsey? She went over and, remembering what Lara had taught her, pressed the intercom button. 'Hello?'

'It's me.' A moment later, Kelsey hurried into the

apartment, head bent, a mobile telephone clamped to her ear, a camera strung over one shoulder. 'OK, right,' she was muttering.

Beatrix was delighted to see the camera. Kelsey had had the same idea!

With the mobile telephone still held to her ear, Kelsey nodded. 'I'll wait,' she said. 'Call me as soon as you know.' She pressed a button and gave Beatrix a wide smile. 'That's the hair stylists. There's been a cancellation so we might – just *might* – get an appointment today.'

Beatrix's heart thudded. She wasn't ready to go to the hairdresser's. It was too sudden.

Seeing her expression, Kelsey put a hand on her arm. 'Don't look so scared, honey. Don't you want to get your hair done?'

Beatrix nodded. 'Yes, yes, but I didn't think it would happen so soon.'

'The sooner the better,' Kelsey insisted. Suddenly her gaze dropped to Beatrix's hands. 'What are these?' she demanded, putting a thumb under Beatrix's wrists and lifting them up disdainfully.

Startled, Beatrix looked from one limp hand to the other. 'Rubber gloves,' she mumbled. 'I'm just cleaning the kitchen floor.'

'No! No! No!' Abruptly Kelsey released her wrists. 'You do *not* clean kitchen floors, you do *not* wear aprons and you do *not* wear rubber gloves. A man must never – *never* – see you in these things, unless . . .' She hesitated for a moment. 'Unless, of course, he specially requests them. OK?'

Beatrix nodded, not quite sure what she was agreeing to, and began to peel off her gloves.

'I think at this point in your life, you need a role model. Someone like me.' Kelsey pointed a long pink fingernail at herself. 'So listen up. You do not wear slippers, especially tartan ones with furry balls.' She made a face and shuddered, causing Beatrix to laugh. 'And you never go into a supermarket with a handsome man.'

Although Beatrix could never imagine going anywhere with a handsome man, she still had to ask, 'Why not?'

'The lighting, of course. Do you want to look as if you've been dipped in formaldehyde?' Kelsey marched into the centre of the room and spun on her toes. 'Now, the schedule for the day. If this hair appointment doesn't come through, we'll check out an optician's; see what they've got in the contact lens department.'

Contact lenses? Beatrix balked at this. Last night Lara had mentioned fashionable spectacles but she had not said anything about contact lenses.

'Is there a problem with that?' Kelsey had noticed her worried expression.

'Well, there might be. I did try them about nine years ago but I found them very uncomfortable.'

'They've changed since then. Now they're just these tiny plastic throwaway things. With a little practice you'll soon get used to them.'

Hearing the concern in Kelsey's voice, Beatrix smiled, grateful that this new and wonderful friend was trying to help her. At that moment, she strengthened her resolve to be brave, to take change in her stride and not to voice objections.

Kelsey grinned. 'Now, is there anything special you want to do? Anywhere you want to check out?'

'I wouldn't mind . . . um . . . checking out Big Ben.'

'Big Ben?' Kelsey frowned. 'I don't know that one. Is it a shoe store?'

'No, it's a clock.'

Kelsey stared at her.

'It's a *big* clock. Next to the Houses of Parliament.'

'O-h-h, *Big Ben!*' Kelsey laughed at her misunderstanding. Suddenly she stopped and looked confused. 'Why do you want to go there?'

'I just thought it would be nice to do a bit of sightseeing.' Beatrix turned to her map on the table and opened it out. 'I've calculated that we can walk there from here. It would take about an hour. Then . . .'

'Wait up.' Kelsey pushed out her palms. 'I don't walk.

Especially for an *hour.* You might get me crossing a sidewalk and into a cab, but that's *it.*'

'Oh! It's just that I saw your camera and thought . . .'

Kelsey glanced down. 'This is to take before-and-after pictures, so your grandmother can see the awesome stuff we've achieved.'

'Oh.'

Witnessing her disappointment, Kelsey sighed impatiently. 'Maybe we'll go see Big Ben,' she muttered. 'Some time. But I can't promise anything.'

Beatrix smiled, suspecting that Kelsey would relent; of course, she would probably go with dragging heels but she would do it anyway, out of kindness.

Suddenly there was the sound of bleeping and Kelsey clamped the cellphone to her ear. 'Kelsey Howitz speaking.'

Not wanting to eavesdrop, Beatrix went back into the kitchen and hung the rubber gloves over the sink, before tearing a square of clingfilm from a roll and stretching it over a bowl of chicken pieces. There was a loud exclamation. '*Great!* We're on our way.'

Beatrix's heart leapt into her mouth, knowing by the triumphant tone in Kelsey's voice that the hair appointment had been confirmed. Kelsey rushed in, staring down at her watch. 'Quick, honey we've got exactly twenty-two minutes. Just grab your coat.'

With a thumping heart, Beatrix lifted her frumpy raincoat from the back of the chair. This was too sudden. She wasn't ready for it. But Kelsey had the apartment door open. 'Let's go!' she cried.

Frantically, Beatrix changed into her shoes.

'Have you got your latchkey?'

'Oh, no.' Beatrix dashed to the mantelpiece and grabbed it.

Seconds later they sat side by side in a taxi. 'If we're just one minute late,' Kelsey fretted, staring fixedly ahead as if willing the taxi to go faster, 'he'll refuse to see us.'

Beatrix buttoned up her raincoat, breathing deeply to calm herself. Although nervous of what lay in store, she couldn't understand why Kelsey was so worried. After all, they were only going to the hairdresser's. Sylvia in the village at home never minded when her customers were late; in fact, she always seemed quite happy to wait with a cigarette in her mouth and a magazine open on her knee. Unless, of course, she was doing a perm. Was this what all the panic was about – a perm? Beatrix's heart sank, remembering the time when she had emerged from Sylvia's, her face scalded red, her hair frizzy. She glanced at Kelsey, wanting to know what lay in store.

'Um . . .' she coughed. 'Kelsey? Do you have any idea what sort of hairstyle I should have?'

'That's up to Gavin. He'll know what's best.' The

American girl tapped an impatient finger on her knee, then craned her neck to look over the driver's shoulder.

Beatrix had to know. 'Will I have a perm?'

'No way.'

Relieved, Beatrix sat back. Now she studied Kelsey from the corner of her eye. It was the middle of the day and yet she wore four strings of pearls and bright red nail varnish. She did not have the dainty features of Lara; she was more rounded, statuesque, her bright blonde hair and wide red mouth making her striking rather than beautiful. Beatrix understood that she was sexy; she had seen the way that the men on the street had looked at her.

As the taxi turned the corner, Kelsey visibly relaxed. 'Nearly there,' she said, smiling at Beatrix. 'How about, afterwards, we pick up a sexy little number. Short skirt, tight top. What's your colour?'

Beatrix could hardly breathe with fear and excitement. 'Pink?' she hazarded.

Kelsey judged her through narrowed eyes. 'Yeah. Sounds good.'

The taxi swerved into the kerb and stopped. 'It'll be quicker if you walk from here, luv,' the driver shouted back.

'OK.' Kelsey flung open the door and stepped out, thrusting a twenty-pound note at the driver.

Beatrix was quick to protest. 'Let me pay.'

'My treat,' Kelsey said quickly, shoving the change into her bag.

They set off at a brisk march, Beatrix tripping to keep up with her new friend while side-stepping oncoming pedestrians. For someone who doesn't like walking, she thought, Kelsey's pretty good at it. They had crossed a side street and now approached a glass-walled building on the corner. Beatrix could see everything that was happening inside, customers in black smocks, hairdressers wearing platform shoes and purple lipstick cutting hair, brushing hair, painting hair. With the potted palms and sofas it looked like someone's sitting room.

Inside, there was the smell of bleach and the chatter of voices vying with the ear-splitting volume of thumping music. Within seconds she was robed and sitting in front of a huge mirror with only a plateglass window between her and the pavement. Being on display made her feel uncomfortable. She didn't want all those people staring at her. Preoccupied with this, she was startled to feel the touch of hands on her shoulders and looked into the mirror to see a small, spiky-haired man standing behind her. He wore a string vest and an earring and looked like a window cleaner.

'Hi!' he said. 'I'm Gavin.'

Gavin? 'Hi,' Beatrix murmured, embarrassed at using the word. 'I'm Beatrix.'

Kelsey had been speaking to someone at the reception desk but now she broke off and hurried forward. 'Gavin!' she cried. 'Thank you so much for seeing us.'

'My pleasure.' He turned back to Beatrix, swiftly removing the grips from her hair. 'So Beatrix, what are we going to do for you today?'

'Um . . . I'm not quite sure.' Her hair was now being brushed in long, firm strokes.

'Hey!' Kelsey exclaimed. 'I didn't realise you had such long hair. Jeez, it goes down to your waist.'

'And it's starved of nourishment,' Gavin said sternly. 'I can tell this hair has not seen conditioner in years.'

Overcome with guilt, Beatrix dropped her gaze.

'Will you be able to do something with it?' Kelsey asked.

'Of course. It's strong – we can keep the length.'

'Beatrix wants to be transformed,' Kelsey told him. 'She wants to go for a sexy, feminine look.'

Thoughtfully, Gavin stood back from Beatrix and struck an artist's pose, tapping a finger on his lower lip. 'Would you mind taking off your glasses, Beatrix?' he asked her. 'So I can get a better look at your face.' She did as he suggested, her surroundings becoming a blur.

'We're going for a full make-over,' Kelsey told him. 'You've got to try and imagine her after three hours in a beauty salon, yeah? Eyebrows shaped, facial hair zapped, contact lenses, a pink halter-neck jumper . . .' Her words trailed off.

Gavin was nodding studiously. 'Sexy and feminine,' he repeated. He ran his hands back through Beatrix's hair, his fingertips firm against her scalp. 'You've got thick hair,' he said. 'So it can take colour.'

Kelsey interrupted again. 'What about white-blonde,' she suggested. 'The Marilyn Monroe look, sort of fifties' Hollywood.'

Gavin hummed indecisively. 'I'm thinking more along the lines of Rita Hayworth. We keep the length and go for red, soft and wavy.'

Beatrix sat like stone, her heart thumping so hard that it hurt. *Red! Rita Hayworth!* She knew it was only polite that she should join in their discussion and make some observation, but she was too stunned to speak. What were they going to do to her?

'Sounds good to me.' Kelsey's face was now in her line of vision. 'Does that sound good to you, honey?'

Beatrix swallowed hard, her mouth dry. 'Yes,' she breathed.

Gavin handed her her spectacles and she put them on, staring at herself in the mirror, unable to imagine herself with long red hair. With a click of his fingers, Gavin was immediately surrounded by assistants. A cup of coffee appeared, a trolley on wheels arrived, a pile of magazines was placed on the shelf in front of her.

Happy and excited, Kelsey patted her hand. 'Isn't this just so thrilling?' she beamed.

Beatrix gave her a nervous smile while slipping an arm into the black smock held out for her. 'Yes, it certainly is.'

Kelsey took out her mobile phone. 'Look, I'm going to try the beauty salon again. They might be able to fit you in this afternoon.'

Beatrix watched her. Everything was happening so quickly. Kelsey's words came back to her: *Imagine her after three hours in a beauty salon. Eyebrows shaped, facial hair zapped, contact lenses . . .* Up until this moment, she had never been too concerned with her looks, but now she could feel a growing determination to change, to blossom out of these middle-aged clothes and sensible shoes, to wear lipstick and perfume. To be pretty.

'Honey!'

Beatrix looked up to see Kelsey grinning at her. 'We've done it. You're booked in for two o'clock.' She crouched down, leaning her arms on the side of the chair. 'It's all going to happen today! What do you think about that?'

Beatrix caught her breath, thrilled but scared. 'Oh, thank you.'

'Don't thank me. I haven't had so much fun in years. But I can't promise whether we'll have time to get you a new outfit. It depends on when we leave here.' She studied her watch. 'Yeah, we should be in here four hours, that means we're out at one twenty.'

Four hours! They were going to be here for four hours! What on earth were they going to do with her in all that time? And she wanted to use the lavatory, too. 'Kelsey,' she asked, blushing, 'Would Gavin mind if I spend a penny?'

Kelsey looked at her. 'Spend a penny?'

There was a chuckle behind them. It was Gavin. 'That's English for going to the restroom,' he explained, pulling back Beatrix's chair to let her out.

Kelsey's face spread into a grin. 'I was going to say Gavin would want you to spend more than a penny.' She winked at him. 'Wouldn't you, darling?' He laughed.

'Actually,' Beatrix began, turning to him. 'How much will it all cost?'

'No more than three hundred,' he assured her.

She stared at him. 'Pounds?'

He nodded.

'Wait up!' Kelsey had the camera to her eye. 'Let's get a photo.'

Beatrix gazed into the lens in a state of shock. *Three hundred pounds!*

The camera flashed. Then Kelsey's grinning face appeared above it. 'I tell you, Lara is going to get the surprise of her life!'

Lara

Lara hurried up from the tube station and strode purposefully along the pavement, her head bursting with new and exciting ideas; cross-promotions, listings, accessing young collectors, extended openings. For the past four days she had spent an hour before work with Pamela – a friend-of-a-friend and an established dealer – who had revealed the secrets of running a successful gallery space in Stepney. It had made Timothy's gallery seem almost Dickensian in comparison but now, thanks to Lara, it was about to move into the twenty-first century. He was going to be so impressed that he would no longer keep reminding her that he really did need a bilingual assistant who knew the rules of the game. Ha! Lara thought scornfully. That was one thing she had learnt: there were no rules to selling contemporary art. Anyone could do it as long as they had contacts, charm to befriend new artists and imagination to promote. Contacts, charm and imagination: the three attributes she held in abundance. Timothy would soon find her indispensable, eagerly offering her a pay-rise or commission, which would inevitably lead to a partnership: Smith & Bayley. Sounded good.

She crossed the road to the gallery. I don't need a wealthy husband, she thought triumphantly. I can survive on my own. Admittedly, she had been content to accept money from her father, but that money had been given without ties, without penalty. Marriage would be different. Her pride would not allow her to live on the whim of some spoilt, petulant playboy.

Anyway, marriage always ended up in a messy court battle. Look at her parents. Look at Kelsey.

Pushing open the gallery door, she saw Timothy standing at the light box with a magnifying glass in his hand. He turned at her entrance. 'Good morning, Lara. How are you today?'

'Extremely well, thank you.' She dropped her briefcase by her desk before going to stand beside him, eager to reveal all she had learnt. 'I've got some ideas for the gallery.'

'Oh, really?' He lowered the magnifying glass and turned to her. The light shone harshly on the broken veins on his cheek.

She had heard the flat tone in his voice but ignored it. 'I

think we should become less parochial. Open up. Try and attract a younger clientèle by extending the opening hours to, say, eleven p.m. We could provide pastries and coffee in the morning and wine and music in the evenings. What do you think?'

'Coffee and pastries!' he chuckled. 'This is not a car showroom, Lara.'

As he turned back to the light box, she was quick to keep his attention. 'I've been to see a gallery – in Stepney. It had drawers and drawers of unframed-works-on-paper affordable for young, new collectors.'

He shook his head, bending forward to peer through the magnifying glass at a row of transparencies. 'That will consume valuable space for a small return.'

Lara could feel her eagerness evaporating. 'How about cross-promotion?' she suggested, instead. 'This dealer that I saw, she worked with Smirnoff and exhibited Russian icon paintings.'

He sighed and straightened up, looking at her with weary eyes. 'This is not a circus. I understand what you are telling me, but my methods of business are quite different to some prints-and-poster establishment on the outer reaches of London.'

'But—'

'No, Lara. I sell to global industrialists, not to some teenager wandering in off the streets. Our customers speculate. They buy paintings purely as an investment and not to fill wall space.'

'Oh.' Silenced, Lara remained for a moment, trying to collect her thoughts. Obviously, a listing in *Time Out* would not be a welcome suggestion. But she had so many ideas, wonderful ideas. Disheartened, she turned away, all hopes of fabulous pay increases and commissions dwindling fast. Partnership! How naïve. At this rate, she would be lucky to keep her job.

'I appreciate your enthusiasm, Lara.' He waved a limp hand. 'If you want to put some ideas down on paper, I might consider them.'

She knew he was merely placating her, giving her something to do to fill in her time. 'You never know what might come of it,' she said, trying to keep her voice light. 'You might end up making me a partner.'

He smiled absent-mindedly as he glanced at his watch. 'Talking about partners, I'd better get a move on. I'm meeting Vittorio for lunch.'

'Vittorio?'

Timothy closed the lid of the light box. 'Yes, the chap I was telling you about. He has the most marvellous gallery in Milan and has agreed to join forces with me.'

'You mean a partnership?'

'That's correct.'

She watched him put on his jacket and head for the

door. 'If I'm not back by five,' he said, 'just lock up and go home. I'll be on my mobile if you need me. See you tomorrow.'

'Is there anything you want me to do?' she asked.

'Just look pretty,' he called back. Then he was gone.

Angry and humiliated, Lara sat down at her desk and stared out at the street. *Window dressing.* Kelsey had been right about that one. Timothy had not given her a chance; he was merely waiting until her 'trial period' was at an end before replacing her.

But she had to keep this job. Once again, her imagination spiralled down in a vortex of anxiety, landing with a thump at the thought of a flock-walled bedsit in Streatham. I mustn't panic, she told herself. I've still got Beatrix; as long as she stays, everything will be paid for. But what happens once she's gone? Surely, Grandmother will come to my rescue – especially after I've agreed to help her?

Thoughtfully, she picked up a pencil and began to draw a zigzag shape on her notepad realising that – for the moment – she could do little for her cousin, but all that would change next Thursday when they went to the hairdresser's. Lara had thought long and hard about this and she had finally decided on the look for her cousin: gamine. Short, boyish, honey-blonde haircut, cool designer spectacles, soft tailored outfits in cream and white, understated but elegant. This look would be the closest match to her personality, hopefully masking her timidity by making her appear reserved and intellectual.

Lara gazed out of the window once more, absent-mindedly prodding the soft end of her pencil into her cheek while trying to imagine Beatrix and Kelsey together at that very moment. Were they leafing through magazines? Or walking up and down the living room with a pile of books on their heads? Or sightseeing? Lara reached for the telephone and dialled home. No answer. Grinning, she replaced the receiver, picturing Kelsey at that moment staggering – knock-kneed and in three-inch heels – from one London tourist trap to another.

Just then, a middle-aged couple entered and began to browse among the sculptures by the sofa. They were followed by a trickle of customers, looking but not buying, which gave Lara an opportunity to write out an invitation list for Nick Thornham's launch. Taking Kelsey's advice, she would ask Oliver Marchant to organise it. After all, he was wildly creative, using his skills to produce lavish, headline-grabbing parties – all of which conveniently paid for his global travels.

Throughout the afternoon, she tried Kelsey on her cellphone but the line was dead. The battery had probably run out with overuse! At five she locked up the gallery and headed home, imagining that Kelsey was now sitting with Beatrix in her favourite watering hole, glugging ice-cold

Pouilly Fumé down her parched throat while her hot shoes steamed gently on the floor beside her.

But Lara was about to be proved wrong. As she opened her apartment door, there stood Kelsey, grinning. 'Hi!' Lara said, throwing her briefcase against the wall. 'Had a good day?'

Kelsey lifted her shoulders up to her ears, her smile widening to almost maniacal proportions.

Lara shot her a look. 'What's the matter with you? You look demented.' She glanced over to see a girl standing by the window, looking out. It was one of Kelsey's friends, her long artificial-red hair cascading down her spine, almost to the hemline of her short, too-tight black leather skirt. The spiked heels on those stilettoes looked lethal. Typical Kelsey friend; too busy eyeing-up the talent in the street to look round and say hello.

Lara turned back to Kelsey. 'You should have phoned, let me know what was happening. After all, Beatrix is my responsibility.' She threw her jacket over a chair. 'Where is she anyway?'

Lara stopped and frowned suspiciously. The American girl's eyes were practically bulging out of their sockets and she was hopping from foot to foot as if desperate for a wee. Something odd was happening and Lara didn't like it. 'Have you been taking drugs?' she whispered fiercely.

Kelsey shook her head so violently that her pearl necklaces rattled.

Lara called out, 'Beatrix?' There was no answer. Maybe she was in her bedroom. 'I'm going to check on my cousin,' she muttered menacingly and headed for the bedroom. The red-headed girl was now slowly turning from the window, a tight pink roll-neck showing an ample chest. Lara gave her a perfunctory nod as she opened the bedroom door. Then she stopped dead. Her brain had registered something, something important. That girl had the same shy smile as . . . as *Beatrix*?

Lara turned round, feeling a tremulous excitement. Again, the girl gave that same shy smile, showing neat white teeth: her cousin's teeth. No! It was impossible. Lara looked her up and down; the girl's smile might be Beatrix's but the rest of her was pure porno queen. Lara's lips moved on their own volition, the word floating softly through the air. 'Beatrix?'

The lovely face nodded, the vivid blue eyes shining with joy.

Lara's astonishment was so great, she could hardly draw breath. 'I can't believe it,' she whispered. 'You're . . . you're *beautiful!*'

'Oh, thank you.' With a dazzling smile, her cousin hurried forward. 'What do you think?'

Lara looked her up and down, then looked her up and

down again, noting the full pink glossy lips, the finely arched eyebrows, the heavy blue eyeshadow. This couldn't be Beatrix. Her cousin didn't have such long legs. She didn't have that hair, those slim hips, that chest, that face!

'Do you like my hair?' Beatrix asked, touching it.

Dumbstruck, Lara could only nod. This was Beatrix's voice, her awkward mannerisms and fluttering, nervous hands. Lara gazed at the curtain of red hair falling over one eye, the perfect oval-shaped face, the pink eyelash bag gripped in one hand. Beatrix had been transformed. No, Lara shook her head at this thought. Beatrix had been *transplanted.*

'Doesn't she look fabulous?' It was Kelsey, jumping into her line of vision. She now stood beside Beatrix. 'The hairstyle was Gavin's idea,' she chattered excitedly. 'He got a cancellation and – boy – we were in there like a shot, weren't we, honey?'

Beatrix nodded vigorously.

'But . . .' Lara didn't know where to begin. 'Her hair – it's so long!'

Kelsey laughed delightedly. 'I got a shock, too.'

Lara touched it. 'Is it extensions?'

'No, it's all real.' Kelsey said this with pride in her voice.

Lara's gaze moved over Beatrix's face. 'What happened to your glasses? And your eyes – they're *blue!*'

'Contact lenses,' Kelsey said briefly. 'Indigo. We also

got some jade ones. Then we came back here and I did her make-up.' She grinned at Beatrix. 'It's been one busy day!'

Lara let her gaze travel over Beatrix once more, seeing the bright red nails, the thickly mascaraed eyelashes, the beauty spot on her cheek. 'Is that a real beauty spot?' she asked.

'We cheated,' Kelsey admitted. 'Looks good, huh?' She brushed something invisible from the sleeve of Beatrix's jumper. The gesture was almost proprietary. Now she pointed to the black leather mini-skirt. 'Do you like the skirt? It's Trussardi.' She ran her fingers through the pink fronds on the handbag. 'It looks a bit like some pink oversized bug, doesn't it?' she chuckled. 'But it's fun. What do you think?'

Lara thought it looked tarty . . . so did the skirt . . . and the hair. Everything did. And why change the colour of her cousin's eyes? They were beautiful enough as they were. She could feel her fury steadily mounting. Kelsey had deliberately gone against her wishes. Beatrix was meant to look elegant and sophisticated. Now – *now* – she looked like a cross between some biker's moll and a lap dancer!

Seeing the expression on Lara's face, Kelsey's bubbling self-congratulations trailed away. 'What's wrong?' she asked.

Lara wanted to stamp her foot in vexation. 'I didn't want this.' She planted her hands heavily on her hips. 'I wanted gamine, not garish.'

'Hey, slow down,' Kelsey protested. 'What's *gameennot-gerish*?'

'I wanted gamine,' Lara repeated slowly and firmly. 'Boyish but feminine. Short, dark-blonde hair. Cool specs. Squared-toed mules. Clamdigger pants with a silk cream blouse – Betty Barclay or something.' She tutted irritably as she threw up a hand. 'Not violent red hair and spiked stilettoes! It's garish.' She saw Beatrix's look of distress and immediately repented, putting her hand on your cousin's arm. 'You look a million times better though,' she added hastily. 'But we have to think of Grandmother. Do you honestly think she would want you to look like this?'

Beatrix looked down at herself and slowly shook her head. 'No. No, she wouldn't.'

'But she looks great!' Kelsey exploded. 'I can tell you this – if she went home right this minute she would get her man back just like,' she clicked her fingers, 'that!'

Lara tensed. She didn't want Beatrix going anywhere.

Obviously struck by this idea, Kelsey spun on her heels to face Beatrix. 'What do you say, honey? Do you want to go home – get your man back?'

Beatrix's eyes had widened in alarm. 'I—'

Hastily, Lara stepped forward. 'She can't go back just yet. She's not finished. What about her social skills? Her personality?'

'Personality?' Kelsey exclaimed, her voice incredulous.

Now she threw her hands at Beatrix as if presenting a magician's trick. 'Look at her! Who needs personality when you look like *that*? What do you say, Beatrix, honey? Do you want to go home or do you want to stay and get some more help?'

Holding her breath, Lara waited for the answer. 'I want to stay,' Beatrix mumbled, her eyes wide, almost fearful. '*Please*. If that's convenient?'

'That's fine with me,' Lara said, relieved. 'But we're going to have to change her appearance all over again.'

'Why?' wailed Kelsey indignantly.

'Think about it. Our Mr X is not like our average man, is he? He's into stuff like philately and—'

Kelsey stiffened in outrage. 'Whadda you telling me?'

Despite her mood, Lara had to smile. 'Philately,' she repeated slowly. 'Stamp-collecting.'

'O-h-h.' There was relief in Kelsey's voice.

Lara sat on the edge of the coffee table. 'So,' she continued, 'given that our Mr X is into stamp-collecting and cricket, he might be more than a little intimidated by Beatrix turning up on his doorstep looking like this. It might scare him off.'

'Mm.' Kelsey bit her lip thoughtfully. 'OK, we could try asking Gavin to tone her down a bit but he's not going to like it.'

'Forget Gavin. I've got an appointment booked with Anabelle Walters for Thursday.'

'Anabelle Walters!' Kelsey crossed her arms and made a petulant face. 'Now you're going to destroy everything we've achieved.'

'No, I'm not. We'll keep the beauty spot, the roll-neck, um . . . the foundation – although we'll have to rethink that shade of eyeshadow.' Seeing her friend's expression, Lara got up and put a hand on her arm. 'You've done brilliantly. Really. It's just one or two things we're going to have to change. It's not what *I* want. It's what Grandmother wants. And, of course, Mr X.'

Kelsey threw her a resentful look.

'I've got my orders,' Lara explained, beginning to lose patience. 'And I've got to stick to them, haven't I? Yeah? For Beatrix's sake.'

Kelsey nodded sulkily. Then she unfolded her arms and grinned, her face lighting up in mischief. 'Boy! Did you get the shock of your life, or what?'

'I certainly did!' Lara laughed, relieved that Kelsey had accepted the situation. 'At first, I thought she was one of your friends.'

Immediately, Kelsey threw her arm around Beatrix's shoulders and squeezed tight. 'Whadda you talking about? She *is* one of my friends.'

Beatrix's face had become pink with pleasure, her grin

wide across her face. Then, to Lara's horror, she saw the grin dissolve and the face crumple as if in grief. Aghast, she cried out, 'Beatrix, what is it? What's wrong?'

Those glossy pink lips trembled. 'I . . . I . . . am so . . .' A sob broke free. 'So happy. Th-thank you.'

Overwhelmed with this display of emotion, Lara too felt a tear prick her eyes and immediately threw her arms about her two friends, enfolding them both. 'Don't cry, Beatrix,' she wailed. 'Or I'll start.'

Beatrix lifted her head high, laughing through her tears. Her face shone and her eyes sparkled.

Lara stepped back. 'Oh, I wish we had some champagne to celebrate.'

'Champagne? No problemo.' Kelsey swung away and headed for the kitchen. 'We got a couple of magnums on our way home, didn't we, Beatrix? And I've booked a table at La Porte des Indes for eight-thirty. My treat.'

'Brilliant.' As Lara followed behind Beatrix, she saw how those long legs wobbled, the thin ankles snapping as she tried to keep her balance on her high heels. She looked like a newborn foal finding its legs for the first time. It didn't help that her skirt was wrapped around her like a surgical dressing.

In the kitchen, they giggled as the champagne foamed up over their glasses. 'Cheers!' Kelsey cried. 'Here's to Beatrix!'

Lara raised her glass. 'And here's to Mr X. May she knock him off his perch!'

Half an hour later, they left the building, hiccuping with champagne and chattering. As they crossed the road, Lara and Kelsey flanked Beatrix, as if protecting their new and very precious toy.

'Lara!' At the sound of her name, Lara looked round. It was Mario standing in the doorway of his bar, waving a brown envelope. 'A letter for you,' he shouted.

The letter had come. 'Oh, God!' She pressed a hand to her beating heart. The polo player!

Mario protested. 'Hey, Lara. You must not take the Lord's name in vain.'

'Sorry.' She thanked him politely, resisting the urge to snatch the letter off him. Then she marched along the street, distractedly searching for somewhere secluded where she could devour the contents. Kelsey and Beatrix had to run to keep up with her.

'What's happening?' Kelsey asked breathlessly.

'I've got a letter.'

'We can see that. Who's it from? And why did Mario have it?'

'It's from a man, a man who advertised himself in a Lonely Hearts column.'

Immediately, Kelsey grabbed her arm. 'Are you crazy? He could be some psycho!'

Lara shook her off and dived into an empty cybercafé, the spotty youth behind the counter too involved with a computer to take any notice of them. As she sat down, the others clustered around her. 'I can't believe you're doing this,' Kelsey began.

'Well, it's your fault.' Lara opened the envelope with shaking hands. 'Since you were the one who told me to find a wealthy man.'

Kelsey was staring intently at the letter that was now emerging. 'Is that what he is?'

'Yes.'

'Well, *hurry!*' the American girl squealed.

Lara went straight for the photograph. A tall, broad-shouldered man stood beside a car. He looked to be in his mid-thirties. The image was blurred. Although the face was turned to one side, she could tell that his features were regular. He stood leaning against an antique car, a tweed cap covering his hair and a gun held loosely under his arm. The clothes looked shabby but, naturally, this was the casual dress of a country gentleman – shabby yet rich. Too rich to care what others thought. He dressed for comfort, that was obvious. But the dog at his heels said it all. It was obviously pure pedigree with a glossy black coat and regal bearing; in fact, it looked exactly like the dog that Asprey's used to model their diamonds.

Feeling a breath on her cheek, she turned to see Kelsey

and Beatrix straining to look over her shoulder. 'Nice,' Kelsey murmured.

Lara looked back at the man, trying to bring him to life, trying to imagine him moving, talking, but it was impossible. Her eyes sought further clues. Behind the car could be seen the corner of a house covered in a trelliswork of climbing yellow roses. How big was the house? Was it a mansion? In the distance, hills rolled away to the horizon. She could almost breathe the fresh, fragrant air, hear the birdsong in the silence.

Now the letter . . . Passing the photograph into Kelsey's eager hands, Lara picked up the letter and unfolded it. Her eyes scanned down the page of neatly written words: *fields of lavender* – until she came to the signature: Jack Havers. She began to read the letter from the beginning, digesting and dissecting every line.

Manor Farm

Harnet, Nr Wool

Dorset

Manor Farm? That sounded promising.

Dear Lara,

Thank you very much for your letter and photograph. Yes, there is such a thing as a harvest moon and, no, lambs don't gamble. Not my lambs anyway! Although my bull's a bit of a card shark.

She laughed at this and carried on reading.

I would very much like to meet you but first you will want to know a little more about me. I live on the edge of a small hamlet, ten miles from Dorchester. My property extends to three hundred hectares . . .

Lara stopped. What was a hectare? Her country cousin would know. 'Beatrix, what's a hectare?'

Beatrix looked up from the photograph in her hand and thought for a moment. 'It's about two acres.'

'How big's an acre?'

'The size of a small meadow.'

Lara gazed at her. What was the size of a small meadow? Forget it, she told herself. This line of questioning could go on for ever. Well, whatever a hectare was, this guy had three hundred of them.

The majority of the land is lying fallow because I am converting to organically grown crops.

Crops? She wasn't too sure about that. So the guy was an actual farmer. Mmm. But, if he were rich, he wouldn't actually grow the stuff himself, would he? He had people to do that. Organic? It made her think of Planet Organic, fashionable but expensive. Yep, sounding good.

This year I will have two fields of lavender.

Lavender! Oh, how divine. Now she could see herself

running through a fragrant, sunny meadow of purple blossoms.

I breed Tamworths. In fact, Cleopatra, my champion of champions, is about to give birth any day now.

Tamworths? What were they? Dogs? No! They would be polo ponies. Now she could see Cleopatra galloping over the hills, her jet-black coat gleaming in the sunshine, her proud thoroughbred nostrils dilated. How silly of me! Lara thought suddenly. I've got this all wrong. Cleopatra wouldn't be galloping anywhere if she were pregnant! She carried on reading.

Manor Farm has views over the Purbeck Hills to the sea. Apart from the main house, there are two barns, a glass house and a tied cottage.

Glass house? Of course, that would be a Victorian conservatory where the head gardener would grow pomegranates. But what was a tied cottage? 'Beatrix?' she asked. 'What's a tied cottage?'

'They were built to house servants on an estate.'

Lara squeezed her eyes tight in ecstasy. Servants! No more cleaning agencies, no more boil-in-the-bag suppers, no more trudging down to the drycleaners with sacks of clothes. She opened her eyes to see that Kelsey and Beatrix were staring at her. 'What do you think of him?' she asked, a grin spreading from ear to ear. 'Don't you think he's dishy?' She was pleased to see them nod. 'He's a polo player. Stinking rich!'

Kelsey rolled her eyes to heaven, her voice high with relief. 'Thank the Lord for that.'

With pounding heart, Lara returned to the letter.

May I suggest we meet and get to know each other better? If this is acceptable to you, I can either come up to London or you can come here. If you wish to pursue this, please telephone me at the number above. I look forward to hearing from you.

Best wishes.

Jack Havers.

That was it. There was no more to learn. She looked at the signature once more, trying to analyse the neat, even curves, the whorls on the capital letters. What did they mean? That he was precise, stuffy, pompous? Or flamboyant, carefree, zany? She gave the letter to Beatrix and took back the photograph and gazed at it. It was a pity the image was so fuzzy but he looked kind, he looked normal, but should she meet him?

She leant sideways, her shoulder pressed against Beatrix's and looked down at the letter in her hand. 'What do you think?' she asked.

'Oh, Lara.' Her voice was fearful. 'I don't know.'

Kelsey jumped up. 'Do it!' she cried. Then she frowned. 'I presume he doesn't know your address?'

'Oh no, absolutely not.'

'Good. Then you've got nothing to lose.'

All at once, Lara went cold. If he were truly wealthy, wouldn't he be inundated with female attention? Perhaps, unbeknown to her, she was up against stiff competition; a vivacious polo championess, perhaps. 'I'm phoning,' she declared. 'Kelsey, give me your cellphone.' It was in her hand in an instant.

'I'm so nervous,' Lara moaned as she dialled the number. There was the ringing tone and then a click and a man's voice.

'Manor Farm.'

'Hello.' She could hardly speak. 'Is that Jack Havers?'

'It is. Is that Lara Bayley?'

He had remembered her name! Good sign. 'Yes, that's right,' she answered in her sweetest voice. 'I've just received your letter.'

That's great.' His voice was deep and resonant, his tone warm and friendly. 'I've been hoping that you would.'

She was surprised by his accent. She had imagined a haughty voice with rounded vowels but, on the contrary, he sounded quite ordinary. 'I . . . um . . . I haven't done anything like this before,' she admitted.

He laughed. 'Me neither. Scary, isn't it?'

She, too, laughed. He sounded really nice – understanding and sensitive. Just by listening to him, she knew that this was no psycho.

'Would you like to meet up?' he asked.

She replied quickly, blanking out her fears, as if throwing herself into a cold swimming pool. 'Yes, I would.'

'Brilliant!' His joy was apparent. Did that mean there was no vivacious female polo championess to worry about? 'I'm coming up to London on Monday,' he continued. 'How about meeting for dinner?'

She thought fast. Monday? 'That sounds perfect. Where do you want to meet?'

'You tell me.'

'L'Escargot,' she answered. 'It's a little bistro near South Kensington tube station. Any taxi driver will know it.'

'Right,' he said. 'I've made a note of that. Lara?' His voice had become urgent. 'I'm sorry about this, but I've got to dash off. Do you remember my mentioning Cleopatra?'

Once again, she saw the black mare galloping over the hills. 'Of course.'

'Well, she's just about to farrow so I need to get back to her.'

She frowned. Farrow? Her brow cleared instantly; of course, that meant Cleopatra was just about to give birth.

'She's having babies,' she said, wanting to show off her newfound knowledge.

'That's right – and making a great deal of fuss about it, too. But I've got my boys to help me . . .' He paused at this, as if waiting for a response.

'They'll come in useful.' She laughed. Not only did this guy have servants, he also had stableboys.

'It would be nice to have a chat before we meet up,' he said. 'So I will ring you back over the weekend.'

'No, no,' she said airily. She had learned all she needed to know. 'We can have our chat on Monday.'

'But . . .' He seemed to hesitate, sounding uncertain.

Picking up on his tone, Lara tensed. Was he getting cold feet? She mustn't lose him now. 'You'll be in London,' she said casually, trying to keep the panic out of her voice, 'and I'll be in London, so, one way or another, we might as well meet up. Getting to know each other over a glass of wine is much nicer, don't you think?'

'Oh, yes, definitely.'

'Good. So I'll see you Monday?'

'I'll look forward to it.'

'Well, goodbye.'

'Goodbye.'

Lara disconnected the call then slumped forward as if winded from a long race. Kelsey crowded her. 'What did he say? What did he say?'

Lara could only stare at the telephone, her thoughts buzzing. Jack Havers was nice and amusing and sensitive. And now he'd gone off to help his horse have her babies, tiny little shiny black ponies, just like their mum. How she longed to be there with him, to help. It was all so perfect. Suddenly she was filled with trepidation. What if this all went wrong? She gazed at the spotty computer nerd, seeing the green hills rolling down to the shimmering sea, smelling the fragrance of lavender, touching the soft skin of baby ponies. And hearing the birdsong in the silence. It was all so perfect . . . too perfect.

Impatiently, Kelsey grabbed her arm. 'So? What?'

This action snapped Lara out of her trance. 'I'm meeting him Monday evening,' she told them, body quivering with anticipation.

'That's great.' Kelsey swung to Beatrix. 'Isn't that great, Beatrix?'

Beatrix sat at the table with the photograph in her hand. 'Yes,' she answered softly. 'That's great, Lara.'

Jack

Swiftly, Jack turned away from the telephone, trying to avoid Patsy's eyes. This was awkward. She had arrived only minutes before and must have heard everything.

'You didn't tell her, did you?' she accused.

'I did,' he muttered, picking up the pail of hot water from the sink and heading for the door. 'I said my boys were helping me.'

'So she knows you've got children?'

With a sigh, he stopped and rested the pail on the side. 'No, she doesn't know,' he admitted. 'But I wanted to tell her. I suggested I phone her back over the weekend so we could find out more about each other, but she preferred to wait.'

Patsy gazed away, a worried frown crumpling her brow. 'I see. But why did you tell her you were going to be in London when you're not?'

Jack straightened up and grinned. 'That's where you're wrong. One of the galleries phoned this morning wanting to see more of my work. I've got an appointment at two o'clock on Monday. In Bond Street!'

She clapped her hands in delight. 'Oh, Jack, that's wonderful.'

He carried the pail of hot water and newspapers outside, hoping that this news would divert her attention, but he was wrong.

'Look, I'm not sure about this girl.' Patsy shadowed him closely as he walked across the yard. 'She's very beautiful; I can see why you fancy her. But the letter! Oh Jack, love she's not your sort at all.'

He tried to jolly her along. 'But she's a barmaid – just like you.'

'Yes, but she freely admits that she can't cook and it's obvious that she knows nothing about farming.'

He stopped and turned to her. 'We're just having a drink. Like she said, I'm going to be in London and she's going to be in London.'

'But what if you fall in love with her? Can you imagine the problems that would cause?'

He carried on walking.

'And will you tell her then? About the boys?'

He nodded. 'Yes, Patsy, I promise you one thing: I will tell her on Monday.'

'Daddy, Daddy!' It was Sam, running round the corner, his muddy trainers skidding on the loose gravel. 'Quickly – she's started.'

Jack smiled at Sam's state of excited panic. 'Calm down,' he ordered. 'It's not going to help matters if you carry on screaming like that.' He started off across the yard, little Sam dancing around him.

'What are you going to wear?' Pasty demanded, trying to keep up.

He called back over his shoulder. 'I'll find something.'

Then he heard her running up behind him, her voice suddenly louder, breathless. 'But what about your tooth? You can't go without your tooth.'

He turned with a rueful smile. 'There's nothing much I can do about it now, is there? I'll take one of my old photos and show her what I normally look like. How about that?' Evidently, this idea did not impress her. She began to shake her head slowly as if foreseeing tragedy. 'It will be OK,' he said impatiently, moving off.

Confronted by a slick of pig slurry, Patsy could follow no further.

'Don't worry,' he shouted back. 'Everything will be OK. You'll see.'

Monday

Beatrix

Her toes throbbed from a morning's shopping in high-heeled shoes, her eyeballs felt dry from wearing contact lenses, her earlobes ached with the pressure of her earrings and her 'uplifting' bra felt like an iron band around her ribcage. But she didn't care. Oh, no! As if mesmerised, she gazed at her reflection in the dressing-table mirror.

Was this truly her?

She was beautiful – she still couldn't believe it. Slowly, she tilted her head, admiring the upsweep of a finely plucked eyebrow, the apricot sheen of a cheekbone, the vivid blue eyes against black mascara and the glossy lips parted in a smile. But, most of all, she couldn't believe the cascade of shiny red waves sweeping over one eye and tumbling down around her shoulders.

On leaving the hairdresser's, she had sought her reflection wherever she could, glancing into car windows, stainless-steel name plaques on walls and shop windows – and tripping over Kelsey's heels in the process! After that, there had been a whirlwind of activity. The salon with white-coated beauticians, plucking, tweaking, filing, painting, cleansing and toning. Then, without a chance to admire her new face, she had been whisked off to the opticians. Her transformation had been so dramatic that she had gone straight to a mirror as soon as she'd arrived home. 'If you're shocked,' Kelsey had laughed, 'just imagine how Lara's going to react!'

That had been the best bit: Lara's expression of incredulous disbelief. Beatrix hugged the memory to her. In that moment, as she toasted her friends with champagne, she had felt reborn.

Now she saw herself entering the restaurant, more concerned with trying to keep her balance than anything else, and it was only when she was sitting at the table that she became aware of the open stares directed towards her. At first, she had blushed self-consciously but, after two glasses of wine, she had sat back in her seat and soaked up the admiration like wet peatmoss soaking up the sun on a hot day.

With a sigh of contentment, she turned her attention once more to the bottles and compacts spread out before her. Here was a vast array of make-up; some donated by Kelsey on Friday, the remainder bought earlier that morning after a lengthy make-over demonstration in Harvey Nichols. 'Now I want you to go home and take it all off and start again,' Lara had said as they came out into the street, their arms laden with carrier bags. 'You need to practise over and over. Forget about cleaning the apartment, just concentrate on *you.* You've got a lot of catching up to do.' With this, she had put Beatrix in a taxi. 'I'm going straight out after work,' she had said. 'I might be late in so don't wait up.'

Don't wait up? Of course she was going to wait up. How could she sleep? She wanted to know every detail about the handsome stranger from Dorset.

But, for now, she was alone with her new make-up, not knowing where to begin. She picked up a small purple compact; *Urban Decay* it read, *Pot Holes.* Alongside that was a bottle of russet-coloured liquid labelled *Salmonella* and a cologne spray banded in brown with a silver screw-top, called, simply, *Dirt.* And what was *Benefit Lightning*? And what was she meant to do with *Longo Crème Shadow*? With so many bottles and tubes, she couldn't remember what had been used that morning. Was it the *Light Lucidity* or the *City Base Compact*? Finding the make-up remover and the packet of cotton wool, she began to cleanse her face.

If only Kelsey was here to help, but she'd gone back to New York to see a lawyer. The call had come over dinner on Friday evening, Kelsey remarking on it as if she were merely taking a bus into the village rather than a supersonic flight across the Atlantic. 'Post-divorce adjustment phase,' she had explained before turning to Lara with a stern warning: 'Don't make any more changes to Beatrix until I get back. I'll be round Tuesday morning, first thing.'

There had been no more changes, apart from a pair of horse-hair, kitten-heeled mules and three simple outfits. She glanced down at the glossy carrier bags on the floor – Ferragamo, Chloë, Iceberg – each holding an elegant tailored outfit wrapped in tissue paper. As yet, she had not dared to calculate the total spent so far, but she knew it would be a lot, an awful lot. Every time she signed the Mastercard slip her chest had tightened in anxiety.

She would have to telephone Grandmother, she decided; hint at the expenditure without giving details, prepare her for the shock. Admittedly, the old lady had told her to spend, spend, spend, but – coming from someone who would only buy the brand of cream crackers marked 'with 10% extra' – it could give her a heart attack.

In the past four days, Beatrix had been too wrapped up in herself to give more than a fleeting thought to Grandmother and Daphne. Now she tried to picture them together. Were they shouting at each other at this very moment? Perhaps Daphne was suffering in silence? Was Grandmother, faced with household bills, garden maintenance, grocery lists, church cleaning rotas, WI meetings and the problems with the upstairs plumbing, beginning to feel overwhelmed? Beatrix's shoulders sagged, burdened by the thought of it all. Even though she was hundreds of miles away, the shackles of home still tugged at her.

As she stared at her reflection once more, a warm smile spread across her face. She was beautiful. That was what mattered. No one could take that away from her. She thrilled to imagine everyone's reaction: John Chadwick, Daphne, Grandmother, Susan Dobbs. Although, by then, she would no longer have red hair; instead, it would be short and blonde. However it looked, she knew she would be stunning and quite capable of winning back John's attentions and – finally – wiping the arrogant sneer from the face of that woman! But what would happen when all the initial excitement had died down? She would still have John Chadwick as a boyfriend, a boyfriend who would now be more insistent with his wet lips and pawing hands. And she would still be living at Castlemaine with the same day-to-day duties . . .

Refusing to think about it, she carried on with her make-up practice, identifying the tube of concealer and putting it to her face. This was one thing she could remember from that morning's demonstration. Carefully, she smoothed the flesh-coloured lipstick over a broken vein and around the crease of her nostrils before choosing a bottle of pale beige liquid and applying it in blobs to her cheeks, nose and brow, and blending it in with her fingertips.

As she worked, she thought back over the weekend. On Saturday she had tidied up the apartment while Lara had spent the day at the gallery. Then, yesterday, she had cooked a roast lamb dinner while Lara sat at the table in the sitting room, carefully writing out her work notes, diligent and conscientious. Once again, Beatrix found it hard to believe that she was the same person that Grandmother had described.

Using a sponge-tipped applicator, Beatrix spread shadow over her eyelids. It was too thick. Now she looked as if she had a black eye. She wiped it away and started again. By mid-afternoon, she had finished and sat back to study herself. Mm, she thought, Lara was right. I *do* need to practise.

'Right,' she sighed, getting to her feet. 'Time to phone home.' It was Daphne who answered.

'Beatrix! How are you?'

'I'm great.'

'You sound so different!'

Beatrix smiled. 'I *am* different.'

'What's happened?'

'I've got red hair down to my waist, that's what's different.'

'No!'

'And I'm wearing horse-hair, kitten-heel mules.'

'That sounds barbaric!'

Beatrix chuckled. 'Yes, it does a bit. And I'm wearing cologne called *Dirt* and *Urban Decay* eyeshadow.'

'You sound as if you're going to a Hallowe'en party! Honestly, tell me, have you really got red hair?'

Beatrix did not want to spoil the surprise when she returned home. 'Not really, no. Just joking. How are you getting on with Grandmother?'

Daphne answered wearily. 'Up and down. She's out buying bananas at the moment. We've discovered this great promotion. If you buy a certain amount of bananas you get free air miles. So we've calculated that if we buy two thousand kilos, we can fly to the Caribbean and back – free.'

Beatrix couldn't imagine what two thousand kilos of bananas would look like, but it sounded a lot, an awful lot. Surely, Poppy's down in the village didn't stock that much. 'You must be keeping Poppy's busy?'

'Oh no, we're banned from there. We're having to drive miles to buy them. That's where she is now. Out with Reverend Beardsley buying bananas.'

'Oh.' Beatrix didn't know what to say. Contrary to all expectations, Daphne and Grandmother did not appear to be missing her in the least. 'So, everything is running smoothly?'

'Yep. Although I'm starting to get a bit sick of bananas. I've suggested to your grandmother that we set up a stall in the village and she thinks that's a good idea. Even if we sell them half-price, at least we're getting some of our money back.'

Our money. 'So you're both in on this, then?'

'Half and half. I've always wanted to go to the Caribbean.'

'Oh.'

'I think that's her now.' There was a pause then her voice called out, 'Mrs Bayley? Beatrix is on the phone!'

There was a brief muttering of voices and then her grandmother's clear, imperial tone. 'Hello, Beatrix. Did Daphne tell you about our project?' She sounded breathless.

'Yes. That's a lot of bananas.'

A chuckle. 'It certainly is. We're taking two boxes down to the Women's Institute tonight. Sell them off at half price.'

Obviously, Grandmother was coping splendidly without her. 'Did you get the plumber in?'

'Oh, no, no, no,' Grandmother answered airily. 'I simply handed Reverend Beardsley the plunger and let him get on with it. Worked a miracle.'

'Good. Um, Grandmother . . .' Beatrix hesitated, choosing her words carefully. 'I am finding that I am spending far more than I anticipated. Do you think it might be wise if you set a limit?'

'No, no, no. You just carry on. You're a sensible gal, Beatrix, I know you'll do what's right.'

'I just don't want you to get a shock when the bill arrives.'

'As you know, I cannot bear wasting money – perhaps it has something to do with the war. But in your case, this is not a waste of money.' Her grandmother's voice had softened. 'You deserve it. After all, you have never spent a penny on yourself, and I have to agree with Daphne, this London visit is long overdue.'

Beatrix smiled. So, Daphne had a hand in this. 'Thank you, Grandmother.'

'No, my dear. I want to thank *you*. You've been a good girl to me over the years. I've never told you before, so I'm telling you now.'

Even though this was meant to be a heartwarming compliment, it sounded like a military instruction. Beatrix smiled. Grandmother could be a cantankerous old devil sometimes, but she still loved her.

The voice picked up briskly. 'Well, I can't stop and chat. There's boxes of bananas clogging the entrance hall.'

'Of course. I'll phone you again next week.'

'I don't want you worrying about us,' Grandmother interjected. 'Just enjoy yourself.'

'I will, I promise. Goodbye.'

Beatrix replaced the receiver and grinned. *Just enjoy yourself*. It was as if a weight had been lifted from her shoulders. Suddenly, she felt free, reckless.

Irresponsible!

Lara

The tube train slowed to a halt with the sound of grinding metal. As the doors slid open, Lara stepped into the carriage, jostled from all sides by the mass of frantic humanity. Every seat was taken so she had to stand, the metal pole in one hand, her case in the other. It contained her favourite Chloë suit and matching shoes, which she would change into straight after work.

As the train picked up speed, her thoughts zoomed ahead to the night, to the broad-shouldered man sitting at the marble-topped table in L'Escargot. Would he be her saviour? Would he take her away from all this and give her a life free from responsibilities? Would she spend her days picking strawberries and counting fluffy white clouds floating across a sky of perpetual blue? Over the past four days, she had thought about him so much, that she now had a vivid image of him in her head. He would be very handsome, shabbily rich but assured, familiar with the rush of city life.

The tube train had stopped and now the doors went back to reveal a tired-looking mother with a little girl in a buggy. Since there was no space for them, Lara made no attempt to move. But the mother had other ideas. Grimly, she pushed the buggy into the carriage, forcing the other passengers to shuffle back, packing themselves in tighter. Lara could hardly breathe! She shot a resentful look at the mother before dropping her gaze to the child. The small chubby face was dirty, the thin blonde hair matted, the nose snotty. Suddenly a pair of baleful red-rimmed eyes looked up at her and, not knowing what else to do, Lara gave a tentative smile. Immediately, the little face crumpled like a paper bag and a loud wail burst from that chocolate-coated mouth, ricocheting through the carriage. Guiltily, Lara looked away, only daring to glance back when the noise had subsided to see a packet of jelly babies clutched in that small hand.

Unobserved now, Lara studied the little girl, thankful that she lived a child-free life. They were like tiny aliens, she mused, with their own code of behaviour and all communication impossible. If a kid had a problem it simply opened its mouth and screamed. Which was a pretty effective means of communication, she decided on an afterthought. She glanced up at the mother, feeling a wave of sympathy. What a life. The responsibility for a child was *total.*

The train was slowing. Bond Street at last. Pushing towards the door, Lara gave that dirty little face one last look whilst thinking that the mother should make some effort to keep it clean.

Five minutes later she entered the gallery to see Timothy and a young Oriental-looking couple staring at Thornham's *Oil Slick on Water*. Timothy was in full flow and, not wanting to disturb him, she went straight through to the kitchen. Meryl was there, shrugging into her coat, ready for departure. 'Going off somewhere nice?' she asked, nodding towards the case.

Lara pushed it under the sink. 'I'm meeting a guy tonight on a blind date and this is the gear I'm changing into.'

Meryl stepped forward expectantly. 'So, tell me everything – but you'll have to be quick because I'm meeting Terry.'

'I saw this advertisement –' Lara began. Hearing footsteps approaching, she clamped her mouth shut and took the lid off the coffee pot.

Timothy entered. 'Good afternoon, Lara. I'll have a cup if you're making one.'

Reluctantly, Meryl picked up her handbag, obviously disappointed by the interruption.

'I've just met the most talented artist,' Timothy said chattily, taking the jug of cream from the fridge.

'And such a nice man,' Meryl enthused. 'A real charmer. You must've missed him by seconds.'

Timothy headed back towards the door. 'Come and take a look at his work, Lara. Quite enchanting.'

'He certainly knows how to paint,' Meryl agreed, following them into the gallery. 'Well, I'm off. Have a good time tonight, Lara.'

'Thanks, I will.'

Timothy had opened out a cardboard portfolio on the lightbox. With growing interest Lara began to leaf through the sheets of tinted Ingres paper. There was a bull worked in charcoal and chalk, the power of the muscular black body almost tangible. There were pastel sketches of landscapes and brooding storms, a barn, a stone wall and a further two sketches of the bull. With strong confident strokes the artist had brought his subjects alive, capturing the mood of the moment.

'They're excellent,' she exclaimed, propping the bull against the wall and standing back to view. It was powerful. Raw. It would sell. Noticing a pile of colour photographs, she picked them up.

'He sent them in last week. They're mostly large-scale oils and acrylics. The dimensions are on the back.'

'Wow!' she breathed at last. 'We are going to represent him, aren't we?'

'I would need to see the rest of his work before I decide, but I should imagine so. We will probably share him with Vittorio.'

She looked up. 'But why?'

'Vittorio and I are partners. He has already seen these photographs and has expressed a wish to show the artist in a selected group exhibition.'

'But why don't we have sole representation?'

'It's all about supply and demand; we do not want to flood the UK market and devalue the work, so I am quite happy for Vittorio to take his share back to Milan.' Timothy glanced at his watch in irritation. 'In fact, he should have been here for the meeting.'

Lara studied a landscape, the pastel blended to a smooth texture. 'Is he showing anywhere else?' she asked without taking her eyes from the paper.

'On the contrary. He's never exhibited before, which will certainly please Vittorio.' Timothy looked at his watch again. 'Where on earth could he be? He's almost three hours late!'

'Where's he coming from?'

'The Channel Tunnel. He doesn't fly.'

Lara had propped up an ink-wash of a drystone wall and stepped back to study it, noticing the initials JP neatly marked in one corner. 'What's the artist's name?' she asked.

'He uses Penfold as his pseudonym but his real name is—' He was interrupted by the ringing of the telephone. 'Smith's Galleries.' There was a moment's silence in which Lara could faintly discern a man's voice protesting rapidly, almost hysterically. 'Oh dear,' Timothy murmured. 'Oh dear. I'll come at once. Yes. Yes.' He hung up, whipping his jacket from the back of the chair. 'That's Vittorio. His car's been clamped and he's furious. I don't know how long this is going to take, Lara. If I'm not back in time, just lock up.'

As the door closed behind him, Lara turned back to the sketches scattered across the cardboard portfolio. 'At last,' she muttered, 'some decent work.' Carefully, almost tenderly, she put the sheets back into their folder.

Jack

Marble-topped tables and wrought-iron chairs covered a floor of umber-coloured tiles, and from the rafters hung ropes of fat onions. Inside, this could have been a café in Montmartre; outside, the rain drizzled down on a London street with its red double-decker buses and black taxis.

Through the rain-streaked windows, Jack watched the pedestrians hurrying to and fro, shoulders hunched beneath dripping umbrellas. From which direction would she come? Was that her? No. His heart hammered in his chest. Would her face light up as soon as she saw him? Would this be love at first sight? His Black Lion marriage advisers had strong doubts, but he was about to prove them wrong. From his years at college, he knew himself to be attractive to females. He had personality, a sense of humour, and his own house and land. Perhaps if he could just earn Lara's affections, then he would have more chance of winning her over to the idea of children.

Once again, he swung a look at the young couple at the far corner table. Was this their first date? The girl was talking rapidly, her cheeks flushed while the boy stared in open adoration, his eyes never leaving her face. Jack felt a fluttering of anticipation. Would he and Lara look like this an hour hence? Would he look longingly into her eyes while she talked excitedly about her life? His gaze darted back to the door. So far today he had been lucky – but would that luck continue?

He thought back to that morning, remembering how he had taken a deep breath before entering Smith's, a swanky Bond Street gallery. He had presumed that the owner, Timothy Ashley-Smith, would be both cool and patronising but, to his relief, he was greeted with warmth and friendliness. 'Call me Timothy,' the man had said at once. He had then gone on to study the portfolio pieces whilst apologising for the absence of his business partner. 'Quite enchanting!' he exclaimed at last, which made Jack's knees almost buckle with overwhelming relief.

After that, there was talk of forthcoming exhibitions in London and Milan, general prices of contemporary art which made Jack's head reel. He had immediately agreed to Timothy's suggestion of a visit to his studio but, at the same time, he wanted to admit the truth, to say: 'I haven't got a studio, I've only got a shed. I'm not a real artist. Nobody's going to pay those prices for my work.' But he remained silent, resisting the urge to bellow out a shout of triumph and whisk Meryl the bookkeeper around the floor.

Now, out of habit, he glanced down to check his portfolio, only to remember that it was no longer with him. At Timothy's request, he had left it behind to be viewed by the Italian partner. Would he, too, like his work? Would it really fetch such vast sums of money? If so, there was a slim chance that he would have sufficient funds to make a bid for Old Matthew's land.

And if that happened, it would be thanks to the Colonel and his constant encouragement. Admittedly, the Colonel had the annoying habit of trying to run his life, but, on this occasion, Jack was grateful. He was also grateful to the others for placing the advertisement. He recalled Patsy's last-minute instructions: 'Don't tell any of your jokes, don't wipe the back of your hand across your mouth, say 'yes' instead of grunting and make sure your fingernails are clean.' Despite her doubts, he knew that she wished him well. He had noticed the fine lines on her face puckered in apprehension, but she needn't worry. He had a good feeling about this . . .

He looked at his watch. If all went to plan, Lara would walk through that door in two minutes flat. He took another swig of beer, thinking of his basement room in the Earls Court guesthouse, damp and dark, but it was cheap and it had a mattress, which was all he needed for the night. Growing hot and uncomfortable, he stretched his shoulders in the too-tight jacket, the collar of his shirt digging into his neck. Earlier he had felt smart but now, looking around him, he felt unfashionable, provincial. The gap between his teeth didn't help his image, either.

As he put his hands up to loosen his tie, the door opened and a dark-haired woman appeared, dressed elegantly in a cream-coloured suit. His heart missed a beat. *It was her.* He recognised the pale, heart-shaped face, the large wide eyes. He saw how her gaze travelled across him to the far reaches of the room before once more – like the beam of a lighthouse – it began its return journey.

Coming to his senses, he stood up swiftly and grinned, lifting a hand in welcome.

With her attention caught, she looked directly at him and frowned in uncertainty, her eyes scanning him from head to toe. 'Jack?' He did not hear his name above the chatter around him, but he saw her mouth move to form the word. He nodded and smiled, gesturing to the empty chair in front of him.

Slowly, almost doubtfully, she walked towards him, eyes never leaving his face. As he extended a hand, she cautiously put her own in his but gave no grip as he shook it. Her hand felt feather-light and cool and fragile. Witnessing her dismay, he kept his smile fixed to his face even though his intestines had knotted into a spasm of anxiety. 'Lara?' he asked, trying to sound jovial.

She nodded, her eyes dropping reluctantly to the chair that she would have to sit on.

'Please, take a seat,' he invited.

She sat and put her handbag on the table, glancing around as if fearful of being watched.

'What would you like to drink?' He looked for the waiter.

'A dry white wine, please.'

Her voice was soft, perfectly enunciated. A rich voice. It didn't sound like the voice of a barmaid. When he had placed the order with the waiter, he turned and caught her staring at the scar on his eyebrow. He touched it, grinning. 'That was a little argument between me, a bull and a barbed-wire fence.'

'Oh.' Her eyes darted away.

'So, you're a barmaid?'

She frowned. 'Absolutely not. Whatever made you think that?'

'Oh. I just thought, you know, from your address . . .'

Her voice was cold when she answered. 'I don't work there.'

Silence.

'So, the country life appeals to you?' he asked in a desperate attempt to start a conversation and to clear that tension from her face.

'Um . . . yeah.'

She sounded doubtful. This was not the girl he had chatted to on the telephone. That girl had been animated and friendly, but now . . . He tried to remember all the topics of conversation that he had so painstakingly rehearsed but his mind was a blank. All he could think of was her. Her face was exquisite, with its small, pointed chin, her pale skin framed by waves of conker-coloured hair. But it was the eyes that held his attention, they were big and brown. In fact, this was like confronting a fearful kitten, which caused his male instincts to rise up to protect her, to smooth the anxiety from that beautiful face. OK, it was obvious that she didn't like his looks, but maybe she would like his personality? 'This is a bit nerve-wracking, isn't it?' he suggested lightly.

'Yes.' She watched the waiter approach with her glass of wine. 'Thanks,' she said and he didn't know if this was spoken to him or the waiter. Now she held the stem of the glass loosely in her hand, staring at it as she twisted it around and around on the table top.

He had to say something that would put her at her ease, make her open up and start talking. 'So, where do you live?'

She darted him a look of fear, and immediately he

understood. 'I'm sorry, I shouldn't be asking. After all, I'm still a complete stranger, aren't I?'

'Yes, you are.' She knocked back a big slug of her wine and put the glass on the table. 'Can I just check something with you?'

'Sure. Go ahead.'

'Are you PO Box 2176?'

He felt sick. 'You can call me that if you like,' he said, easing a chuckle into his voice. Unsmiling, she waited for his answer. 'Yes,' he replied. Everything was going horribly wrong. She didn't fancy him. But he was charming, polite, good-looking. However, gazing at her expression, his doubts set in. Why hadn't he taken time to go into Dorchester and buy some fashionable clothes? Why hadn't he got his tooth fixed last week? He ran his hand back over his head, feeling the stubble of hair, regretting the fact that he had shaved it instead of going to the barbers.

As she continued to sip her wine, her eyes moved down over his clothes and came to rest upon his hands. She didn't like them, he could tell. OK, maybe they weren't his best feature, but they had always served him well. He could pick up a fifteen-stone heifer with these hands.

'So,' she murmured casually. 'You're a polo player?'

His heart thudded to a stop. Polo player? This was a mistake! A serious mistake. A voice screamed inside his head and now the page of newsprint loomed up before his eyes: *Gentleman farmer. Handsome polo champion.* She wanted the polo champion – not him! He dropped his gaze, knowing that she was waiting for an answer. Should he lie?

'I think you've made a mistake,' he said slowly, lifting his head to look her squarely in the eyes. 'I'm not a polo player.'

Her eyes hardened suspiciously. 'But you told me you were!'

His brain spun at this accusation. 'No, I didn't!'

'Yes, you did. You even told me your polo pony was having babies.'

'I haven't got a polo pony,' he protested. Then he remembered their telephone conversation. 'It wasn't a horse having babies. It was a pig.'

Her face screwed up in confusion. 'A *pig*?'

Jack took a deep breath. 'I think you've got this wrong. I don't think it's me you want, it's the polo player. His advertisement was above my own.'

Lara frowned in bewilderment then suddenly she gasped and pointed a finger at him. 'You, you're the pig farmer!'

The words hit him like a mulekick to the chest.

Suddenly, her shoulders slumped forward. 'I don't believe it,' she whispered to herself, as if he were not present. Although her face turned towards him, her eyes looked right through him. 'I must have written down the wrong box number.'

His face was burning with shame. He wanted to get up and walk out. Her accusation continued to echo in his brain: *You're the pig farmer!* She had said it as if it were an insult. But what was wrong with being a pig farmer? OK, it didn't match up to the glamour of a polo champion – that was for sure. Anyway, he was more than a farmer now, he was an artist. He had a top London gallery owner coming to the farm to see his work. He would tell her that, impress her.

'I—' he began.

She cut him short, 'So, all this time I thought . . .' She picked up her handbag, ready to leave.

'Obviously you got the wrong number, but don't rush off,' he protested. 'Now we're here we might as well make the best of it and have a chat.'

'A *chat*?' The look in her eyes appalled him. She stood up abruptly. 'This has been a complete waste of my time!'

'*What*?' he thundered, gazing up at her. He couldn't believe what he was hearing. *She* was blaming *him*. 'A waste of your time?' he demanded, feeling the first flush of anger. 'I've come all the way up to London for this meeting, wasting time and money, and all because you got the wrong number. I think *I* deserve an apology.'

She dropped down onto her chair and leant forward across the table with eyes blazing. 'I . . . don't . . . think . . . so,' she said, every word spoken like a hammer blow.

He was speechless.

'You deceived me. I might have written down the wrong number but you blatantly lied to me, pretending to be *lord of the manor*. If you had only told me the truth, I would have immediately realised my mistake. Instead, you fed me all that stuff about hectares and glass houses and tied cottages!'

'But that's all true.'

'Is it? So tell me, who lives in your tied cottages? Servants – or *pigs*?'

She didn't understand. He hadn't lied.

'So?' She was waiting.

He looked away. 'Chickens,' he answered softly.

'*Chickens!*' She spat out the word as if spitting out poison. 'Now I know why your photograph was so blurred. If only you'd had the decency to send me an *honest* photograph.'

'There was nothing wrong with the photograph.'

She snorted derisively. 'So what do you breathe down there, pea soup?' She eyed his scalp. 'And now I understand why you wore a cap.'

Self-consciously, he ran his hand back over his shaven head. 'I admit it's a little short,' he said.

'Let's just say I don't go in for the ginger convict look.'

'I'm not ginger, I'm sandy.'

'Does it matter?' She sighed and stood up as if suddenly bored with their argument. 'I'm leaving.'

He shot to his feet, his fists balled on the table. She had humiliated and insulted him and now she was just going to walk off. 'That's all that matters to you, is it?' he said, his face hot with anger. 'A man's haircut?' It was his turn to snort derisively.

She looked at him steadily. 'You know what I mean.'

'No, actually, I don't. I've never had complaints before.'

'Really? So why were you advertising yourself in the Lonely Hearts?'

This knocked him sideways but immediately he regained his balance. 'So why were *you* looking in the Lonely Hearts?'

'For fun.'

'Yeah, I bet. With your sort of charm, men are going to run a mile!'

She, too, balled her fists onto the table and leant towards him, her nose only inches away from his. 'Tell me, was that your car in the photograph?'

Taken by surprise, he shifted his eyes guiltily.

'Ha! Thought not.' She stood straight. 'And the dog?'

He didn't answer.

'I don't care what you say, you lied to me. Jesus! I should have known by the blurred photograph that this was a set-up.'

'I didn't take it, my friends did.'

'Oh, right, so this is all a schoolboy prank, is it?'

He stiffened indignantly. 'Definitely not.'

'You deceived me. I came here to meet a handsome polo player, not some . . . some *half-witted hillbilly!*'

His mouth fell open in astonishment. Now she began to rifle in her handbag. 'I'm paying for my drink.'

'No, don't.' He held up a hand, trying to prevent this final humiliation.

Ignoring him, she brought out a five-pound note and slammed it down on the marble-topped table. 'I don't want you to waste any more of your *money*.'

It had happened so suddenly. Dazed, he could only watch her march out of the door, along the pavement and out of sight. She had gone. This was like coming into the kitchen after walking the hills in a gale-force wind. His brain was numb, his ears buzzed. Now he gazed down at the five-pound note on the table. Slowly, like sun burning through the early-morning mist, anger began to burn through his stupor. How dare she? He crumpled the note in his great fist and snarled at the door, only thankful that he would never see the likes of *her* again.

Tuesday

Beatrix

Kelsey glanced up and gave a smile of reassurance. 'Don't look so scared. You'll do fine.'

Beatrix sat beside her on the sofa, her hands clasped tightly in her lap. 'It's just that, well . . .' Moments ago Kelsey had breezed into the apartment, excitedly informing her that they were going to a party that night, 'your first London party!' How could Beatrix explain that she wasn't ready for it? 'I don't know how to talk to people,' she said at last.

Kelsey continued to take out plastic bags from the leather trunk that sat on the sofa between them. 'Yes, you do.' She put a handful of black lace on the coffee table. 'You talk to me.'

'But you're different. You're not a stranger. You're my friend, I know you.'

Kelsey laughed. 'Everyone's a stranger until you get to

know them.' She paused and looked up with kind eyes. 'It'll be practice, that's all. Practice in helping you win back your Mr X. Just remember that whoever you meet tonight, you will probably never see again. So, you might get a little nervous.' She shrugged. 'You might get a little tongue-tied, but does it matter?'

'But I won't know what to talk about.'

'You don't *need* to talk.' Kelsey leant forward as if sharing a secret. 'Do you know who the most interesting people are?'

Beatrix shook her head.

'People who *listen*. As long as you can appear interested in what someone's saying, you'll do swell.' Kelsey suddenly gave a wicked grin. 'How about I fix you a couple of New York Slammers before we go?'

Beatrix smiled at this, remembering how she had chatted and laughed on her first night in the apartment, the pink intoxicating liquid swiftly loosening her tongue and inhibitions. That had been six short days ago. It was hard to believe. The time had gone so fast.

'Listen, Beatrix.' Kelsey's voice had become earnest. She paused as if weighing the words she was about to speak. 'At the moment you are still that shy country girl. Let's face it – you haven't got a personality.'

Beatrix looked away in shame.

'No! Don't look like that. It's good. Think of it like

. . .' she cast her eyes about as if seeking inspiration . . . 'like you're a blank canvas. Nothing there. Now, it's up to you to choose the personality that appeals to you. You practise, get a taste of what you want, perhaps make a few wrong moves but then it'll all fall into place. Think of it as a pick'n'mix personality.'

Beatrix took a deep breath. Kelsey made it sound so simple. Like filling a bag of sweets in Woolworths.

'We've got a saying in the States,' Kelsey continued. 'You can take the girl out of Idaho, but you can't take Idaho out of the girl.' She grinned. 'Well, let's just prove them wrong, whadda you say?'

Beatrix felt the first tentative thrill of the challenge.

'As I said to Lara, you're beautiful – you don't need a personality. So, if you do end up talking, think of it as a bonus.' She dipped her hand in the bag and brought out a packet of cigarettes. 'What we've got to do now is to sort out your,' she stopped and lifted her chin haughtily, speaking through stiff pouting lips, 'persona. That's my impersonation of your Queen,' she explained. 'Good, yeah?' Beatrix giggled. It was impossible not to be happy in Kelsey's presence.

Her new and glamorous friend was now taking out magazines. 'How did Lara's date go last night?' she asked.

'He didn't turn up.'

'Oh, what a drag.'

'Yes, that's what I thought but she didn't seem too disappointed.'

'She probably realises that he went to the wrong place and that he'll try again.' Kelsey brought out sheets of paper, drawings of women in various fashionable clothes. 'I've sketched out some ideas,' she said, handing them to Beatrix.

'Gosh, you're so talented.'

'Do you think so? I was always good at art. Actually, I wanted to be a sculptress.'

'Really? So why didn't you?'

The American girl shrugged. 'When you're arm candy you haven't got time for a career.'

'Arm candy?'

'Yeah, that's when you spend all your time on self-improvement so you can look good on some rich guy's arm.' She had searched in the bottom of her bag and now held up a cigarette in one hand and a round, Cellophane-wrapped lollipop in the other. 'OK,' she said, waggling the lollipop. 'Lara wants *gamine*. Me?' She waggled the cigarette. 'I go for ultra vixen. But it's your choice. Think: pick'n'mix.' She put the cigarette between pouting red lips while giving a sultry, eyes-half-closed stare.

Beatrix chuckled.

Kelsey spat the cigarette onto her lap. 'Hey, this is a serious business.'

Beatrix kept her face straight although her eyes danced. Now the cigarette was given to her and she took it uncertainly. 'But I don't smoke.'

'It's not to smoke, it's for effect.'

Obediently, Beatrix put it between her lips and waited for approval.

'No,' Kelsey shook her head dismissively. 'It's not you. Try this.' She unwrapped the lollipop and gave it to her. 'Go on – lick it.'

Tentatively, Beatrix licked it, staring at Kelsey with big eyes.

'Great!' the other girl exclaimed. 'It's definitely you. Pretty but innocent. Hey, Lara was right. That look is pretty effective.'

Beatrix was not so sure. She stood up and faced the mirror above the mantelpiece. 'Do you really think so?' she asked doubtfully.

'I'm positive – trust me. You're gamine.' Kelsey slotted the cigarette back into the packet. 'It's going to be Capri pants with a white, school-uniform-type shirt. Sneakers, perhaps. And your hair tied back in a ponytail. Whadda you say?'

Beatrix nodded absent-mindedly and rolled the lollipop over her tongue.

Kelsey continued, 'I was going to give you some more of my tips on flirting but now I won't bother. You've got a naturally shy, please-help-me sort of look which is far more effective.'

Beatrix sat down feeling proud of herself. She hadn't even tried and yet Kelsey was showering her with praises.

'Right,' Kelsey continued. 'Now: sex. I guess you know the basics?'

Beatrix was silent, too embarrassed to admit the truth.

Kelsey's eyes had narrowed. 'What's up?'

'Actually, Kelsey, I haven't done it before.'

'*You haven't*? Jeez, where have you been all your life? An old folks' home?'

Beatrix gave a tremulous smile. 'Well, yes, that's exactly where I've been.'

The American girl sighed, shaking her head. 'No wonder your guy left you. OK, we'll talk birth control next time, and I'll bring condoms.' She paused. 'You know what they are, don't you?'

Beatrix nodded.

'Good. Safe sex is not a padded headboard. It means taking responsibility for your own body and not leaving it up to the guy.'

Beatrix nodded dutifully. So far, she'd been having fun but now with the mention of sex, she felt the ground shift beneath her feet.

'OK,' Kelsey declared. 'What's next on the agenda? Drugs. Lara is not going to agree with me on this but I think you should be aware of them. There's a lot of dangerous things in life, like speeding trains and drinking bleach, yeah? Imagine you've just come out of the jungle and you've never seen traffic before. The first thing you'd probably do is to step off the sidewalk and get hit by a truck. So, all I'm going to do is to show you what drugs look like and what they can do to you.' With this she brought out a small silver-foil package and opened to reveal something that looked like chocolate. 'This one's OK. This is a soft drug, so it's not dangerous; in fact, it has medicinal qualities. You can call it marijuana, ganja, spliff.

'Now this one . . .' Kelsey had taken out a small bag of white powder, 'is a different ball game. This is cocaine. I don't want you taking this 'cos it'll fry your brain. OK?'

Beatrix gazed down in horrified fascination. Drugs! Never in a million years would she have thought she would ever be doing this.

After that came capsules, tablets, grey powder and more capsules. Listening dutifully, Beatrix picked up the black lace from the coffee table and held it up. It looked like a pair of underpants but with three leg openings.

'They're crotchless,' Kelsey murmured, now replacing the contents of her bag.

'Crotchless?'

Kelsey nodded abstractedly.

With sudden understanding, Beatrix flung them back, a

blush spreading up over her body to the roots of her hair. She could never wear anything like this. Never! She was a country girl. She belonged to Castlemaine, with her dungarees and headscarf, with her potting shed and secateurs, her wheelbarrow and her heated windowsill propagator.

She could never be the girl that Kelsey was trying so hard to create. *Never*!

Lara

Lara stared grimly out at the traffic beyond the gallery window. What a creep, she thought furiously. Then, with a big effort, she looked down at the words before her, beginning once again to check Zorka's 'List of Works' against the printer's proof.

11. Dog, Eye and Chair, 1999

Opus 10. Oil on canvas 72 × 60 in/183 × 152 cm

12. Dog, Eye and Oil Tank, 1999

Opus 12. Oil on canvas 48 × 60 in/122 × 152 cm

Damn. However hard she tried, she could not get that man out of her head. How dare *he* demand an apology? She should telephone *Country Living* and complain. Tell them that this creep was advertising in their dating column. He had lured her into *L'Escargot* under false pretences and then he had had the nerve to think that she would want to stay and chat. What a joke! What would they have talked about? *Swine fever?* She squeezed her eyes shut against the humiliation.

She had simply written down a wrong number, that was all, and look what had happened. Thank goodness she would never see him again, never have to worry that he could trace her address. The whole sordid incident was over . . . so why couldn't she stop thinking about it? Why did it keep going round and round in her head? It was like a mouse in a wheel; the more it ran, the faster the wheel spun until eventually, it couldn't get off.

Distractedly, she picked up a pencil and began to make a row of crosses along the margin, the image of his face appearing before her. She saw that shaved ginger hair over a pale scalp, the eyebrow divided by a white scar and the gap in his front teeth. He was no more than a bar-room brawler! Would he continue to ensnare innocent females from the dating column of magazines? Maybe she should telephone the police? No. She didn't want to get involved, couldn't take the risk of revealing her address.

At the sound of the gallery door opening she glanced up, the look of fury still stamped upon her face. It was a young couple. At her expression the man stopped dead. 'Come in, please,' she cried, flustered and smiling wildly to compensate. 'Are you looking for anything special?'

The man shook his head. 'We're just browsing.'

Lara left them alone and turned back to the List of

Works, startled to find that in her furious reverie, she had drawn a row of heavy black crosses right along the edge of the paper. No wonder! Just the thought of that man made her blood boil. The minute she had clapped eyes on him, she'd known that he was not wealthy. The jacket was too tight, the collar of his mustard-coloured shirt digging into his thick neck, the polyester tie shiny and old-fashioned. And those hands! She shivered to think what those hands would have done to her if they had been alone in some dark alley.

The young couple were coming closer, moving from painting to painting. She could tell by the way they shot furtive glances at the price tags that everything have was beyond their means. If only she had works-on-paper to show them, something that they could afford, something that would start them off on a lifetime of collecting. But this was not the gallery for them.

'Do take a catalogue,' she offered brightly. The woman shook her head and in the next moment they had gone. It was demoralising when this happened. It made her want to grab them back and talk them into buying, but she couldn't. She wasn't some stall-holder in Brick Lane market.

She gazed at her surroundings, uninspiring but elegant, the large canvases overhung with tiny halogen spotlights, the vast picture window looking out onto one of the finest streets in the world. Bond Street. Exclusive. Fashionable. Since Timothy was spending the day with his new partner, she had the place to herself. It was pleasant not having him around; it gave her a sense of being in charge. Feeling slightly happier, she continued with her work, all thoughts of That Man pushed forcefully out of her mind.

Some time later there was a crack of thunder and a shadow moved over the sun. Rain hammered down on the slow-moving traffic, bouncing off metal and into the gutter. Drivers became nebulous figures behind misty glass and shoppers vanished from the pavement. Inside, the gallery suddenly seemed cavernous, the glow from the spotlights ineffectual against the heavy gloom. Lara got up and turned on the overhead lights. Then she returned to her desk and shuffled her papers in a folder. Evidently, Timothy would be late back and she had no intention of staying one minute longer than was necessary. Kelsey had telephoned that morning to report excitedly: 'Beatrix's first party! Tonight! This is her chance to start building up her confidence.' Lara had agreed wholeheartedly. Yesterday, she had spent three hours with her cousin, choosing a selection of clothes and shoes, and now she was eager to get home and dress her the way she had so carefully planned.

Swiftly, she went over to the door, locked it from the inside and turned the card to Closed. As she was about to put the cash box in the safe, there was the sound of a knuckle knocking on glass and she turned to see Timothy with his nose pressed to the door. He looked soaked. A black Porsche was parked outside, with a man bending over it. Who could it be, the new partner? When she unlocked the door, Timothy fell in gasping and giggling, his breath smelling of stale wine, his eyes bloodshot and his hair plastered to his skull.

'It's positively a deluge,' he exclaimed, swaying past her.

Her baleful eyes followed him, noting how his coat tails dripped rainwater onto the floor. 'I thought we were going to discuss Thornham's exhibition?' she reminded him tartly.

With hand on heart, Timothy gave her a sorrowful look. 'I'm truly sorry.' Then he smirked. 'It's all his fault,' he declared, suddenly pointing a finger over her shoulder towards the door. 'Blame him.'

Irritably, she swung on her heel. Then stopped. Stunned. Before her stood a black-eyed Adonis, his smile revealing strong white teeth against smooth, sun-bronzed skin. His face was alive with laughter, his eyes sparkling with mischief. Now he swept the jet-black hair from his forehead, his eyebrows converging in a look of sincerity, his smile fading swiftly. 'I am sorry,' he said softly.

She quivered at the sound of his voice. It was Italian, soft and smooth, sweeping over her like the caress of a silken sheet.

Timothy suddenly jumped into her line of vision. 'I am dreadfully rude,' he cried. 'Lara, this is Vittorio de Fiorell:, my new business partner. Vittorio, this is Lara.'

The man smiled in puzzlement. 'Lara?' Her name floated from those lips as if carried on a soft breeze. He extended a hand towards her, his warm, strong flesh closing about her fingers, squeezing gently. 'I am pleased to meet you, Lara.'

L-a-r-a. She had never imagined that her name could sound like this. If he said it once more, her knees would buckle beneath her. He continued to hold her hand in his, his eyes showing open admiration. 'I did not know that you would be so beautiful.'

She blushed and dropped her gaze to the floor. Jesus! What was happening to her? She hadn't felt like this since having a crush on Henry Plunckton at school. So this was Vittorio; and all this time, she had never once paid attention when Timothy had talked about him.

Suddenly Timothy's dripping face loomed up in front of her. 'Cat got your tongue?'

She shook her head, the quick movement snapping her out of her trance. 'No, I'm sorry. I was just thinking about . . . um, my cousin.'

Timothy peered at her. 'Oh yes – the country mouse.' He stood back and paddled his hands towards the door. 'Right. Off you go.'

At this, Vittorio stepped forward. 'Please, Lara,' he begged. 'Do not go so soon.' He held up a bottle wrapped in tissue paper. 'Perhaps I can tempt you with a glass of wine?'

You can tempt me with anything you like. She knew she should get back to Beatrix but the pull of this man was too great. 'That would be nice, thank you.'

'*Bravissimo!*'

They followed Timothy into the kitchen, where he produced a corkscrew and began to open the bottle. 'Why didn't you tell me that your assistant was so beautiful?' Vittorio berated.

Timothy winked at her. 'And she is also charming and full of excellent ideas.'

Lara glanced at him, surprised at this unexpected praise. Perhaps, after all, he was beginning to value her worth.

As Vittorio presented her with a glass of wine, his gaze locked onto hers and he gave her a warm, secretive smile, as if they were conspirators.

'You had better be careful, Timothy,' he said, his eyes still on Lara. 'Or I might steal her from you.'

Lara made a show of staring down into her glass of wine while her brain screamed, *Steal me! steal me!*

'Lara would be an asset to any gallery,' Timothy continued, taking out a packet of pretzels and tipping them onto a plate. 'Isn't that right, Lara?' She nodded.

Then a thought struck her: He wants to get rid of me! He's tried everything to get me out of the gallery and now he wants to palm me off on Vittorio.

In silence, she sipped her glass of wine, gazing speculatively over the rim at the handsome Italian. Well, that would suit me fine, she decided. Just fine!

'Let's have a look at Penfold's work, shall we?' Timothy ushered them out into the gallery to where the cardboard portfolio lay on the desk. As Vittorio studied the drawings, she studied him, noting the curve of a nostril, a beauty spot high on his cheek, the angular shape of his profile.

'They are magnificent,' Vittorio said at last. 'Magnificent. You were right to bring this to my attention. You see, Timothy, our partnership is working already.'

'Delighted, old chap.' Timothy clinked his glass of wine against Vittorio's. 'I have suggested to Penfold that we drive down to visit him. He has a lot to show us – mostly large-scale works in oils and acrylic.'

'Excellent.'

Timothy picked up his diary. 'How about this Sunday?'

'Perfect.' Vittorio turned to her. 'And you, Lara?'

'*Me?*'

He nodded. 'I presume that you will be accompanying us?'

She had not anticipated this. 'Well, of course, yes.'

He gave her that secret, conspiratorial look once more.

Boy, was he sending out signals! With no thought to the time, Lara fell deeper and deeper under his spell, listening enraptured as he described the family palazzo and the reasons why he refused to have a chauffeur; the expense of installing bulletproof glass in his Porsche and the purchase of a new yacht (it didn't take an Einstein to realise that this was not some dinghy with *Daisy* painted on the side). It was family wealth, handed down through generations of powerful men, although, from what he said, his mother sounded extremely powerful, too. In fact, she sounded quite scary. 'She rules us like a Tartar,' Vittorio admitted with a laugh. 'Only last week, she gave me strict instructions to find a wife.' He raised an eyebrow, the corners of his mouth turning down at the sides in mock despair. 'My playboy days are at an end.'

Lara made sympathetic noises but all the while her brain screamed, 'This guy's a stinkingly rich aristocrat who needs a wife! Why didn't Timothy tell me? And all this time – while I'm yelling at some slack-jawed pig farmer – this hunk of Italian film star was just around the corner!'

Then a thought hit her. Surely Vittorio would have to marry an Italian woman, someone from a similar background? How could she, Lara Bayley, marry into such a family when she couldn't even speak the lingo? Well, she wouldn't give up without a fight. As Timothy topped up her glass once more, she glanced at the clock. 'Gosh, I've got to go!' There would be no time to dress Beatrix now.

'Let me drive you,' Vittorio offered, standing up.

She made noises of protest but, thankfully, he ignored them. Taking a bunch of keys from his pocket, he followed her to the door, speaking over his shoulder to Timothy. 'I'll meet you at The Canteen in, say, about an hour?'

His Porsche was sleek, sexy and black, the offside wheel parked up on the pavement. With a gallant flourish, he helped her into the car and she fell back against the soft, sweet-smelling leather. As he got in beside her, he grinned boyishly, stuck the key into the ignition and pressed the accelerator hard, the engine roaring dangerously, like a chained beast howling to escape.

'I'm back that way,' she explained. 'Fulham Road.'

In one movement, he released the clutch and swung the car into a U-turn, causing oncoming vehicles to blast their horns in protest. Unperturbed, he moved the gearstick into second, the force of the sudden acceleration pushing Lara back in her seat.

He remained silent, concentrating as he weaved in and out of the traffic, braking sharply and accelerating hard. Lara clung to the edge of her seat, her body stiff with tension as she anticipated one collision after another. Gosh, he was certainly a fast driver! But of course, he was Italian. She gazed at him from the corner of her eye.

Wouldn't it be lovely to think that he could marry an English girl? Someone like her.

Outside her apartment block, he pulled up sharply with a squeal of brakes, yanked on the handbrake and turned to her, resting an arm along the back of her seat. 'Lara,' he breathed, 'I have been rude. I have talked about myself and, yet, I know nothing about you. I have invited Timothy to dinner tomorrow night and it would please me greatly if you would join us.'

'I would like that.' She gazed at his lips, so close. Now they were coming closer. He was going to kiss her on the mouth! Her heart thumped, her body tense and waiting but, just at the last second, his lips veered to her cheek. Then they moved to her other cheek. '*Ciao,*' he whispered.

She could hardly breathe. '*Ciao.*' Blindly, she opened the car door and got out. Then she watched him drive off in a shriek of tyres and a blare of horns. On the numberplate were the letters MILANO.

Deep in thought, she climbed the stairs to her apartment, and it was only when she saw the note lying on the table, that she remembered. The party! *Where are you? Why didn't you phone? I want to get Beatrix to the party early so that she can settle in. We'll meet you there. Kelsey.*

Half an hour later, Lara arrived at the party, eager to inspect her cousin. Brushing past Oliver, she gave him a quick peck on the cheek but he seemed distracted, gazing beyond her to something in the centre of the room. Kelsey, too, seemed distracted. 'Where's our party girl?' Lara asked excitedly, coming up and kissing her on the cheek.

The American girl stared fixedly ahead. 'Over there.'

Lara followed the direction of her gaze. If not for the mane of red hair, she would not have recognised her cousin. Beatrix was walking away from them, heading towards a sofa at the far end of the room. Her hair was pulled up high in a ponytail, the tip of it swaying gently across her buttocks as she moved with slow sensuous strides. She wore grey Capri pants, so tight that they looked as if they had been airbrushed on, and a white shirt with the sleeves rolled up to the elbows. With every lift of her legs, the pink fluffy mules snapped back against the soles of her feet. In one fluid movement, she turned and slowly, effortlessly, sank to the sofa, curling one long leg beneath her. Lara's mouth fell open in astonishment. Where did she learn to do *that*?

'Pretty good, eh?' Kelsey whispered from the side of her mouth. 'Look at that innocence.'

Lara was looking! She had expected to see Beatrix's face plastered in make-up, but, on the contrary, her cousin wore a touch of pink lipstick and a flick of mascara – nothing more. She looked so . . . young. What was it? The ponytail? The Barbie doll shoes? The bow at the back of her head? Or was it the school-uniform shirt and tie?

'What do you think?' Kelsey murmured.

Lara didn't know what to say. The men around the sofa were looking at her cousin with undisguised approval. And what on earth was she doing now? It looked as if she was removing the wrapper from a lollipop. As Lara stared, she saw a round red lollipop emerge from its Cellophane wrapper and then, to her astonishment, Beatrix began to lick it. 'Kelsey!' she whispered fiercely. '*What the hell is she doing?*'

'Don't you think it gives that extra touch?'

Lara couldn't believe it. Furiously, she turned on Kelsey. Seeing this, the American girl took a step back. 'What's up?'

Lara swung to take another look at Beatrix. The men in the room were now eyeing her cousin lasciviously, lust having replaced all polite conversation. She glared at Kelsey, angry words jostling one another in an attempt to form a sentence. 'You've made her look like a schoolgirl *hooker!*'

Kelsey considered this. 'No,' she said, 'I don't agree with the hooker bit, but you have to admit I got the schoolgirl bit to perfection.'

Lara's voice came out in a strangled shriek. 'This is not some fetish party. Christ, you could get her arrested. I wanted gamine, for God's sake.'

'Yeah, and that's what you got. You said young – you got young.'

'I said *boyish!*'

'Boyish, girlish – same thing.'

'No, it's not.' Lara was alarmed to see that everyone in the room was now looking at Beatrix. 'You're going to have to take that lollipop from her. It's sending out the wrong signals.'

Kelsey folded her arms mulishly. 'I did exactly what you told me: no false eyelashes, no thick make-up, no black leather, no suspenders, no plunging neckline. I've tried, I've really tried, and this is all the thanks I get.'

'But—' Lara paused. Kelsey was right: it was obvious that she had tried, but, with strict instructions to make Beatrix attractive, she had gone about it the only way she knew how. Sexual allure, not elegance. She had successfully made Beatrix into a man magnet.

But there was no harm done, so why get so uptight? Grandmother would never see her darling granddaughter like this. 'I'm sorry,' Lara relented. 'You have tried hard, I can see that. Gosh, the way she walked across the room! That was amazing.' She laughed suddenly. 'Her backside looked like two peaches wrapped in clingfilm.'

Kelsey smiled stiffly. 'I just don't know what you want. If only you took time out to supervise us, we wouldn't be in this position.'

'Yeah, *you're* right,' Lara agreed. 'I shouldn't be complaining.'

'No, you shouldn't,' Kelsey mumbled resentfully.

Lara reached over to take a glass of kir from a side table. 'Anyway, I don't know why we're arguing. It's not as if she's going to go home looking like that. I think we've nearly got the look we want.' This was not true; as yet, they were far from it.

As her gaze shifted, she was surprised to see Justin emerge from the crowd to her right. This unexpected sight of him gave her a jolt because she had not seen him since the night of Amelia's charity bash. He hadn't changed, there was still that familiar lick of black hair, the pale tired face, the tie loosened at the neck which she had always found so sexy . . . but compared to Vittorio he looked positively anaemic.

Suddenly, she realised where he was heading. The sofa. And Beatrix! Now he stopped to say something to her before sitting down alongside and, although Beatrix was pink in the face, she was beginning to *talk!*

Lara looked on, seeing him for what he was: a dull corporate man in a smart suit with all the allure of a computer print-out. She nudged Kelsey. 'Look. She's making conversation with a complete stranger and yet she told us it would be impossible. Isn't that great!'

'Mm,' came the uncertain response. 'Don't you mind that your ex is chatting her up?'

'Of course not.' Lara was surprised at her friend's expression. 'What's up?'

'I don't like the way she's staring at him.'

'Oh, don't worry. She's not going to fall in love, if that's what you're thinking. Don't forget, she's got gorgeous Mr X waiting for her at home.'

At that moment, Oliver appeared beside them, his blue eyes vivid against his tan as he gazed at Beatrix. 'Kelsey,' he said. 'That girl you came in with . . .'

Kelsey put up a hand as she set off across the room. 'Forget it, Oliver, she's engaged.'

Lara saw the dismay on his face and felt sorry for him. Although charming with women, he was mainly a man's man, his broken nose a legacy from his rugby days at Eton, his skin tanned to leather from an African sun whilst leading expeditions across the savannah to save the rhino. Never once had Lara seen him look at a woman the way he was looking at Beatrix now.

Lara laughed. 'Oh Oliver, what a face!'

He seemed startled by her exclamation.

'You haven't even spoken to her, so why are you looking so lovesick?'

'I've never been lovesick in my life,' he said forcefully, and turned on his heels.

With the lollipop in her hand, Kelsey returned, eyeing Oliver's abrupt departure. 'What's up with him?'

'Nothing.' Lara took her friend's arm. 'Let's go eat.' But Kelsey dug in her heels. 'Leave her,' Lara exclaimed. 'There's nothing to worry about. He might be whispering in her ear, but it ain't sweet nothings – more like stock-jobbing and bull accounting. I tell you what – by the time we get back, she'll be bored stiff.'

But Lara was wrong. When they saw her cousin again, she was dancing with Justin, her body held against his as they swayed gently to the music. They were talking as if they had known each other for years.

'Oh,' Lara said in surprise. She anticipated a dart of jealousy, but nothing happened.

'I thought you told me she'd be bored stiff?' Kelsey stood with her arms folded, studying them. 'I don't like this, Lara. I don't like this at all.'

Just then, Oliver strode up to them, eyes blazing. 'Is that the guy she's engaged to?' he demanded, pointing a finger at Justin.

'No.'

'Well, in that case, I don't think she should be dancing with him like that, do you?'

Kelsey put her hands on her hips. 'You got *that* right!'

Jack

Jack stepped down onto the platform, closed the carriage door and headed for the car park, waving briefly to Arnold but not stopping to chat. He opened the picket gate and went through, his shoes crunching on cinders. Overhead, thunderclouds had gathered and the air was still. Yesterday, there had been sunshine and birdsong and he had been excited, longing for the moment when he would finally meet the girl with the big brown eyes . . .

Unlocking the driver's door, he climbed into the pickup and threw his overnight bag onto the passenger seat before putting the keys into the ignition. Suddenly he stopped and gazed out at the train track, seeing her face before him. Fiercely, he blanked it out.

He started the engine and headed for the exit. He needed to pick up the boys from the Black Lion before returning home. They would be there now, Patsy no doub fussing over them with bags of crisps and pint glasses of lemonade.

Driving past the greengrocers he saw the Colonel tying Persephone's lead to a lamp-post but Jack did not stop to speak. He didn't want to confront him, not yet. If not for the meeting with that girl, he would now be coming home victorious, ready to tell the whole village that a top London gallery had shown interest in his work. But now that glorious sense of triumph lay buried deep beneath humiliation and anger.

What right had she to look at him like that, as if he were repulsive? He wasn't repulsive; he was good-looking, he was tall, strong, with his own farm. There were a great number of women who would go out with him at the drop of a hat. There was Linda in Harcome, Janice down at the feed store, Sharon at the garage. He sighed, knowing it was useless to pretend. The Lindas and Sharons of this world did not have skin like buttermilk nor glossy chestnut curls nor the smell of sophistication. The beautiful, brown-eyed girl was out of his league. It was as simple as that.

As he turned into the pub car park, he saw Sam and Jamie feeding the ducks down by the river. Up on the lawn sat Patsy and Trevor.

'Afternoon,' he called out, coming across the grass.

'How did you get on?' Trevor asked.

'Great! I couldn't believe it. The gallery owner was

bowled over. In fact, he was even talking about coming down to see the rest of my work.'

'Let me get you a pint,' Patsy said, swiftly getting to her feet. 'And don't say another word till I get back. I want to know *everything.*'

Trevor grinned. 'The Colonel will be pleased to hear the news.'

The boys had seen him and now came running. 'Hi, Daddy,' Sam cried. 'I got a house point for my reading.'

'Clever boy.' Jack knelt down and kissed them in turn, his great arms going around them and pulling them close. It didn't matter about some snooty stuckup female, he thought. He had his boys and that was all that mattered.

Jamie offered him a crust of bread. 'Do you want to feed the ducks with us?'

'I will in a minute, Jamie. Just let me talk to Trevor and Patsy first.' He straightened up, absent-mindedly watching his sons race down to the river. It looked cool down there, the willow trees overhanging the shallow water.

If only he could get that woman out of his mind.

'So, you're going to be a celebrity then?' Trevor remarked.

'What?' Jack looked at him. 'Oh, the paintings.' He sat down and ran his hand back over his scalp. 'Well, let's hope so.'

'Tell us about your date.' It was Patsy. She put the pint

of beer in front of him and sat down expectantly. 'Are you going to see her again?'

Jack picked up his glass, unable to meet her gaze. 'She didn't turn up,' he lied casually.

Patsy's eyes widened in surprise and disappointment. 'Oh, what a shame. Didn't you phone her? Oh no,' she corrected herself, 'you didn't have her number, did you?' Her voice softened. 'Maybe it's for the best, eh?'

'Maybe.' He felt a lump in his throat, remembering how he had first seen the photograph of the beautiful, brown-eyed girl and how he had taken the torn pieces home and had tenderly Sellotaped them together before putting them away in the dresser drawer. He had been so sure that she was the one, but he couldn't have been more wrong.

Patsy had been watching him closely. 'Don't let it get you down, love. Perhaps she'll get in touch with you again. There's still a chance you two will meet.'

'Perhaps.' He gazed down to the river where the boys were dropping pebbles into the water. There was one thing he was sure of; he would never see that girl again.

Saturday

Beatrix

Beatrix followed Lara out onto the pavement, putting a hand to her collar. Without the mane of thick hair down her back, the nape of her neck felt chilly. She liked the style, though. It was short, amazingly short, but attractive, the honey-blonde colour making her face look brighter. Although bedazzled by her Rita Hayworth look, she had never been relaxed with it. Now, she felt different. This style not only suited her but it also felt right. But would Justin like it? And would he like her wire-rimmed spectacles?

'I'm sorry I haven't had much time to spend with you,' Lara began. 'It's just all the work at the gallery.'

'Please, don't apologise,' Beatrix answered. 'You have done so much for me already. I will always be grateful.'

'I've enjoyed myself.' Lara smiled. 'How do your glasses feel?'

'Compared to my old ones, they feel so light.'

'Yeah, I bet.' Lara smiled. 'So, do you think your Mr X is going to like the new you?'

Every time that name was mentioned, Beatrix felt a dragging sensation in her chest. 'Yes,' she replied evenly. 'I'm sure he will.'

'Good.' They paused at the kerb, ready to cross a side street. 'You certainly seemed to be having fun with Justin the other night.'

Beatrix blushed. 'Yes, he was very nice.'

'He and I used to date. Did he tell you?'

Beatrix was horrified. 'No, he didn't. Oh Lara, I didn't realise!'

Lara laughed at her expression. 'It's OK,' she said reassuringly. 'Don't worry about it.'

'But if I'd known, I would never have—'

'I don't mind. There was nothing between us.'

Beatrix was overwhelmed with relief. She would never have behaved the way she had if she had known that Lara and Justin had once been in love.

'This is it,' Lara said, moving towards the entrance of a small café.

Beatrix followed her in and they took a table by the window. As Lara studied her menu, Beatrix gazed out at the busy street. Justin, she sighed. Would they ever see each other again? He had promised they would. He had sounded so certain.

Lara spoke, breaking into her thoughts. 'What are you having?'

'Coffee, please. And a chocolate éclair. But this time let me pay.'

'OK.'

As Lara placed their order, Beatrix once more gazed out at the street. She loved London. She loved the bustle, the noise, the smell, the excitement. She knew that she had so little time left here, but everything that had happened would stay with her for the rest of her life. The way she had danced slowly with Justin, her body pressed up against his. The way that they had sat together on the sofa while he told her all about his business deals with Japanese clients. It was strange, but she had not felt her usual shyness. Instead, his exhausted face had filled her with pity, making her want to lay him down on the sofa and tuck him up!

'Did you tell him you've got a boyfriend?'

Beatrix swung round. 'Pardon?'

'It's only fair that if you meet a guy you should be straight with him, so he doesn't get the wrong idea.'

'Oh, yes, of course.' Beatrix nodded her head. But she didn't want to tell Justin the truth. If she did, he would not want to dance with her, to laugh with her, to . . .

'I've met the most gorgeous man,' Lara remarked, taking out a book and putting it on the table. It was an Italian dictionary, the cover showing a bottle of red wine and a plate of salami. 'He's Italian.'

'Is he handsome?'

'*Mamma mia,* is he handsome! He's wealthy, charming and sexy. And he's looking for a wife.'

Beatrix gasped. 'That's wonderful.'

'Not that wonderful,' Lara said ruefully. 'Because of his background, I suspect he's going to have to choose some Italian contessa. But,' she held up the dictionary, 'I'm not going down without a fight!'

Beatrix smiled, hoping dearly that her cousin would have more success this time. Heading home in the taxi last night she had, once again, mentioned the blind date with the polo champion and was perplexed by the monosyllabic response. Yet, only days before, Lara had been full of excitement about the meeting. Why had she lost interest so abruptly?

'His name's Vittorio de Fiorelli,' Lara continued proudly. 'He's invited me and Timothy to dinner tonight. Then, tomorrow, he wants me to go with them to check out a new artist.' She groaned. 'I hope he's not going to be the one who's driving. He goes so fast, my eyeballs shoot out the back of my head!'

Beatrix laughed.

'So, how are you enjoying yourself in our fair city?'

'I love it!'

'A bit different from the Welsh borders?'

Beatrix nodded solemnly, her eyes dancing. 'Just a tiny bit.' For a moment, she gazed at the people coming in and out of the café; foreign businessmen, women in designer clothes, two workmen in overalls, a dark-skinned man in heavy sandy-coloured boots and brightly coloured knitted waistcoat, his black hair hanging from under a cap in long plaited strands. This was what she loved most about London: all the different types of people – Africans, Chinese, Americans, Spanish, Asians. Looking at them made her imagine fragrant orange groves and slumbering hilltop villages; the heat haze of an African sun shimmering low over the horizon; calypso music; the Oriental spices and fruit of a floating market . . .

'So what do you do with yourself at home?'

Beatrix sighed, reluctant to think about it. 'Well, I've recently been elected Treasurer for the Woman's Institute.'

'Wow,' Lara teased her gently. 'That sounds pretty serious stuff.'

Beatrix carried on: 'I also organise the church-cleaning roster and help out at the Sunday School and with the Cub Scouts.'

Lara whistled. 'Sunday School? Cub Scouts? Sounds like a nightmare.'

'It's not too bad, although the boys can be a bit uncontrollable.'

Suddenly, there was a shout. 'Hey, Lara!'

Beatrix looked up to see a man approaching their table, a wide grin spread across his suntanned face. He was tall and slim, moving with an easy grace, and in the next moment he kissed Lara on the cheek, smiled at Beatrix and sat down, his vivid blue eyes staring at her in open curiosity.

Under that intense gaze, Beatrix wriggled uncomfortably. Now she remembered where she had seen him before. He had been staring at her during the party on Wednesday evening.

Lara made the introductions. 'This is Beatrix, my cousin from the Welsh borders. Beatrix, this is Oliver.'

His hand came across the table and in the next moment, she felt his grip, tight against her own. Although slim, his shirt sleeves were rolled up to reveal strong, sinewy forearms. 'I saw you at the party the other night,' he said. Now his eyes moved over her hair. 'But I hardly recognised you just now.'

Beatrix smiled at this, shyly putting a hand to her neck.

'What do you think?' Lara asked him.

'Terrific!'

The force of his exclamation made Beatrix blush.

Feeling the hot blood in her cheeks, she was annoyed with herself. Why couldn't she react to this man in the same way she had reacted to Justin? Friendly, interested and without a thought to herself. Now, she must look like some idiotic schoolgirl.

'But I thought your eyes were blue?' he queried.

Lara answered for her. 'No, those were contact lenses. This is her real colour.'

'Topaz,' he whispered.

Beatrix was glad when the waitress arrived and diverted his attention. She had put their coffee and cakes on the table and now turned to Oliver to take his order. 'No, thanks,' he said. 'I'm not staying long.'

Lara laughed. 'That should be engraved on your headstone.'

Oliver grinned. 'Talking about not staying long, what happened to you the other night? You shot out of Amelia's front door like a bullet out of a gun.'

Lara smiled. 'I just felt a bit ill. Did I miss anything?'

'Not much,' he replied 'apart from Rupert Billington bidding two hundred pounds for *Scream Speed* tickets. I didn't realise he was a head banger on the quiet.'

Lara laughed. 'Don't be ridiculous. They'll be for his grandchildren.'

Oliver's face had become serious. 'Do you know, I can't help thinking that with all the poverty in the world, it just seems crazy to be so hung up about a few floor tiles.'

Lara shrugged. 'I never thought of it like that.'

Suddenly he grinned. 'I've got a joke for you girls. What have floor tiles and men got in common?'

Mystified, Lara and Beatrix shook their heads, Beatrix now studying him quite closely. His lower lip was full and yet his top lip was quite thin, tilted up in each corner in a ready smile.

'If you lay them properly the first time, you can walk all over them for life.'

Lara burst out laughing but Beatrix took a moment to understand.

'Lay!' Lara said, nudging her. 'It means . . .'

'I know, I know,' Beatrix retorted, feeling the hot blood flood her cheeks again. Lara's friend was now looking at her in puzzlement.

'Kelsey told me you're just visiting?' he said.

Beatrix nodded.

'So how long are you staying?' Oliver was cut off by the sight of a man outside knocking on the window. Quickly he stood up. 'I've got to go.' He stared down at Beatrix. 'I'll see you again,' he said. 'Won't I?'

Lara answered for her. 'Oh, yeah. She means to party every night, don't you, Beatrix?'

She nodded.

'Great!' Oliver seemed relieved. 'I'll see you soon, then.' And he was gone.

'Oliver's a really nice guy,' Lara said, slipping her Italian dictionary back into her handbag. 'But he's *wild* – boy, is he wild!'

Lara

At the sound of squealing brakes, Lara leapt to the window and looked down into the street. 'He's here!' she cried excitedly, wheeling from the window and bumping into Beatrix who had dived forward to get a look. Lara gave her face a final, breathless inspection in the mirror. Perfect. With her hair piled up on top of her head and the row of pearls against the bodice of her black velvet dress, she looked every inch an Italian aristrocrat-to-be.

Now she grabbed her bag and headed for the stairs. 'See you later, Beatrix.'

'Good luck,' her cousin called without turning from the window.

As Lara stepped out of the building, she saw Vittorio leaning against his Porsche, his arms crossed casually as he surveyed the street with the air of a contented man.

He smiled when he saw her, unfolding his long limbs

and holding out his arms in welcome. '*Bellissima,*' he murmured, waiting for her to come forward before kissing her on the cheek. Now his eyes roamed her body, her legs. 'Lara, you look exquisite.'

Her chest heaved as if she had run a five-mile race. 'Thank you.'

Opening the passenger door of the Porsche, he guided her in. There was the same smell of expensive aftershave, the same soft touch of the black leather. As the car sped off, she lay back, savouring the moment, thrilling to his presence beside her. He drove fast, his eyes narrowed in concentration as he zig-zagged through the evening traffic. He's so masterful, she thought, admiring the way he cut up a motorbike. This is the sort of man who grabs life with both hands.

Outside the restaurant, he slowed and swung the steering wheel to park in front of the door.

Timothy sat waiting at the bar. 'Good evening, Lara, good evening, Vittorio.' He gave them a paternal smile and slid down from his stool. 'Where would you like to sit, Lara?'

But it was Vittorio who answered. 'My usual table.' From that moment, he took complete charge, leading them to a corner table and pulling back a chair for Lara. She was surprised to find herself facing the wall, which had never happened to her before. Vittorio sat opposite, smiling broadly at the approaching waitress who held out a menu. He waved it away. 'I will order for all of us,' he declared. 'We will have minestrone soup, followed by artichoke risotto. And wine, plenty of wine. Barolo.' He waved the waitress away and then turned back to his guests. 'You will like it here,' he told them. 'The kitchen is immaculate, and look,' he held up a wine glass to the light. 'Do you see how clean it is?' He picked up a chunk of lemon wrapped in muslin. 'Nice touch, eh? You do not get juice on your fingers.'

Lara gazed, entranced by the sound of that voice.

During the meal, Vittorio dominated the conversation. He talked of his horses, his vineyards and the army of guard dogs that patrolled his vast estate. She knew that he was making polite conversation for Timothy's benefit, sensing that, if they had been alone, he would have asked her all about herself. Oh, how she wished that they were alone. Resentfully, she glanced at Timothy, wishing he were a cartoon character and that she could just snap her fingers and watch him disappear in a puff of smoke. Instead, she had to make bland, polite conversation, unable to dip into her vast repertoire of flirting techniques. At this very moment, she should be pouting gently while running a moist fingertip over her bottom lip. But, knowing Timothy's cackhanded reaction to this, he would probably remark, 'Your cold sore coming back?'

Perhaps, though, she should be concentrating on giving a more sophisticated impression. With this thought, she sat straight-backed, lifted her chin and began to issue orders to the waitress as if well accustomed to marshalling a battalion of hired hands. By the time they left, Lara couldn't help but feel guilty at the look of cold resentment the waitress threw at her.

Vittorio offered to drive them home. They stopped first at Lara's block and he escorted her up the stairs, leaving Timothy in the car which had been conveniently parked further along the road.

In silence they mounted the steps, then Vittorio spoke in an urgent whisper. 'Lara, I want to kiss you.'

She tensed; her hand trembled as she inserted the key in the lock. 'Do you want to come in for a moment?' she asked casually. Once inside, she turned to him, her lips parted in invitation. Slowly, he came towards her, his mouth brushing one cheek, then the other, his breath hot and smelling of wine and garlic.

'Lara,' he murmured, drawing back to gaze at her. 'I think I have fallen in love with you.'

She could hardly draw breath to speak. 'But you can't,' she protested weakly. 'You have to find a wife.'

He came close once more. 'Yes, I know.'

'And I guess you have to marry a *contessa* or something,' she said lightly, trying to appear nonchalant.

He shrugged. 'No, why? My mother can tell me to marry, but she cannot dictate my choice.'

Hope soared like a rocket. She could almost taste the Chianti and hear the chatter of elegant Italian women window shopping on the Via di something-or-other, smell the espresso and strong cigarettes on a busy piazza.

'Oh, Lara,' he murmured. 'Somehow, I sense you are my kindred spirit. You share my passion for art – that is evident. I saw how your eyes shone when you discussed Penfold's work.' He moved closer, his lips lightly brushing down her neck until she felt she could melt into a heap on the carpet. 'I want to know you, Lara. Do you want to know me?'

'Yes, oh yes.'

'Beautiful Lara,' he murmured, tracing a fingertip down over her lower lip, around and under her chin, down her throat to stop, tantalisingly, at her breastbone. 'I will see you in the morning,' he said, and was gone.

She fell back against the wall, listening to his footsteps on the pavement, the roar of the Porsche fading into the distance. If his touch could make her react like this, how would she feel when he made love to her? She skipped up the stairs, ready to shake Beatrix violently awake and tell her everything!

But Beatrix was not asleep. She wasn't even in bed. Lara read the note.

I hope you had a good time tonight. Justin has just phoned to ask me out to dinner. Is that OK? I won't be late. Beatrix.

Him – again? She shrugged, imagining them now, Justin with his tired, earnest face eagerly explaining corporate mergers; Beatrix with her big, puppy-dog eyes listening to every word with a childlike rapture. Well, at least Justin had found an audience for his boring monologues, she decided. And Beatrix was having a chance to meet people, instead of being tied to Kelsey's apron strings. Kelsey in an apron – that was something that would never happen! Suddenly, the telephone shrilled and she picked it up, chuckling at the thought of her friend done up like Mrs Mopp.

An imperious and all-too familiar voice boomed into her ear. 'Lara? Is that you? I would like to speak to Beatrix.'

'*Grandmother!*' Lara panicked, wildly thinking up a suitable excuse for Beatrix's absence – alone – at eleven-thirty at night. 'She's out walking the dog,' she said quickly.

'Good gracious. I didn't know you had a dog. What sort of dog?'

'A Rottweiler.'

'Really?' Her grandmother sounded uncertain.

'Yes,' Lara continued brightly, resurrecting her imaginary pet. 'He's called Chardonnay.' Now taken up on the roller-coaster of lies, she was unable to stop. 'He needs a lot of exercise – so Beatrix won't be back for a while yet.'

'I see.' The old woman paused as if thinking about this then carried on briskly: 'Is everything progressing as planned?'

She made it sound like an army invasion. 'Yes, fine. No problems.'

'Have you any idea, yet, when she can come home? I've just discovered some fifty-per-cent-off vouchers on Bliss Bridal Wear. It would be a shame to waste them.'

Lara paused. Beatrix's continuing presence would mean all bills paid, her departure the promise of a substantial reward. 'I'm not quite sure,' she prevaricated. 'Shortly, I should imagine.' She knew she would have to let Beatrix go home soon; it would be unfair to keep her from the man she loved, but surely an extra week or two would make no difference to their romance?

'I hope you've got her out of that ghastly headscarf,' the old woman muttered.

'Oh yes, Grandmother,' Lara said. We've certainly done that, she thought.

'Is she entertaining?'

'Yes, she's great fun.'

'No, no, you misunderstand me. Has she had the opportunity to play host to her new acquaintances?'

'Not yet, but we're planning a dinner party next week.'

'Jolly good. Make sure she does finger food. Always a hit at the WI Christmas get-together.'

'What a great idea.'

'I'm going to bed now,' the old lady stated. 'Tell Beatrix that I will speak to her another time. Goodnight, Lara.'

'Goodnight, Grandmother.'

Lara replaced the receiver and fell back on the sofa. She yearned to recapture the thrill of Vittorio's touch, but it was impossible with that imperious, cut-glass voice still ringing still in her ears.

She glanced at the clock. Eleven-thirty. When would Beatrix be home? Impatiently, she stood up and put her hands on her hips, not knowing whether to wait up or just forget about her and go to bed. She felt like a mother waiting for her teenaged daughter. I'm going to bed, she decided. Beatrix is old enough to look after herself.

An hour later, she lay awake in the darkness, her mind playing over the dangers that could befall her cousin. It was with relief and annoyance that she finally heard a key in the door.

Beatrix was startled to see Lara standing at her bedroom door. 'I'm sorry I'm late,' she hiccuped, struggling to get out of her jacket.

'Are you drunk?' Lara demanded.

Beatrix nodded sheepishly. 'Yes, I think I am.'

'I don't mind you having fun,' Lara continued sternly, 'but I've been worried sick. It's one o'clock in the morning and I've got to be up at six. You should've called.' Heavens!

she thought in alarm. Now I'm beginning to *sound* like a mother.

'I'm sorry.' Beatrix swayed as she came into the room, her face puckered in concentration as she attempted to walk in a straight line. 'Actually, could I just get something to eat? I'm starving.'

'I thought Justin took you out to dinner?'

'He did, but I'm still starving.'

Lara frowned suspiciously. 'Don't tell me. You've got the munchies?'

Beatrix peered at her. 'Pardon?'

Of course, Cousin Beatrix was new to the drugs scene. 'Have you been smoking dope?'

Beatrix nodded guiltily, eyes downcast. 'But I only tried a few puffs.'

Lara sighed in exasperation, annoyed at herself for being bad-tempered, annoyed at Beatrix for causing it. 'Go on,' she said more gently, not wanting to dent her cousin's newfound confidence. 'Fix yourself something to eat, and I'll have a glass of mineral water.' She followed Beatrix into the kitchen and sat up on the stool, wanting to gloss over her lecture of a moment ago. 'So, did you have a good evening?'

Beatrix took the bottle of Perrier from the fridge. 'Yes, thank you. Did you?'

'I certainly did! All this time, I thought Vittorio would

have to marry an Italian girl but I was wrong.' She grinned, taking the glass of water. 'I'm definitely in with a chance.'

'Did you practise your Italian on him?'

Lara snorted. 'Are you kidding? I don't want to frighten him off!' She sipped her water, contemplating Beatrix from over the rim of her glass. The girl was really gaining in confidence – her movements were more assured, her manner more relaxed, her eye-contact more direct. 'So,' she enquired, 'where did you and Justin go tonight?'

'A restaurant. Bibendum, I think it was called. Then we went to an apartment overlooking Chelsea Harbour where I met some of his business colleagues.'

'Sounds fun,' Lara lied, knowing the sort of in-depth financial analyses Justin and his friends would have eagerly discussed. 'You're looking great,' she said. 'That outfit really suits you. I bet you can't wait to get home to show off. Your Mr X is going to have the shock of his life!'

'Yes, yes he will.'

'I presume you've told Justin about him?'

'I completely forgot.' Beatrix's voice had become hesitant, a reminder of her old self.

'Kelsey's right,' Lara said gently. 'You should tell him, in case he starts getting the wrong ideas.' Hell! she thought irritably, I'm sounding more like a mother by the minute. 'Grandmother phoned earlier,' she trilled, wanting to lighten the mood. 'Boy! Does she scare me!'

Beatrix glanced up from buttering bread. 'Her bark is worse than her bite.'

'Talking about barking, she asked where you were and I told her you were out walking the dog.'

'The dog?'

Lara shrugged. 'That's my usual excuse. I call him "Chardonnay" – my invisible Rottweiler.'

Beatrix raised her eyebrows in surprise.

'That's all I could think of. I couldn't say: "Oh, Beatrix? She's out somewhere smoking dope with a strange man".'

Beatrix giggled. She was now loading the bread with anything she could lay her hands on. 'I will always be grateful to her for sending me here.' She turned and smiled shyly. 'And I will always be grateful to you for letting me stay.'

Lara went pink with pleasure. 'I've enjoyed it. I just wish I could have had more time with you.' She glanced at the clock and swiftly got down from the stool. 'Taking about time, I'm meeting Vittorio tomorrow morning – *at six!*'

'Oh, that's right,' Beatrix recalled. 'You're going to meet the new artist.'

Lara hugged herself and began to waltz in a circle. 'Which means a whole day with Vittorio.' She stopped and smiled indulgently. 'Well, I'd better get my beauty sleep.' She walked to the door. 'I'll see you some time tomorrow.'

'Goodnight, Beatrix.'

'Goodnight, Lara. And I'm sorry I was late.'

'That's all right. You may as well make the most of it while you're here.'

Jack

'Goodnight, Daddy.'

'Goodnight, Sam.' Jack tucked the duvet under the mattress before bending forward to give his youngest son a kiss.

'I still wish I could have a Crushhammer cake,' Sam repeated wistfully.

'I know you do, and if I could get you one, I would.' Jack stroked the curly hair back from the little boy's forehead. He yearned to give Sam the world but he couldn't even give him the birthday cake he wanted.

Sam persevered. 'Couldn't you ask Cameron's mum to make it?'

'No, sweetheart, I can't. They live miles away now. It just wouldn't be possible. Maybe we can sort something out for next year, eh?'

Sam was silent. Next year to a little boy was light years

away. Jack closed the curtains. 'Goodnight, Sam. Goodnight, Jamie. Now go to sleep.' He left the door slightly ajar and softly descended the stairs. He entered the kitchen to see Ernest gazing into space as he picked his nose.

'Don't do that!' Jack growled. 'You're worse than the boys.'

Ernest turned sharply. 'Eh?'

'Picking your nose.'

The other man looked surprised. 'Oh, sorry.' He wiped his fingers on his woollen waistcoat and picked up his glass of beer from the table. 'They asleep, then?' he asked.

Jack laughed. 'Give them time.' Ernest knew all there was to know about lambs but he had no idea about children. As Jack took his unfinished roll-up cigarette from the ashtray, he glanced over at his friend. Ernest's general misogyny and unappealing habits had made him an unattractive specimen to the opposite sex. It was doubtful that he would ever marry. Perhaps that was the reason why he was so against Jack finding a wife; he didn't want to lose a bachelor friend, an ally.

'It doesn't look good about the landfill, does it?' Ernest muttered.

Jack pulled on his roll-up, drawing the smoke into his lungs. 'No, it doesn't.'

'So, do you think you're going to make enough money from this painting lark to outbid?'

Jack shook his head slowly. 'I don't know. Some of those prices I saw at that gallery had my head reeling, I can tell you. Ten thousand pounds for a white canvas with black dots on it!'

Ernest lowered the glass from his lips. 'Pff, even *you* can do better than that!'

Jack smiled wryly and began to gather up Sam's drawings, wanting to get the place tidy for his London visitors. 'Anyway, I'll get a better idea of things tomorrow. The fact that I've got two gallery owners coming to see my work gives me a better chance.' He looked beyond the fluttering curtains to see the sun sinking in a ribbon of scarlet. The swifts were out, their screeches echoing in the still, balmy evening. 'But I've got to get that money soon,' he whispered. 'Or it will be too late.'

Ernest nodded. 'It's not going to help matters if you run around chasing after women, is it?'

Jack's voice was sharp. 'I'm not chasing after women.' He forced the image of the brown-eyed girl from his thoughts.

'So, what actually happened about that barmaid – the one in London? Patsy said she didn't turn up.'

The mere mention of that episode made Jack shiver. 'That's right,' he said evenly. Distracted now, he slid the pile of papers towards him across the counter and into the dresser drawer.

'They're all the same,' Ernest said knowingly. Suddenly, he stopped and bent forward to pick something up. 'Hello – what's this?'

Jack looked on in alarm. It was the photograph of Lara, the two pieces held together with Sellotape. 'It's nothing.' He went to snatch it but Ernest was too quick for him and jerked it away.

'This is her, ain't it?'

Jack sighed. 'Yes, it is.'

'Pretty.' He flipped it over and looked at the name. 'Lara Bayley,' he read aloud.

Jack took it from him and dropped it in the bin.

'So, she never turned up,' Ernest said heavily. 'Probably for the best, if you ask me.' He lifted his glass of beer to his lips. 'I knew it was a bad business, right from the start.'

For a moment, Jack gazed down into the bin. Yes, he thought bitterly. For once, Ernest, you were right, dead right.

Sunday

Beatrix

Grimacing with the pain in her head, Beatrix eased herself out of bed; her mouth felt dry and stale. She put on her new Kata spectacles and opened the curtains, blinking against the bright light. 'Oh,' she moaned. 'My head!' She turned for the bathroom, going straight to the Paracetamol tablets in the cabinet. She had never taken so many headache tablets as she had in the last week.

As she crossed the sitting room, she caught sight of herself in the mirror above the mantelpiece. Her short blonde hair stood out from her head in spikes, her lipstick was smudged and her mascara lay in dark patches beneath her eyes. Within a matter of days, she had gone from seventy-year-old spinster to seventeen-year-old raver! She smiled at the thought of it, only thankful that Grandmother could not see her like this. She remembered the old lady's words: *Indeed, with your influence, Lara may learn to be a bit more sensible*. Beatrix chuckled at the irony of it. Here she was, getting out of bed at midday, hung over with drink and drugs while Lara had risen at the crack of dawn to go on a business trip!

She made a cup of coffee and carried it into the sitting room. Here she slid the *Eagle Eye Cherry* album into the CD player, fast tracking to 'Save the Night'. This was her favourite tune. It would always remind her of Justin . . .

Last night, she had opened the door to him, smiling at the astonishment on his face. Her long red ponytail and blue eyes had been replaced with cropped blonde hair, designer spectacles framing her hazel-coloured eyes, red lipstick and a black figure-hugging jacket and skirt. 'Wow!' he had exclaimed. After worrying that he would only fancy her as a redhead, his reaction came as a relief. In fact, he liked her new look even better. 'I didn't recognise you at all,' he admitted as he leant forward to kiss her on the cheek.

What a wonderful evening. Over dinner in a candlelit restaurant, he had told her a lot more about his work as a corporate financier; he had even won a million-dollar deal with the Japanese! He was clever, charming, and handsome. A million miles from John Chadwick in his butcher's shop.

A cloud of depression settled upon her as she recalled Lara's words: 'Your Mr X is going to have the shock of his life! Have you told Justin about him?' Beatrix sighed, not wanting to think about it – not yet. She only had a couple of weeks left and in that time she just wanted to pretend that London was her home, that Justin was her boyfriend and that racing from party to party in the early hours of the morning was something that would never end. 'You can't start to get interested in other guys,' Kelsey had warned, 'You have to tell Justin you've got a boyfriend waiting back home. It's only fair.' Boyfriend! Huh! She gave a harsh laugh. John Chadwick would never again be her boyfriend. She no longer cared about him, or Susan Dobbs or the Corwyn Marrow Title or the WI meetings or the upstairs ruddy plumbing. She didn't care about any of it. All she cared about was Justin . . . She moved over to the mirror and gazed at her reflection.

She was here as an instrument of revenge against the Dobbs family. But once she had fulfilled her rôle couldn't she then come back to London and continue to stay with Lara? Would her grandmother continue to pay their expenses? No. The old lady never parted with money unless it was of direct benefit to herself.

Beatrix wandered over to the window and looked down on the street. Naturally, she could get a job to support herself – but doing what? Then doubts overwhelmed her. Could she really desert her grandmother? Could she blank out the fact that the old woman had been like a mother to her, taking her in after the car crash, giving her love and kindness? Beatrix bit her lip thoughtfully. Could she abandon her now, now that she was getting on in years? Now that she would need, more than ever, a companion, a helper?

This was hopeless. She was deceiving Grandmother *and* Lara and Kelsey, and Justin, too. Yet she hardly knew him. How could she base the rest of her life on a man she had met twice?

Suddenly, the telephone rang and she picked it up. 'Hello?'

It was Justin. 'Beatrix? Hi, it's me. Are you doing anything at lunchtime?'

At the sound of his voice, her heart skipped a beat. 'No, no, I'm not.'

'Great. I've got a couple of hours off. Why don't you come over and meet me at my office?'

'That's a wonderful idea!'

'I knew you'd think so. Just get the tube to Holborn and I'll meet you by the newspaper stand. One o'clock, sharp.'

'I'll see you then.' She put the phone down and ran into the bathroom, hurriedly wiping the mascara from her face. The excitement in Justin's voice had matched her own. He had only a few hours spare and yet he wanted to spend them with her and not some important business client.

He liked her, she knew that, knew by the way he had kissed her slowly, softly down in the hall last night. For a moment, she imagined herself lying in his bed, feeling his hand on her naked breast. She shut her eyes in trepidation, overcome with fear. She would have to get drunk. But, if she truly loved him, surely she wouldn't need to? She wouldn't worry about it now, she decided, brushing her teeth. Today, she would just have fun.

At Holborn station, she came up into the bright sunshine, pausing to gaze in awe at the towering buildings around her. The City. Impressive slabs of white brick, polished steel and reflecting glass. For a Sunday, the area was surprisingly busy. As instructed, she waited by the newsstand. And waited. It was one-thirty when he finally appeared, hurrying towards her.

'Beatrix!' he exclaimed, cupping her head between his hands and kissing her on the lips. 'I'm afraid I'm running late so we've only got twenty minutes.' He grabbed her hand and swung her around. 'Let's get some sandwiches and I'll take you up to see my office.'

She skipped along, feeling the sun on her bright blonde hair, her white-looped earrings dancing against her neck. She wore a yellow polka-dotted dress that billowed out from her waist, light and summery, and knew she looked pretty, thrilling to the admiring glances from passing men. It was such a lovely day, she would have much preferred to sit down by the river but she also understood that Justin wanted to show off his new computer system.

Suddenly he grinned back at her. 'Do you remember what I said about the Nikkei index hitting rock bottom?'

She couldn't quite remember but she nodded anyway.

'Well, I was right. It's dropped from a peak of thirty-eight thousand to fifteen thousand. Wait till you see the graphs!'

Lara

Without taking his eyes off the road, Timothy said it again. 'A milk float!'

Arms folded tight, Lara threw him a savage look. She was irritated enough without having to listen to him repeating himself. Although still annoyed with Vittorio, she felt it only right that she should stick up for him in his absence. 'Maybe it wasn't his fault.'

Timothy glanced into the rearview mirror as he changed lanes. 'We're not talking about a hi-jacked juggernaut speeding through the streets of London, we're talking about a milk float standing at the kerbside. Of course it was his fault!'

Lara remained silent. They were heading westwards along the flyover, the soft morning sky promising a sunny day. Vittorio should have been here, she thought bitterly. She had got up at the crack of dawn for nothing.

'It doesn't surprise me in the least,' Timothy continued. 'The man's a maniac in a car.'

Lara kept silent. She was not prepared to believe anything bad about Vittorio. It had been an accident, nothing more.

'It was lucky the milkman wasn't in the float at the time,' Timothy nagged on. 'Otherwise, Vittorio would be on a manslaughter charge. He wrote off a Lamborghini last year, can you believe it?'

'Let's forget about it, shall we?'

'If you wish.' He slid a CD into the player and immediately the interior of the car was filled with the soft, gentle strains of an aria. 'Since he's going to have to make this trip in the next week or so, I shall need to ask you to drive him, is that all right?'

Immediately she sprang up in her seat. 'I'm sure that won't be a problem.'

'Good. I can't risk having him involved in a mass pile-up. Don't get me wrong,' Timothy drawled, 'Vittorio's not some kind of nutter – not at all. As long as he's nowhere near a steering wheel, he's perfectly level-headed. In fact, he's a shrewd businessman with an unerring eye for fresh talent and he's positively passionate about art.'

Lara gazed out of the window, seeing Vittorio's lips so close. *You share my passion.* Oh yes, Vittorio, and I'm going to prove it to you. She began to form a plan. Today, she would make friends with their new artist, win his trust, learn all she could about him and his work, so that when she eventually brought Vittorio to meet him, she would appear knowledgeable and encouraging; in fact, the perfect wife for a successful gallery owner. Perhaps, after all, it had been for the best that Vittorio had been forced to stay behind because now she had the whole day in which to quiz Timothy about him while making inroads with this Penfold guy. Yes, it was all going to work out for the best.

The sun shone as they breezed along in Timothy's vintage Rolls-Royce, free of London and heading for the south coast, a Fortnum & Mason's hamper on the back seat and the sound of a romantic aria surrounding her. When she saw the sign to Southampton, Lara smiled contentedly, gazing out at the fluffy white clouds on the horizon. Yes, she decided, this is going to be such a lovely day. And yet, forty minutes earlier, she had almost refused to come, silently fuming at the sudden change in plan.

As Timothy began to chatter about the building work to his house, she daydreamed, seeing herself in a billowing white wedding dress standing at the entrance to some huge Italian cathedral.

'So,' Lara remarked smugly, glancing at Timothy, 'Vittorio's got to get married, has he?'

'That's right. He has strict instructions from his mother to produce sons and heirs.'

Lara thought about this. Sons. That didn't form any part of her plan. Marriage was acceptable to her – but children? Of course, she thought swiftly, I won't have to look after them. He's rich enough to have a battalion of servants. I will be there solely to kiss them goodnight and to exude an aura of maternal discipline, kind but firm.

Timothy loosened his cravat. 'It might be an idea if you were to remember the route for next time,' he suggested. He pointed to the glove compartment. 'There's directions in there.'

Lara emerged from her daydreaming and removed the scrap of paper. 'Take the M3,' she read.

'We've done that. We're on the A31 now, heading for Ringwood.'

'Good. Ten miles beyond Ringwood,' she continued, 'turn off for Bere Regis.'

With gentle prompting, Timothy answered all her questions about Vittorio and it was not until she saw the Bere Regis sign, that she remembered the directions in her hand. 'Turn off to Wool,' she read. 'Then take the A352 to Appleby.'

They carried on, Timothy remarking on the landscape. Soon afterwards they reached a small town; the main street was deserted, the shops closed. In the distance, church bells were ringing. There was a Sunday feel about the place that you could never get in London.

'Where next?' Timothy asked.

'Take the first left to Harnet.' She rolled down her window and leant out, savouring the warm, fragrant breeze on her face. Everything was so green and fresh.

'Harnet,' Timothy stated.

She saw the sign. 'Go straight through the village, over a humped-backed bridge. Fifty yards up on the left is a sign saying *Strawberry Picking*. Go on for another fifty yards.' At this point, she turned over the paper to read the rest. 'Manor Farm is on the left as you come round . . .' Her words trailed off into silence. Hang on – she knew a Manor Farm. That pig farmer! Where was it he lived? Devon, wasn't it?

Timothy was laughing. 'What's the matter with you? You sound as if your battery's running out.'

'Timothy.' She tried to keep her voice light. 'Are we in Devon, by any chance?'

'I certainly hope not,' he chuckled.

She breathed with relief. How silly of her! Her imagination was running away with her again. They had turned off onto a rough track and now drove slowly through an orchard of pink blossom. Ahead stood a sprawling white-washed cottage, the diamond windowpanes winking in the sunshine, the thatched roof hanging down like a fringe over a friendly face. It was the most beautiful house she had ever seen. Doves, white against the blue of the sky, fluttered like falling handkerchiefs to land on the roof. Over the door trailed yellow roses and beside it was a bench seat tucked amongst stone pots of pink and yellow flowers. There was a wishing-well – a real one – and around it lay a green lawn sprinkled with daisies. At the sight of it all, Lara felt her chest swell with inexplicable joy. 'This has to be the most beautiful place on earth,' she whispered.

'It's certainly very pretty,' Timothy remarked, surveying their surroundings. 'Come to think of it, this place does remind me of Devon. I've frequently been through Dorset but never this far south.'

'Dorset?' Her voice trembled.

'Yes, that's right.' Timothy glanced at her. 'Is there something wrong?'

Lara stared straight through Timothy, shocked rigid. Now she remembered. It wasn't Devon, it was Dorset! She twisted her fingers together, feeling a growing apprehension. *Dorset. Manor Farm.* Why did she keep thinking of that pig farmer? Why did she have this cold feeling of fear? Could she honestly imagine that that man could be their artist?

'Timothy,' she asked, trying to keep her voice light, 'does Penfold have pigs?'

'Yes, I think he does. Why do you ask?'

In an instant she had the window rolled up. There could

easily be more than one Manor Farm in Dorset with strawberry-picking and pigs, she told herself. In fact, there could be hundreds of them.

As Timothy parked the car alongside a pickup truck, she noticed a tweed cap on the dashboard, identical to the one worn by that man in his photograph. She gazed at it in horror. 'Timothy?' she began.

'Hang on, Lara.' He had opened his door and now stepped out, looking towards the house and smiling. 'Jack!' he called, raising a hand in greeting.

Lara froze; only her eyes moved, swivelling in their sockets. Swiftly, she folded forward and began to rummage in her handbag on the floor, pretending to hunt for something. 'Go on without me,' she called to Timothy. 'I'm just looking for something.'

'OK. We'll see you inside.'

Her ears strained to identify the man's voice, but at this distance it was impossible. Could it be him? Maybe not. She had to know. Slowly, very slowly, she turned her head and peeped over the back seat. *It was him!* He towered head and shoulders above Timothy, his short hair shining reddish gold in the sunlight, his smile showing a missing tooth. 'Oh shit!' she breathed. 'Shit, shit, shit.' This was unbelievable! How could she not have known?

The farmer had paused on the doorstep, shading his eyes from the sun as he scanned the orchard. Quickly, she ducked forward and out of sight. When next she looked the doorstep was empty. Exhaling a deep breath, she sat back in her seat and stared out of the windscreen. If he saw her, he would be shocked and angry, refusing to have her on his property. He might even become violent! She shivered, remembering the look in his eyes when she had left him standing alone in L'Escargot.

What was she going to do? Instinctively, she glanced towards the gate. She could sneak off through the orchard, find a taxi and head for the nearest train station. There would be plenty of time to think of an excuse to give to Timothy. It would be an extreme move, she had to admit, but there was no alternative. She shut her eyes tight against the unfairness of it all. At this moment in time she should have been in that house chatting confidently with their new artist. Bonding. Making a lifelong friend. Instead of which, she was hiding out in the car with sweaty armpits, too scared to move. This was a nightmare!

Suddenly, two little boys appeared up ahead, skirting the edge of the lawn. They wore shorts and T-shirts; the taller one was holding a ball. They smiled shyly at her and she responded with a tentative wave. Now they were walking towards the car. They stopped outside her door, the smaller one shuffling to half-conceal himself behind his older brother.

To her horror, the older boy began to shout through

the window. 'Hello,' he called. 'Have you come to see my daddy?'

Lara frowned. That man had a family! What a nerve.

The older boy nudged the smaller one. 'Go and get Daddy,' he ordered.

'No!' she screamed, feeling the veins almost explode from her neck. The little boys jumped back, frightened. She lowered her window a fraction, giving them her best smile. They were so sweet, she didn't really want to scare them like this. The little one had mud on his chubby knees, the older one placing a protective arm around his shoulders. 'Listen,' she began, wishing she had sweets to bribe them with. 'I—'

At that moment, there was a shout from the house. 'Jamie! Sam! Come in and say hello to our visitors.'

A mischievous look spread across the little one's face and he began to dance on tiptoe, backing off and circling the front of the car. No! she wanted to shout. Go away! The little boy was now peeping over the bonnet of the car with a come-and-get-me expression. In the next instant the man was there, scooping him up and planting a kiss on his cheek. Then he grabbed the older one around the waist and began to carry them both towards the house, the two boys struggling playfully.

He's going, Lara thought, weak with relief. Oh thank God. As the man passed, there was a loud bang at her window and she spun round in terror only to discover that it had been a boy's shoe that had kicked out. She glanced up and what she saw made her heart thud to a stop. The farmer had stopped and was looking down at her, a frown of astonishment forming on his brow. She could only smile weakly.

The game was up.

Slowly, timidly, she opened her door and stepped out. Now she stood before him, glad those massive arms were occupied. The guy was enormous. 'Hello, Jack,' she said sweetly, desperately trawling her entire store of charm.

'*You!*' Without taking his eyes from her, he released his sons. 'Go inside,' he told them. 'Both of you.' Something in his voice made them obey instantly.

Oh no, he was going to hit her! This was like confronting a killer convict. 'I bet you're surprised to see me,' she said lightly, edging away. He was obviously too stunned to do more than gape at her. This was the moment to introduce a measure of civility. 'It's nice to see you again, Jack.' She thrust out her hand for him to shake but he ignored it.

He jerked his head back to the house. 'Are you the assistant he's talking about?'

She smiled winningly. 'That's right.'

'You've got a nerve coming here!'

She was rapidly beginning to lose patience. Why should

she be the guilty party? '*I've* got a nerve!' she cried. 'That's a joke. I'm not the one with a family!'

At the sound of brisk footsteps they turned sharply to see Timothy approaching the car. He opened the boot then flopped his hand against his chest. 'For an awful moment there I thought I'd forgotten the camera.' He reached in and took it out. 'I see you two are getting acquainted. Lara, this is Jack Havers, known to us as Jack Penfold. Jack, this is my assistant, Lara Bayley.' His introduction prompted them to shake hands politely, Lara grateful to realise that the man was in no position to reveal their sordid first meeting.

'I'll get the picnic hamper out while I'm at it,' Timothy said, opening the car door.

Lara would have stamped her foot in vexation. After all her plans to win the artist's friendship, *this* had to happen. It was unbelievable! She had met this man through an advertisement and yet only days later she was to meet him again. Was this destiny telling her something? And if so, what?

Happily unaware of the tension in the air, Timothy said, 'Come along. Let's get all our business chat out of the way so we can have lunch.'

Lara and Jack followed in silence, the latter eyeing her suspiciously as he stood to one side of the doorstep to let her enter. Jesus! she thought irritably. You'd think I was some axe murderer. If he keeps looking at me like that, Timothy's going to start asking questions.

She was relieved when the farmer broke his heavy silence by offering her a cup of tea. 'That would be lovely, Jack, thank you,' she gushed, smiling widely at the boys by the sink. She sat down at the table and looked around.

To one side stood an antique dresser, its shelves stacked with flower-printed plates, chipped mugs, a row of childish egg cups, a foil packet of tobacco and a beaker of felt tip pens. At the very top, half hidden behind a vase, was an ugly china dog with a moustache and a gold chain around its neck. No wonder it's been relegated up there, she mused. She continued to look about. Every spare inch of the whitewashed walls had been covered in childish paintings held in place with Sellotape. This is more than a kitchen, she thought; this is the heart of the house. A black cat lay stretched out on a battered yellow sofa, lifting its head to view her briefly while a dog sat and scratched its ear with a back paw. There was an old green Aga in the corner, looking more in keeping here than the one Poppy Tomkins had in her pseudo-rustic Notting Hill house.

The two boys had dried their hands on a tea-towel and now stood gazing at her as Jack introduced them as Sam and Jamie. So, he had sons? The guy had tricked her. Not only had he pretended to be lord of the manor but he'd also forgotten to mention kids. Aha, she thought, *and* he's got a wife, too. Any moment now some dumpy, rosy-cheeked woman in an apron would appear, fussing over the boys while producing a freshly baked fruitcake from the oven. She couldn't wait to see the embarrassment on Jack Havers' face!

As the older boy approached, he put out a hand and she shook it. 'Hello, Jamie,' she said. 'Nice to meet you.' The small chubby one was not so bold and she was quick to cover up his embarrassment by taking his hand and shaking it vigorously, speaking in an adult voice. 'Hello, Sam.' Now she pointed to the robot cartoon character on his T-shirt. 'I love your T-shirt.'

Startled, he looked down at his chest, then back up at her. 'It's Crushhammer,' he explained.

'Yeah, I know,' she replied. Not so long ago, she had spent many an afternoon tuned into the children's channel. 'The space crusader of the universe,' she added in an American drawl. 'Destroyer of the spawn warriors!'

The little boy grinned in surprised delight, his shyness completely forgotten. 'I'm six next week,' he confided.

'Great!' she enthused. 'Are you going to have a party?'

'Yes.' Suddenly, the little face lost its brightness. 'But I wanted a Crushhammer cake just like Cameron Cole's but we don't have anyone to make it.'

'What about your mummy?'

The room went silent. In surprise, she looked from Sam

to Jamie and then to their father. 'They don't have a mummy,' Jack explained. 'My wife died six years ago.'

She stared at him. Then she stared back at the two boys, a hollow feeling in the pit of her stomach. I had no idea, she wanted to tell them. I wouldn't have said anything if I'd known. Suddenly, she yearned to put her arms around them and hug them to her but, as a stranger, this was something she could not do. Instead, she looked over at the plate of biscuits on the table. 'Could I have a biscuit, please?'

The two boys dived for the plate, Jamie getting there first and proudly offering it towards her. She studied the biscuits, making a show of indecision. 'They all look so yummy, I don't know which one to choose.'

'What about this one?' Sam suggested, pointing to a pink wafer. 'They're my favourite.'

'Mine, too,' she exclaimed, picking it up. Seeing the expression on the little boy's face, she felt a tear prick her eye. He was such a darling. They both were. And they had no mummy! That was terrible! Not wanting to let her feelings show, she smiled brightly instead. 'Did you see Crushhammer when Zorka melted the ice mountain and the—'

Timothy coughed. 'I'm sorry to interrupt, Lara, but perhaps we should remember why we are here?'

For a moment she had forgotten completely. 'Of course,' she said, flustered. 'Sorry.'

Timothy turned to Jack and began to apologise for Vittorio's absence before going on to explain their working partnership. Meanwhile, the two boys had quietly settled themselves at the table and, although Lara sat back with a studious air, wanting to give Jack the impression of professional art assistant, she couldn't help but tip the boys a surreptitious wink.

After a brief discussion, Timothy stood up, slipping the camera from his shoulder. 'Right, Jack. Let's see where it all happens.'

As Jack got to his feet, he looked down at himself anxiously. 'I didn't think you would want to take a photo of me,' he said. 'Should I go and put on a suit?'

'No, no,' Timothy assured him. 'We want you just how you are, don't we, Lara?'

She was forced to look at Jack, forced to nod in agreement. 'Um, yes,' she mumbled, feeling her cheeks grow hot. For an awful moment, she witnessed the hard glint in his eyes. Then he turned for the door.

With Jack in the lead, they walked across a cobbled terrace and past the wishing well, the boys skipping beside her. At the edge of the lawn, two white sheets fluttered from a clothesline, dazzling white against the green grass. She sniffed, savouring the scent of crisp cotton baking in the hot sunshine. 'We've got a brilliant rope swing across the stream,' Jamie chatted, as they entered a thicket of trees. 'Daddy made it for us.'

Jack immediately shot up in her estimation from 0 to 5. 'That's great,' she answered.

'You can have a go on it if you want,' Sam invited her.

She gestured at her Armani suit and Manolo shoes. 'Oh, I'm sorry, Sam, but that's impossible. I'm not dressed for it.'

'Oh.'

She heard the disappointment in his voice. 'Next time, eh?'

'OK.'

Would there be a next time? she wondered. Probably not. Although Jack was behaving courteously, she could sense the smouldering anger coming at her in waves. He would not want her to return. And could she blame him, after the things she had said to him that night in the wine bar? *You're the pig farmer! I came here to meet a handsome polo player, not some half-witted hillbilly!* She shuddered at the memory of her cruel words.

They had followed a well-worn path through the trees and now came out into a sun-dappled clearing. In the centre stood a shed, the walls made of breeze blocks, the roof hung with sheets of corrugated metal. 'You two boys can go and play,' Jack said as he opened the door. 'I'll give you a shout when we're finished here.'

They glanced at Lara, shuffling their feet in uncertainty. 'Go on,' Jack repeated. 'We won't be long.'

Lara watched them run off. In that moment, she dearly wanted to go with them, to run across the lawn sprinkled with daisies, under the apple trees pink with blossom. Where were they going? The rope swing? How she wished she could kick off her shoes and run with them. Instead, she followed Timothy into the shed.

Inside, a mixture of pungent smells met them – turpentine, beeswax, tobacco. Overhead, a section of the roof had been cut away and covered with a sheet of Perspex to allow the daylight to enter. Directly under this stood an easel with a half-finished sketch thumb-tacked onto a wooden board, and beside it was a table littered with rags and paintbrushes in jam jars. There was a sunken-seated armchair in the far corner and a shelving unit loaded with books and odds and ends. On the floor to Lara's right, large painted canvases had been stacked neatly.

Timothy was in like a shot, kneeling down to flick through the paintings. 'Wonderful,' he muttered, straightening up to study a landscape. 'Let's have this on the easel,' he suggested, handing it to Jack. 'And you can stand in front of it as if you're finishing it off.' As soon as Timothy had arranged this to his satisfaction, he put the camera to his eye and began to take photographs.

Lara waited, noting an abandoned coffee mug, a plate

with a curled-up crust of bread, an old swivel chair with dirty yellow sponge showing through the shredded leather. Behind her, there were more shelves holding bottles with neat handwritten labels: *Linseed Oil, Walnut Oil, Sun Bleached Poppy Oil, Turpentine*. She recognised the writing, the whorls on the capital T, the loop in the a's. How could she not have known that this man was Penfold? Surely, there must have been clues!

Suddenly she was annoyed with herself. Would she never change? Would she always be that empty-headed girl with her thoughts in the clouds? No, she told herself firmly, she was being unfair on herself. After all, she'd had a lot to deal with in the past couple of weeks; bills to be paid, worries about the future, her plans to impress Vittorio by making friends with the new artist. Fat chance of that now! She knelt down and began to go through the paintings on the floor. They were excellent. It was hard to imagine that someone with the appearance of a road digger had the skill and sensitivity to create such beautiful pieces.

Timothy now laid down the camera and began to make notes on a writing pad whilst questioning Jack. 'I make my own charcoal,' Jack said, holding up a long black twig. 'Luckily, I'm surrounded by willow trees.'

Lara straightened, listening as he explained his working methods and the materials he preferred. Could she succeed in winning this man's friendship? It seemed doubtful. But did she want the friendship of a man who ensnared unsuspecting females? As she looked at him, she felt a thud of horror. He had not been ensnaring females, he had been searching for a wife – a mother for those two little boys! Oh God, and after the way she had behaved, he would probably never try again! What had she done?

Now he stood confidently, eyes clear and intelligent as he talked with Timothy. Without those bushy eyebrows lowered over hard eyes, he looked quite pleasant. In fact, without the gap in his teeth and the short hair, he could easily find himself a wife. It didn't help, though, that he wore a mustard-coloured nylon shirt buttoned up to the neck and baggy corduroy trousers. Admittedly, he did look like a hillbilly but he didn't need to. With such a beautiful house and orchards and fields, he must have *some* money. In fact, if he were to wear some fashionable clothes, get his teeth fixed and do something with his hair, he could be quite a catch. His advertisement had been badly worded, though. *Pig farmer*! That was enough to turn any woman off.

She frowned. But there was one problem . . . the boys. No woman in her right mind would want to take on a ready-made family.

Timothy closed his notepad. 'OK, Jack, do you mind if I lay your canvases out on the floor here?'

'Go ahead,' he answered.

Timothy pushed the swivel chair to one side to make more space before laying the second canvas on the floor directly under the skylight.

'Do you need my help?' Jack asked.

'No, dear chap, I'm fine.' Once again, Timothy had the camera to his eye. 'This shouldn't take too long.'

Lara was startled to see Jack staring directly at her. 'Perhaps your assistant would like to see some piglets?' he suggested.

Seeing the look in his eyes, she was tempted to cling to Timothy and refuse to go. But common sense prevailed; she had seen how lovingly he had kissed his boys, how tenderly he had stroked the hair back from Sam's forehead. He would not harm her. He might look as if he would, but he wouldn't.

'That's a nice idea,' Timothy replied absent-mindedly.

Jack waited for her answer. If she intended to make friends with him, this was an ideal opportunity to clear the air between them. 'I would love to,' she beamed.

Jack handed her a pair of Wellington boots as she stepped out of the shed. 'You'll need to wear these,' he explained, closing the door behind them.

She changed into the boots, leaving her Manolos in the grass by the step. 'Isn't it a lovely day,' she exclaimed, walking along beside him. Perhaps if she pretended that nothing had happened between them, then he would do the same. But she was wrong.

'Why did you come here?' he asked, his voice deadly calm.

'I liked your work,' she said quickly. 'I thought to myself, Gosh—'

'I want the truth.' He stopped and looked at her coldly.

'I didn't know it was you,' she blurted out. 'I didn't know that you and Penfold were the same person.' Her eyes fell before his. 'I'm sorry about . . . you know.' As she looked up she saw a flicker of pain cross his eyes, and in that moment, she was gripped with a terrible shame.

He carried on walking. She tripped to catch up with him and put a hand on his arm, wanting to explain.

'I don't want you to come here again,' he said, pulling his arm away.

Oh no! This was terrible. She wanted to be forgiven, to wipe away the memory. And what about her plans? She had to come back! She had to bring Vittorio here, to impress him, to win his respect. 'I am *so* sorry, Jack,' she said. 'Really. It was all my fault. I wrote down the wrong number, I know that now.'

'I think we should just forget about it.'

'What – just forget everything?' she asked hopefully. 'Does that mean I can come again?'

He stopped and looked at her. 'For someone who put me lower than an earthworm, I'm surprised you would want to come back.'

'I do, I do,' she said eagerly. 'Honestly.' His eyes moved over her face. It made her think of how she had recently gazed at a pair of kitten-heeled mules in Petras, knowing that she could no longer afford to buy them.

'I don't want to see you again,' he stated and moved on.

'But you must,' she cried. 'Don't you want to sell your paintings?'

He frowned. 'So?'

'I am the best person to help you.' This was a lie but she was desperate.

'I believe Timothy is the one to help me,' he said.

'In London, yes. But you want to sell your work on the Continent, don't you?' He nodded. 'Well, I have the contacts,' she said confidently, thinking of Vittorio.

They were approaching a row of long, low huts, the farmyard smell that had hung heavy in the air now overpowering. Lara wanted to put a hand across her nose, but she had other, more important, matters to think of. Then suddenly they had stopped and she found herself looking down into a straw-filled pen. A mother pig lay on her side, her head half-buried in straw and along the curve of her belly lay a row of tiny pink piglets, their fat bodies wriggling to get a better hold on the mother's teats. 'Oh!' she exclaimed in wonder, forgetting everything else in that moment. 'Aren't they gorgeous! Can I stroke one?'

He nodded perfunctorily. 'Go gently. The mother can be over-protective.'

One of the piglets had fallen asleep. She touched its warm soft body. Then she put her fingers around its tummy and picked it up.

Immediately, Jack put out a hand. 'Watch your clothes!'

With this warning, she remembered her Armani suit and held the piglet away from her. 'Oh, isn't he just wonderful?' The piglet had the teeniest corkscrew tail and trotters, its ears like tiny seashells, pink inside and curled to a fine point. 'What's his name?'

'We haven't given them names yet,' Jack answered, his voice flat.

She wanted to give them names. 'This one could be called Merlot,' she suggested hopefully.

He shrugged, his manner cool and unforgiving.

'What's the mother called?'

'Cleopatra.'

Cleopatra. She was stunned, remembering his letter and how she had imagined Cleopatra as a thoroughbred polo pony galloping over the hills. Not this fat snoring pig with stubby legs. How wrong could she have been! She glanced across at Jack's hard, miserable face. It had all been such a terrible mistake – for both of them. If only she had written down the right number. If only . . .

She looked away across the rolling emerald hills under a

blue cloudless sky. To her left, she could see the back of the house with an overgrown garden, a bench seat and a lily pond. Beyond that was a valley, the hills folded into one another like a woman's plait, leading down to the sea. Suddenly, the boys appeared, running and jumping over a stream to grab a rope that hung from a tree. Their rope swing.

'Let me put him back,' Jack said, gently taking the piglet from her, his rough hand brushing her own. He's got more consideration for this animal than he has for me, she thought. But is it any wonder?

'Jack,' she began. 'I—'

There was a shout from behind them. 'Yahoo!' It was Timothy. 'I'm finished,' he called.

'OK, we're on our way,' Jack replied.

Lara wanted to stop him. This was her last chance to be alone with him, to repair the damage she had done, to persuade him to let her return. Instead, she could only watch him walk away.

Timothy came out of the trees and up the hill to meet them. 'Vittorio will be delighted.'

Jack smiled. The dull expression of only a moment ago was now beginning to lighten.

'I calculate that he will want to take away with him at least fourteen large-scale canvases,' Timothy continued.

Jack's smile faded. 'But I don't have that many.'

'I know,' Timothy replied. 'That's why it is imperative that you put everything aside and concentrate on your art. You have less than a fortnight.'

'But that's impossible!'

'You must try,' Timothy insisted. 'What you have is excellent but it is not enough. Apart from Vittorio's requirements, I will want to show your work. Therefore I will need a total of ten large-scale oils or acrylics, ten or so small temperas and as many sketches as you can manage.'

'What?' Jack looked aghast. 'I honestly don't think I can do that.'

'You must.' Timothy flung out a hand. 'Forget the farm. Forget everything.'

'How can I? I'm a single parent with two small boys.'

'Surely you have a relative or a friend who can help?'

Jack shook his head. 'I've already asked around, but there's no one.'

'What about an agency?' Lara suggested. 'A nanny agency.'

Jack turned to her. 'I've already made enquiries but it's too expensive.'

'Dear chap,' Timothy admonished. 'We will pay for all that.'

Jack nodded slowly, considering this. 'There's an employment agency in Dorchester,' he murmured, evidently thinking hard. 'I'm sure they can find me a childminder.' He furrowed his brow in consternation. 'But how long will that take?' He shot Timothy an anxious look. 'And you think this Vittorio will be here in two weeks?'

'At the most.'

'I might be able to do it,' Jack began hesitantly, 'but only if I've got someone to help me. What I've got to consider is that the agency might not be able to find someone immediately. What if it takes a week, or more? And, for the boys' sake, I could only take on someone they liked.'

Lara nodded in sympathy. In her estimation, Jack went up from 5–8.

'Mm.' Timothy tapped his chin with the knuckle of a hand.

In the silence, Lara gazed towards the stream. Little Sam swung on the rope, lifting his knees sharply to avoid the water below. She smiled. The water would be cold. They were two adorable little boys and she only hoped that the woman who came to look after them would be kind and gentle. And fun. 'Jack is right,' she said. 'He can only take on someone that the boys really like.'

'*You!*'

At the sound of Timothy's exclamation, she turned, mystified to see him pointing a finger at her chest.

'Yes, you!' he repeated. 'You can help him until we find a proper nanny.'

Lara stood stunned, feeling the first stirrings of alarm. She knew that Timothy wanted her out of the gallery but this was absurd. 'Hang on, hang on,' she cried, halting the situation before it spun out of control. 'I can't even cook!'

'I'll order a delivery of oven-ready meals,' Timothy assured her.

Now she was frantic. 'I don't know the first thing about little boys.' She looked to their father, thankful to see that his horrified expression matched her own.

But: 'I think you underrate your capabilities,' Timothy responded. 'I couldn't help but notice that you had a certain rapport with them back at the house. Anyway, it would only be for a few days, until we find a replacement.'

'But—'

'Just a minute.' Jack had a hand up. 'This isn't going to work.'

Lara was quick to agree with him. 'He's right.'

Timothy persisted, 'Of course it will work. In fact, I have a better idea. Why doesn't Lara stay until Vittorio arrives?'

Ideas and images began to flash through Lara's brain. *Vittorio. Wife. Boys. Making friends with the artist.* Of course! It was so obvious. This would be the ideal setting in which to demonstrate to Vittorio that she would make the perfect wife. Not only would he see her as a gentle but disciplined mother, he would also realise that her passion for art was so great that she could sacrifice herself to help a struggling artist.

She gazed around. And would it be so bad staying in such a beautiful place? In that moment, she saw herself pegging crisp white sheets out in the sunshine . . .

She took a deep breath before she spoke, giving herself a moment in which to change her mind. But she didn't change her mind. 'I think Timothy is right.' Jack gazed at her in astonishment. 'And I am prepared to stay on until Vittorio's arrival. However, I shall need to go home and pack a suitcase. I could be back here by tomorrow.'

Her boss looked up at the big man for approval. 'What do you think, Jack?'

Perplexed, Jack was slow to take his eyes off Lara. 'No, I'm sorry, I would rather get someone locally.'

Timothy cocked his head. 'But you've just said you can't get anyone locally.'

'Without sufficient artwork, there can be no chance of exhibitions,' Lara cautioned. 'You could stand to lose thousands of pounds.'

Jack stared at the ground, distractedly running a hand back over his head. 'I suppose you're right.' Now he was looking at her, his eyes clouded with anxiety.

'Absolutely,' Timothy agreed. 'Lara can be our liaison officer, making sure you do your work.' He smiled, waggling an admonishing finger. 'But, more importantly, the boys will be happy. What do you say?'

'OK,' Jack said quietly. 'Let's do it.'

Although Lara gave him an encouraging smile, she could tell it had no effect on him. Well, she had less than a fortnight to change all that.

Jack

Jack picked up Scruffy and tucked it under the duvet beside Sam. 'Less noise,' he said sternly. The boys were excited. Lara was coming to stay and already they were making plans. He wished he could share their enthusiasm but instead, all he could feel was this heavy sense of dread. He moved across the landing and into the bathroom. Why had he agreed to let her stay?

He kept remembering her words to him that night in L'Escargot. '*I came here to meet a handsome polo champion, not some half-witted hillbilly!*' He closed his eyes against the sting of it. What right had she to talk to him like that? He would phone the gallery tomorrow, tell Timothy he had found someone else. He sighed hopelessly; the trouble was, he needed money – quickly – and the only way he was going to achieve that was to paint night and day, with no thought to cooking, shopping, homework, or clean school uniforms.

Whether he liked it or not, he had to have help.

He picked up Sam's toothbrush from the floor and pushed the bucket of bath toys under the sink. The boys had taken an instant shine to Lara. Proudly they had shown her Charlie, the stick insect, their drawings and toys and vegetable patch, and she had seemed truly interested. Surely, the most important thing was that they liked her. He paused, gazing down at the yellow rubber duck in his hand. And, after all, he was going to be so busy, he would have little contact with her.

Looking up, he met his reflection in the mirror. His hair had begun to grow and his face had a light tan from the spring sunshine. He grimaced, drawing back his lips from his teeth, inspecting the gap. That would be fixed tomorrow morning. He might not be a wealthy polo champion but he was determined to show Ms Lara Bayley that he was no half-witted hillbilly!

Monday

Beatrix

Beatrix shook drops of lavender oil into the bathwater, put on a shower cap and lowered herself into the water, topping up her glass of champagne before lying back. Although it was only four in the afternoon, she wanted to give herself plenty of time to get her make-up right for the party.

After taking a sip from her glass, she began to coat her face with a mud pack whilst dreaming of Justin. Yesterday, she had gone into the City, overawed by the towering blocks of steel and glass. He had been so keen to show her his office, his computer system, his wall charts while talking about bull markets and beefing up positions in money market funds, tightening fiscal policy and loosening monetary policy. And although she hadn't understood a word of it, she had been impressed. He was not only handsome and charming but also very, very clever. So clever, she couldn't even understand him!

She smiled fondly, seeing the tired eyes and the thin face, pale with exhaustion. From what he had told her, she knew that he had always worked hard – at school, at university, as a junior analyst and now as a top corporate financier. In some ways they were similar. He, too, had a strong sense of family duty and had never known those teenage years of irresponsibility and freedom. But, in other ways they were different. Whereas she wanted to make the most of her newfound freedom, he was firmly entrenched in his work ethic, determined to reach the top of the career ladder. But, she supposed, who could blame him? He had a corner office, thirty floors above the City, with his own secretary and flashy computer. He was clever and handsome – and she was going to see him tonight. Once again, he would talk excitedly about the deals he had struck that day, after which, he would take her in his arms and they would dance slowly, their bodies pressed together . . .

Slowly her smile faded. Soon he would want more than a slow dance and a kiss. He would want to make love. She gazed down at her long slim body with the triangle of pubic hair between her legs. She wanted so desperately to become a 'proper' woman, but she was scared. She liked being with Justin and she liked him kissing her, but did she want to go further?

But if she truly loved him it should come naturally, shouldn't it?

She sighed. And where would they do it? At his apartment, or here? Now that Lara had gone to Dorset, she had the place completely to herself. If she were going to do it, it would be here, in her own surroundings. But, for some reason she couldn't imagine it. Why? She found him attractive and charming – but was that enough to propel her naked into his arms?

She drained her glass before wiping the mud from her face. Then she stood up, pulled out the plug, slipped into a towelling robe, and padded into the sitting room to put the champagne bottle on the table. The place was a mess but she just hadn't had time to clean it up. The morning had been spent window-shopping in Kensington High Street, then she had been lured into Petras by the vision of gold sling-backs. An hour later she had emerged into the sunshine to bump into one of Kelsey's friends who had suggested lunch.

Thinking about it now, she wondered how Lara – with her busy job – had managed to fit it all in.

Putting on a new Eagle-Eye Cherry album Beatrix went into the kitchen but there was nothing to eat except for a jar of truffles and almond-stuffed olives in the back of a cupboard. What was happening to her? She had been too busy buying gold sling-backs to even think about buying something as simple as bread. She nibbled an olive, deliberating whether to go out to the supermarket or simply eat when she got to the party. She would eat at the party.

With that decision made, she went into her bedroom, settled at her dressing table and selected her make-up. Lara had been right; it was important to experiment in order to understand what suited her best. Just like clothes. Lara had suggested beige tones, soft and flowing, while Kelsey veered between outrageous vamp and innocent ingénue – neither of them giving a thought to what *she* herself wanted.

Now she would make her own choice, and tonight she would be techno-peasant with a white organdie off-the-shoulder blouse and a multi-coloured gypsy skirt, finished off with her new gold sling-backs.

Kelsey was not impressed. At seven o'clock that evening she stood in the doorway and looked Beatrix up and down. 'You look like a hippie,' she cried. 'Where's the foxy look I've been moulding?'

Beatrix twirled on the spot. 'I thought I'd try something different.'

'Hmph.' Kelsey picked up the champagne bottle and headed for the kitchen. 'Is Lara ready?'

Beatrix followed. 'Oh, no. She's not here. She's gone to Dorset.'

'Dorset? But I thought that was yesterday? Wasn't she checking out some artist guy?'

Beatrix leant on the doorframe, watching her friend pour champagne into a glass. 'She did but she went back this morning to look after his boys.'

'Boys?'

'Yes. She's looking after them until he finds a replacement, which might take a week or so.'

With the glass to her lips, Kelsey stared at her as if trying to work this out. Now she lowered her glass. 'I don't understand. Can you run that by me again?'

'Yeah.' Beatrix extended a leg, admiring her new gold sling-backs and pink-painted toenails. 'Because her artist will be busy, he needs a housekeeper. So, she's volunteered to help out. She said she'd also be doing other things like feeding chickens and—'

'Feeding chickens?'

At this exclamation Beatrix looked up. 'Yes, she's staying on a farm.'

Kelsey gazed at her blankly. 'Is this Lara we're talking about?'

'Yep.' Seeing a saucer of butter uncovered, Beatrix automatically reached for the clingfilm but stopped herself. For some reason, Kelsey didn't like her using it; it tended to make her impatient, irascible. 'I'm trying to mould you into arm candy,' she would lecture. 'Not Homemaker of the Year.'

'Of course!' Kelsey grinned. 'She's playing out her fantasy.' With the mystery solved, she raised the glass once more and drank heartily. Then she banged it down. 'Can you see Lara feeding chickens? What will she wear? Versace and rubber boots?'

Beatrix chuckled.

'I've an idea,' Kelsey continued, 'since she's not here, why don't we rethink your image?'

'What do you mean?'

'You're not blonde enough. A guy's not impressed by the natural look – he wants platinum. He wants to be able to find you in the dark.' She grabbed a biro and began to sketch on the back of an envelope, the biro moving swiftly and lightly over the paper. 'Imagine that in satin.'

Beatrix stood beside her, studying the drawing of a woman in a backless, side-slit dress. Kelsey was certainly a talented artist, and it was flattering that she took so much interest, but Beatrix did not want to change any more. Apart from letting her hair grow to shoulder length, she was happy with what she had.

Suddenly, she felt like a doll in the hands of two squabbling little girls. At some point she was going to have to make a stand. 'I want to start thinking for myself,' she insisted.

Kelsey put up her hands as if accepting her opinion but

doubting her judgement. 'OK, but I just want you to think – Marilyn Monroe.'

No, Beatrix thought firmly to herself. I am not going to think Marilyn Monroe or Jackie O or anyone else. I'm going to think Beatrix Metcalfe!

Ten minutes later they settled themselves side by side in the back of a taxi. 'Since you've always wanted to be a sculptress,' Beatrix began, 'why don't you pursue it?'

'Me? Can you imagine me as an art student?'

'Yes, actually I can.'

Kelsey chuckled, taking out a compact and lipstick and retouching her lips. 'Yeah, I guess I would've liked it but I've left it too late.'

'No, you haven't. You could become a mature student.'

Kelsey's eyebrows shot up in mock horror. '*Mature*?' She shuddered delicately. 'Don't say that word unless you've giving me cheese.'

'I think you should try,' Beatrix persevered. 'I think you're really creative, with your ideas and drawings.'

The other girl wrinkled her brow. 'Well, maybe. But for now, *you're* my creation. Let's get you sorted out first.' She dropped her lipstick in her bag. 'I think Justin might be there tonight.'

Beatrix knew for a fact that he would be there. 'Oh, really?' she murmured, feigning disinterest.

'I suppose you've told him why you're in London?'

'Oh gosh, I keep forgetting!'

'You can't go stringing him along.'

'Absolutely,' Beatrix agreed, knowing that she was not about to blow her cover.

The taxi drew up in front of a rose-pink Georgian terraced house and they stepped out, Kelsey insisting on paying. 'It's going to lead to complications if you spend all your time with him,' she said, opening a wrought-iron gate onto a brick pathway. 'You're here to learn how to mix in society. You've suddenly become beautiful – right? – so I can understand why you've been bowled over by the first guy who's shown interest.'

Was Kelsey right? Beatrix pondered, following her up the path. Had she been bowled over by the first man who had shown his interest? On hearing the sound of loud thumping music and squeals of laughter, Beatrix felt a surge of adrenalin, immediately forgetting her friend's words of warning.

She saw him as soon as she entered. He grinned, breaking off from a conversation with a group of people and coming forward. 'Hi!' he murmured, not taking his eyes from her. For a moment they stood in silence, smiling at each other as if the whole world had gone away.

'OK! OK!' It was Kelsey. She grabbed Beatrix by the wrist and began to lead her away. 'I'm sorry, Justin, but you can't monopolise her.'

'Monopolise her?' he thundered. 'But I haven't said a word!'

Suddenly, Beatrix felt Justin grab her other hand and pull her towards him and she found herself in the middle of a tug of war, and laughed.

Abruptly, Kelsey released her and marched up to Justin. 'There's a reason why Beatrix is in London,' she whispered fiercely. Beatrix tensed. But thankfully Kelsey was not about to admit the truth. 'She's had strict instructions from her grandmother to *mix*.'

He folded his arms stubbornly. 'I don't see why her grandmother should tell her what to do. Surely Beatrix can make her own decisions?'

Beatrix sensed that the truth would come out at any moment. 'I did promise her,' she said regretfully.

His face softened when he looked at her. 'Fair enough.' He turned back to Kelsey. 'I would only ask Beatrix for a favour. The other night she told me about her culinary skills and so I have a business proposition to put to her.' He turned to Beatrix. 'I desperately need someone to cater for my Japanese clients on Tuesday. Could you help me?'

Beatrix smiled to herself. What a clever ruse. 'I'd be glad to.'

Kelsey could only relent with an angry growl. And so it was that five minutes later, Justin and Beatrix were sitting side by side on the sofa. 'What a fib!' Beatrix exclaimed softly.

'I'm serious. I really do need help. Five very important Japanese businessman are coming to my place for lunch, and I don't know what to feed them. Unfortunately, all the catering agencies are booked solid and I don't think take-away fish and chips would be a good idea.'

She laughed. 'Finger food,' she stated. 'That's what you need. I don't know much about the Japanese but I do know they are not stodgy eaters. How about tidbits of contrasting flavours? Walnut-stuffed dates and courgette cups.'

'Sounds great!'

Beatrix couldn't help feeling rather smug. She was thrilled to be catering for sophisticated jet-setting businessmen instead of the usual WI get-togethers. She might be inexperienced in the bedroom but she was an expert in the kitchen!

Lara

Lara removed her sunglasses to view the world in its true colours and not through tinted lenses. All was green, shades of green. High rounded hills of emerald sloped down to wooded valleys, and along the edge of the railway track lay a broad smooth stream overhung with weeping willows, the leafy fronds reflected so clearly in the still, smooth water that there seemed to be a forest growing beneath its glassy surface.

Lara missed none of it, her excitement so acute that if she'd been alone in the carriage she would have bobbed up and down in her seat, thrown open the window and stuck her head out to feel the air on her face. But she was not alone. Once more, she glanced at the two dumpy flower-frocked housewives with their flat sturdy shoes and deep wicker baskets, their eyes continually sliding curious glances at her. They're probably wondering who I am, she thought complacently. I doubt whether they've seen many elegant females on the Dorchester to Appleby line.

For the first time in her life, she wore her hair coiled neatly into a chignon at the nape of her neck and, although it was proving to be uncomfortable, she was determined to ignore it. She was here to mould herself into the perfect wife. No more slobbing on the sofa with a mega-bucket of Kentucky Fried Chicken, no more standing at the fridge door spooning ice cream straight from the carton. No, that life had ended.

As she lifted up her Italian dictionary once more her eyes strayed to her two enormous suitcases in the luggage bay. She smiled at the thought of their contents:

Tattoos: 2 packets of vipers curled round bloodied daggers (for Sam)
4 pairs of shoes. Manolo's, Jimmy Choo and Christian Louboutin
1 Supersoaker gun (Sam's birthday present)
1 pack of Pokémon cards (for Jamie so he wouldn't feel left out)
1 Versace cream-coloured cocktail dress (for Vittorio's arrival)
1 short red Japanese dress (in case she suddenly felt exotic)
3 bottles of Barolo wine
12 TV dinners (to feed her new family)
1 jewellery box of Cartier, Erickson Beamon, Asprey
2 huge bags of sweeties

Beatrix must have thought she was leaving home!

Once more, Lara went over her plans, honing every detail. Firstly, she would become friends with Jack, winning his affection and loyalty whilst learning all about his art. Secondly, she would practise her nurturing skills on the boys so she could begin to evolve a Madonna-like aura. After all that had happened, Vittorio would arrive to be met by a clean and tidy house, candles and jugs of flowers dotted about the old farmhouse kitchen, Italian wine open and breathing on the table and the aroma of Osso Bucco coming from the oven. (Of course, this would have to be made by some local restaurant.)

The only drawback to this clever plan was that, in the interim, she would have to keep three people from starvation. How long would twelve TV dinners last? Three days. Then she would have to start cooking for real. And would she have all the essentials of a modern kitchen? A microwave, a dishwasher, a coffee grinder, a washing machine? Would she have to toss the laundry and washing powder into the bath and pulverise it with bare feet? She sighed, only hoping that Vittorio would realise the sacrifice she was making.

Suddenly, she felt the train begin to shudder and slow. There was the sign *Appleby*. Gathering her belongings together, she hurried to the door, pushed down the window and looked out. The station was so cute, like something out of a nursery rhyme book; the small honey-coloured brick station overhung with a steeply pitched roof, the chimney pots tall and crooked. Then she saw Jack and waved cheerfully. His answering wave was formal rather than friendly.

As the train drew to a standstill, he opened the door and helped her down. 'Hi, Jack!' she trilled. 'My suitcases are just there.'

One by one he swung them down onto the platform. 'Did you have a good journey?' he asked stiffly.

'Fabulous!' She didn't want him to be like this. She wanted him to be friendly and happy – just like her.

He picked up her suitcases and moved off. 'I'm parked over here,' he muttered. She followed, delighting in the warm scented air, the baskets of flowers hanging from the crenellated eaves of the station building, the small birds darting and screeching across the blue summer sky. Now she caught the smell of woodsmoke and heard the sound of church bells from some distant hamlet.

Jack backed up against a white picket gate, holding it open for her. 'I want to thank you for coming to help us out,' he stated.

As she walked past, she smiled up at him. 'I just hope I will come in useful.' She could sense his awkwardness, his forced politeness. Perhaps winning his friendship was not going to be as easy as she had anticipated. Why, oh why, did they have to have that disastrous first meeting? What bad luck!

He let the gate swing shut before leading the way across the rough ground. The train had chugged away and now there was silence. 'How's the painting going?' she asked.

'Slowly.'

'Don't worry. I'm here to take some of the load off your shoulders.'

More silence. Heavens! This was going to be hard going. She groaned inwardly. How could she repair the damage that she had done? She would have to apologise – big time. 'Jack?' She stopped abruptly and took off her sunglasses so that he would see the sincerity in her eyes.

'Yes?' He paused and looked back at her.

'I want to apologise,' she said sorrowfully, dropping her gaze to illustrate her regret. 'I didn't mean what I said . . . in London.'

'I think it's best we forget about it, don't you?' He began to move on.

This was not the result she had hoped for. Suddenly, she felt annoyed with herself. No matter how much apologising she did, her cruel words could never be eradicated; they would always be there as if etched in stone between them. 'But I want you to know how sorry I am,' she insisted. No answer. Suddenly, she lost patience.

'This is ridiculous,' she snapped. He stopped and stared at her in surprise.

'This is *not* all my fault. OK, I'm sorry I called you a hillbilly.' She put her palms out as if conceding this point. 'And I understand – now – that you were trying to find a wife, but you've got to admit, you did make yourself out to be a gentleman farmer!'

'I wasn't making anything out. Everything I said was true. OK,' he admitted, 'the photograph was misleading. That wasn't my car and neither was the dog, but everything else was true.'

'Except you forgot to mention your sons,' she reminded him, shaking her head in mild reproof. 'Jesus! Any woman hearing that would *run for the hills!*'

'I was going to tell you about them when we met, but I didn't get a chance.'

She stared up at him, remembering how she had stormed out of the door. 'I'm sorry,' she said quietly.

'And I'm sorry not to have sent you a clearer photograph of myself in the first place. I half-suspected that my shaven head would be less than appealing, but I had brought a photo along to show you how I would normally look.'

She grinned. 'A shaven head and a couple of scars on a man can look really sexy.' Was she pushing this too far? With relief, she saw his expression soften. 'In fact,' she said glibly, 'the *Action Man* look is back in fashion!' Now he was smiling. Wow! She stared at him in astonishment. He looked so handsome. It was his smile. 'You look different,' she began.

At this he bared his teeth, showing a row of perfect white. 'I've had my front tooth fixed.'

Of course, that was it. What a difference! No longer did he look like some half-crazed yokel. But there was more than this. His hair had grown, covering that pale scalp, and his skin had a healthy golden colour. Instead of that grisly mustard-coloured nylon shirt, he wore a blue denim shirt rolled up at the sleeves, which accentuated his hard, muscular forearms. 'You look so much better,' she said honestly.

'Thank you.' His soft brown eyes continued to gaze down at her.

This guy has no idea how handsome he is, she thought, feeling a strange fluttering in her tummy. She ignored it, taking advantage of the moment. 'Can we start again?' she asked.

He nodded, his eyes not leaving her face. 'OK.'

Smiling triumphantly, she stuck out a hand. He took it, his big strong hand engulfing her own. Then she had a better idea. Standing on tiptoe, she put her lips to his cheek and kissed it. 'That's more friendly, isn't it,' she declared, standing back down.

He was blushing! She laughed at his discomfort. Then,

suddenly, she shifted uneasily, watching his face come down towards her. It was his turn to laugh. 'Hey! You can kiss me, so why can't I kiss you?'

'Well—' She didn't get any further before his rough lips pressed against her skin. 'There!' he exclaimed. '*Now* we can start again.'

She, too, found herself blushing and feeling that strange fluttering sensation in the pit of her stomach.

'Let's go,' he said cheerfully. 'I don't know what you've got in these suitcases but they're about to pull my arms out of their sockets!'

Lara put on her sunglasses and fell into step beside him, pleased that she had overcome this first hurdle and yet, at the same time, confused by her feelings. Before she had time to analyse them, they had reached his pickup truck. In the back stood his dog, Rosie. Lara remembered her from their last visit, when the bitch had kept obediently to Jack's heels. Now she wagged her tail in greeting as Jack dropped the tail-gate and slid the suitcases inside. At the sound of the Louis Vuitton calf hide scraping across the floor of the truck, she shuddered. But what else could she expect – a stretch limo?

There was a clean towel laid across the passenger seat and for that she was grateful, dreading the thought of getting her Betty Jackson skirt covered in dog hairs and God-knows-what-else. Two clean arcs had swept through the coating of dust and dead flies on the windscreen, and on the floor by her feet lay an enormous canvas glove caked in dry earth. From under the dashboard hung electrical wires joined together with black tape. This vehicle had not been bought to impress a female.

Jack got in beside her, his huge bulk filling the cab. 'Excuse the mess in here,' he said. 'If you'd come two weeks ago, I would've had a Volvo Estate but I've had to sell it.'

'Oh, why?'

'I needed the money for the farm.'

'Forget farming!' she exclaimed. They were now heading out of the car park. Without suspension the truck bumped over the rough ground, every stone jarring her spine. 'You're an international artist now,' she continued. 'You never need get your boots muddy again.'

He chuckled. 'It's not that simple. Of course I enjoy painting, but farming is my life. Without it, I would be lost for inspiration.'

'I quite understand,' she said knowingly, wanting to give the right impression.

'Having this chance to sell my work has come as a godsend,' Jack told her. 'You see, for the past seventeen months I've been converting to organic farming methods, which meant I couldn't farm until all the chemicals had gone from the soil. Without a steady income, it's been a hell of a battle.'

'So why bother?'

'It all started a couple of years ago. There was ringworm in the heifers so I went and got the usual drugs from the vet. I knew that stuff was strong, but then I happened to read the packaging. It said: "Not to be handled by women of childbearing age." It got me thinking. From then on I never allowed the boys with me when I was spraying.'

She shuddered. 'Gosh! You're converting me to organic now.'

'I hope so.' He braked gently as the pickup rounded a bend. 'In the long run the organic method is cheaper, and the results taste better. With any luck, my decision will influence other farmers in the area.'

'I think it's really good, what you're doing.' In Lara's estimation he had gone up from 8 to 10+. 'So when can you start farming again?'

'Within six weeks, but I won't start making a profit for at least seven months after that.'

'Gosh – you must be really glad that Timothy came along.'

'You can say that again!'

Suddenly, Lara saw her plans changing. No longer would she be showing interest in Jack's work simply to impress Vittorio, she would also be doing it out of a strong sense of commitment, determined that Jack's talent would make him a fortune and thus help him win his battle. With this in mind, she asked: 'I would love to see your latest painting – if you've got the time to show me?'

'I'd be honoured. We'll have an hour before dinner, although the boys will want to drag you off me. They're over the moon that you're coming.'

'Really?'

He chuckled. 'I don't know what you said to them yesterday but whatever it was, you made yourself a couple of fans.'

She grinned. 'All I did was to discuss the finer points of *The Fifth Element* with Jamie, then I shot Sam to smithereens!' Jack laughed, the sound rumbling deep within his chest.

She carried on happily: 'I've got a couple of surprises in store for them, too. I've bought Sam a pump-action Supersoaker for his birthday and a pack of Pokémon cards for Jamie, so he doesn't feel left out.'

'That's really kind of you, but you didn't have to.'

'It's all my pleasure.'

'You certainly know what they want.' He sounded suspicious. 'I hope they didn't ask you for them?'

'Oh no, not at all. I knew what would appeal to them because I used to watch a lot of kids' TV.'

'So *that's* how you know about Crushhammer?'

'That's right.'

'Lara?' His voice had become hesitant.

'Yeah?'

'Do you remember the birthday cake that Sam mentioned yesterday?'

'Crushhammer!' she exclaimed in an American drawl. 'From the Planet Zorg. Fighting the spawn warriors for universal supremacy.' She chuckled, waiting for Jack's laughter, but instead, his brow crumpled in thought. 'What wrong?' she asked.

'It's all he can talk about at the moment. You see, his best friend had a Crushhammer cake for his birthday and he wants the same.' Jack slowed as he turned the corner. 'I've told Sam to wait until his next birthday, but to a child, that's a long time to wait.'

Lara nodded wisely. 'I was exactly the same when I was a little girl. A birthday cake is so important.'

'But there's no one to make it.'

'Who made his friend's cake?'

'The mother, but she's moved to Yorkshire.'

'That's a pity.'

'Up until yesterday, Sam seemed to have accepted the situation but then, suddenly, he started talking about it again.'

'Oh, why?'

'Because he's got it fixed in his head that *you* are going to make it.'

'*Me?*' The force of her exclamation had her sitting bolt upright.

Jack shook his head regretfully. 'I told him he can't expect you to do it, but for some reason he's got this absolute confidence in you.'

'But why?' Her voice rose shrilly.

'I've no idea.'

Now she saw herself sitting on the grass with the picnic spread out before her, chatting to Sam. Oh no! She felt rising panic at the responsibility thrust upon her. She loved the little boy, she really did, but who did they think she was – Delia Smith? 'I've never baked a cake in my life,' she said firmly. 'I wouldn't be able to – even if you held a gun to my head.'

'Don't panic,' he assured her. 'I understand completely. I'm just forewarning you in case he mentions it.'

'Get a cake person,' she cried, suddenly realising her salvation. 'A baker.'

'That's what I intend to do, although I suspect the result will not be exactly what Sam had in mind.' Jack changed gears as they approached a crossroads. 'So, what about jelly? A green rabbit, to be specific. I can never get it right.'

She stared blankly at him. He saw her expression. 'For Sam's party,' he prompted.

'But surely you've got caterers coming?' As soon as she had said this, she realised how ridiculous it sounded.

'Oh no,' Jack answered. 'I'm going to do it all as usual, but I can never get jelly to set properly.'

'Well,' she began hesitantly. 'I'm prepared to give it a go.' Suddenly she felt buoyed up with the challenge – and of course she would have Jack to help her. Between them they could give Sam the best party of his life!

'Before I forget,' he added, 'Jamie has painstakingly written out in his best handwriting a list of things that will help you, such as how to work the washing machine and oven – things like that.'

For the first time in her life Lara was glad to hear the words *washing machine*. At least the place wasn't totally primitive.

'And I've made up a timetable,' Jack continued. 'Normally, the boys have dinner well before six on a school night so that they can get to bed early, and I always make sure they do their homework as soon as they get in.'

Lara felt a sense of dread, that suffocating sensation of responsibility. Instantly, she put a halt to it. I can do this, she told herself firmly. Everyone's so keen to tell me how hopeless I am, but this time it'll be different. 'I've brought TV dinners with me,' she said brightly. 'We could have some tonight if you like.'

'Don't worry about cooking on your first day. I just thought I'd put a lamb joint in the oven.'

'OK, but leave me to do everything else.'

'Are you sure?'

She grinned. 'Sure I'm sure.'

They had come to a halt in a small village of honey-coloured stone houses. There was a village green with a duck pond, and across the road stood a stone wall encircling a school.

As she and Jack joined the group of mothers walking in through the gate, Lara became aware of curious glances in her direction. Spotting Sam waiting by the front door, she waved and, for good measure, pointed two fingers into the shape of a gun and shot him. He grinned and did the same, causing the elderly teacher beside him to glare at Lara. Silly old bat, Lara thought rebelliously. We're only pretending. What does she think he's going to do? Ram-raid the sweet shop?

'Hi, Sam,' she said, taking off her sunglasses to kiss his cheek. He blushed furiously and for a moment looked like a miniature of his father. Jamie came over to join them, looking serious and older than his nine years. He's so handsome, Lara thought. Give him seven years or so and there'll be a line of lovesick girls queuing at the front door. But without a mother's influence, would he know how to treat a girl? Jack had better hurry up and get himself a wife.

She shook Jamie by the hand, knowing better than to kiss him on the cheek. 'Hi, Jamie. How you doing?'

'OK,' he answered gravely, obviously desperate to hide his shyness.

She sensed this immediately. 'Have you seen *Toy Story Two* yet?' she asked casually.

Immediately his face brightened. 'No, have you?'

'Yeah,' she lied, seeing as it was in a good cause. 'It was cool.'

'Wow!' he exclaimed.

'But not as good as *The Fifth Element,*' she added.

Immediately, they began to chat like old friends, Jack carrying the satchels as they headed for the gate. Then she felt a small warm hand slip into her own and looked down to see that Sam was holding on to her with an obvious sense of ownership. It felt nice, really nice. She squeezed the small hand fondly, resisting the urge to kneel before him and nuzzle up against that chubby neck. Yes, she was going to make sure that he had the best party – ever!

Reaching the gate, Jamie turned to his father. 'Can we walk home, Dad? I want to show Lara the ducklings under the bridge.' As he spoke, he took a handful of bread crusts out of his school shorts. 'I've saved some bread.'

'Not today,' Jack replied. 'Lara's just arrived. She'll want to get home and settle in. And, anyway, I've got the truck here.'

'I don't mind going with them,' she interjected.

Doubtfully, he looked down at her shoes. She followed his eyes and realised that she was wearing her best Manolo's. Why did I have to wear these? she thought in annoyance. But they were not going to stop her! She promptly handed her sunglasses, jacket and handbag over to Jack and took Sam's hand. 'Lead the way, Jamie.'

As Sam pulled her along the road, she glanced back over her shoulder. 'Won't be long,' she shouted. 'Get the kettle on.'

They were just leaving the village when the truck went by with a toot. They waved and watched it disappear around a bend. Now there was silence. Overhead hung a canopy of trees, the sun filtering through to throw spots of dancing light about them. Crossing over a hump-backed bridge, the trio went down a grassy slope to the water's edge. It was cool here in the shade with the tinkling sound of water on pebbles and, following the boys' lead, Lara slipped off her shoes and waded into the clear shallow water. From under the bridge paddled a mother duck and her tiny brood. 'Quick!' she whispered frantically. 'Give me some bread.'

After exhausting their supplies, Lara tried to pick up a duckling but the brood raced away, skimming frantically across the surface of the water and into the shadows beneath the bridge. 'We'd better get home,' Jamie said, making for the riverbank. 'I've got science homework tonight.'

'Oh-h-h,' Lara moaned. 'Don't do homework. That's a pain. Let's go for a paddle down the river instead.'

Jamie put on a sock. 'I can't, otherwise Dad'll get angry.'

Disappointed, Lara watched the boys put their shoes back on. Then they started up the road, Jamie beginning to tell her about the wildlife while Sam slipped his little fat hand into hers once more. She carried her shoes in the other hand, enjoying the sensation of warm tarmac against her cool wet feet. Birds sang overhead, the air becoming warmer as they moved away from the river. Suddenly, there was a clip-clop sound of hooves behind them and she turned to see a horse-drawn cart coming up the hill. A solemn-looking man sat on the bench seat holding the reins.

'It's Ernest,' Sam cried. 'Ernest!' he shouted, waving. Without a change of expression, the man pulled at the reins, slowing the horse to a halt. He wore a dirty Fair Isle waistcoat and an oilskin cap, his large ears sticking out from beneath it. He stared at her with open suspicion. Goodness, she thought in surprise. Hasn't he ever seen a woman before?

'Hello, boys,' he said, without taking his eyes off her. 'I see you've got a visitor.' He made her sound like the she-devil from hell!

'This is Lara,' Jamie explained. 'She's come to look after us.'

'Oh yes?' the man replied slowly. To Lara's ears he sounded almost disbelieving; weighing her up as if he would make his own decision on the matter. 'How do?' he said, touching his cap.

The boys seemed to like the man, so for their sakes she would force herself to be pleasant. 'I'm fine, thank you.'

He turned to the boys. 'I'm going up to see your dad; do you want a lift?'

'Yes, please!' They ran to the back of the cart and scrambled up onto the bundles of straw. Caught up in their excitement, Lara followed but then stopped dead. She could not possibly climb up there in such a tight skirt. 'What the hell!' she exclaimed, lobbing her shoes aboard. She hitched her skirt up around her thighs, put her hands down on the wooden planks and levered herself up. At the same moment, the boys pulled at her arms and she fell face forward in the straw, gurgling with laughter. The boys, too, were laughing, rolling around with their hands clutching their tummies. Only the man retained his composure, watching her with a long, measured look. Then he turned in his seat and shook the reins and they moved forward.

Lara scowled at the back of his head. But it was such a lovely afternoon; the cart was rolling steadily beneath them, the birds were trilling in the trees and the sun was shining. She would make friends with him, she decided, feeling expansive.

'This is a beautiful area,' she began.

'Yup.'

She tried again. 'Have you lived here all your life?'

'Not yet.'

This made her pause. Sod him! she decided, lying back on the straw. She would talk to the boys instead. 'This straw is so soft,' she murmured, putting a stalk into her mouth.

'It's not straw,' the man answered gruffly. 'It's hay.'

'Oh.'

'It's grass that has been dried for fodder,' Jamie explained.

'Fodder?'

'You don't know what fodder is?' the man demanded, his voice high with disbelief.

Jesus! Who was this guy? For the boys' sakes, she bit back a retort.

It was Sam's turn to explain. 'It's animal feed.'

'Right,' she muttered.

The man spoke again. 'So you don't know much about animals then, eh? That's no good if you're helping out on a farm, is it?'

She couldn't believe this! 'I do know about animals,' she retorted. 'Because I have a Rottweiler.'

The man made a noise in his throat and fell silent.

Lara sat straight, ready for battle. Then she realised that they had turned into the driveway of the house. *Manor*

Farm. Her heart lifted with joy. There was the same sprawling cottage with its shaggy fringe, the same white turtle doves, and the blossom coating the grass like a sprinkling of pink snow.

As the cart stopped, the boys scrambled off, leaving her stranded and holding a shoe in each hand while anxiously considering the distance to the ground.

'Jump!' Jamie cried eagerly, looking up at her.

'I can't.'

Jack grinned as he approached across the gravel. 'What have you two boys been doing with Lara?'

Immediately, she realised what he meant. Her elegant bun had come undone and, from the corner of her eyes, she could see strands of hay sticking out from her hair. Ernest had got down and was now staring up at her with the same blank face and suspicious eyes. Although the merriment of the boys and Jack did not make her feel foolish, the look on that man's face did.

'I see you've met Ernest,' Jack said.

She nodded coldly at the man.

'I'll go and get a chair to help you down,' Jack suggested, moving off.

'But Daddy, why don't you lift her down?' Sam suggested.

'No, no.'

Ernest had pushed the cap back from his forehead. 'Go

on, just lift her down,' he instructed. 'You've had to lift heavier loads before now.'

Lara eyed the man. Now she definitely knew she didn't like him. She turned her attention once more to the stony ground below. 'Out of the way, boys, I'm going to jump.'

'No, you don't!' Jack turned back, put his great arms around her thighs and carried her carefully over to the lawn, and here he released his grip and she slid down onto the soft ground. She grinned up at him but for some reason he suddenly seemed distracted. 'I'll go and pour the tea,' he muttered and turned away.

Under Ernest's expressionless scrutiny, she put on her shoes, smoothed down her skirt and walked past him with as much dignity as possible, feeling his eyes boring into her back like red hot coals.

'I've put your bags up in your room,' Jack said as she stepped into the kitchen. Now she looked round, seeing the yellow knitted tea cosy over the teapot and the childish drawings taped onto the far wall. The black cat lay stretched out on the battered sofa, lifting its head to inspect her with lazy curiosity while the sun streamed through the diamond-shaped windowpanes and onto the honey-coloured flagstone floor.

Jack set mugs alongside the box of vegetables on the table. 'Jamie, could you please show Lara up to her room.'

'OK, Daddy.'

They scampered ahead of her, glancing around continually as if fearing she would disappear. At the threshold to her room, she stopped and gazed about. The ceiling was low, the whitewashed walls seeming to buckle beneath the weight of it. The bed had a carved wooden headboard, and a thick flowery quilt, and on this lay her sunglasses, handbag and jacket. She walked to the little window set low in the wall, wide open to let in the warm breeze which fluttered the faded cotton curtains. 'Oh!' she exclaimed softly. She could see the horse and cart below, the green meadows beyond the gate, the blue sky. The boys stood on either side of her looking out of the window in silent companionship. 'This must be the prettiest place on earth,' she whispered.

'Do you like the flowers?' Sam asked, leading her across to the dressing table to where a bunch of buttercups had been jammed into a chipped cup.

'They're lovely,' she gurgled. 'You and I share the same floristry techniques!'

'Do you want a go on our rope swing?' Jamie asked, his eyes bright and expectant.

'That's the only reason I'm here.' She recalled the events of the previous day and how she had imagined that she would never return. How things had changed.

Jamie made for the door. 'I've just got to do my homework first but it won't take long.'

She opened the lid of her suitcase. 'I'll unpack and get changed.' Then she stopped. 'Oh, hang on. I don't have anything to wear.'

Sam pointed to the contents of her suitcase. 'Yes, you have,' he said helpfully.

'No, sweetheart, I haven't. These are my smart clothes. I can't wear them to play on a rope swing.' She saw their disappointment and was angry with herself. Why had she been so concerned with looking smart? After all, Vittorio wouldn't be arriving for at least a week.

'You can borrow some of my clothes,' Jamie offered.

She compared herself to him. He was at least twelve inches shorter and a lot slimmer. 'I don't think they'll fit.'

'We can try.'

'OK, but I don't think this is going to work.' She followed him into the next room and watched as he opened up drawers and took out handfuls of clothes. She selected a pair of vividly-patterned stretch shorts and put them up against her. 'These might fit.' Next, she held up a large T-shirt with a photo of a football team across the front. 'This will definitely fit but what am I going to wear on my feet?' This silenced them for a moment, until Jamie ran off and returned swiftly, holding a pair of flip-flops. 'They're Daddy's but he won't mind you borrowing them.'

She grinned. 'This is better service that Harvey Nicks! Now – where's that rope swing?'

Jamie grimaced. 'I still have to do my homework first.'

'See you in a little while then,' she said. As Jamie picked up his books, Lara and Sam returned to her room where she began to unpack her clothes, fitting them on hangers in the wardrobe.

Sam sat on the bed watching her. 'I like that one,' he said, pointing to her red Suzi Wong dress.

'Do you?' she asked. 'It's real Japanese.'

'Did you go to Japanese to buy it?'

She smiled at his mispronunciation. 'No, a friend brought it back for me.' For a moment, she thought of Justin, seeing his pale, tired face. They had been so wrongly matched. What he needed was a wife, someone who would be interested in his work, who would make his home comfortable, who would not berate him for falling asleep at two o'clock in the morning.

Sam brought her back to the present. 'But I don't like that one,' he said, pointing to the cream-coloured cocktail dress – the one she would wear for Vittorio's visit. She smiled. Sam was only five years old and yet he was sitting there like some fashion doyen giving his undisputed opinion on her wardrobe. Then he spotted her black jewellery box in the corner of her suitcase and took it out. When he saw what was inside, his eyes lit up and he dipped his chubby hand into the mass of gleaming metal. 'Cool,' he squeaked, picking out a rope of amber stones and draping it about his neck with a very serious expression.

Smiling benevolently, Lara continued to unpack, taking the plastic bags of oven-ready meals down to the fridge in the kitchen. When she returned, she found he had hung five assorted earrings over one ear and was busy putting on a bracelet while glancing solemnly at his reflection in the mirror on the dressing table. Although he was happy to walk around loaded down with guns and bazookas, he was too young to realise that jewellery was only for females: he made no distinction between the two. Now he looked like a tiny Maharajah.

'I like these,' he said, holding up one of her party earrings. 'Are you going to wear it?'

'Tonight,' she promised.

'And your Japanese dress?'

She chuckled. 'If you insist.' It didn't matter what she wore tonight because there would be nobody to impress. But the minute that Vittorio arrived . . . She began to drift off, seeing that noble profile once more.

'I can fart with my hands,' Sam told her. At this, Lara blinked, snapping out of her reverie. She watched as the little boy proceeded to demonstrate by putting the heels of both hands over his mouth and blowing hard. Sure enough, there was the distinctive sound of flatulence.

Lara didn't know what to say. Did she praise him, or

what? But his aren't-I-clever-smile told her that congratulations were in order. 'That's great,' she said hesitantly. 'But do you think you should be saying "fart"? Isn't it more polite to say something like . . . *poo-puff*?'

To her surprise, the little boy burst into a fit of giggles. 'Poo-puff!' he chortled. 'Poo-puff!'

'Shh!' she hushed fiercely. 'Don't let the whole house hear.'

'Can I tell Daddy?'

'No!'

This sharp outburst seemed to subdue him. 'Oh, all right.' Then he brightened up. 'Can I tell Jamie?'

She nodded reluctantly, wishing that she had kept her mouth shut.

Again, there was a companionable silence as Lara continued to unpack. 'Cameron Cole's mum wears Santa Claus earrings at Christmas,' Sam remarked wistfully, gazing at a gold sun-shaped earring in his hand. 'And they flash off and on in the dark.'

'Lucky mum,' she lied. She spoke gently now, regretting her sharpness of only a moment ago. With the suitcase empty, she closed it and pushed it under the bed. Then she glanced at Sam and was dismayed to see that he was gazing sadly at the floor. She knew what he was thinking. 'Do *you* wish you had a mummy?' she asked softly.

His silent nod made her heart ache. Should she take out

the bag of sweets and give them to him now? No. This was not the time to gloss over what was obviously a deep sadness. And she should know. Her parents had always been too busy to give her their time; instead they had given their little girl sweeties and presents. Later on, when the arguments started, she was given her own sound system. But no one ever listened.

Now, Lara went over and sat beside Sam on the bed; she put an arm around his small shoulders. 'You've got a daddy, and you've got a big brother. Some kiddies don't even have that.' She stroked his cheek. 'I'll let you into little secret,' she whispered. 'I know that your daddy is trying to find a mummy for you.'

Sam's big eyes stared up at her. 'Is he?'

At his expression, she hesitated. Maybe she was raising his hopes in vain. Admittedly, his daddy had been looking – but after the way she had treated him, he might have given it up as a bad job. Again, she felt a terrible guilt.

'Listen, Sam,' she told him, 'it's important to talk to somebody when you feel sad. I'm only here for a few days but after I've gone, you can phone me at my place. Any time. I'll be there to listen if you need me.' On a sudden impulse, she tipped her jewellery onto the bed and held the empty box before him. 'And then I can put all your secrets in the box and close the lid on them. Good plan?'

She gazed down at his little nodding face, so serious

against the bizarre accumulation of earrings and necklaces. Feeling a tear prick her eye, she hugged him to her so that he would not see her sadness, but, as she turned she saw the two of them reflected in the mirror. It seemed strange, seeing herself like this.

Suddenly, there was a thundering of footsteps on the stairs and Jamie burst in. 'Are you ready?' he gasped.

His rush of exuberance triggered her own. 'I've just got to get changed.' She jumped up and began to unzip her skirt. Then she stopped, aware that the boys hadn't moved. They were simply standing there, waiting for her as if she were just another pal. 'Look, guys,' she requested, 'could you wait outside?'

With a start, they realised her meaning and bustled out of the room, closing the door behind them. She heaved on the stretch shorts, then pulled the T-shirt over her head, stuck her bare feet into the flip-flops and removed the grips from her hair. 'Great!' she mumbled, staring at herself in the mirror. 'I've gone from Milan catwalk to Wembley dogtrack – in one easy move.'

On the way to the door she picked up the bags of sweets, her sunglasses and her pink cardigan. She had planned to spend time with Jack, but that could wait until tomorrow. Half an hour on the rope swing would do no harm.

On the way through the kitchen, Jamie picked up a

handwritten list and showed it to her. 'Look, me and Daddy wrote out a note to help you.'

She took it and briefly scanned the words: *The boys do small household chores, like setting the table, drying the dishes, putting away their toys. Sweetie day is on a Sunday.*

Would it matter if she gave them sweets today? Surely not. Lara put the note back on the table. 'I'll read the rest when we get back. Come on, boys. Let's go have *fun!*'

Jack

Once again, he saw her standing barefoot on the edge of the cart, her hair tumbling loose about her shoulders and covered in hay, her face a picture of anxiety.

Smiling, he began to clean his brush on a piece of rag, remembering how his cheek had brushed against her breasts as he'd lifted her down from the cart, how his senses had been overwhelmed by the smell of her, the feel of her soft body moving down against his . . . Abruptly, he stood up, concentrating now on tidying up while forcing all thoughts of Lara out of his head.

Gradually, his movements slowed until, once again, he was sitting and gazing sightlessly out of the window, not seeing the long shadows across the woodland clearing but the sheen of a stockinged leg . . .

He sighed wistfully and reached for a Rizla paper, trailing a fine line of tobacco along its centre. As he rolled it tight he recalled her look of delight when she'd stepped into the kitchen and looked around. Then came Ernest, bristling with indignation, his voice a fierce whisper. 'Where's she gone?'

'The boys are showing her to her room,' Jack had replied.

'She's that girl, isn't she?'

'Yes, that's right.'

'So what's she doing here?'

'Keeping house.'

Ernest made a phlegm-clearing noise in his throat. 'I know all about her – the Colonel told me. Flighty piece. Does *he* know she's here?'

'No, but I'm sure you'll tell him.'

This was answered with a firm nod. 'That I will.'

'Meeting her was just a coincidence,' Jack tried to explain. 'She happens to work for the art dealer who's selling my paintings. It was he who suggested she stay and help me find a housekeeper. This is purely a business arrangement.'

But Jack knew that Ernest had already formed his own, unfavourable opinion. Now he looked at his watch. 5.30. He turned towards the open doorway, searching the fringe of willow trees, expecting to see her. For two hours he had been waiting, listening. Why hadn't she come? And yet she had been so eager to see his work. Perhaps, understandably, she had been too busy peeling potatoes. More than likely she was now putting the dinner on the table, the boys scrubbed and brushed, Sam setting out the knives and forks while Jamie slotted his finished homework into its folder.

But when he entered the house, he found the kitchen empty, the table untouched, the hob cold and Jamie's homework scattered on the sofa. 'Hello?' he called out, but the word was met by silence. The smell of roasting lamb nagged his hunger. *Where could they be?*

He went out the back door and onto the lawn. Lara's sunglasses lay on the sundial. Further on he saw a pink cardigan draped over the branch of an apple tree. As if following a trail he carried on, discovering his flip-flops in the grass between the hedges. Suddenly there was a shout from Jamie and an ear-piercing shriek from Lara. Immediately, he was running towards the sound, his heart banging fearfully. When he saw the scene, he stopped. Lara stood barefoot on the knot at the base of the swing with both hands clutching the rope as she swung wildly backwards and forwards across the stream. Her screams pierced the stillness, sending the rooks flapping and cawing high into the skies, while below stood the boys, shouting encouragement from the riverbank.

Jack breathed with relief. She was all right. For a moment he smiled, pleased that she was getting on so well with the boys. Then he felt the first stirrings of jealousy. From the moment she had stepped off the train, she had been enthusiastic about seeing his work but now it was obvious she much preferred to be with the boys. And why weren't they out of their uniforms? And why had Jamie abandoned his homework? Frowning, he strode to within earshot and shouted: 'Jamie. Sam. Lara.'

They came running, Rosie happily bounding along beside them as if part of the gang. But Jack only had eyes for Lara. She was shouting and laughing, her hair bobbing about her flushed cheeks, her legs glistening with water, her feet dirty. The fact that she was barely ten inches taller than Jamie made her look like a child, so different from the cool, elegant female he had collected at the station only hours ago. Sternly he waited, ready to demand an explanation. Why was he behaving like some mean-spirited ogre? Had it something to do with the fact that she had not given him a thought in the last two hours?

Now she stood before him, breathing hard, eyes bright and expectant. Jack felt a warm, melting sensation in his limbs. How he yearned to pick her up in his arms, but instead he frowned. 'The boys have to have their dinner by five-thirty,' he stated.

Immediately she clamped a hand over her mouth. 'Oh shit! I completely forgot!'

His brow lowered. 'And I don't allow swearing in the house.'

'Oh God, sorry.' In meek apology, she looked at the boys in turn. 'Sorry.'

'That's OK,' they assured her.

It was then that Jack noticed Sam's black-rimmed mouth. 'What have you been eating?' he demanded.

Guiltily, Sam stared at the ground. 'Sherbert fountains.'

Jack did not need to ask where they had come from. 'I'm sorry,' Lara interjected again. 'That was my fault.'

He turned and began to walk up the hill. 'I don't usually allow them sweets during the week,' he muttered. Why was he talking like this?

'Can I take these?' Lara asked softly.

He felt the flip-flops being taken from his hand and looked down to see her slipping her feet into them, aroused to see that each of her toenails had been painted pink. He studied her shorts. They looked very much like Jamie's. And that T-shirt?

She saw his puzzlement. 'I've borrowed some of Jamie's clothes. Is that OK?'

'Yes, of course.'

Back in the kitchen, he lifted the box of potatoes onto the draining board. 'We'll have to have mash,' he said, beginning to peel them. 'It's quicker.'

'We don't mind,' Jamie trilled, setting out his homework once more.

In silence, Lara helped Thomas. He didn't want this tension and now he felt guilty for dampening their fun. When there was nothing more to do, Lara turned for the door. 'I'd better get changed,' she said in a small voice. Immediately, Sam put his hand in hers and they left the kitchen.

When they reappeared fifteen minutes later, Jack was setting the cutlery on the table. Seeing her, his breath caught in his throat. She was beautiful. She wore a shiny red Oriental frock with red high-heeled sandals, red lipstick, made-up eyes and big shiny earrings. Sam walked on ahead of her smiling proudly as if, in fact, she belonged to him and they were going out on a date. Jack knew he should be amused, but instead felt again that dart of irrational jealousy. Sam had spent the last fifteen minutes with Lara, watching her get dressed, allowed into that inner sanctum of her bedroom, while he himself would have more chance of getting into Fort Knox.

'Lara let me choose her dress,' Sam declared. 'Do you like it, Daddy?'

Jack had no choice but to cast his eyes up and down the satin fabric that flowed over Lara's breasts and hips. 'Very nice,' he muttered. Abruptly, he turned away and continued to lay the table. 'You'd better hurry up with your homework,' he told Jamie.

'I'll help him,' Lara offered, moving towards the sofa. With Jamie on one side of her and Sam on the other, she proceeded to show a keen interest in the science diagram but only minutes later, the three of them were giggling. Jack looked over to see that she had drawn a sketch of the back view of a naked lady bending over in a bath tub. He frowned. 'The boys need to eat early on a school day,' he reiterated.

Lara looked suitably repentant. 'I'm really sorry. I just forgot.'

'Lara swung from the top of the tree,' Jamie interjected, as if trying to steer his father's anger away from their new pal.

Lara rolled her eyes to heaven and flopped back, her long, slim legs splayed out before her, the split in the shiny red dress parting to reveal a smooth thigh. 'I can't believe I did it!' she exclaimed. 'I've never been so scared in all my life.'

Jack tried not to look at her thigh, tried not to look at those pink-painted toenails bound by the thin red straps of her shoes. God, how he wished that he could sit next to her, bathe in the scent of her, feel the touch of her thigh against his. 'I'm going to feed Cleopatra,' he mumbled, marching to the door.

'The piggies,' Lara cried, jumping up. 'Let's go feed the piggies!'

'*No!*' At the startled look on her face, Jack softened. 'Jamie hasn't finished his homework,' he explained.

'Oh.' She stood there, obviously torn between staying with Jamie and going to see the piglets.

Jamie looked up. 'You can go with Daddy. I'm nearly finished.'

She looked up at Jack as if waiting for his approval. Suddenly he wanted her all to himself. 'Sam,' he said firmly as the little boy slipped his hand into Lara's once more, 'I want you to stay and put all your toys away.' Sam looked up in puzzled disappointment but Jack didn't care. They had had Lara all afternoon, now it was *his* turn.

'There's some Wellingtons here you can wear,' he told her. As he bent down to pull them out from under the coat-stand, he felt a hand on his shoulder and turned to see that Lara now stood beside him, casually using his shoulder for support while slipping a slim naked foot into a boot. At the sight of her thigh only inches from his face, he felt his breath quicken.

Lara was unaware of this. 'We won't be long, fellas,' she called, walking past Jack and out of the door. He picked up a pail of vegetable peelings and led the way. This was his chance to amuse, to make her laugh but his mind was a total blank. During his years at agricultural college, he had been popular with the girls, charming them with his wit and intelligent conversation. Evidently that had long gone. Now he felt like a dullard.

They were approaching Cleopatra's pen. Lara hurried forward to look down at the piglets. 'They've grown,' she complained, looking up at him with big, reproachful eyes. In the sunlight, he saw that they were flecked with shards of copper.

He couldn't help but smile at her indignation. 'I'm afraid that's what piglets tend to do.' With her attention taken by the animals once more, he was able to stand back and watch her, noting how the sunshine picked out the reddish strands in her hair. Her upper arm was pale and slim, so slim that he knew his hand would easily encompass it. Her back was straight, curving into a tiny waist before widening out to her buttocks, and, with every movement, the red shiny fabric of her dress slid over those buttocks. He looked away, feeling hot and breathless. He was going to have to get a grip on himself.

Suddenly, there was a shout from below. 'I've got some parsnips for Cleopatra,' Jamie cried, racing up the hill with Sam close at his heels. As he handed them out, the sow lumbered to her feet while emitting a spluttering sound of flatulence, which caused the boys to fall against each other in gales of laughter. 'Cleopatra's done a poo-puff!' Sam chortled.

Jack frowned. 'Poo-puff?' he demanded. 'Who taught you that?'

'It was me.' Lara's face was crimson with embarrassment. At the sight of this, Jack felt a sliding sensation in his chest. Oh God, she was so lovely. Quickly he turned away. 'Dinner's ready.'

During the meal, he made an effort to appear jolly and relaxed but even to his own ears his voice sounded forced. Eventually, he gave up and let the boys take over. When the plates had been cleared away, Sam begged to play Blind Man's Buff but he shook his head firmly. 'Not tonight.'

'Oh, *p-l-e-a-s-e*, Daddy.'

Encountering a barrage of pleas, Jack finally capitulated and resigned himself to being blindfolded with the black cotton apron over his head. How was he going to appear witty and intelligent with an apron over his head?

As usual there were squeals of fear and delight as he began to shuffle into the middle of the kitchen, his hands outstretched and probing for his victims. The boys were good at the game, silently slithering from one area of the room to the other, but Lara had none of their stealth. He identified her giggling immediately, her heels clicking rapidly against the stone floor and within seconds he had grabbed her round the waist, feeling her slim, satiny body against his. 'Got you!' he cried in triumph. As her buttocks moved against his groin, he felt the first stirrings of an erection and let go of her as if she had been hot coals. 'You're dead!' he told her sternly. 'Go and sit on the sofa.'

He carried on with the game, banging his knee against the table leg and, knowing the impossibility of catching his sons, he pulled the hood from his head in exasperation. 'I give up,' he muttered, suddenly feeling exhausted. His emotions had never taken such a battering as they had that afternoon. 'OK, boys, time for bed.'

When they had said goodnight to Lara, he took them upstairs and settled them into bed. 'Lara told me you're going to find a mummy for us,' Sam whispered, hugging Scruffy in his arms.

Jack hesitated, not knowing how to answer. She should not have told them that. 'We'll see. No more talking now. Goodnight.'

He found Lara in the kitchen washing a pan at the sink and gazing out of the open window at the twilight. 'Sam thinks that I'm going to find a mummy for him,' he stated, picking up a tea-towel and beginning to dry the plates.

She turned swiftly, biting her lip in consternation. 'Gosh, I'm sorry. I shouldn't have raised his hopes.'

He sighed regretfully. 'I'm afraid it's not a good idea. Finding a mother for them is not the easiest thing in the world.'

'Especially when you end up meeting someone like me,' she added quietly.

He shrugged.

'I'm sorry, Jack.'

'Better luck next time, eh?'

'You'll find a wife, Jack. I know it. You're handsome and clever. You have all this land and a truly beautiful house.'

'Do you think so?'

'Oh, yes.' She turned to face the kitchen. 'This is such a lovely room. Magazine editors probably spend a fortune on top stylists in order to get a room looking like this. Except, they wouldn't include that dog up there.'

He followed her eyes to the china dog on top of the dresser. 'It is a bit ugly, isn't it?'

She nodded. 'Why don't you throw it away?'

'Because, many years ago, an antique dealer told me that if I ever found its partner, the two together would fetch a fortune.'

'And you believed him?'

He laughed. ' 'Fraid so.' He looked down at her, feeling the smile fall from his lips as he gazed into her eyes. She was the first to break off, turning away sharply.

'Yes, this is certainly a lovely place,' she said briskly, taking up the scourer once more and rubbing hard at a pan.

At that moment, a soft breeze wafted in through the open window, bringing the smell of damp earth and nettles. Did she really like it here? he wondered. Or was she simply being polite? Before he knew what he was doing he was saying: 'You can come and stay whenever you want.'

Her gratitude astonished him. 'Can I? Really?'

In the dull electric light her eyes seemed darker, shadowed by her thick lashes. He wanted to paint those eyes, those lips.

She handed him a dripping plate. 'And can I watch you at work – tomorrow?'

He imagined how they would have to stand close together in that small shed. He would smell her soft perfumed skin, feel her breath on his cheek, know that it would only take a split second for him to catch her in his arms and kiss her. He could imagine her reaction to that! 'Not tomorrow. No.'

'Oh.' She sounded surprised, disappointed.

After that they fell quiet. When the dishes were put away, she said goodnight and went upstairs. He stayed below, listening to her movements overhead and when there was silence, he turned off the lights and climbed the stairs. At the top, he heard her call his name. 'What is it?' he asked softly, going to stand outside her door.

Her voice was hesitant, fearful. 'That noise. What is it?'

He listened. 'Foxes.'

'Foxes!'

'They're harmless. Don't worry about it. Goodnight.'

'Goodnight,' she murmured.

In his room, he stripped naked, got into bed and lay looking up at the ceiling knowing that he would be unable to sleep. Over and over again, he kept seeing her pink-painted toenails, her legs splayed open on the sofa.

'Jack?'

He sat up sharply. Lara was knocking at his door! Before he could speak, the door creaked open and she stood there, her white pyjamas illuminated in the light from the moon. 'Jack?' she whispered. 'I think there's bats outside my window.'

He tried to calm his ragged breathing. 'They're nothing to be afraid of.'

'What?' Her voice rose shrilly. 'So they *are* bats!'

'Ssh, keep your voice down. You're going to wake the boys. Yes, they're bats but they're harmless.'

'But they might come in by accident. They might get tangled up in my hair. I know, I've seen it.'

'Where?' he asked impatiently. 'In a horror movie?'

'Yes.'

'That can't happen.' He sighed. 'Why don't you just close your window?'

She advanced into the room. 'I can't sleep on my own in there. Can I sleep in here?'

'No!' The word exploded from his lips. 'I mean, no, I don't think that's such a good idea.' He thought quickly, doggedly refusing to entertain the idea of her sharing his bedroom. The temptation would be too great. 'Listen, I'll put Jamie in your bed and then you can have his bed. Then you won't be alone. You'll have Sam.'

'OK.' She sounded slightly relieved. 'But can you make sure the window is shut first?'

He had swung the duvet aside before recalling his nakedness. Swiftly, he threw it back over himself and stretched down to pick up his shirt from the chair. But how was he going to reach his trousers without her seeing him? 'Could you just wait outside for a moment?' he asked.

'No.'

Angered by his feelings of frustration and confusion, he growled at her. 'Well, can you *please* turn round?'

Finally catching on, she swung to face the door. 'Sorry.'

Zipping up his fly, he walked barefooted towards her and out of the door. She followed close behind. 'I'm sorry,' she whispered. 'I'm not used to this sort of thing.'

He did not trust himself to speak, let alone express sympathy. He put Jamie in Lara's bed and waited until Lara had climbed into Jamie's bed. In the light from the corridor, her eyes were enormous and it made him want to kneel down beside her and tell her that there was nothing to fear. Instead, he said goodnight one last time and left the room.

'Could you leave the landing light on,' she pleaded softly.

'Yep.' Entering his own bedroom, Jack closed the door firmly behind him and got back into bed. There was no way he would sleep now.

Tuesday

Beatrix

Beatrix smiled fondly. Justin was trying so hard, his lips pulled back from his teeth in concentration as he carefully piped the crème fraiche mixture into a green grape. With his task completed, he placed a piece of walnut on top and stepped back to admire his handiwork.

'You're treating them like works of art,' she exclaimed, laughing. This was true. He had completed ten stuffed grapes in the time she had taken to make thirty courgette cups, thirty stuffed tomatoes, thirty miniature chicken satays with peanut sauce, thirty rice balls and thirty miniature assorted sandwiches. But, of course, it had not helped that his mobile phone kept ringing every five minutes.

Now, he bristled in mock indignation. 'They *are* works of art!' With great ceremony, he carried the last plate over to the table and laid it down. 'I'm going to be stuffing grapes in my sleep,' he complained.

She chuckled, pleased that she had been able to get him to focus on something other than his work for a change. Unfortunately, their few hours of childish banter would be short-lived because, that afternoon, he would be taking a flight to Japan on a three-day business trip. Earlier, she had packed his suitcase, teaching him the best way to fold his shirts.

She gazed at him now. He so desperately needs a wife, she thought, someone efficient yet amenable, someone who would support him in his struggle to the top.

His gaze moved over the room, coming to rest on her. 'The place looks fantastic,' he said softly. 'You have worked a miracle.'

'Thank you.' She glowed with pride. Of course, she had often made this type of buffet but never with this sense of achievement. A blush spread over her cheeks as she watched him come towards her, the intensity in his eyes making her look down at her hands. Suddenly she didn't know what to say, didn't know what to do. Up until this moment, they had been busy but now everything was done and they had time to themselves. Not a lot of time – perhaps twenty minutes or so.

She felt his finger under her chin, lifting it softly until she was forced to look into his adoring eyes. 'Beatrix,' he whispered. His lips came down, slowly brushing from side to side against hers. She could smell grape and crème fraiche on his breath as he spoke. 'You are beautiful, talented and kind. I can't believe that some love-struck Welshman hasn't had the sense to snap you up. Or maybe I'm wrong? Do you have an admirer? A lover?'

Nervously, she glanced away and then back again, meeting his eyes squarely. 'I don't have a lover,' she began, knowing that this was the moment to tell him the truth, but as she opened her mouth to speak, his lips came down on hers. However, there was one question she needed to ask. 'Justin,' she said, pulling back. 'I know you went out with Lara, but did you love her?'

Vehemently, he shook his head. 'Absolutely not. I promise you, I was never in love with Lara.' Now his arms enfolded her to him, pulling her up against his body. She could feel his hot lips, his tongue filling her mouth. Automatically she put her arms around his neck, desperately wishing she could abandon herself to him.

His hand moved over her breast, down over her hip and over her buttock, drawing her in tighter. Now she could feel the hardness of his penis. 'Oh God, Beatrix,' he moaned. 'I want you so badly.'

The shrill ringing of a doorbell pierced the air and she broke free. The guests! They were here! Panting hard, Justin stared wildly at the intercom. 'It's too early,' he cried, his voice strangled.

They stared at the intercom for a moment, a second ring

prompting Justin to answer it. Keen to disappear before the guests arrived, Beatrix raced into the kitchen to gather her bags ready to make a quick departure. Justin stopped her as she headed for the door. 'Don't go,' he begged. 'I want you to stay. Please.'

She shook her head fiercely. His eyes pleaded with her. 'Show a united front?' he whispered hopefully.

'I can't, Justin. I can't.' She was scared of meeting his high-powered business clients. Right from the start she had felt no shyness towards him, so how could he understand her terrible lack of confidence with everyone else? She had to slip away – now. 'I'm sorry.'

He released her, disappointment on his face. 'Maybe next time?'

She yearned to have the confidence to stand by his side, but she did not have the power to fight against this debilitating shyness. 'Maybe.'

Suddenly there was a tap on the door and he glanced at it before turning back to her. 'I'll understand if you don't want to stay, but just say hello to Hanna before you go. I've been wanting her to meet you.'

She nodded, trying to calm her pounding heart. Satisfied with this, he opened the door wide. 'Hanna!' he said warmly.

Beatrix could only stare as a beautiful Nordic-blonde girl stepped across the threshold and pressed her cheek to

Justin's. The woman's sapphire-blue eyes saw her and glittered. Then she advanced into the room, those hard eyes raking over her in mild contempt. At this hostile confrontation, Beatrix was dismayed to feel her confidence sliding away, leaving her feeling awkward, uncomfortable . . . inferior. Once more that tongue-tied girl whose life revolved around a potting shed.

'I guess you must be Beatrix?' the woman drawled, her voice overlaid with a guttural edge.

Beatrix nodded, feeling Justin's hand come around her waist. 'That's right,' he answered. 'Beatrix, meet Hanna. She works in our Stuttgart office.'

'It's nice to meet you at last.' The woman's gaze scanned the room before settling on the food. 'This looks cosy,' she sneered. 'Justin said you were good in the kitchen and it seems he was right.'

Beatrix looked to the door, wanting to go. Justin had seen this. 'I'm afraid Beatrix can't stay,' he explained.

'What a pity.' But the voice sounded almost triumphant. The woman stepped towards Justin and linked her arm through his. 'It's probably for the best,' she said. 'Since we still haven't managed to plan our strategy.'

Beatrix hesitated. All her instincts warned her against leaving Justin alone with this predatory woman.

Hanna now swung to Justin and pouted. 'Darling, I'm dying of thirst. Fix me my usual, will you?'

Beatrix stiffened, alert to the proprietary note in that silky voice. She felt the touch of Justin's lip at her ear, heard him whisper: 'Just have one drink – before you go?'

This time she nodded firmly, her jaw set hard.

As Justin turned for the kitchen, Hanna followed. 'Are you packed?' she asked him.

Beatrix frowned. This Hanna made it sound as if they were travelling together?

'Beatrix has done it all for me,' he answered.

'How convenient.' The woman smoothed the curtain of white-blonde hair back from her face. 'I've booked the cab to pick us up at four.'

They *were* travelling together! Seething with fury, Beatrix spun on her heel, wanting to storm: 'Justin is *my* man, leave him alone!' It was as if that one kiss with Justin had released her animal responses and now she was ready to fight for him – tooth and nail!

'Isn't it revealing,' Hanna began, 'that only a handful of companies on the Nasdaq provided almost double the index's ten per cent year-to-date gain, while all the rest produced an eight per cent loss.'

Justin put up a hand to politely interrupt. 'Beatrix,' he asked, 'what would you like to drink? White wine?'

'Yes, please.'

Hanna glanced at her as if she were an irritating nuisance before continuing. 'I don't care what you say,

Justin. We are in a bear market. Alexander Mulholland is shifting to portfolio stocks. He says Humana is good at eighteen per cent growth and a p/e of eleven.'

Beatrix accepted her glass of wine, unable to join in with their conversation. Then the realisation struck: this woman was purposefully trying to exclude her. Admittedly, Beatrix was accustomed to Justin and his friends discussing business, but this was different. She gripped her wine glass in impotent fury.

Suddenly, Hanna turned to her. 'Oh, you poor thing, you don't understand a word I'm saying. At least you've got the sense to leave – otherwise you would be bored to tears.'

'I disagree,' Justin argued. 'She would enjoy herself. This lunch is about bonding – nothing to do with business.'

'Nothing to do with business!' Hanna gave a high, girlish snicker. 'But, darling, you live and breathe business. You wouldn't know what else to talk about!'

A look of indignation rippled across Justin's face. Then Hanna stepped forward and kissed him on the cheek. 'What a crosspatch you are! I'm only teasing.'

Beatrix wanted to shout: 'Why don't you bugger off, you stupid cow!' This sudden hostility amazed her – she was beginning to think like Daphne! Now she coughed nervously, marshalling her courage to fight back. 'I wouldn't be bored to tears,' she told the other blonde.

'I'm interested in Justin's work. And, although he doesn't know it,' she threw him a shy smile, 'I've been studying the financial news.'

'Good girl!' The woman swung to Justin. 'Isn't she a good girl? I think you've struck gold this time. You said you wanted a clever woman who was good in the kitchen and now—' she flung out a hand. '*Voilà!*'

Beatrix felt uneasy. She had an image of herself being placed into a box, compartmentalised, categorised. Would she always be branded a 'good, sensible girl' just because she could cook and keep house?

At the sound of the doorbell, Hanna put her glass on the side. 'They're here,' she declared. 'It was nice meeting you,' she said over her shoulder, as if dismissing Beatrix in order to get on with more important matters.

As Beatrix picked up her bags, Justin put a hand on her arm. 'Please stay.'

She saw herself surrounded by his important international clients, blushing furiously and stuttering nervously. It would be too awful. But she *wanted* to stay – if only to wipe that smug superior look off the woman's face. 'You had better go and greet your guests,' she suggested quietly.

She was alone now, trembling at the sound of chattering voices getting nearer. With a hammering heart, she put her bags on the side, took off her jacket and hung it over the back of a chair before taking out her lipstick and mirror to retouch her lips. Then, taking a deep and calming breath, she pulled herself up to her fullest height and walked out of the kitchen, her grandmother's words ringing in her ears: 'Where's your Dunkirk spirit?'

Beatrix smoothed her clammy palms down over her skirt and came out of the kitchen. Ready – for the first time in her life – to do battle.

It was five o'clock by the time Beatrix got back to the apartment. She came in just as the telephone started to ring.

It was Kelsey. 'That was a long lunch.'

With the telephone receiver cradled to her ear, Beatrix smiled indulgently, happily floating on a cloud of self-congratulation and the afterglow of five glasses of white wine. The lunch had been an outstanding success – the clients complimenting her inspired choice of delicacies, the President of Kanasaki even taking her to one side so they could discuss at length the merits of propagation units and the viability of glass-housing bonzai trees. She had been gracious and charming, softly-spoken and attentive, more than a match against Hanna with her hard eyes, her loud, strident voice and domineering opinions.

Beatrix sighed luxuriously. 'Oh Kelsey, I wish you could have seen me. You would have been so proud.'

'So it was a business arrangement?' Kelsey enquired.

'Oh yes!' For a moment Beatrix shivered, remembering Justin's hand on her breast. What would have happened if Hanna had not arrived at that moment?

The American girl's voice broke into her thoughts. 'So how much did he pay you?'

'What?'

'If it was a business arrangement – how much did he pay you?'

'Well, um, he paid for the ingredients.'

'So you did it for free?'

'Yes.' What else could she say? 'But I wanted to help him. I didn't need to be paid.'

There was a moment's silence before Kelsey spoke again. 'I just want to know the score, OK? You're supposed to be in London for a reason: to win back your Mr X – right?'

'Right.'

'And Lara faithfully promised her grandmother that she would help, right?'

'Right.' The word was spoken in a whisper.

'Sure I'm helping too, but when it comes to the crunch, you're Lara's responsibility. Whatever you choose to do will reflect on her.'

Beatrix felt the stirrings of guilt, not wanting to hear more.

'Then we've got to think of your grandmother. I don't

know the total cost but I guess she's spent a small fortune on you. And I know why.'

'You do?'

'Yeah. She wants to see you settled before she dies.'

Beatrix's heart stopped. 'She's *dying*?'

'No, no.' Kelsey's voice was impatient. 'I mean, she's old, she's gonna die. Some time. So she wants to see you settled.'

'Oh yes, I see.' Beatrix breathed with relief but then frowned; Kelsey had it all wrong. Now was the time to admit the humiliating truth that her closest relation was an eccentric miser. 'To be honest, my grandmother is helping me for her own reasons.'

'Her own reasons?'

'Yes. She's helping me for . . .' How could she explain it? 'Let's just say she doesn't like the woman who's gone off with my boyfriend.'

'Well, of course she doesn't,' Kelsey retorted. 'Because it's messed up her agenda.'

Beatrix thought about this. Was Kelsey right? Did Grandmother want to see her settled? With hindsight it did seem a bit ludicrous that she was prepared to spend a fortune in exchange for a free weekly delivery of ten lamb chops and a pound of mince.

'I don't want to be a bore,' Kelsey sighed, 'but it's not fair on any of us if you start fooling around.'

'But I'm not fooling around.'

'So what're you doing?'

Overwhelmed with guilt, Beatrix tried to explain it to herself. She had made a friend in Justin, that was all. She was simply building her confidence, learning to talk to a man. Wasn't that what Kelsey and Lara had wanted all along? 'Grandmother wanted me to gain confidence in society,' she explained. 'So what better way to achieve it than by my hosting a lunch for international businessmen?'

Silence. Then: 'OK,' Kelsey conceded, 'I understand that, but you mustn't start changing the rules of the game. Lara's my best friend and I don't want her getting into trouble.'

Kelsey was right. Lara had been kind to take her in, while Grandmother had indeed spent a small fortune. And Kelsey herself . . . 'I'm sorry,' Beatrix whispered. Suddenly she felt a surge of rebellion, but she couldn't be expected to foresake Justin for someone like John Chadwick! That was ridiculous. She had changed so dramatically that she would be out of his league. Let him have Susan Dobbs – with her blessing! She bit her lip, thinking hard. This charade would soon have to stop.

'So what's it to be?' Kelsey was waiting.

'I promise I will tell Justin,' Beatrix murmured. 'He will understand.'

'Good, I'm glad to hear it.'

Beatrix gazed off into the distance, feeling a dread settle upon her. She couldn't go back to her old life at Castlemaine and yet, she couldn't desert her grandmother. Who would keep her company? Who would look after that vast house? For a moment she imagined the old woman sitting alone in the twilight, friendless and sad. Maybe, once she was dead, she could start a new life. Why was she thinking like this? It was horrid! What was happening to her sweet, selfless nature?

'Have you spoken to Lara?' Kelsey asked now.

'Sorry, what did you say?'

'Have you spoken to Lara? Did she get to Dorset OK?'

'Yes, she phoned last night. She said she arrived in the back of a hay wagon.'

'Mm,' Kelsey murmured. 'I wonder how long that little fantasy will last?'

Beatrix wasn't listening, as once more she began to worry about her future. Could she desert the woman who had given her a home? But, at the same time, could she return to Castlemaine and pick up the threads of her life?

'. . . so Oliver will pick you up at eight instead.'

Kelsey's words broke into her thoughts. 'Sorry, what did you say?'

'I'm saying I can't make it tonight, so I've asked Oliver to take you.'

Beatrix gazed blankly at the wall.

'You know Oliver – Oliver Marchant?'

'Yes, but—'

'You're going to have to wear pants because he's got a motorbike.'

Her thoughts still full of complications, this caught Beatrix unawares. '*Motorbike?*'

'Yes, those things on two wheels that go brrm, brrm. You're going to be riding to the cocktail party on a motorbike.'

'Oh.'

'Are you OK with that?' Kelsey sounded impatient. 'I'm sorry I can't make it but Oliver's a great guy. He'll look after you. So, I'll see you tomorrow, honey. Bye!'

Suddenly registering that she would be alone with Oliver that night, Beatrix opened her mouth to protest but it was too late, the line clicked dead.

Slowly she replaced the receiver. Did it really matter who she went out with that night? Did anything matter? All she wanted was her freedom. With little enthusiasm, she began to get ready, desultorily applying her make-up before choosing a pair of lime-green Capri trousers and a white shirt. When she stood back to study herself in the long mirror there was a frown between her finely shaped eyebrows. It was not only her face and hair that had changed over the past weeks; the strength in her ever-expanding personality filled her with fear and exhilaration.

There was no way she was going back to a spinster life in Castlemaine.

When the doorbell rang, she put on her jacket and headed down the stairs, her thoughts revolving on the future, one moment feeling awash with guilt, the next filled with rebellion.

She opened the door to see Oliver standing on the step dressed from head to toe in black leather. 'Ready?' he asked, handing her a helmet.

She took it nervously, glancing beyond him to the huge black motorbike parked at the kerbside, the streetlight gleaming on the black metal. 'I think so.'

'Your first time?'

She nodded.

'You'll love it.'

She felt his rough hands against her cheek as he buckled the helmet strap under her chin, conscious of the smell of warm leather and diesel. Now she followed him. Effortlessly he swung his leg over the seat and sat grinning at her. 'Come on! You can do it.'

Putting a hand on his shoulder for support, she swung herself up behind him and the engine roared.

'Put your arms around my waist.'

Since he was almost a stranger to her, she did so tentatively but as the motorbike roared away from the kerb her grip tightened. With her cheek pressed to his back, she closed her eyes against the surge of fear and adrenalin pumping through her veins. When she opened them again, she saw shops and wine bars flashing by in a kaleidoscope of lights. Then the engine dropped to a hum as they slowed behind a double-decker bus.

When he accelerated, she felt the full roar of the engine between her legs, felt the hardness of his body, the jerk of his shoulder as he changed gears. He was in total control, and she felt safe. What had Lara said about him? He was wild. But she knew he would look after her – she had sensed that by the gentle manner in which he had put on her helmet.

By the time they came out into Piccadilly, her grip on him had eased and now she looked around with wide, excited eyes. Never in a million years would she ever have imagined that she would be roaring through the London night on the back of a motorbike. Daphne would never believe it.

The traffic was heavy now, the motorbike angling from side to side as it weaved in and out. Gaining confidence, she relaxed and let her body move with Oliver's. At a traffic light, they stopped and she sat straight and looked around so that people would notice her. She could just imagine how sexy she looked, with her svelte figure and that blonde fringe peeping from under a black helmet, riding with a strong, handsome man on a powerful and dangerous machine.

Gradually, they left the bright lights of the city behind,

taking dark narrow alleyways until they finally come to a halt outside a grim, dilapidated warehouse. As Oliver cut the engine, there was an ear-ringing silence. 'I hope you like dancing,' he said, taking off his helmet.

Perplexed, she looked around at the silent, shadowy buildings. Dancing? Here?

'Don't look so worried,' he laughed, unbuckling her helmet strap. 'You're OK with me.'

Minutes later they opened a door to be met by a blast of lights and music. 'I thought we'd come here first,' he offered. 'But if you don't like it, we can split.'

Dazed by the journey and this sudden eruption of life, she could only nod. Oliver handed the helmets to the girl behind the bar and then stripped off his leathers, emerging like James Bond in a dinner jacket. Then he turned with two bottles, handing one to Beatrix.

'Cheers!' he said, and put the bottle to his lips.

Never having drunk from a bottle before, Beatrix hesitated and looked around for a glass but seeing that everyone else was drinking from bottles, she shrugged and knocked back the icy cool lager.

The music was too loud to make conversation and so they stood side by side, watching the throng of people on the dance floor, Oliver tapping his foot to the music. 'Do you like rock and roll?' he asked, leaning close to shout in her ear.

She nodded with a smile. Up until that moment she would not have known the answer but now she did. She loved it. Suddenly the bottle was taken from her hand and, in the next second, Oliver was leading her towards the dance floor. Oh no! she thought wildly. I don't know how to dance to this!

She had no time to remonstrate before he had turned, pulled her towards him and spun her under his arm. Now she was facing him again, giddy on her feet and laughing. He grinned down at her and she grinned back. In that moment, she knew she would forget all her worries, all her responsibilities, for – tonight – she would have *fun*!

Lara

'Where's the rest of your uniform?'

Whispering voices brought Lara to consciousness. With her brain thick with sleep it took her a moment to realise what was happening: Jack was getting the boys ready for school. This was her job, but she was too tired. At the sound of the door closing softly behind them, she drifted back to sleep.

Much later she awoke once more and lay staring up at the strip of sunshine on the ceiling. What a God-awful night! Yelping foxes, hooting owls and howling dogs – like a soundtrack to some Gothic horror movie. Then, when everything had become silent and the sky was tinged with the pearly light of dawn, the birds went hysterical. In one full blast they chirruped, trilled, warbled, whistled and, not to be outdone, the cockerel joined in. Now, at last, there was peace. She strained her ears to identify some sound but there was only silence.

Swinging out of bed, she went to the window and gazed out on the sunny garden. The boundary hedge burgeoned with bright blossom in the morning sunshine, looking so different from the skulking shadows of the night before. 'How am I going to get through another night like that?' she muttered.

A football lay abandoned on the lawn. The boys would be at school, she calculated, and Jack would be painting in his shed. Her thoughts went back over the previous evening, remembering the sight of his powerful torso illuminated in the moonlight and how he had flipped back the bedclothes to get out of bed. He had covered himself quickly, but not before she had glimpsed his penis hanging heavy between his legs. It was strange how that glimpse of him had introduced a new ingredient into his personality. Up until that moment she had simply thought of him as a gifted artist with two small sons; now she saw him as an attractive man, a sexually attractive man. Did he have a girlfriend? she wondered. And what would he be like in bed?

She quickly shook these thoughts away. Vittorio was the man she desired – not some pig farmer. She smiled to herself, knowing that Vittorio would be a tender lover, experienced in whipping a female up to a pinnacle of sexual climax. How she longed to feel his hands on her naked body, hear his husky voice whispering words of desire.

With a delicious shiver, she slipped off her pyjama top and headed for the bathroom. Once inside, she threw it over the back of a chair, picked up her toothbrush and toothpaste and then paused, admiring her breasts in the mirror above the sink. What would Vittorio think when he saw her naked?

Suddenly, from the corner of her eye she saw something that made her blood run cold. On the wall above the toilet cistern was the biggest spider she had ever seen. It was black and hairy and as big as a fist. Slowly, very slowly, she backed out of the room. This was no English spider! It was too big. Maybe it had escaped from the local zoo. She had seen *The Really Wild Show* enough times to suspect that this creature was some sort of Amazonian deadly poisonous bird-eater. It was monstrous – unbelievable – like something from a joke shop. The answer hit her. It *was* from a joke shop. The boys were playing a trick on her. She stopped in relief and chuckled. Wait until they got home . . . Now she saw the spider for what it was: a clever imitation in black rubber. How could she have been so gullible? She would ask to borrow it, take it back to London and scare the shit out of Kelsey!

As she went to take it off the wall, she stopped and frowned. Wait a minute. She bent forward to take a closer look. Those hairy legs looked incredibly real. Suddenly the spider scuttled up the wall and she screamed, terror pinning her feet to the floor. It had stopped and now watched her malevolently. From below came the sound of thundering footsteps on the stairs. 'Lara?' It was Jack.

She couldn't move, couldn't speak. She heard the door bang open, heard his exclamation, 'What's happened?' Then he, too, must have seen the creature because his voice stopped dead. Now he spoke slowly, his breathing laboured. 'What's happened?'

Was he blind? As she put out a hand to point at the spider, it scuttled down towards the floor. 'Ahh!' she screamed, jumping back and colliding with Jack. Although the spider had stopped, she sensed it was coming for her. It was going to run down the wall, along the floor and up her legs! She had to get out of here – fast! Carefully, without alerting it, she began to back off but once again she came up hard against Jack. For heaven's sake, why didn't he get out of the way? She felt his hand on her naked arm, felt the buckle of his belt cold against her back. Christ! She was half-naked. She had completely forgotten. Grabbing her pyjama top, she pushed past him. Now he would kill it and they would be safe.

Outside the door, she put on her top, waiting to hear the bang of a shoe smacking the spider flat against the tiles, but there was no sound. She peeped in to see him closing the window. 'Is it dead?' she breathed.

'No. I've just put him out of the window.'

'What?' She stared with incredulity. 'You mean it's still alive?'

He nodded impassively.

She pointed a quivering finger at the window. 'And it's outside?'

'It's harmless,' he stated, and moved by her towards the stairs.

She followed him quickly. 'You're wrong. I don't know much about insects, but I do know a bird-eating spider when I see one.'

With his hand on the banister, he paused and looked back at her. 'It's English. And like all spiders in England, it's completely harmless.' Then he turned and headed down the stairs.

He had spoken with such a weary conviction that she was tempted to believe him. Now she felt stupid. How was she to know? And why hadn't he given her some sympathy, taken time to explain away her fear – instead of being so cool and impersonal? But surely this was out of character? She had seen how loving and caring he could be with his boys, so why hadn't he been the same with her?

His voice called up from the foot of the stairs. 'Would you like a cup of tea? I'm just making one.'

'No, thank you,' she retorted, her voice stiff with anger. She didn't want his tea. If he wasn't going to be nice to her, then he could stuff his tea! She stood on the landing, staring at the bathroom door with uncertainty before deciding to brush her teeth at the kitchen sink instead. With her toothbrush in one hand and her toothpaste in the other, she headed down the stairs. But what if that thing sneaked in through a window during the night. Imagine waking up with it crawling over her face. Well, first thing this morning, she would go around the whole house and make sure every window was shut tight, then she would find a can of insecticide and fumigate the building. Then, this evening, she would get paralytically drunk and collapse unconscious into bed.

And Jack wasn't even trying to understand her fears. He had been exactly the same last night, treating her as if she were some hysterical air-head. Well, she didn't care. *She* would show *him*! If he was going to be hateful to her, then she was going to be hateful to him! With her mouth set in a grim line she entered the kitchen and threw a haughty sneer in his direction. Without acknowledging her presence, he took the teapot from the shelf and set it on the table.

It was as if she were invisible. Well, if he was going to ignore her, then she was going to ignore him! She wet her toothbrush under the tap, violently squeezed toothpaste over the bristles and proceeded to brush her teeth, whipping up a lather as she glowered at him.

This silence was too much! 'Tell me, Jack,' she said, mumbling through a mouthful of foam. 'Do I annoy you?'

Without looking up, he spooned tea-leaves into the pot. 'No,' he said coldly.

He *was* annoyed with her! Fury boiled, ready to erupt. 'Well, I'm very sorry to be a nuisance,' she spat, 'but it's not my fault I'm scared of spiders – so you've got no right to be annoyed with me.'

'I'm not.'

'Yes, you are.'

'No, I'm not.'

'Yes, you are.'

He banged down the tea caddy. 'This has got nothing to do with spiders!' he shouted.

She stared at him, her foaming mouth hanging open in astonishment.

'I am a man,' he said angrily. 'How do you think I feel when I come into the bathroom and see you half-naked?'

As his fury gathered momentum, she held her breath, not daring to move.

'You are a beautiful and desirable woman. You can't just come into my bedroom at night and—' He stopped, abruptly averting his face as if having said too much.

In the silence, Lara felt the strangest sensation; it was as if a tiny Irish dancer was merrily leaping about in her chest. At the sound of the door creaking open, she turned sharply.

'Um . . . sorry.' A woman was leaning into the room, waving a white envelope. She was plump but pretty with a faded beauty and bleached blonde hair. 'Don't let me interrupt,' she said, placing the envelope on the dresser and quickly withdrawing.

Jack stepped forward. 'Patsy, it's OK. Come in.'

The woman did not need a second invitation. She stepped in with alacrity, smiling a welcome at Lara as if eager to be introduced.

'Lara, this is Patsy – a friend from the village,' Jack said. 'Patsy, this is Lara. Lara's the assistant to the gallery owner I was telling you about, and she has kindly volunteered to act as my housekeeper until we find a replacement.'

The woman nodded repeatedly, her eyes bright and intelligent.

Lara tried to smile. *What must I look like?* Foaming at the mouth and dressed in pyjamas in the middle of the day whilst embroiled in a shouting match with my client. She turned to the sink and rinsed out her mouth, covering up her embarrassment with a carefree smile and a nonchalant wave of a hand. 'I haven't quite got into the swing of things.'

'Of course,' the woman answered. 'It takes time.' She had kind, youthful eyes, only the grey hairs at her temple indicating her age. She wore big gold earrings, too shiny to be real.

Lara had wiped her mouth and now smiled hesitantly, uncomfortable under the woman's scrutiny: she was as bad as the man in the dirty woollen waistcoat. Didn't anyone have manners in the country?

Faced with this awkward silence, Jack coughed. 'Would you like a cup of tea, Patsy?'

'Yes, please.' The woman sat down, her gaze still fixed on Lara. 'So you're here to help our Jack, then?'

Lara nodded. *Why is she staring at me like this?*

'And you're from London?'

'Yes.'

At that moment the telephone rang and Jack crossed the kitchen to answer it, leaving Lara alone with the woman.

'So how are you two getting along?'

'Fine.' Lara coloured, knowing that this woman would have heard them shouting only moments before.

'That's kind of you, to be the housekeeper. I suppose you can cook then?'

'Yes,' Lara replied defensively.

'That's good. And—'

Lara was grateful to be interrupted by Jack. 'That was Timothy,' he said quickly. 'We're in for a bit of a surprise today.'

'Oh, yes?' she enquired stiffly, her resentment of him still at boiling point.

'Vittorio's arriving – today.'

'Today?' Lara could only stare in horror. *But she wasn't ready! What about her plans?* 'Oh shit!' she breathed, pressing the knuckle of her hand against her teeth.

Jack looked alarmed. 'Don't worry,' he assured her. 'He's not coming to pick up any paintings; he just wants to meet me.'

'What time will he get here?'

'Timothy doesn't know.'

Lara bit her lip. She had to take control of herself, ignore this rising panic. Would she have time to clean the house, take a bath, wash her hair, do a full beauty routine, fill the kitchen with flowers, arrange an elaborate dinner? 'Food!' she cried. 'What about food?'

'We can knock something together,' he offered.

Knock something together! This wasn't one of his prized pigs they were feeding! She took a deep breath to calm herself. Apart from a lamb bone in the pantry and a box of vegetables, there was nothing else. 'Vittorio is important to us,' she began. 'I think it will be necessary to give a good impression, don't you?'

Jack nodded. 'Definitely.'

Patsy spoke. 'Listen, Lara, just pop down to the stores in the village,' she suggested. 'They mightn't have caviar but they've got everything else.'

'I'd better get back to work,' Jack said quickly. 'Are you going to be all right, Lara?'

She nodded distractedly, and when the door had closed behind him, she looked to the woman. 'Can you help me?'

'I'd be happy to.'

'You see, I can't really cook.'

Patsy nodded in understanding. 'I can bring you something up from the pub where I work. Steak and ale pie do you?'

This was all wrong. Lara wanted to weep. 'Don't you have Osso Bucco?' she pleaded. The woman shook her head. 'Canneloni?' Lara asked hopefully. 'Spaghetti? Penne? Any pasta at all?'

Patsy continued to shake her head.

Lara gave in. 'Steak and ale pie will be great.'

'Good. I'll be back at what time – around five?'

Lara nodded.

After Patsy had gone, she stood slumped in the middle of the kitchen. Oh, why had Vittorio decided to come today? What about her plans? She and Jack were more at loggerheads than ever before. For a moment, his words echoed in her brain. *You are a beautiful and desirable woman.* Did that mean he desired her? Again, she felt those tiny feet leaping about inside her chest. Angrily, she pushed these treacherous thoughts from her head. What the hell was she playing at?

Now she set off upstairs to wash her hair in the bathroom. Spider or no spider; her future hung in the balance!

For the next few hours she worked rapidly, her energy fuelled by thoughts of Vittorio's *palazzo*, his servants, the vast terrace shaded with mimosa. All to be hers! In fact – she paused with a hair roller halfway to her head – she could return with Vittorio to London, tonight. She would never have to sleep in this house of horrors again. But what would Jack do about a housekeeper? He needed her. 'Oh hell,' she muttered, knowing that she could not desert him and the boys.

Not yet, anyway.

At two o'clock, she carried a tray loaded with cheese sandwiches, biscuits, sliced Madeira cake and a mug of tea into the shed, putting it down on the bench beside Jack and giving him her best smile.

He looked up briefly, his voice friendly. 'Thanks, Lara. I'm sorry about my outburst earlier.'

Immediately, she quashed those dancing feet. 'Don't worry about it,' she replied sweetly, grateful that his cold aloofness had gone. Together, they would show a friendly, united front to Vittorio. 'I thought I'd make the house look nice,' she suggested.

'Good idea.' He told her where to find the candlesticks and vases, but stood firmly against the use of insecticide. 'That stuff does more harm than good.'

After hoping to nuke every creepy crawlie in the house, this came as a bitter disappointment. Well, she would just have to keep the windows shut. She hurried back to the house, put on an apron and began to clean the kitchen, dusting every shelf on the dresser – even standing on a chair to dust the ugly china dog. After that, she went upstairs and changed into her cream-coloured cocktail dress, her Cartier watch and De Beer diamond earrings before giving a final check to the elegant mass of curls pinned neatly at the top of her head. Perfect!

At three-fifteen, there was the sound of the truck returning, followed by the boys' footsteps running towards the house. 'First one to the rope swing!' Jamie shouted, throwing his satchel down next to Rosie and looking expectantly at Lara. She dropped the branch of apple blossom on the table and turned to catch him.

'There will be no rope swing today,' she told them both. 'Didn't your daddy tell you? We've got an important visitor arriving any minute. I want you two to look your very best.'

They gave her a blank look.

'You have to look smart,' she reiterated, 'so I want you both to have a bath and change into your best clothes.' And when the boys looked doubtful about this: 'It'll be fun,' she enthused. 'Don't you like getting dressed up?'

They shrugged. 'We never get dressed up,' Jamie admitted.

Jack came in, scooped the cat up from the sofa and put

it outside the door where it stood dazed, only the tip of its ear twitching. As he turned he saw Lara and stopped dead. 'You look lovely,' he said softly.

His expression made her breathless. 'Do I?'

They gazed at each other in silence. Then, abruptly, he turned away. 'Come on, boys,' he ordered. 'We've got to get washed and changed.'

She watched him go. Why was he being like this? One minute he was adorable and the next he was horrid! Refusing to think of him, she fussed about, tastefully repositioning the candlesticks around the room, brushed the petals of apple blossom from the table and plumping up the pillows on the sofa. Everything was ready.

Then, she noticed Rosie, who stood over her dinner bowl looking up with big mournful eyes while the cat curled around the leg of a chair, wailing. 'Jesus,' Lara muttered. 'What's up with you two?' Calculating that they were hungry, she opened a tin of tuna fish, tipped it upside down on a plate and frizbee-ed it across the floor towards the cat. Then she grabbed the lamb bone from the pantry and tossed it into the dog's bowl. There! Two animals fed. *Easy.* She was totally in control of a difficult situation. How she wished that all those people who had branded her hopeless – her mother, her teachers, Meryl, Kelsey, Timothy, Grandmother Bayley – could see her now!

As the boys trooped down the stairs, she checked them

in turn, giving their hair a final comb and trimming Sam's fingernails. 'Rosie shouldn't be eating a lamb bone,' Jamie remarked. 'She might get sick.'

Lara waved this off. 'She's a dog. Dogs eat bones.'

Jack hurried by, telling her he needed to tidy up the shed. 'And Jamie,' he said over his shoulder as he went out the door, 'don't forget to feed the chickens.'

'Stop!' Lara put a restraining hand on Jamie's shoulder. 'I don't want you getting grubby.'

'But I won't.'

She didn't trust him. 'I'll do it,' she said. 'What do I need?'

'Laying mash,' Jamie answered. 'Here.' He pulled back the curtain under the side table, brought out a plastic bucket and peeled back the lid to reveal oatmeal-looking flakes. 'You just shake a little bit in their trays.'

'OK.' Taking the bucket, she marched out to the chicken enclosure and pushed back the gate. The chickens were waiting, surrounding her immediately, clucking and flapping wildly. In fright, she threw the entire contents over their heads, flung the bucket away and dashed back into the kitchen.

'Are you OK?' Puzzled, Jamie stepped towards the door to look out but she stopped him. A herd of maniac chickens was not going to interfere with her plans. 'Don't worry about them – they're fine. Now I want you—'

A voice called from the doorway. 'I'm back!' It was Patsy, coming into the kitchen carrying a cardboard box containing a golden crusted pie and a bowl of mashed potato. When she saw Lara, she stopped and stared. 'You look fantastic!' she exclaimed.

A bit different from this morning, eh? Lara took the cardboard box, suppressing the urge to bundle Patsy out of the door. She didn't want Vittorio discovering that someone else had made his dinner. The woman hesitated for a moment, taking a good look round. 'Well, I've got to get back,' she said reluctantly. 'Have a nice dinner.'

'Thanks again.' Lara went to the door to wave her off. Good – everything was going to plan. She put the pie in the oven, opened the two bottles of Barolo and placed them on the table. Suddenly she heard a retching sound and looked down, puzzled to see the dog's neck thrust forward, her ribcage heaving. In the next moment a pile of dog sick was deposited on the floor.

'Oh, for God's sake!' she yelled, clawing the air with her hands. *The dog was still retching!* Sam grabbed Rosie by the collar and pulled her outside while Lara snatched up a bundle of newspapers and knelt down to clear up the mess. 'Please, Vittorio,' she begged. 'Don't come now.'

'I told you,' Jamie muttered, wiping the flagstone with a wet rag.

'How was I to know?' Lara wailed. She ran upstairs for

her perfume, returning to liberally shake *Chanel No. 5* over the damp patch. Finished, she fell back on the sofa, exhausted and breathless. Why on earth had she chosen a farm as the stage on which she would act out her role as perfect wife and mother! Was she crazy?

The minutes ticked away.

She tried to imagine how Vittorio would walk in through that door and see her there, poised, elegant and beautiful. Should she cross her legs or angle them to one side like the Queen? Should that candle be brought closer or pushed further away? She got up and went to the window and looked out. Again, she sat down on the sofa, sniffed her armpits, checked that there was no chicken poo on her shoes, plumped up a pillow then watched Sam shuffle his Lego bricks into a box. This excitement was unbearable.

At the sound of an engine, she leapt to her feet and raced to the window, but it was just a car passing along the lane. With this false alarm, she felt faint and, wanting to take her mind off her anxiety, she called the boys to sit with her and talk about their day. After a while, the three of them grew silent, staring towards the blue sky beyond the window, each with their own thoughts.

'Can't we just go out and have a little play?' Jamie asked.

'No, definitely not.'

He sighed and flopped back.

'What about your homework?' she cried, remembering her plan. She would sit beside the boys while patiently helping them with their homework. She would even smudge ink on her finger to give the impression that, although she was innately elegant, some things were just more important. Yeah! One look and Vittorio would think to himself – *I was right. This is the woman for me.*

'But I don't have to hand my homework in until Friday,' Jamie told her.

'We could make a start.' She jumped up and went to the table, giving Jamie an isn't-this-fun look as he slumped down in a kitchen chair and put his chin in his hands. 'You said homework was a pain,' he moaned.

'I was being silly.' She opened up his school folder. 'Oh look, here's a letter.' She took it out, scanning the page.

'Dear Parent,

NITS

Unfortunately, I have to report that there is an outbreak of head lice in the school.

Head lice? Lara gazed at the words, a cold fear rising up through her body. She continued breathlessly, as if a great hand were pressing down on her chest.

Head lice are highly contagious so please inspect your child's hair for infestation. Any child found to be infected will be sent home immediately. Please use the recommended treatment to eradicate this problem.

Yours faithfully,

The Headmistress.

Highly contagious! Lara sat frozen. This couldn't be happening. She stared at Jamie's hair. Sam's hair. Did they have head lice? Were there tiny creatures crawling over their scalps at this very moment?

Did *she* have head lice?

Oh God, yes, she could feel something moving. Her hands tore at her hair. They were all infested! Oh no! Panic gripped her by the throat.

Taking a deep, calming breath, she walked over to Jamie and parted his hair. 'I am just going to check your hair for—' She couldn't say those words. As hard as she looked she couldn't see anything.

She wanted to succumb to this mounting panic and let out a scream. Instead, she swiftly checked Sam's hair. Nothing. But maybe the nits were invisible to the naked eye? Desperately, she spun to the window and stared out with wild eyes. 'Please, Vittorio, don't come now,' she prayed, clutching the edge of the sink. If any one of them had head lice they would give them to him. Handsome, elegant, aristocratic Vittorio – with *head lice.*

She swung into the room. 'Jamie, quick – get your daddy. He's in the shed. RUN!'

As his brother raced out of the kitchen, Sam looked up at her. 'What's wrong, Lara?'

She answered casually, 'Oh, nothing. I just want Daddy to check your hair.'

'We don't have head lice,' the little boy assured her.

He had spoken those words! Immediately she dropped to one knee before him. 'Darling, sweetheart, you like me, don't you?'

He nodded firmly.

'Good. So will you make me a promise? Promise not to say those words in front of our important visitor?'

He nodded again. 'OK.'

Now the door burst open and Jamie fell in, evidently enjoying this sudden drama. 'Daddy's not in his shed.'

'Try somewhere else. You too, Sam. Go, quick!'

Lara bit down into the knuckle of her hand. This was a catastrophe. Why ever had she volunteered to come here? She must have been out of her mind! Suddenly, she thought of Beatrix. She was a country girl – she would know what to do. Lara dialled home, annoyed to hear her own voice on the answermachine. Maybe she was at Kelsey's? On the third ring Kelsey answered.

'I must speak to Beatrix.' Lara cried. 'It's terribly urgent.'

'Sorry, she's not here. Can I help?'

In that instant, Lara pictured her friend lying back on her reclining leather chair, her body swathed in silk, her hand held out to a manicurist. Unhurried, pampered and utterly content. Lara gave a bitter, hysterical laugh. 'I don't think so.'

'How do you know?' Kelsey replied tartly, obviously offended.

'OK then. Tell me what head lice look like.'

'Head lice?' Kelsey sounded defensive. 'Is this some sort of joke?'

'Yeah,' Lara drawled. 'This is how I get my kicks. I like to phone my friends and ask them what head lice look like. Of course this isn't a joke!'

'Hell, Lara, you're right – I can't help you.'

Lara spoke from the depths of her soul. 'I hate this place!'

'Bad, huh?'

'A nightmare! As soon as I'm de-loused, I'm out of here. Listen, Kelsey, I've got to go. Bye.' With this, she replaced the receiver. Next, she phoned the gallery.

'Good afternoon. Smith's.' It was Timothy.

'Is Meryl there?' she asked quickly.

'No, she's left for the day. May I help?'

'No, no, it's simply a domestic hiccup, that's all.'

'I've got to say it, Lara, you've surprised us all.' Timothy's voice was indulgent. 'Meryl is positively thrilled with the outcome. She predicts that you and Penfold will get along admirably.'

'*Really*?' At the sound of the door opening, she turned and saw Jack with the boys. 'Timothy, I've got to dash.' She slammed down the phone and rushed over to Jack. 'Can we go outside for a moment?' she asked urgently.

He looked perplexed. 'Sure.'

Once outside she told him about the letter. 'Do you know what head lice look like?'

'Yes, but I doubt whether the boys are infested. I use a nit comb on their hair every time I wash it.'

'But what about *me?*' she cried.

'You've only been here two days. Even if you had become infested, the eggs take almost ten days to hatch.'

Infested? Eggs? Hatch? Her brain reeled. 'But I've been brushing my hair, so I would have brushed them all out.'

He shook his head. 'If you had them, an ordinary brush wouldn't get them out because they cling to the hair shaft. You need to use a proper nit comb and thick hair conditioner – or an insecticide, which I never use – to remove the lice and their eggs.'

She lunged for the door. 'Where's the nit comb?'

To her astonishment, she heard him chuckle. 'Don't worry, you won't have them but if it makes you feel easier,

I'll check the boys, show you how it's done.' Once inside the kitchen, he took a piece of white paper and held it under Sam's fringe and began to comb through his hair with a small steel comb. 'The eggs are dark in colour,' Jack explained. 'And if Sam had them, they would now be falling onto the paper.'

Hawk-eyed and breathless, Lara watched. Nothing. One down, two to go. 'Try Jamie,' she said.

Jamie sat at the table and the procedure was repeated. Nothing. 'I told you,' Jack said.

'Now me.' She nudged Sam off the chair and sat down, unpinning her hair and letting it fall about her shoulders.

Jack slowly and gently pulled the comb down through her hair, making her want to shout, 'Hurry – for God's sake!' There was silence.

Suddenly Jamie cried out, 'What's that?' The comb stopped.

She went rigid. An egg must have fallen out on the paper and they were inspecting it! She dropped her forehead on the table and gave out a wail of anguish. 'I hate this place,' she sobbed. 'I hate it.'

'It's OK, it's OK,' Jack said quickly. 'It's nothing. In fact, it looks like a piece of laying mash.'

Lara slowly raised her head. That made sense. 'Are you sure?' she asked, standing up to inspect the paper.

'Absolutely. Look for yourself.'

Released from the build-up of fear and tension, she burst into tears, her shoulders heaving as she put her hands over her face. 'Oh God!'

Jack gripped her by the arms. 'Lara! Hey!' She felt his arms come around her, drawing her up against his hard chest. 'Shush now, there's nothing to cry about. You'll be fine.' She felt safe in his arms, soothed by his hand tenderly stroking her hair. He smelt of turpentine and tobacco. It was a lovely smell, comforting and solid.

'Jamie, go and get some toilet paper.' Gently, Jack held her back from him and bent low to look at her tearful face. 'How about a glass of wine, eh?' She didn't want a glass of wine, she wanted him to carry on holding her, to comfort her, but already he was moving away.

As Jamie handed her a huge ball of toilet paper, she gave him a tremulous smile. The boys looked stricken. 'Do you want to have a look at my miniatures?' Sam offered, obviously trying to take her mind off her distress.

She laughed, wiping the tears away. 'That's really sweet of you, darling, but not just now.'

Taking the glass of wine from Jack, she looked up to see him give her a small, encouraging smile. She noticed that the whites of his eyes were very white, the lashes thick and dark. He had beautiful eyes . . .

Suddenly the telephone rang and he moved past her to pick it up. 'Hello?' he said. 'What a pity . . . That's OK

. . . Oh, I'm sorry to hear that. . . . Yes, no problem . . . Yes, she's just here.'

Lara went to the phone knowing who this would be.

'*Cara mia.*' Vittorio's voice was soft, wistful. 'I am desolate. I had so much hoped to see you this evening but I have been called back to Milano. I telephoned you earlier but there was no reply. How are you?'

'Fine.' Even to her own ears, there was a hard edge to her voice. He wasn't coming – after all her anxiety!

'But I have good news. I will be with you on Saturday instead. Only three more days. How I long to see you.'

She set her jaw. His voice sounded creepy. Had he always sounded like this?

'*Ciao, bellissima.*' His words were fading into sad regret.

'I look forward to seeing you on Saturday,' she said in her best businesslike voice, not wanting Jack to suspect her feelings for Vittorio. 'Goodbye.' She put the phone down and exhaled slowly. 'He's coming on Saturday,' she told Jack, her voice flat.

'Yes, he said.'

She felt deflated, exhausted. She picked up the oven gloves. 'Shall we eat?'

As they settled themselves at the table, she served the food, aware of an unusual silence. 'You can start,' she told the boys. They seemed strangely subdued. Then she realised why. *I hate this place!* Oh hell! Why had she said those words? She cringed with mortification, angry at her stupidity.

'I didn't mean what I said.' She saw the boys look up at her with big, hurt eyes. 'I *do* like this place. I just said it because I was frightened. You see, I'm not used to the countryside and all the insects and noises . . . and head lice.' She gave them a wry grin.

'But don't you have insects in London?' Sam asked.

'Not like the ones here,' she shuddered. 'This morning I saw a spider as big as a . . . as a *dinner plate!*' She had expected them to laugh, but instead, their little faces remained grave.

She tried again. 'I thought I had horrid creepy crawlies on my head. You see, ladies don't like things like that. I'm sorry for what I said. I do like this place and I love you both. Really.' She leant towards them. 'You're fun and sweet and kind. I just wish I could take you back to London with me.' This produced tentative smiles. Thank goodness. She would hate more than anything to hurt them. She stroked a finger under Sam's chubby chin. 'Would you two like to come and live with me?'

They nodded eagerly, their eyes bright. She had won them back.

Jack coughed and immediately she sensed his meaning. She shouldn't be promising something she could not deliver. Quickly, she backtracked. 'Well, at least you can come and visit.'

She smiled at their eager faces but when she glanced at Jack, he did not meet her eyes. She didn't want him to look like that. She was fond of him. He was kind and sensitive and funny. In fact, they could all come and visit her, and she could come and visit them. Although the spider situation would be a problem. And the bats, and the foxes . . .

Released from the fervent excitement of Vittorio's visit, she came back to earth with a bump, foreseeing a long, fearful night ahead of her. She lifted the glass to her lips. Well, the only thing I can do, she decided, is to drink myself into oblivion.

Jack

'How do you use an Egyptian toilet?' Jack asked.

Everyone shrugged.

'Toot and come in!'

Lara shrieked with laughter, the corkscrew of hair, which had fallen over one eye, now bouncing up and down. It was a funny joke but not *that* funny. He viewed her empty glass. She was really knocking it back. Did she normally drink like this?

Admittedly, he was pleased that she was having a good time but now she was becoming quite reckless. First, she had joined Sam in making farting noises through her hands, then she had scared the cat and now she was striking a match to the wrapping from her macaroon biscuit. With a sense of unease, he saw it sail up to the ceiling in a ball of flames. Jamie was helping, striking match after match until suddenly they were surrounded by a flotilla of flaming paper.

Sam gazed up in awe. 'C-o-o-l!' he breathed.

'Why don't we play another game?' Jack suggested quickly.

'Can we play Blind Man's Buff?' Sam asked.

'No!' The alarm in his voice startled even himself. 'No,' he said more gently. 'Not tonight.' He felt uncomfortably hot and, looking towards the window, saw that it was shut. As he went to open it, Lara forestalled him.

'Can we keep it closed?'

Now he realised *all* the windows were shut. 'But why?' he asked.

She looked away.

'Is it something to do with our little visitor this morning?' he enquired.

'Yes.'

'Come on,' he ordered. 'Everybody outside. I've got an idea.' They followed him out of the door. 'Right, boys. First one to find a spider . . .'

'OK, Daddy,' they chorused and began searching the walls. Lara had raised her hands in protest. 'I don't think—' she began.

'Got one!' Sam came running, his little hands cupped together.

Jack put his hand on the small of Lara's back, gently pushing her forwards. 'Lara wants you to put the spider on her hand, don't you, Lara?'

With the force of his hand on her spine, she was unable to retreat. Sam held up his cupped hands. 'It's not a very big one,' he apologised. 'Does that matter?'

'I've got a *gigantic* one!' Jamie shouted, stumbling towards them. 'It looks like a tarantula!'

'Right, Lara,' Jack said reasonably. 'Which one is it going to be?'

She gazed at Sam. 'Is it very small?' she asked him.

He nodded regretfully. 'But I can find a bigger one,' he promised.

'No, no. This one will do.' Tentatively, she held out a palm and in the next moment a tiny spider dropped onto it, ran over her thumb and launched itself into space. She bent forward in curiosity. 'It's made a rope,' she exclaimed.

'That's how they make their cobwebs,' Jamie explained.

'Amazing,' she murmured, still gazing at the tiny spider hanging from her thumb.

Entering into the mood of things, Jamie dumped a large slug on her palm. 'Urgh!' she yelled, causing the boys to fall around in gales of laughter. 'Take it off! Take it off!' She was definitely hamming it up now, Jack realised. She may have overcome her fear of spiders but there were also her nighttime terrors.

'Come on, boys,' he said firmly. It had been a long day. 'Time for bed.'

They complained all the way up the stairs, eventually

quietening down when he finally tucked them up. 'Do you fancy Lara?' Jamie asked suddenly. Sam giggled, then stopped and waited for the verdict. They were studying him intently.

'Why do you ask?' Jack felt embarrassed.

Jamie frowned as if trying to work something out in his head. 'Well, Ian's brother Rupert fancies this new girl and when he looks at her, he goes red and smiles really weirdly. And that's what you look like with Lara.'

Jack blushed. Damn! Was it that obvious? 'Yes, I think that Lara is very pretty,' he began. Should he lie or tell the truth? They were still surveying him, making him suspect that this had been discussed at some length. He sighed and threw up his hands in capitulation. 'Yes, Jamie, I do fancy her.'

They smirked in triumph. 'But don't tell her!' their father ordered. 'She mustn't know.'

They nodded in complete understanding. 'Does she fancy you?' Jamie asked.

He shook his head. 'No, I'm afraid she doesn't.'

'Why not?'

'I expect I'm not handsome enough.'

'I think you're handsome,' Sam said stoutly.

'Thanks, soldier.' Jack smiled, bending over to kiss the boys in turn. 'Goodnight now. No more talking.' He switched off the light, left the door ajar and headed back down the stairs. To Lara. So far, the boys had acted like chaperones, but what would happen now they were out of the way? He prayed that he would not do anything foolish; it would be so easy to take advantage of her, now she was drunk.

She sat at the kitchen table, her feet bare and resting on a chair. He tried not to look at the gleam of satin skin along her thigh.

'Jack?' She leant forward across the table. 'I've got a problem. It's not just spiders that scare me.' She shot a fearful glance towards the window.

'Yes, I know.'

'Can you help me?'

He nodded. 'I'll try. Come on, let's go outside again.'

Once more, they stood on the driveway. 'The only way to overcome your fears is for me to prove to you that they are unfounded.' He looked up at the darkening sky. 'The bats are coming out.' As she made to dash for the house, he caught her arm. 'Stay. I want you to stand with me and watch them. Listen to them squeak. Did you know that they suckle their young?'

She shook her head, hunching her shoulders and nervously eyeing the black shapes flitting through the dusk.

'You see?' he said after a moment. 'They have no intention of harming you. Now tell me, what else frightens you?'

She pointed to the end of the lawn. 'Those bushes.'

'Bushes?' He was astonished.

'Yes. Last night I saw shapes moving across them, like hunch-backed men.' Her voice was shaky.

He took her by the elbow and led her forward. 'Look closely; see? It's just the breeze blowing through the leaves, making the shadows move.'

'Oh yeah, you're right.' She crossed her arms in front of her. 'Then there's the foxes.'

'They're scared of humans.' He laughed. 'They're even scared of the cat. Can you imagine anything being scared of that fat ball of fur?'

She giggled. Then she was silent, as if waiting, her gaze moving over her surroundings. 'I think it's working,' she said slowly. She looked up into his face, her eyes soft, her lips parted. What would it be like to feel those lips under his? He could hear her breathing, smell her hair, her perfume. He moved closer, his hand . . .

'*Daddy!*'

The shout startled him and he looked to the house. Sam stood in the doorway, silhouetted against the kitchen light. 'You've forgotten to brush my teeth,' he called out.

All at once, lights came on upstairs. Jamie waved from his bedroom window, and Rosie began to bark while the glare of headlamps cut through the blackness as the Colonel's car pulled into the driveway.

Jack gazed around at this sudden frantic activity. Now Lara was moving away. He wanted to grab her, pull her back to him and kiss her. They had come so close, so very close. She had been waiting for him – he *knew* it. Damn!

'Evening, Jack.' The Colonel banged the car door shut and turned to watch them approach.

Jack made the introductions. 'Colonel, I would like you to meet Lara Bayley. Lara, this is Colonel Stirling.'

The Colonel nodded watchfully, extending a hand. 'Delighted.' As she took it, Lara stumbled. 'Sorry,' she slurred. 'I'm a bit drunk.'

Jack saw the tension in the old man's jaw, recognised the look of disapproval. It had just been a matter of time before Stirling came to inspect his housekeeper. Trevor would probably be the next to arrive and mutter the usual dire warnings. They all disapproved – Patsy, Ernest and now the Colonel – but they need not fuss themselves. How could they imagine that someone like Lara could ever fall in love with someone like him?

Sam continued to wait at the kitchen door. 'Go back to bed,' Jack told him. 'We won't bother with your teeth tonight.'

As Lara reached the door, she ran her fingers through the little boy's fringe. 'I'll come up and read you a story in a minute, OK?'

'Yes, please,' he answered eagerly and shot off.

Jack felt sick with longing, knowing that he would never feel those delicate fingers brushing through *his* hair. Oh yes, Lara had been ready to kiss him but only because she was drunk. In the cold light of day, she would have remembered their kiss and cringed with embarrassment. Perhaps, after all, this sudden interruption had been for the best.

'Just come back from the Council Chambers,' the Colonel began, following them into the kitchen.

With a jolt, Jack remembered: the meeting on the landfill site. 'How did it go?' he asked anxiously.

'They've proposed two sites – one of them being old Matthew's. We're meeting down at the pub tonight to organise a protest group. I thought you'd want to come.'

'Definitely!' Then Jack paused, remembering Lara's night-time terrors. She would not want to be left alone. He turned to her, seeing the look of enquiry in her eyes. 'Do you know the meadow beyond the rope swing?'

She nodded.

'A company is proposing to turn that area into a landfill site.'

'A landfill site? What's that?'

The Colonel answered. 'It's used for dumping waste. If we don't fight this, Lara, there will be lorries coming up that lane every hour of the day. It's not just the noise and the destruction of the countryside, it's also the contamination by methane gas.'

'But they can't do that!' she exploded. 'It's beautiful down there. They can't spoil it!'

The Colonel shrugged. 'I'm afraid they can.'

Jack saw Lara stiffen, her face set with indignation. 'You've got to stop them! Jesus – I would!'

Jack was glad that she cared so strongly. 'That's what we're going to try and do,' he told her. 'I'm determined to buy the land from under their noses, but even if I do succeed, we've still got to form a protest group to stop them setting up elsewhere in the area.'

'Good!'

'So, do you mind being left alone with the boys so I can go to the meeting?'

She shook her head forcefully. 'Not at all. I'll be fine, don't worry about me.'

With a smile of gratitude, he left her there, standing in a pool of light at the kitchen door. Just like *his* woman. Well, he could dream, couldn't he?

'So that's Lara Bayley,' the Colonel murmured, accelerating as he swung the car out into the lane. 'She's prettier than her photograph. I just hope you're not taking a fancy to her.'

'Of course I'm not – she's here in a business capacity, nothing more.'

'I certainly hope so.'

Jack sighed. 'I don't know why you are all worrying so

much. There's no way in a million years she would ever consider marrying someone like me.' He gazed out at the fields, their furrows shadowed by moonlight.

'Well, I've got to say I'm glad to hear it,' the Colonel stated. 'She is totally unsuitable. First off, Ernest informs me that she doesn't know the meaning of fodder. Then Patsy tells me that she can't cook. Now, tonight, I see her drunk on her feet and done up as if for an ambassador's reception.'

'And she's scared of spiders, too,' Jack added wearily. 'Look, I know she's not suitable, but there's no point in raking over her faults.'

'Yes, old chap, you're right there. We'll just file this under "bad business", shall we? Then try again.'

No, Colonel, Jack thought sadly. You're wrong there. I will never try again.

Friday

Beatrix

'I can't believe it!' Astride her exercise bike, Kelsey peddled furiously, her anger fuelling her legs. 'I've every right to that apartment. Where am I going to stay now? The YMCA?'

Knowing that her friend was having a one-sided conversation, Beatrix allowed her thoughts to drift off. Last night, she had waited an hour outside the cinema. When Justin had finally appeared, it had been too late to see the film. He'd made no apology, as if his activities took priority over everybody else's.

It was beginning to annoy her.

Now she thought of Oliver and smiled, remembering her fear at that first sight of his motorbike. By the end of the evening, though, it was as if she had always travelled pillion behind him.

Yesterday, she had mentioned Big Ben. 'Let's go!' he'd

exclaimed and within minutes they were roaring through the traffic. For the rest of the day, they had behaved like sightseeing students, roaming the streets with no plans, no schedule, eating frankfurters from a street stall at ten in the morning, buying matching Union Jack bowler hats, feeding the pigeons outside Buckingham Palace. Yes, they had been like students, footloose and fancy-free. Living for the moment.

At midnight, they had gone to the Ministry of Sound, a cavernous place, dark and throbbing with music. Seeing it empty, she had presumed that they were too late but, on the contrary, they were too early! She had been startled when Oliver explained that the place didn't get going until three in the morning!

Then, in the early hours, he had taken her down to the beach at Barnes, the lights of London twinkling across the inky-black river as he escorted her into a rowing boat and pushed off. It was only when they were floating in the middle of the water that she discovered the boat didn't even belong to him! Exhausted with laughing, they lay back in the boat and looked up at the stars in silent companionship, their bodies rocked by the motion of the water.

'I've never been an escort before,' he murmured.

She looked at him. 'What do you mean?'

'Kelsey has asked me to be your escort for the rest of your time in London.'

'Oh.' She felt bitter disappointment knowing that he was only with her as a favour to Kelsey, not out of choice. 'You didn't have to.'

'But I wanted to.' He rolled onto his elbow and stared into her eyes. 'I think Kelsey is worried that some man is going to whisk you away.'

She smiled, suddenly shy of him. He was so close that her breathing quickened. Was he going to kiss her? She parted her lips, ready. Instead, he rolled away leaving her confused and disappointed. All evening she had wanted him to kiss her – and he'd had plenty of opportunity – but still he held back. Why?

He spoke as if to the stars. 'I'm going back to Nepal on Sunday.'

Her heart lurched. 'How long will you be gone for?'

'Six months. Maybe more.'

Six months! For some reason she felt gripped by a sense of panic.

'I'll be spending the first four months white-water rafting,' he told her. 'I'm setting up a small travel company specialising in dangerous sports. After that, I go on to Kashmir to organise a party for some Indian billionaire.'

She felt a strange sadness lying heavy on her chest, but she kept her voice light. 'White-water rafting?' she echoed. 'Is that when you take a boat down a river?'

He chuckled. 'It's when a boat takes *you* down the river.

White-water means the foam created by the powerful rapids. It's one of the most exhilarating things you can do. It makes you feel *alive!*'

Silence. From a distance, a barge gave a mournful hoot.

'I wish you could come with me,' he said softly.

The words were so low that for a moment she wasn't quite sure if she had heard them correctly. Then the meaning hit her like a punch to the chest, taking the breath from her lungs. He wanted her to go with him! That was madness! She would be extremely lucky, indeed, to break free from Castlemaine and settle down in London. But to start a life in Nepal? White-water rafting? Organising extravagant parties? It was laughable – and yet . . .

Kelsey's voice brought her back to the present. 'Are you listening to me, or what?' She had stopped peddling and now tossed her sweat band onto the floor.

'Yes, I'm listening.' With her head resting on the arm of the sofa, Beatrix watched her friend climb down from the exercise bike. As usual, Kelsey was on to her favourite topic: divorce/husbands.

'An attorney is the only person who can put together a twenty-thousand-word document and call it a *brief!*' The American girl joked bitterly, picking up her high-energy fruit drink from the shelf and slugging it back.

Beatrix sighed. Normally she would be enthralled by Kelsey's chatter, but today she could only feel listless.

Kelsey lowered the bottle, wiping the juice from her chin. 'What do you call that soft useless thing at the end of a penis?'

'I've no idea.'

'*A man!*'

Beatrix forced herself to chuckle. 'Have you heard from Lara since the head lice?' she asked, sitting up and rubbing her hands down over her face.

Kelsey took off her trainers. 'No, I haven't. She's probably too busy plucking chickens.'

Beatrix smiled. 'I'd love to be a fly on the wall.'

'Me, too. Well, this time, her fantasy has taken her over the edge. She's probably holed up in some shack in the middle of a field.'

'I hope not.'

'That reminds me. This Castlemaine place you live – is it a castle?'

'No, it's just a very large house.'

'And will you inherit it?'

'Oh no. It's been willed over to an old soldiers' charity.'

'Doesn't that bother you?'

'Not at all. I've always known that it would never be mine. Anyway, I wouldn't want it. It's too big. When Grandmother dies, I'll move into a small bungalow in the village.'

'What do you mean?' Kelsey cried. 'You're going to be married to your Mr X and living in splendour.'

Beatrix failed to respond.

'So.' Kelsey stood admiring her figure in the wall-to-wall mirrors. 'Has Oliver been showing you a good time?'

'Yes, he has.'

'You'll be safe with him,' Kelsey assured her, screwing up her face to inspect a back tooth, 'because I told him you're engaged to be married.'

Beatrix stared at her. Now she understood why he had not wanted to kiss her!

Lara

'Happy birthday, darling!' With a loving smile, Lara went down on one knee and threw her arms wide. Sam grinned and rushed into them. 'Six years old!' she said, hugging him tightly. 'What a big boy!'

She stood up and led him to the table. 'And you're going to have the best party – ever!' At this he smiled and she was glad, anticipating the look of sheer pleasure on his face when he came in from school that afternoon to see his Crushammer cake. Unlike all his friends, he didn't have a mummy to make his birthday special, so it was up to her. And Jack.

She helped the little boy into his chair. 'Rice Krispies?' she asked.

'Yes, please, Lara.'

As she shook the cereal into his bowl, her eyes strayed to Jack. With a jolt, she caught him staring at her with an expression of sadness. Then it was gone and he was smiling again.

'I hope you have better luck with the jelly than I do,' he remarked cheerfully.

She laughed at this. Anyone watching them would think that they were an established couple, very friendly and always polite; but it was a charade to mask something much stronger, something that neither of them could admit to.

It's Sam's birthday today, she told herself firmly, and I'm going to concentrate on him alone. She would refuse to think of Jack, refuse to dwell on that twilight evening when their lips had almost touched. Deep in thought, she reached for the butter dish. Jack had been doing the same and in the next moment their fingers touched. It was as if they had both been electrocuted, their hands recoiling in shock.

'You go first,' he offered.

'Thank you.'

She was exhausted with this display of politeness, dismayed by her feelings towards him. Had she wanted him to kiss her that night? Yes. But she had been drunk, she told herself. Drunk and scared, simply confusing love with lust.

As soon as she found her replacement she would leave. But this was not proving to be easy. Yesterday, she had interviewed two women sent by the agency in Dorchester. The first one had been matron-like; walking into the kitchen with an air of control and darting a disapproving look at the leftover pie sitting on the side. 'That should be covered in clingfilm,' she had muttered. 'Or the flies will get to it.'

The woman had waited, and irritated beyond belief, Lara had had no choice but to do something with the pie. She's a harridan, Lara had thought, peeling the clingfilm from its roll. How can I leave the boys with someone like that?

The second woman was young and very pretty with a freckled nose and a big wide smile. Too young, Lara decided before the girl had had a chance to speak. Obviously the irresponsible type. The boys needed someone who would *care.*

In the last few days, Lara had spent time talking to them, dismayed to discover that Jamie was desperate to talk about his mother's death. The accident had happened so suddenly that he still couldn't comprehend how his mother had been stepping off the pavement one moment and lying dead in the road the next. Lara had also understood that Jack must have been so deeply hurt by the tragedy that he had been unable to face up to his loss; blinded to the fact that his eldest son wanted to keep his mother's memory alive. Now it was up to her to discuss this with Jack, make him understand that his son was desperately reaching out for someone to talk to.

But she would not bring it up today. It was Sam's party that afternoon and everybody was going to be happy. The cake was scheduled to arrive at ten, after that there would be plenty of time to get the place ready.

'Would you like another cup of tea, Jack?' she asked, picking up the teapot.

'No, thanks.'

She filled her own cup and added milk. In the last two days she had been careful not to be left alone with him. She would leave his tea tray on the step of his studio, giving the excuse that she didn't want to disturb him. Evidently, this was fine with him.

They barely exchanged words during the day. Once, when she was hanging out the washing, she had noticed him sitting on a low wall nearby, a sketchbook on his knee. 'Hi!' she had said simply, before putting the washing basket on her hip and heading for the house.

Now she stood up. 'Who wants more toast?' she asked. Glancing towards the window, she saw the baker's van pull into the driveway. The cake! Going to the door, she turned to Jack, mouthing the word *cake*. He understood her silent warning and nodded.

Stepping outside, Lara saw that the van had come to a halt. A fat lady was now opening the back doors. 'I've made it sponge like Mr Havers wanted,' she said, and slid a square box towards her.

Lara took it in her arms. 'Thank you very, very much.'

'Don't forget this.' The woman placed the Crushhammer man on top of the box. 'I couldn't make it standing up, so I made it standing up but lying down.'

Lara nodded, wanting to hide the box. Quickly, she thanked the woman once more and dashed for the shed. Inside, she put the box on the table and opened the lid. What she saw made her heart thud. This was all wrong! This was no mean-looking android destroyer but an iced white sponge with a green robot shape stuck on top. With the broad smile and jolly eyes, it could have been a little girl's cake. Was this what all the fuss was about? Surely not. She glanced round as Jamie hurried in.

'Is this what Sam wants?' she asked him.

Jamie shook his head vehemently. 'No way. This is a baby's cake.'

'Oh God.' She threw back her head and gazed up at the ceiling. What a disaster! All this time, she had imagined that the cake would be a perfect copy of the model, with a grim face, metal helmet and jacket, air pipes and consul buttons.

Just then, Jack popped his head around the door. 'Oh Jack,' she cried. 'It's all gone wrong!'

He frowned. 'This is not what I asked for. I knew she wouldn't be able to do it.'

Lara could have wept. 'And this was meant to be such a brilliant surprise.'

Jack ran his hand through his hair. 'Look, I've got to drive the boys to school. We'll talk about it when I get back.'

As Jamie climbed into the truck beside Sam, he called out to her, 'I've forgotten to feed Charlie.'

'Don't worry, I'll take care of him.' She waved them off, then turned, picked a handful of ivy and went inside and lifted the lid of the vivarium and stuffed it in. If only life was as simple as keeping a stick insect happy!

Next, she brought the cake and the Crushhammer man into the kitchen and placed them side by side on the table. They were so unalike. In fact, if the robot had been red, he could have been Father Christmas!

With Jack's artistic talent, maybe he could repaint it? No, they would have to start from scratch. But they needed advice. Hang on – Beatrix was the ideal person for that. Lara tried her flat but there was no answer. Next she tried Kelsey and, after a considerable wait, the phone was answered by a drowsy voice. 'Hello.'

'Kelsey, is Beatrix there?'

'What?'

Remembering that her American friend was not her

brightest in the morning, she started again. 'This is Lara. May I speak to Beatrix, urgently?'

'She's not here.' Kelsey yawned.

'Oh, damn.'

'Can I help?'

Lara snorted. 'I don't think so!'

'I'm getting sick of you talking to me like this,' Kelsey retorted. 'After all the times I've helped you out of a jam.'

'This is not a matter of simply losing my lip gloss.'

'Try me.'

Lara suddenly had a thought. Kelsey had always wanted to be a sculptress – maybe she *would* have an idea. 'I need to make a cake,' she told her quickly. 'It's got to look like a robot warrior with airpipes and stuff.'

'Sorry, no can do.'

'But you haven't even given it a second's thought!' Lara yelled.

'Why are you getting shitty with me? It's the crack of dawn, for Christ's sake, and you're asking me how to bake a cake. Just because you're living some freaky farmer's-wife-fantasy doesn't mean you've got the right to shout at me. Anyway, how come you think I suddenly know how to bake a cake? Have I missed something?'

'It's not simply about baking a cake. It's more about constructing one. You've always said you'd make a good sculptress so I thought you might have some ideas.'

'Yeah, sure I wanted to be a sculptress, but I wanted to sculpt in marble, not Victoria sponge.'

Lara sighed. This was a waste of time. 'Look, I've got to—'

'Hang on,' Kelsey interrupted. 'What about Oliver's sister, Linette? She's got a cake business. The only thing is, she's usually got a two-month waiting list. When do you need it by?'

'This afternoon.'

'Oh.'

'Exactly. Listen, Kelsey, I've got to go. I'll speak to you later.' Lara put the phone down and leant back against the sideboard. On the shelf in the pantry she could see packets of plain sponge cake wrapped in Cellophane, a bitter reminder of the situation she was in.

Suddenly, the phone rang and she grabbed it. 'Beatrix?'

'No, it's me, Kelsey. I've got an idea. It's a robot, right? So, basically, you're going to have to create a series of building blocks – think of styrofoam cubes – which you—'

'A birthday cake is meant to be edible,' Lara said wearily. 'I should imagine a mouthful of styrofoam would probably kill the average kid.'

'No, you don't understand. If you've got chunks of sponge, you can use them like styrofoam blocks. All you've got to do is to cook about eight blocks of sponge and—'

'Oh, is that all?' Lara cried sarcastically. 'I'll just pop off and do that, shall I?'

'Do you know something,' Kelsey said slowly. 'I don't think I want to be your friend anymore.'

'Good.' How many times had she said that in the past? But she didn't have time to sweet talk her now. As she turned, her gaze fell on the sponge cakes in the pantry. *Blocks of sponge.* That was it!

'I mean it,' Kelsey was saying. 'You're horrid.'

'What was that you said?' Lara was excited now, swiftly trying to recall Kelsey's suggestion of a moment ago.

'I said, you're horrid.'

'No, I don't mean that. I mean about the blocks of sponge. When I've got them, what do I do next?'

Silence. Then: 'I'm not telling you.'

Lara tried to placate her, her voice dripping with sincerity. 'Listen, sweetheart, I'm sorry for being so horrid. Really. I think you're very clever and talented.'

'No, you don't.'

'Yes, I bloody do. Remember the time you did my face for the Egyptian Ball?'

'Mm.'

'Just tell me how to do this, and I will love you for ever.'

'All right,' came the petulant reply. 'You cut the sponge into blocks and then join them together by pushing those long wooden barbecue sticks through them. What colour do you want it?'

'Green.'

'Right. You buy this marzipan stuff, mix it with green food colouring and then roll it out thin, like plasticine and cover the sponge with it. *Finito.*'

'But what about air pipes? See, this robot has air pipes and consul buttons and a belt.'

'That's easy. You get your farmer guy – he's an artist, isn't he? OK, you get him to paint all those things in with food colouring. Easy.'

Lara paused. 'How come you're suddenly an expert on cake decorating?'

'I'm not, but when I get really, really bored I hang out at Linette's place and watch. Of course, they normally make wedding cakes.'

Lara chuckled. She owed her friend an apology. 'I'm sorry for being so snappy.' At the sound of the door opening, she turned to see Jack walk in. 'I've got to go, Kelsey. I'll phone you later.' Immediately, she grabbed a pencil and paper. 'Jack, I've solved the problem. Look.' She sat down at the table and sketched the shape of the robot, repeating Kelsey's instructions. As she spoke, she was alive to the fact that Jack had one hand resting on the table, the other hand on the back of her chair. So close, it made her tummy flutter while hot waves radiated out from her breasts.

'Brilliant,' he declared, staring down at the drawing. 'But we don't need barbecue skewers because I've got plenty of thin willow sticks. How tall shall we make it?'

'I don't know. What do you think?' She turned in her chair, lifting her face to his but he had taken the piece of paper and now stood back, studying it.

'Eighteen inches. Any higher and it's going to topple over.'

'That sounds good.'

'Let's get cracking.' He grabbed a handful of ten-pound notes from the jug on the shelf. 'We're going to have to go into Dorchester. Make up the shopping list as we go.'

Now that their plan was set in motion, she jumped up excitedly and grabbed her handbag. As she passed Charlie the stick insect's vivarium she saw the lid open and closed it quickly.

Two hours later, they returned with a bag of groceries, a pot of false eyeballs in green slime, a helium cylinder and one hundred coloured balloons. The man in the party shop had gravely shaken his head at these. 'You're going to need help blowing that lot up or you'll still be at it by Christmas!'

Now Jack backed in through the kitchen door, wheeling the cylinder. 'You've got an expert here,' he boasted. 'I'm the one who does the balloon race at the village fête every year.'

Happy and excited, Lara threw him a grin. 'So you mus be full of hot air!' He grinned, his teeth flashing whit against the brown of his skin.

Immediately, they set to work, Jack cutting up chunk of the sponges they'd bought and threading strips o willow through them, while Lara massaged green colouran into the marzipan. When the phone rang, it was Jack wh answered. He listened for a moment and then turned. 'It' your friend, Kelsey,' he said. 'She says we've to cover th sponge with jam before we put the marzipan on, otherwis it won't stick.'

Lara rubbed her nose with the back of her hand. 'Ca you tell her "love you lots".'

Jack repeated this into the phone. 'Lara says to tell yo "love you lots".'

Even at that distance, Lara could hear the squeal o Kelsey's laughter. How could she flirt like that, with a tota stranger? Didn't she have any decency? Lara was unable t make out what her friend was saying, but whatever it was it was making Jack laugh. A lot.

'Jack,' she called loudly. 'We've got work to do.' Sh was glad when he cut short the call and came back to th table.

'She sounds nice,' he commented, taking a jar of ja from the pantry.

Lara felt a dart of jealousy. 'She's married. Twice.'

'Twice?'

'I mean she's been divorced twice.'

'I see.' He had covered the sponge with jam and marzipan. 'Whoops – it's not going to stand on its own for very long,' he observed.

'That doesn't matter, as long as it's standing when Sam walks in.'

'Yes, you're right.' Suddenly, he grinned. 'I think this is going to work!'

Lara grinned back. In that moment, their eyes met. She felt the smile slide from her face, imagined what it must be like to have those lips press down on hers.

As if coming to his senses, he turned away sharply. Picking up a fine brush, he dipped it into brown food colourant and began to paint the details on the robot, adding white streaks to give a shiny look to the green armour. When he had finished, Lara added a cloak made from tin foil and strips of liquorice laces for the air pipes.

Gently, Jack carried the board with the cake on it to the work surface in the corner and propped it up against the wall. Then, side by side, they viewed their achievement. Together, they had recreated Crushhammer in exact detail.

'It's wonderful,' Lara breathed. 'Sam is going to love it.'

Jack turned to her and stuck out a hand, a triumphant smile spread across his face. 'Put it there, *partner*.'

She shook hands with him, feeling the warmth of his

skin, the power in his grip. Oh God, how would those hands feel on her naked body? 'Let's get the table set,' she mumbled, moving away.

After that, they worked in silence, tipping packets of Hula Hoops into bowls, making Marmite and cucumber sandwiches, laying out wafers and Iced Gems. When the table was set, they started on the balloons.

'Have you ever breathed this stuff?' Jack asked, detaching the nozzle from the cylinder.

'No – why?'

'Try it.'

She put the nozzle to her lips and breathed in. Nothing happened; it tasted just like air. 'It doesn't taste—' She stopped in horror. She sounded like Donald Duck! 'Oh, my God,' she shrilled.

Jack had also inhaled from the nozzle. 'Hiya babe,' he squeaked. It was so incongruous – this big, tough man talking like the Chipmunks that she gurgled with laughter. Taking another lungful of helium, she picked up Sam's bazooka and struck a pose. 'You're dead meat!'

Within minutes, they were falling against each other in hysterical laughter.

'Oh, hell!' she cried, realising she needed a wee – and fast. With tears streaming down her face, she dashed to the loo, hitting the toilet seat just in time.

On her return, she held a hand to her aching ribs,

gasping for breath but composed. Jack was waiting with his lips tightly closed, his eyes dancing with devilment, and she knew that whatever he said, it would set her off again. He thumped his chest, looking sinister. 'Me Tarzan,' he squeaked in his Chipmunk voice. 'You Jane.'

She screamed again, doubling forward against the convulsions that rocked through her body.

Eventually, exhausted and panting, they collapsed side by side on the sofa and wiped the tears from their cheeks. 'I've never laughed so much in all my life,' she told him weakly. As their eyes met, she saw his become dark and intent. His lips were so close – he was going to kiss her! A dart of excitement pierced her chest. But then he turned away. 'It's nearly two-thirty,' he said flatly, getting up from the sofa. 'And we've still got a lot to do.'

In bitter disappointment, Lara tried to think of Vittorio, tried to fill her head with him so that she could stop thinking about Jack.

Once again, they began their charade of aloof politeness, Jack blowing up the balloons in silence while she tied ribbon around them. She wanted to ask him what was wrong, but she already knew what the answer would be. He was attracted to her. He wanted to kiss her but feared her vicious rebuff. Perhaps she should talk to him, tell him she liked him a lot and wanted him to kiss her. But where would that lead . . . ? She must not promise something she could not follow through. She was here for one reason only: *Vittorio.*

From the corner of her eye, she watched Jack working. He was kind, funny, clever, and she was sexually attracted to him. But this was no single guy with whom she could slip into a brief relationship. If she committed to him, she would be committing to Sam and Jamie, the farm, the dog, the cat, the chickens, Charlie the stick insect, the pigs . . .

For a lifetime.

'I'm going to have to go and pick up the boys,' Jack said, standing up. He ducked under the ceiling of bright-coloured balloons towards the door. 'Just stop what you're doing and get changed.'

'I haven't got time.'

'At least wash your nose. It's green.'

'OK.' But she didn't bother, wanting instead to give the finishing touches to their arrangements. Then, taking a paper and pen, she wrote out the itinerary. In a way, this was just like a launch party at the gallery, except the food was different.

3.15 – Drinks reception. One carton of Um Bongo each

3.30 – Sam to accept his birthday gifts

3.45 – Musical Statues

4.10 – Hunt the chocolate

4.40 – Birthday buffet

5.15 – Photocall

5.30 – Birthday cake

When she heard the truck return fifteen minutes later, she was still in Jamie's stretch shorts, skull-covered T-shirt, flip-flops and apron, her hair tied back in a head-scarf. There were at least thirty balloons still to do but she would have to leave them. Jumping up, she took one last look at the table set with brightly coloured food, the banner with *Happy Birthday Sam,* the balloons, and the rabbit jelly. Then she took the itinerary out of her apron pocket. Right.

3.15 – Drinks reception

It was 3.20. Already they were running five minutes behind schedule. Suddenly, the door burst open and Sam came rushing in. When he saw the balloons he stopped dead. 'Wow!' he exclaimed. She waited for Jack and Jamie to come in and then said: 'OK, Sam, close your eyes. And no peeking.' Please God, she prayed, standing the cake upright, don't let it fall over. 'Right,' she instructed. 'You can look now.'

He spun round, the smile on his face slipping away to be replaced by an expression of awe, his mouth falling open in breathless wonder. Lara had never felt so proud of herself as in that moment. She had done it! Jack looked at her and their eyes met in a moment of triumph. *They* had done it.

Sam remained speechless. 'Do you like it?' Jack asked.

'Oh, y-e-s,' came the hushed reply. 'It's awesome – a billion times better than Cameron's. His was *titchy*,' he sneered, measuring a distance of ten inches with his hands. 'And it didn't stand up.'

'It didn't stand up?' she queried, exchanging a look of puzzlement with Thomas. 'But I thought it did stand up?'

Sam shook his head.

Although dimly aware of car doors banging outside, she couldn't move, reeling from this information. What in fact had she and Jack achieved – a miracle?

Sam stood inches from his cake, gazing up at it in reverence. 'This is the best birthday cake of my whole life,' he whispered.

Suddenly, the front door banged open and a bunch of chattering little boys piled into the kitchen, swinging plastic carrier bags. Lara went to the door to welcome the mothers but all she saw was a line of cars disappearing down the driveway. Obviously, they couldn't get away fast enough!

To her surprise the noise stopped abruptly and she swung round to see that all their guests – about ten of them – stood gazing in awe at the Crushhammer cake.

'C-o-o-l,' breathed a ginger-haired boy.

'Mega,' said another.

'I wish *my* mum could make me a cake like that,' whined another.

To Lara's astonishment, Sam turned to his classmates and shrugged. 'Yeah,' he drawled. 'It's all right.'

'All right?' She gazed at him in amazement. Jack was looking equally surprised. He caught her eye and shrugged his incomprehension, while his son swaggered through the crowd of friends, pushing them to either side as he made his way to the table. Here, he picked up a carton of Um Bongo, jammed the straw in his mouth, leant his elbows on the table and looked back at the cake with a jaded air. It made Lara think of a ham actor in some third-rate cowboy movie.

All the other little boys were staring at Sam, admiring his cool reaction, which caused Lara to bite back her laughter. Sam was behaving like Clint Eastwood!

Now their little guests huddled closer to the cake, their commentary very pleasing to Lara's ears. 'Look, it's got breathing pipes.' 'Yeah, and it's got a real consul.' As a small grubby finger reached out, Lara realised with alarm that one touch would send the whole thing crashing to the floor. 'Right, men,' she said in the voice of an Android Commander. 'It's time Crushhammer went to zap a couple of Spawn Warriors. What do ya think?'

'Y-E-S!' shouted ten sturdy voices.

With her back to them, she slipped the board into the

far corner and covered it with a tea-towel. Then she spun on her heel and jabbed a finger towards the window. 'Look! There he goes!' She held an imaginary death ray in her arms. 'Zap! Zap! Zap!'

A dozen pairs of eyes gazed skywards. 'Wow!' whispered a voice. Then all hell broke loose, the children screaming and yelling while imitating explosions and the crashing of jet fighters. 'Okay,' she said briskly, remembering their schedule. They would have to skip the *Drinks Reception* and go straight on to *Receiving Presents.* 'Listen everyone.' She had to shout to make herself heard. 'All presents can be arranged on the sofa here.' At this, brightly coloured parcels flew across the room and landed in a heap. Then the boys began to strip naked.

'What's happening?' she exclaimed in alarm.

Jack shouted across: 'They're changing out of their uniforms.'

She saw underpants patterned with jet fighters, Batmen, dinosaurs. Instead of starched white shirts and bow ties, they were now putting on scruffy jeans and T-shirts, which gave her an idea. If they were in old clothes, then Sam could use his Supersoaker on them. After all, it *was* his party. Sam was now ripping open his presents with a fearful urgency but was stopped by Jack, who put out a restraining hand.

'OK, everyone,' Lara shouted. 'Before we start, we will

have a welcoming drink and get a chance to introduce ourselves.' It was as if she had never spoken. All the boys – including Sam – simply streamed out of the back door like a swarm of bees.

'Boys! Boys!' she shouted, flapping her itinerary. 'We've still got Musical Statues!' There was silence. Jack grinned in wry amusement. 'They're just over-excited.'

In weary resignation, she tore up her itinerary and let the pieces flutter to the floor. 'Sod it!'

A warning cough from Jack made her look round. There on the doorstep stood a woman with stiff, lacquered hair and a prim, lipsticked mouth, her thin hands clutching a boy to her hip. 'I'm so sorry we're late,' said the woman, 'but we had to go home for Drew's asthma spray.'

Jack made the introductions. 'Lara, this is Audrey Trip. Audrey, this is Lara, my temporary housekeeper.'

The boy was thin and pale, his face stamped with an air of defeat. A mummy's boy, Lara thought. Poor kid. He wore a starched white shirt and a bow tie and it looked all wrong. 'Come on, Drew,' she said, taking his hand. 'Say goodbye to Mummy.'

The woman tightened her grip on his shoulders. 'Oh no, I'm not leaving. I have to stay to keep an eye on him. He's very delicate, you see.'

Lara sighed inwardly. This woman had no right to stay; she would cramp her kid's fun, she would cramp everybody's fun. One look at that white-collared polyester dress told her that Mrs Trip was a spoilsport; she would have to be kept out of the way. 'I'm so glad you can stay,' Lara said, handing over the packet of nylon ribbons. 'Could you tie the rest of the balloons for me, please?'

The woman took the packet, unable to refuse. 'You sit on the sofa,' Lara suggested, 'and I'll just take Drew to join the party.' As she led the boy away, she heard Jack say: 'Can I make you a cup of tea, Audrey?'

Out in the garden, she saw Sam and his guests down at the rope swing. 'I bet you like rope swings,' she said to the little boy by her side.

He nodded shyly. 'But I'm not really allowed to play on them.'

'Well, today you can.' Entering the mêlée of jostling, quarrelsome boys she threw her arms about trying to create order and was grateful when Jack arrived and took command.

'My head's spinning,' she moaned as they stood back to keep an eye on the orderly queue.

Jack chuckled. 'And this is only the first ten minutes!'

She groaned. Jack was looking down at her, his gaze mellow. 'I want to thank you for everything you've done today. You've given Sam a birthday party that he will always remember.'

'We did it together,' she remonstrated, noticing that his

lower lip looked dry. For a moment, she wanted to wet her finger and brush it over, softening it. He had so many problems in his life, she thought. It just wasn't fair. 'Do you think you'll be able to stop the landfill site?' she asked, gazing at the meadow beyond the stream.

'I hope so. It's ironic really. Here I am, converting to organic farming, and these people come along and decide to dump their waste right next door.'

'It just seems so stupid.'

'You can say that again. Do you realise that in a hundred years' time, people are going to look back and wonder how we could have been so shortsighted as to poison our food and land with all these fungicides and pesticides, and worst of all, organophosphates!'

'Absolutely!' In comparison with him, she mused, I'm an empty-headed bimbo who whines at the first sign of a problem. What did Kelsey call me? *Arm candy!* Well, she was certainly right about that. I'm weak, self-centred and completely hopeless. Then: No! she decided forcefully, I'm not completely hopeless. I've helped to make Sam's birthday a fantastic success.

'So you think Sam liked his cake?' she asked shyly.

'You bet. Wait until he opens your Supersoaker.'

'That reminds me: can he shoot his friends with it?' Seeing his doubtful face, she protested, 'It's a warm day and they're all in scruffy clothes. It'll be fun.'

'Well . . . all right.'

As soon as she heard this, she plucked Sam from the crowd and whispered in his ear: 'How would you like to shoot your friends?'

'Yeah!'

'Come with me.'

Sam skipped beside her as they hurried back up to the garden. 'Stay here,' she ordered and went in to get his presents. 'Hi, Audrey,' she said on passing. The woman looked up from knotting the nylon ribbon. 'What are you going to do with all these balloons?' she asked.

'I don't know yet. Let's think about it.' Lara returned to Sam and handed over his presents. First came the jar of eyeballs in green slime then came the rest of the tatto transfers. 'You've got to keep these secret,' she muttered. 'Or I'll be in trouble from your dad.'

When he saw his Supersoaker, he opened his mouth but no words came out. Miraculous astonishment had taken away his power of speech. He went straight to the tap on the wall and began to fill it up.

'We'll ambush them when they come up the hill,' Lara giggled.

But when it came to the ambush, she had not planned to be a victim. Within minutes, she, Jack and every boy there had become drenched. By now the screaming had reached unparallelled proportions.

It was inevitable, what happened next. 'What on earth is going on?' Audrey Trip stood at the back door, her face like thunder. Seeing her beloved Drew, she dragged him to her side and turned on Jack. 'This is a disgrace.'

Lara intervened. 'Don't blame him. It was my idea.'

The furious glare swung on her. 'Don't you realise that these children could catch pneumonia?'

'But it's a lovely sunny day.'

'You have a responsibility to these children,' Audrey continued, unbuttoning her son's shirt. 'I suggest that all wet clothes should be hung up to dry immediately.' She lifted her head to shout: 'All you boys, take off your clothes.' With alacrity they stripped naked and ran around squealing with this sudden and unexpected freedom.

Audrey had the peg basket and was now pegging up the sodden clothes on to the washing line. Reluctantly, Lara heaved herself over and began to help. On the other side of the bushes, Sam was secretly decorating his friends with tattoos. Ha! That will give Moaning Minnie something to moan about! Lara thought gleefully.

'Do you realise that your nose is green?' Audrey commented through a mouthful of pegs.

Lara felt rebellious. 'Yeah, I know.'

Audrey pegged up the last sock. 'Right, we need more towels.'

'There's some in the kitchen.' Muttering expletives

under her breath, Lara followed Audrey towards the house. Then she saw Jack throw his wet shirt over a low bush, revealing a brown back; a great pack of muscle shifting when his shoulder moved. Now he knelt down to break up a fight. At the sight of him, Lara felt strangely breathless, aware of a tingling sensation in her breasts. How she yearned to go to him and run her hand down over . . . Suddenly she fell into Audrey who had stopped.

'Look at Drew!' she demanded, pointing a finger at her son who stood shivering by the door. 'He's blue in the face.'

Yeah, Lara thought irritably. He's blue in the face because you won't let him run around with the others. As they entered the porch, she spotted the helium cylinder and, as a final act of rebellion, she paused, put the nozzle to her mouth and breathed deeply. This was going to give Audrey Trip a shock!

But it was not only Audrey Trip who was about to get a shock. As Lara stepped into the kitchen, she saw – framed in the open doorway beyond – a jet-black Porsche with the logo *Milano*.

Vittorio!

She could only stare in mind-numbing horror. Vittorio had come a day early! Suddenly, her brain kicked into action, instinct screaming at her to dive for cover. Safely hidden behind the pantry door, she peered out, while

Audrey stood in the middle of the room with her arms full of towels, her mouth open in bewilderment.

Pressing a finger to her lips, Lara shook her head furiously, her eyes wide in terror, trying desperately to convey her silent message, but would the woman understand?

Audrey frowned, baffled. At the sound of footsteps on stone, Lara tensed. If only Vittorio could be lured away from the kitchen, she could sneak upstairs and change.

'Oh, hello,' Audrey said in a voice of surprise. 'Can I help you?'

Lara squeezed her eyes shut in prayer. Please, Vittorio, don't come in. Please, don't come in. This was a nightmare. It was never meant to happen like this. She should be dressed in Prada and silk stockings, her hair elegantly drawn back into a chignon at the base of her neck, smelling of Rive Gauche and looking like a million dollars.

That husky honey-toned voice spoke. 'Hello.'

When Audrey answered it was hardly above a whisper. 'Hello.'

Lara realised immediately that Vittorio was having the same effect on the woman as he'd had on her.

'I have come for Lara,' said Vittorio. There was the sound of his footsteps coming closer. 'Is she here?' he asked.

One more step and he would see her. The game was up.

Smiling brightly, she jumped out, voicing her surprise and delight. 'Vittorio!' The word came out like a hyperactive Chipmunk. Horrified, she clamped a hand over her mouth and stared at him in horror. The helium! She'd forgotten!

His eyes were round in astonishment, his gaze moving slowly and inexorably down over her skull T-shirt, her apron, her leggings, her flip-flops and then back up to her headscarf. 'Lara?' he said. It was obvious from his expression that he could not believe what he was seeing.

She smiled madly, keeping her lips glued together. Maybe he would find it funny. Any moment now he would burst out laughing – just like she and Jack had done. But Vittorio's features remained grave, confused, bewildered. He looked so striking in his white jeans, his white monogrammed shirt, his skin bronzed mahogany against the whiteness. A breath of exotic sophistication against a backdrop of tatty English clutter.

Now he stood back and looked her over once more, his eyes staring aghast at her dirty toenails inside the broken flip-flops. 'Lara,' he repeated. He made it sound as if he were calling the name of a loved one who had died.

Silence. She had hit rock bottom. Nothing could get worse than this.

Suddenly, there was the distant hum of childish voices coming closer, and in the next moment the back door burst open and a dozen naked little boys rushed in screaming, their arms and chests covered in blood-and-dagger tattoos. They punched the balloons, threw themselves across the table and grabbed handfuls of jam tarts and Iced Gems. Vittorio had backed off in alarm and now stood in the safety of the front door staring around in stupefaction.

'We're having a party,' Lara explained dismally, not caring that her voice was back to normal.

She yanked off her headscarf. Oh, why didn't I get changed when I had the chance? All my plans are ruined! Turning to the mirror, she saw her eyes wild and smudged with mascara. With her dripping fringe and green nose, she looked like a madwoman. But she was meant to look like a beautiful and elegant aristocrat – not some crazy bag lady who talked like Donald Duck!

Bowed in defeat, she gazed around the room. Everyone had been right to label her hopeless, because she *was* hopeless. At this moment, she should be sitting elegantly at the table, helping two obedient and silent little boys with their homework while exuding firm but loving control. Instead of which, she had successfully turned twelve school boys into a frenzied mob of naked, tattoed yobs.

Pushing past a dazed-looking Audrey, she ran from the room, sobs breaking free as she dashed up the stairs. She should never have volunteered to stay here. It was all Timothy's fault. *And* Jack's fault. Hurling herself into her bedroom, she began to clean her face, dragging the cotton wool across her skin and muttering furiously. Next, she put on her cream-coloured cocktail dress, the one she was meant to wear tomorrow. She groaned. Why did he have to come *today*? Why hadn't he warned her? Did he assume that she would leap to his beck and call like some slobbering puppy? She kicked her flip-flops across the room and stepped into her Jimmy Choo sandals before quickly brushing her hair and slapping on some make-up.

Returning to the kitchen, she paused on the threshold and took a deep breath before sashaying towards Vittorio. *I am a woman in control. I can rise above any disaster.*

Jack was now talking to Vittorio at the front door, breaking off to bellow, 'Can I have some quiet?' Meanwhile Audrey Trip continued to stand in the middle of the kitchen, gazing at their Italian guest with a love-sick expression and seeming unaware of the chaos around her.

Side-stepping a grubby hand smeared with green jelly, Lara smiled benevolently, twirling a casual hand as she raised her voice. 'Audrey, you can take the children away now.'

The woman looked at her, surprised to be given such a high-handed order, but thankfully she complied. Within seconds, there was silence.

The two men turned to Lara. She didn't see Jack's expression – she was only interested in Vittorio. 'Sorry about that,' she trilled. 'Audrey does tend to whip them up into such a frenzy!'

With a broad smile, Vittorio looked her up and down, relief flooding his face. Then he threw his arms open in greeting. She had been forgiven. Thank goodness! She felt herself folded into his arms, heard the whispered words of endearment, smelt the fragrance of wealth. '*Cara mia*,' he moaned. '*Bellissima*.' Why did his voice sound so sugary? She was beginning to grow alarmed by this show of affection; didn't he want to keep their relationship a secret? Now his lips found hers. She had yearned for this – and yet, now, she felt awkward, not wanting Jack to witness this embrace.

Vittorio lifted his head and spoke over her shoulder at Jack. 'Isn't she beautiful? My Lara!'

Lara could not turn round, mortified that Jack had to find out like this.

'If you'll excuse me,' he murmured, and left the house.

Vittorio seemed surprised at this. 'Is there something wrong?'

'He's probably embarrassed that we're kissing,' she lied.

'Ah, you English!' Vittorio chuckled. 'No fire in your veins.' He pulled her into his arms again, brushing his damp lips over her forehead. 'I want you to pack a bag. Tonight I am taking you to a charming hotel. Oh Lara, I have waited so long!'

She stiffened, perplexed by her feelings of irritation. Why hadn't he telephoned to warn her?

'But first, I must view Penfold's work.' He smiled down at her. 'It won't take long, I promise.'

She lifted the muscles of her face into a smile. 'I'll show you the way.'

At the edge of the clearing she stopped and pointed. 'That's the studio.'

Vittorio raised his eyebrows and chuckled. 'The studio? It looks more like a dog kennel.'

Anger flared inside her. How *dare* he? Inside that dog kennel Thomas had created some of the most beautiful paintings and drawings that she had ever seen. She clenched her fists. Cushioned by his family's wealth, Vittorio could afford to be complacent. He knew nothing of hardship – unlike Jack Havers. Against all the odds, he had single-handedly brought up his sons to be kind and charming. *And* he cared about what was right and good. Because of his ethics, he had forsaken wealth in order to convert to organic farming. Now, he was facing the horror of a landfill site on his boundary land.

'What's the matter, *Lara mia*?'

'Nothing.' She turned away.

'You are not coming with me?'

'No.' She couldn't face Thomas. 'I . . . I have to pack,' she mumbled.

Back in the kitchen, Audrey was making tea. 'What a nice man,' she said dreamily.

Lara gazed at the birthday buffet, the scraps of shredded itinerary lying about the floor. She didn't know what to do. She was meant to be spending the night with Vittorio – wasn't that what she had wanted all along? So, why wasn't she running upstairs to pack?

Instead, she wandered over to the corner dresser and pulled back the towel to gaze down on Sam's birthday cake. Remembering Jack's silly squeaky voice, she smiled. Then she shut her eyes in anguish, knowing the pain he must be feeling at that moment.

She spun away and marched towards the stairs. They fancied each other, OK. And she felt sorry for him. That was all. She laughed bitterly. Their love had to be a helluva lot stronger than *that* if she were to commit her life to him and his children . . . and his farm . . . and his art . . . and the campaign against the landfill site.

Landfill site! Kelsey would laugh her Sergio Rossi beaded mules right off her feet!

On reaching her room, Lara threw a case on the bed and began to pack. Raising a family? That took commitment – and for fuck's sake, that was something she couldn't handle. He would be better off without her. They all would. Tonight, she would go with Vittorio and in the morning she would be back to organise a housekeeper. Then she would get say goodbye to the Havers family and walk out of their lives for good.

Her overnight case packed, she carried it downstairs. At that moment, she felt no desire for Vittorio but given time, it would be rekindled. Tonight he would make love to her and the experience would be so intense that she would forget her irritation that he had not telephoned, forget her anger at his smug complacency.

She found Audrey out in the back garden, sitting on the bench by the fish pond, a tea tray on the table beside her. There was the distant sound of children's voices. 'Drew has gone off with the boys,' Audrey confessed. 'What a rogue. This party has really brought him out of himself.'

Lara accepted a cup of tea and sat down, gazing into the fish pond choked with weeds.

The other woman leant forward. 'I hope you don't think I'm being nosy but I couldn't help noticing that our visitor seems very keen on you.'

'Mm.'

Audrey chuckled. 'And he's certainly got a sense of humour.'

Lara looked at her in surprise. 'What do you mean?'

Audrey gave a high girlish laugh. 'The way you carried on. He must think you such a card.'

Lara nodded once more, gazing down into the neglected pond. For a moment she could imagine fat goldfish lazily swimming in clear water. It was a shame that it was choked with weeds but Jack was too busy to care for it. *Oh Jack, why can't I stop thinking about you?*

'He's very handsome, isn't he?'

'Who?'

'Your Italian.' Audrey began to slice a Madeira cake. 'Here he comes now.'

Lara turned. Jack and Vittorio were walking towards them, Vittorio speaking rapidly while Jack listened, his expression grave. He didn't look at her.

'Oh Jack,' she wanted to cry. 'I'm sorry. I didn't mean it to happen like this.' Now he sat cross-legged on the lawn, picked a daisy and studied it. Meanwhile, Vittorio hovered, obviously not wanting to stain his white trousers by sitting on the grass, and seeing this, Audrey jumped up, snapped a towel from the washing line and laid it out for him.

'*Grazie*,' he said, giving her a lingering smile.

Lara saw how the woman smirked, one shoulder rising in coy shyness. Do I look like that? she wondered. Did every woman blush at his charms?

Jack!' Vittorio patted him on the knee. 'Your work is magnificent. Perfect for my autumn exhibition.' He smiled at Lara. 'But you must make sure he keeps busy.'

She nodded. Compared to Jack, Vittorio suddenly appeared undersized, his neck almost scrawny. And without the usual Armani suit padded at the shoulders, he looked weedy. And that voice – yuk!

Suddenly, Sam appeared, running over the grass. 'Daddy!' Two strong arms came around him as he settled on his father's lap. 'This is the best party ever!' he cried.

Distastefully, Vittorio swung his knee away from the little boy's feet. Unaware of this, Sam turned to him. 'I've got a Crushhammer cake!'

It was as if Sam had not spoken. Vittorio looked over his head and carried on speaking: 'Yes, Jack, I think we will be very successful.'

Sam looked abashed and made to get up. Now it was Jack's turn to ignore Vittorio. 'Sam,' he said, 'I just need to speak to our visitor but as soon as I'm finished, we'll light the candles, OK?'

The little boy nodded happily and raced off.

With a tender smile playing around her lips, Lara watched him go. Then she turned and fixed Vittorio with baleful eyes, fury coursing through her veins. How dare he ignore Sam, a motherless little chap who was just being friendly? Lara could overlook some of Vittorio's faults, but she could not overlook this.

As if a veil had been lifted from her eyes, she really *saw* Vittorio for the first time. The white trousers, the manicured fingernails, the gold neck chain, the long black hair, the smooth unblemished skin and the narrow shoulders. At that moment, he gave her a secretive wink.

She tensed, knowing exactly what she was about to do.

She was about to destroy everything that she had worked for. A part of her brain screamed against it, but she ignored it. When the general pleasantries began to tail off, she stood up and spoke to Vittorio. 'I think we've covered everything.'

He nodded.

'Shall we go?' she asked. As Jack made to rise, she put out a hand to stop him. 'You and Audrey might as well stay here.'

Vittorio got to his feet, bade the others farewell and followed her into the kitchen. Here, she turned with a sorrowful face. 'Vittorio, I have something to tell you. I cannot go with you.' Seeing his shock, she smiled sadly, knowing that she would have to tread carefully. After all, now that she was going to be living with Jack, they would need Vittorio's patronage. 'You need heirs, don't you?'

'Naturally.'

'That's something I can't give you. I'm hopeless with kids. You saw for yourself – I just can't control them. I would make a *rotten* mother.' She paused, seeing a flash of skirt. It was Audrey – eavesdropping! 'Audrey?' she called. The woman appeared, smiling innocently. 'I've just come in for a tea-towel,' she explained and hurried away.

Lara turned back to Vittorio. 'You deserve much better than me. I think we should say goodbye now, don't you?'

She held out a hand for him to shake; a brief ending to a brief romance.

He ignored it. 'You and Penfold are lovers, no?'

'*No!*' This was so close to the mark, she blushed furiously. 'What made you think that?'

Vittorio folded his arms and studied her. 'You are his muse?'

'No, absolutely not. We don't even *talk* to each other.'

Vittorio raised a sardonic eyebrow. 'Then, may I suggest you visit his studio. There, you will find two pastels, an oil painting in progress and an ink drawing. Of a woman.'

Lara pressed a hand to her heaving chest. 'Me?' she breathed.

He nodded, unfolding his arms. 'Goodbye, Lara.' He kissed her on the cheek. 'You are the inspiration to a great artist. How can I fight against it?'

He hesitated, about to say more but she put a finger to his lips. 'Go now before I cry.'

Stunned, she watched him depart. Then, coming to her senses, she clapped her hands in glee. She loved Jack and he loved her! It was all so simple. From now on her life – *their* life – was going to be a challenge, but she could do it! Now all she had to do was to tell Jack how much she loved him.

Then she had a better idea.

Grabbing a black marker pen, she wrote I LOVE JACK

across twenty balloons. Holding them by their ribbons, she headed for the back door. Audrey saw her first, shading her eyes against the sun, but Jack resolutely kept his back to her. Lara smiled, knowing the balloons would float gently across the grass towards him, engulfing him in brightly coloured words of love. Then he would jump up and run to her, swinging her up in his strong arms.

Grinning, she released the balloons but they did not float gently towards Jack; instead, they went straight up into the sky, over the rooftops and away. It had happened so quickly. 'Damn,' she muttered. 'Everyone in the Northern Hemisphere is going to know I love Jack – everyone except him!'

She would tell him to his face. 'Hi,' she said, returning across the grass.

Audrey's voice was cool. 'I thought you were leaving?'

'I didn't want to go.' Lara looked down at Jack, desperately wanting him to look back at her, but instead, he continued to curl a blade of grass around his finger. 'You see,' she whispered, 'I suddenly realised I don't love Vittorio. I love somebody else.'

Silence. 'Jack?' she pleaded.

Without a word, he stood up, put his cup on the tray and walked away.

'Oh, Jack,' she said in despair, watching him go. 'What have I done?'

Audrey looked stunned. 'Are you saying that you love Jack Havers?'

'Yes.'

'But . . . but don't you realise what that will mean? He's got a family. He can't just have some fling!'

'It won't be a fling.' Lara folded her arms, wondering whether to go after him or whether to give him time to cool down.

'He's got a responsibility to his boys.'

'And so have I.'

Audrey gave her a sneer. 'I don't think so.'

Lara grabbed the tray and headed for the house. 'It's nothing to do with you!'

In the kitchen, she carried the cake to the table and began to cover it with candles. 'Bloody woman,' she muttered. She would not upset Sam's party by having a confrontation with Jack. Not yet . . .

Fifteen minutes later, everyone was once more gathered in the kitchen to witness Sam blowing out his candles.

'Make a wish,' Jack told him, kneeling down to put his arm around his son. 'But keep it secret.'

'Can I just give you a clue?' Sam pleaded. 'It's about having a new mummy.' At this, his big blue eyes gazed up at Lara.

She felt a tear prick her eye. *Oh sweetheart, I want to be your mummy. I really, really do.* She yearned to go to them, throw her arms around them both – but she couldn't risk Jack's furious rebuff and an upsetting scene.

After that, Jack barely looked at her. When the last guest had gone, Audrey began filling the sink with plates. 'You two boys had better get yourselves in the bath,' she ordered, taking charge. Drew was happily watching TV in the sitting room waiting for his mother to take him home. 'Don't worry about the dishes, Jack, I'll sort them out. You heard what Vittorio said, you've got pictures to paint.'

Lara watched him go. Now was her chance. 'Audrey, I'm sorry about snapping at you earlier. I . . . I just need to speak to Jack . . . about his work.' Audrey darted her a suspicious look but Lara ignored it. 'I won't be long.'

She closed the door firmly behind her, and ran along the path, through the trees and into the clearing. Dusk had fallen, wrapping the shadowed trees in silence. From the shed roof a light glowed. He was in there. With hammering heart, she tapped on the door. No answer. 'Jack?' she called.

'I'm sorry, Lara, but I'm busy right now.' His voice was hard.

'I need to speak to you.'

'It will have to wait until morning.'

She pushed open the door. In the dim light he sat facing an empty easel. She closed the door and walked softly towards him.

'I'm busy,' he mumbled, making a show of wiping a paintbrush.

As she put a hand to his hair, he flinched. This did not deter her. Now she moved closer, bending down to kiss the nape of his neck. There was a low groan. '*Oh, Lara!*' Suddenly, he was up on his feet and staring down at her with eyes full of anguish.

She lifted her face to him, parting her lips, her gaze telling him how much she loved him.

As if in urgency, his great arms came around her and his lips crushed down on hers, making her want to cry out in pain. Desperately she tried to push him away but his grip only tightened. Now his lips were moving down over her cheek, her neck as his hot breath caressed her flesh. This was her chance to break free of him but instead she closed her eyes as exquisite tremors began to ripple up through her body. His big hand gripped her buttocks, pulling her into him and she could feel his hardness pressing against her stomach. This was too much for her. In one swift movement she slipped off her knickers. 'Fuck me, please, Jack,' she gasped.

His breathing was ragged, his fingers fumbling at her zip. In the next instant her dress slid down to the floor leaving her naked before him.

For a moment, his eyes roamed her body and then he dropped to one knee, his hot lips trailing a burning path down over her belly. His tongue found her clitoris and began to roll it, his hands squeezing her buttocks, pulling her hard against his mouth.

She could only cling to his shoulders, feint with the desire that flamed up from between her legs. She wanted to whisper his name, to make some sound to show her appreciation but it was impossible, her mind blown apart by the sensations raging through her. Suddenly, without warning, she felt an explosion rip up through her belly. A sob broke from her lips as she convulsed forward, helpless against the shockwaves contorting her body.

Tenderly, he carried her over to the old armchair and parted her legs. Then, kneeling before her, he entered her, hard and desperate. Once he had filled her, he relaxed as if savouring the moment.

'Oh Jack,' she moaned. Now he was moving out of her. She could feel her muscles moist but tight clinging to him. Then he was pushing into her once more. Slow and exquisite.

In the distance, she heard the sound of an engine, a car door banging. She heard the Colonel's booming voice, Audrey's welcome surprise. The front door closing. Silence.

Again, Jack pushed his thick, hard shaft inside her. Now he was moving faster and faster, in and out, cradling her buttocks with his hands. Then, with a cry, he shuddered and fell still, panting hard.

Serene and sated, Lara smiled luxuriously, knowing that she had given him pleasure. She felt a drop of his sweat fall onto her brow, smelt the musky perspiration of his armpits and closed her eyes in sheer contentment. This was her man.

'Oh, Lara,' he whispered. This was not spoken in a tone of triumph but in despair – as if he were losing her.

'I love you,' she told him, putting out a hand to touch his ear.

But there was no response as he drew away. Why wasn't he speaking words of love?

'I think we should go back to the house,' he said heavily, avoiding her eyes as he zipped up his jeans.

'Don't you love me?' she asked in bewilderment.

'Of course I love you!' The words seemed to be ripped from his chest. Gently he took her hands and pulled her to her feet, his eyes infinitely sad. 'Please, Lara. Get dressed.'

Stunned, she could only do as he asked. 'Jack,' she put a hand on his arm as he turned for the door. 'I'm sorry about—'

'I don't want to talk about it now.' His voice was low and very sad.

He was right. This was not the time to talk about it, Lara thought. They would talk about it tomorrow and then all their problems would be solved.

Jack

Jack followed behind her, his memory locking away the touch of her skin, her breasts, her lips, the soft moist tightness that had opened up to him. He had gone from despair to exultation. Now he was rapidly sinking into despair once more.

He blinked against the brightness of the kitchen.

'Evening, Lara.' The Colonel stood munching a piece of birthday cake. 'Evening, Jack. Audrey's told me the good news.'

Jack stared in bewilderment.

'About your visitor,' the Colonel reminded him. 'So, you'll be exhibiting in Milan? Well done! Capital!'

'Thank you.' Jack nodded, aware that Lara had paused in the middle of the room and was now looking back at him with big eyes, her cheeks flushed. 'I . . . I just have to pop upstairs,' she stammered, putting a hand to her hair. Then she was gone.

'Jack.' The smile had gone from the Colonel's face. 'Audrey has told me everything.' The moustache bristled. 'Lara and your Italian visitor are in love. Did you know that?'

Jack shrugged and sat down at the table, putting his head in his hands. Everyone could go to hell!

The Colonel had more to say. 'One minute she informs Audrey that she wants to take responsibility for the boys and, in the next, she admits she would make a rotten mother.' He shook his head gravely. 'This is a bad business, Jack, a very bad business. I wish your father was alive to talk sense into you. She's addled your brain, hasn't she?'

Jack gave a harsh laugh. That was a good way of putting it.

'I'm family to you,' Colonel Stirling insisted. 'I care. We *all* care. I just want you to wake up – realise that nothing could possibly come of this.'

'Oh, I'm sure about that,' Jack retorted, laughing bitterly. Then he felt the tears prick his eyes and he swung away. There in the back porch stood the helium cylinder, a reminder of how they had laughed like children. But they were not children . . .

'I think it best for you – and for Lara – that she should leave.' The Colonel's voice softened. 'I feel it's my duty – to you and to your father – to tell you this.'

Jack understood. Thirty-two years ago the Colonel had lain wounded by shrapnel in the Omani desert. It had been Jack's father who had dragged the unconscious body through the sand. Yards from safety, his father had been killed, the Colonel surviving. Seeing the sadness in the old eyes, Jack sighed. 'I understand what you are saying, sir, but rightly or wrongly, I've got to make my own decisions.'

'So what have you decided?'

'That Lara may stay for as long as she wants.'

'And will she? The girl is flighty,' Colonel Stirling insisted. 'We all know that. She might stay for a year, maybe two, but what then?'

Silence.

The Colonel pulled out a chair and sat at the table, putting a hand on the younger man's arm. 'You have always told me that the boys mean more to you than anything else in the world.'

'And they do.'

'So, answer me this: they have lost one mother – is it fair that they should lose another?'

Jack gripped his skull with his hands, feeling that his head would crack open with the pressure of anger, fear, sadness, pain. Then her words came back to him, as clear as if they had just been spoken. *Except you forgot to mention kids. Heavens! Any woman hearing that would run for the hills!*

'You're right, my boy, it's your decision.' The Colonel

moved to the door. 'We will leave you now. All I ask is that you talk to Lara, present her with that one question: "The boys have lost one mother – is it fair that they should lose another?" Unless you instruct me otherwise, I will be here in the morning to take Lara to the station.'

Saturday

Beatrix

With a thumping headache, Beatrix loaded the dishwasher. Last night had been brilliant. With Kelsey's support, she had hosted her first London dinner party. What a riot! And she didn't even have to prepare the food. Instead, Kelsey had insisted on hiring a sushi-bar conveyor belt. Her guests had talked, laughed, danced, played games and, then, at about two in the morning, the police had arrived and instructed her to turn down the music. The police! At her party!

She had come such a long, long way from that pale, timid girl.

Now the air hung heavy with the smell of alcohol, spliffs, cigarette stubs in cans of lager and expensive perfume, and against the door stood two black bin liners full of empty wine bottles. At the beginning of the evening, she had been astounded by the amount of wine and beer that kept arriving at the apartment. 'Oh, Kelsey, this is too much,' she had protested. 'You kidding?' Kelsey had answered. 'If you run out of booze at midnight, they're going to be baying for blood!'

And ice! The bathtub had been loaded with huge polythene sacks of it.

Beatrix chuckled, slugging back her glass of Andrews. What a night! Arriving early, Oliver had given her a pep talk, infusing her with confidence. Then he'd handed her a printed sheet of paper, saying, 'This will get you a few laughs.' They were jokes, some she couldn't understand, the rest she had memorised and repeated at the dinner table.

Q. How many men does it take to wallpaper a bathroom?

A. Three, if you slice them very thinly.

Q. What are a woman's favourite four animals?

A. A mink in the closet, a Jaguar in the garage, a tiger in the bedroom, and an ass to pay for it all.

Q. Why are married women heavier than single women?

A. Single women come home, see what's in the fridge and go to bed. Married women come home, see what's in bed and go to the fridge.

There was one joke which had her mystified, but she felt too shy to ask for an explanation:

> Q. How did Pinocchio find out he was made of wood?
> A. His hand caught fire.

With Oliver by her side, she sparkled. Most of their guests knew him, and eagerly asked him about his most recent travels. One or two of the male guests had seemed envious, deriding his freedom. Oliver had responded with a shrug. 'Let's just say I'm playing Indiana Jones instead of the Dow Jones.'

Beatrix chuckled to herself again as she picked up the wastepaper basket and tipped it into a black bin-liner. Then suddenly she stopped, frowning at a vague memory of a photograph in a wastepaper basket? Yes, a torn photograph of a man's face. Slowly the image came back to her. On the back had been written: *To my darling Lara, I will love you always, Justin x.* She froze. He had vowed to her that he'd never loved Lara!

He had lied to her!

At the sound of the telephone, she marched over and picked it up, her voice sharp. 'Hello?'

'Good morning, Beatrix.' It was Grandmother. 'I have a

little surprise for you. Daphne and I are coming to pick you up tomorrow.'

Through her tired, befuddled brain, Beatrix tried to make sense of this. Grandmother coming – tomorrow?

'Beatrix?'

'But—'

'We will be arriving at two o'clock promptly, so please have your bags packed ready for a quick departure.'

'I . . . um.' How could she phrase it? She couldn't leave. It was too soon.

Mrs Bayley spoke quickly. 'I've got to go, dear. I will see you tomorrow.' The line went dead.

Before she could even begin to make sense of this bombshell, the intercom buzzed. It was Kelsey. Moments later, she hurried in, whipping something out of a carrier bag. 'Oh, Beatrix,' she cried, 'wait till I tell ya!' With a grin, she held a calico apron up against her chest. 'What do you think?'

Still shocked and confused, Beatrix could only stare.

'You're the first to know. I applied to Chelsea College of Art for their life drawing and sculpture class – and they've accepted me! What do you think about that?' Kelsey waltzed around the room with the apron. 'I'm going to be an art student,' she sang, then: 'Hey! do you realise something? This is the only thing in my wardrobe that doesn't need dry cleaning!' She stopped and looked at Beatrix, her laughter disappearing. 'So, from tomorrow, I won't be able to see so much of you because I'll have to get a portfolio of work together.'

Beatrix sank onto the sofa. 'Don't worry,' she murmured, her voice trembling, 'because from tomorrow, I won't be here.'

'*What?*'

'I've just had a call. My grandmother is coming to get me at two o'clock tomorrow.'

Kelsey leapt forward, kneeling to take her hands. 'That's great! You're as ready as you're ever gonna be.' She gurgled with laughter. 'Boy – especially after last night. What a star!' Then she paused, frowning. 'Honey! what's wrong?' At the sound of the intercom, she stood up impatiently. 'I'll get it. Don't go away.' It was Justin.

'I thought he was in Tokyo?' Beatrix said drearily. She remembered the words on his photograph and scowled, angry and betrayed, refusing to get up and welcome him properly.

The next moment, he strode in, giving Kelsey a cautious nod but, for a change, she welcomed him with a smile. 'Do you want a coffee?' she asked, heading for the kitchen.

He nodded. 'Thanks.' He settled on the sofa beside Beatrix and put an arm about her. 'Hi Trix,' he whispered.

'I thought you were in Tokyo?' she responded coolly, irritated by this sudden nickname. It made her sound like a mindless puppy.

'I was, but there's been a change of plan. This is just a stopover. I'm leaving again tonight for New York.'

'I see.'

They were interrupted by Kelsey, who marched out of the kitchen with a mug of coffee in her hand. 'We should be drinking champagne,' she cried, giving the mug to Justin. Now she grinned at Beatrix. 'Can I be your bridesmaid?' she asked happily.

'Bridesmaid?' Justin echoed.

The smile froze on Kelsey's face. 'Didn't you know?' she breathed.

'Know what?' He swung round to Lara. 'What's happening?'

'I thought you'd told him,' Kelsey wailed.

Beatrix felt trapped. 'There's this man back home,' she began. 'He—'

'That's why she's in London,' Kelsey interrupted.

Justin looked murderous. 'A man?'

Beatrix nodded. 'I wanted to tell you.'

'I've heard enough!' Justin leapt to his feet. 'Bloody hell! There I was, thinking you were someone special, and all the time you were just leading me on. Deceiving me.'

Tired, angry and betrayed, Beatrix was on her feet, too. 'You can talk. You deceived *me!*' He recoiled in astonishment. 'Yes!' she snapped. 'You told me that you had never loved Lara – that it had been a one-night fling. But that was a lie. I found a photograph of you, and do you know what was written on the back? *To my darling Lara, I will love you* always, *Justin*.'

He threw her a contemptuous look. 'Well, at least I wasn't leading you on, playing you like a fool.'

'I wasn't playing you like a fool!'

'Ha!' he scoffed. 'And I cancelled a debriefing to come here today.'

'Well, I never asked you to come.'

'Well, that's good, because I'm going.' And with that, he stormed out of the door.

She heard his footsteps pounding down the stairs and the front door banging. Now there was silence. Beatrix flopped onto the sofa once more. Everything had gone wrong.

Kelsey sat beside her, putting an arm around her shoulders. 'I'm sorry, honey.'

'It's not your fault. I should have told him before.' She lifted her head and looked into her friend's eyes. 'Oh Kelsey, I can't go home. I just can't.'

'But why not? This is what we've been working for. Your Mr X is going to just eat you up.'

'But I don't love him.'

Kelsey peered at her.

'He's . . . he's *greasy*.' Beatrix's voice rose shrilly. 'He's got thin, greasy hair over a bald patch.' She swept her fingers over her forehead to demonstrate. 'And his mouth,' she shuddered at the memory. 'When he kisses me, it feels like a slab of dead haddock.'

'*What?*' Kelsey sat back in horror. 'But I thought he was a catch.'

Beatrix laughed bitterly. 'When you're the only man within a twenty-mile radius with your own teeth and hair, *then* you're a catch.'

'Oh, my God!' Kelsey was stunned into silence.

Beatrix was desperate to release all her pent-up fears and grievances. 'This is all my grandmother's idea. She's a miser, an eccentric. For thirty years she's had a running battle with this woman – Edith Dobbs.' Although Beatrix tried to sound coherent, her words tumbled forth, out of control. 'It's ridiculous! They fight over *anything* – the Colwyn Marrow Title, the Christmas Bazaar homemade-jam stall, the number of Christmas lights they can cram onto their front lawns.' She stopped for breath, shaking her head in bitter humour. 'Then, Edith's daughter pinches my boyfriend and Grandmother blows a fuse!'

Beatrix explained everything. When she had finished, she dropped her head into her hands. 'I don't want to go back,' she wailed. 'I don't want to be a seventy-year-old woman again. I want to be young.' She lifted her head and gazed at Kelsey. 'Do you know what I've been wishing all this time? That I could stay in London, go to parties every night and have the fun that I never knew was possible. Can I tell you something? Justin is the first man I've met who doesn't wipe the beer from his mouth with the back of his hand. Oh, Kelsey! I can't go back.'

Lara

'But I don't *want* you to go!'

'I know, Sam, but I've got to.' Lara buttoned his coat, steeling herself against the tears that threatened to engulf her.

'But why?' This was Jamie. He looked bewildered and unhappy.

'I've got my friend Beatrix, waiting at home for me. And, anyway, I was never meant to stay.'

'But we want you to stay,' Jamie insisted.

'Maybe next year, eh?' With the coat buttoned, she continued to kneel, gazing into Sam's eyes for the last time, memorising the little nose, the short fringe, the chubby jowls. Then she wrapped her arms about him and hugged tight, closing her eyes against the pain in her heart. 'Be good for Daddy.' His little body was stiff, unyielding. He was hurt, but could she blame him?

Now she stood up and looked at Jamie. Gosh, he had grown in a matter of days. He was nearly up to her chin. Gazing down into his face, she could see into the future and all the girls who would fall for him. But she wouldn't be here to see it, would she? She took a deep breath, refusing to give in to her tears and rested her cheeks against his. He, too, stood rigid, stubbornly refusing to believe that she was actually leaving.

'Ready, boys?' Jack stood in the doorway.

Dragging their feet, they followed their father out of the door. As they climbed into the truck, they waved sadly. Lara stayed on the doorstep, keeping the smile on her face even though her heart was breaking.

As soon as they had gone from sight, her face crumpled slowly and the tears rolled down her cheeks. She loved them so much. She would have made a good mother, she would have.

Sobbing, she turned back into the kitchen. Last night, Jack had talked to her in a low, sad voice, explaining the reason why he wanted her to leave. 'I love you,' he had said. 'But I can never offer you the life you want.'

'But you can!' she had replied, throwing her hands out. '*This* is all I want.'

'Maybe for a year or two, but what happens after that?' He did not wait for her reply, but asked the question the

Colonel had put to him first: 'The boys have lost one mother: is it fair they should lose another?'

'Of course not!' But the question had made her stop and think, made her doubt herself. For the next hour, he had talked, she had listened and in the end, it had been agreed. She would leave in the morning.

Now she sat at the kitchen table with her suitcases packed, waiting for the sound of the Colonel's car. 'I want to stay,' she whispered. Almost immediately, the doubts set in. All her life her imagination had carried her into a fantasy world. Then reality would strike and she would be left stranded. As a single girl that was OK, but as a mother . . .? She wanted to stay with Jack and his boys, but what would happen if this was just another fantasy? What would happen when the bubble burst?

She would break their hearts.

No! That must never happen. She would never be able to look after her little family here, but she could certainly look after them from afar. She would concentrate on promoting Jack's work. He would become rich, and thus able to spend more time with the boys. In fact – she brightened as the ideas came to her – she would ask Timothy to forward an advance of fees right away.

The sound of a car engine jolted her back to the present. She looked out of the window. It was the Colonel. No!

Suddenly she panicked and looked around wildly: once she had gone, she could never come back.

At that moment, she saw something hanging from high on the wall. Oh, no – it was Charlie. Dead. Caught up in a spider's web. Now she remembered. Yesterday, she had left the lid of the vivarium open: he must have escaped. Stricken, she gazed at his corpse. Then she saw the spider moving slowly along the ceiling and felt no fear at all. She simply wanted to take off her shoe and flatten it! But no. This was *her* fault, *her* responsibility. If she was incapable of looking after a mere stick insect, how could she possibly think she could look after a family?

Taking a scrap of paper, she wrote a note to the boys: *Jamie and Sam. I stupidly left the lid off Charlie's vivarium. Please forgive me. Lara. x.*

Miserably, she picked up her suitcases, and without a backward glance walked out of the door.

As Lara reached her apartment door, it opened and there stood Kelsey. 'Honey!' she squealed, kissing her cheek. 'Welcome home.'

'Hi.' As Lara dropped the suitcases against the wall, she noticed a package by her mail. In curiosity she began to open it. 'Everything OK?' she murmured.

'I wish!' Kelsey answered, glancing towards the bathroom.

Abstractedly, Lara removed a heavy book from its

packaging. *Delia Smith's Complete Illustrated Cookery Course.* On the fly leaf was written: *To Lara, I love happy endings. Your friend, Meryl.* Lara put the book aside. Meryl read too many slushy romances. Real life wasn't a Mills & Boous.

At that moment, Beatrix appeared, her eyes widening in surprise. 'Lara! I didn't know you were coming back?'

'I couldn't stay there for ever,' Lara said lightly.

Her cousin came forward to kiss her and as she did so, Lara couldn't help but notice how gracefully she walked, how confident her movements. That gauche, unattractive girl had finally vanished without a trace, yet Beatrix didn't look happy. 'How is everything?' Lara asked.

Beatrix looked down at the floor. 'I'm leaving tomorrow. Grandmother's coming to collect me.'

'That's a bit sudden, isn't it?'

'Yes.' Beatrix spun away. 'I've got a bath running – if you'll excuse me.' Lara looked after her, puzzled.

'Thank God you're back,' Kelsey muttered. 'We've got a problem.'

Lara took off her jacket. 'Why? What's happened?'

'Beatrix doesn't want to go home.'

'That's OK. She can stay – I really like her.'

'Let's go through to your room,' Kelsey said in a weary voice. 'I've got something to tell you.'

After Kelsey had finished, there was silence. 'But that's not fair,' Lara complained. 'She can't be expected to stay with Grandmother for the rest of her life. Someone else has got to look after that old bat.'

'Apparently there's no one else who can put up with her.'

'That's Grandmother's problem.'

'Yeah, I suppose, but Beatrix can't help feeling that she owes a lot to her.'

'That's a two-way street. Grandmother owes a lot to her, too.'

'Yeah, you're right.' Kelsey sat back in the armchair. 'Poor Beatrix. Do you know what she told me? She said she wants to be young. And she wants Justin.'

'Justin?'

'Yep.'

'And does he want her?'

'He did, until I put my foot in it.' Kelsey bit her lip and gazed into space. 'Do you know? I'm going to phone him tonight. Play Cupid!' Suddenly she put out a hand towards Lara. 'Hey, what's up?'

Lara had been lying on the bed, gazing up at the ceiling and thinking of Jack, unaware that a tear was rolling down her cheek. Quickly she brushed it away. 'It's nothing.'

'Bullshit! What's wrong, Lara?'

At this, Lara squeezed her eyes shut against the flood of tears. 'I love him. I love Jack.'

Kelsey hurried over and sat beside her on the bed. 'But I thought he had kids?'

'He does, and I love them, too.'

'You're way out of line,' Kelsey retorted. 'It's OK to have fantasies, but this is *way out of line.*'

'I know. Trouble is, I don't think it's a fantasy this time.'

'So, if it's not a fantasy, why did you come back?'

'He told me to leave. He fears that I will walk out on them sooner or later.' Suddenly, Lara swung off the bed, picked up her jewellery box from the dressing table and tipped the contents into a plastic bag.

'What're you doing?'

'I've just had an idea. I can sell these to raise money to help Jack.'

'But I thought you just said you'd split up?'

'We have, but I'm not having those boys living next to a landfill site.'

Kelsey was up on her feet. 'Stop it, Lara!' At the startled look on Lara's face, her expression softened. 'You're tired, sweetheart. Have a sleep – yeah? Then, when you wake up, we'll open a bottle of champagne, hit a few clubs . . .'

Lara stood there, tears trickling down her face.

'Oh, Jeez,' Kelsey muttered. 'You really do love this guy, don't you?'

Lara nodded.

'First Beatrix, now you!' The American girl rolled her eyes to heaven. 'What am I going to do with you both?'

Jack

As Jack entered the kitchen, Sam spun on his heels, holding the telephone to his ear, his little face alight with joy. Beside him, Jamie stood grinning from ear to ear. This was strange; when he'd picked them up from school that afternoon they had been silent, even morose. What was going on? He'd never seen them look so happy.

Sam held the receiver out towards him. 'It's Kelsey,' he said carefully. 'From London.'

Jack frowned. Kelsey – wasn't that Lara's friend? Feeling his heart begin to thump, he took the receiver and put it to his ear. 'Hello?'

'Hi, Jack. It's me, Kelsey – remember? Lara doesn't know I'm making this call, OK?' Without waiting for an answer, she carried on. 'You love Lara, right? And she loves you.'

'It's not that simple,' he barked. He couldn't prolong

this agony. For his sake, for his sons' sake, he would hav to finish this off, once and for all. 'I've got the boys t think about.'

'Sure, I understand that.'

'They have to come first.'

'Of course they do – but have you thought about wha *they* want?'

'It's not up to them.'

'Isn't it? So you don't think they should get a vote on this

'Well, yes, but—'

'Good. So come to Lara's place tomorrow. Jamie's gc the address and phone number.'

'But—'

'Just get here!' The line went dead.

Dazed, he replaced the receiver and slowly turned. Th boys stood looking up at him with wide, fearful eyes an bated breath. 'Lara wants to be our new mummy,' Sa whispered.

'Please, Daddy.' It was Jamie.

'No!' The shout startled him and immediately he put hand to his temple, appalled by his behaviour. 'I'm sorr boys.' As he knelt down to hug them, the door opened an Patsy looked in.

'Knock, Knock. Anyone at home?' she asked softly.

'Patsy. Come in.' Jack stood up. Why was she here? T have a go at Lara just like everybody else?

But he was wrong. 'So, she's gone.' Patsy's voice was quiet, almost sorrowful.

He nodded, looking away so that she would not see how upset he was. Patsy put the kettle on the stove and began to spoon tealeaves into the pot. There was silence, and he knew that if he looked down he would see two pairs of eyes pleading up at him. But he wouldn't look down.

'Daddy?' It was Sam.

'Please, Dad,' Jamie began.

'No! I'll find you another mummy, all right?'

'We don't want another mummy, we want Lara!'

This had to stop. 'But she can't be a proper mummy because – because . . .' he wracked his brains. 'Because she can't cook, she can't do the things a real mummy does.'

'But, Daddy,' Sam shook his sleeve. 'She makes the best birthday cakes. And she plays with us.'

'And she listens.' It was Jamie, his voice low and intense.

Jack paused, alert to this new tone in his son's voice. 'What do you mean?'

'She listens to me when I talk about Mum dying,' Jamie replied, his lips quivering.

Jack recoiled in pain, as if a knife had been turned in his stomach. Immediately, Patsy was beside him, a hand on his arm. 'Let's all sit down,' she said. 'I think we've got some talking to do.'

Bewildered and fearful, Jack sat, facing his eldest son and not knowing what to say.

Patsy put the teapot on the table between them. 'So, Jamie, you've been wanting to talk about Mum?'

Shamefaced, he nodded. 'Yes.'

'But you could have talked to me,' Jack pleaded.

'I tried to, but you didn't want to listen.'

'Lara says that I can talk to her, any time,' Sam piped up. 'She said she's going to empty her jewellery box and put all my secrets safe inside.'

Patsy sat down and gazed thoughtfully at the boys. 'And you both want her to be your new mummy?'

They nodded.

'Oh Patsy,' Jack cried. 'We've got to be realistic. I love Lara, but she can never be the mother that the boys need.'

'Oh? Why not? She sounds pretty good to me.'

'What happens . . .' he looked away . . . 'if she walks out on us. It's painful now, but imagine what it would be like after two or three years.'

'Who are you more frightened for – the boys, or yourself?'

He didn't answer.

'Very well,' Patsy declared, pouring tea into a mug. 'She can't cook, she can't dust, but that's nothing. What's important is she *listens*. She's got the imagination to see into a little boy's head and understand his fears.' She thrust the mug across the table towards him. 'Did she say she wanted to stay?'

'Yes, yes, she did, but—'

'Then *go*, Jack – go and find her!'

Sunday

Beatrix

This was like waiting for a funeral cortège. Her mind slipped back through the years, remembering the dim silent room in Castlemaine. The coffins of both her parents arriving . . .

Now she gazed at her suitcases standing ready by the door. Her mother would have wanted her to go back: it was only right. But the time had gone so quickly. She gazed around the room, seeing it for the last time.

Her attention turned to Lara once more. Since arriving back yesterday, her cousin had been pale and listless, moving around the apartment like a shadowy figure, tidying the magazines and dusting the mantelpiece. Now she sat in an armchair by the window, staring out at a distant point.

Meanwhile, Kelsey sat drawing at the dining table, a large sketchbook propped up in front of her. Apart from bright red lipstick, she wore no make-up, her hair pulled back in a spotted scarf, her calico apron tied securely. A new portfolio and discarded sketches lay about her bare feet. Every inch the dedicated artist. Although, in the last half hour or so, she seemed to be rapidly losing concentration. Once again, she glanced at her watch.

'She won't be here for another hour,' Beatrix remarked.

'Who?'

'Grandmother. She won't be arriving until two.'

'Oh, right.' Kelsey glanced at the telephone and then gave her a wide, quick grin.

Beatrix was bitterly disappointed in Kelsey, having expected her to show some sign of regret or even sadness that she was leaving. Instead, she seemed excited, eager almost.

Suddenly, there was a bang at the door and Kelsey nearly jumped out of her skin.

Lara glanced up. 'It's the removal men,' she explained dully. 'The man upstairs is moving out today.'

'Oh, right.' Kelsey regarded Lara anxiously. 'I thought you were going to change?'

'I can't be bothered.'

'But you look awful.'

Lara gave a sad laugh. 'Thanks.'

'No, I mean it. You look really awful.'

'Thanks!' Lara repeated more forcefully.

Kelsey persevered. 'Well, at least put some make-up on.'

'Why?'

'Because . . . because we're gonna have visitors.'

Lara shrugged but made no move. Her usual bouncy, hiny hair lay flat and greasy against her face, and her eyes vere swollen and red. Again, there was silence.

Kelsey fidgeted, darting Beatrix a sharp, nervous smile. 'I et you're going to miss Justin?'

Beatrix sighed heavily. He was now just a memory along vith all the rest. And Oliver? He would be driving to the locks at the same time as she was returning to Castle-naine. She couldn't think about it – it was too upsetting.

Once again, Kelsey glanced at the telephone. 'So, he lidn't phone last night?'

'Who?'

'Justin.'

Beatrix shook her head.

'What about this morning?'

'He'll be too busy,' Beatrix sighed. 'He's got some big neeting at his New York office today.'

Kelsey stiffened visibly. 'New York?'

'Yes, he went over yesterday.' Although locked in adness, Beatrix was beginning to question this interroga-ion. 'Why?'

'Oh, I just didn't know he was going away.' Kelsey sat ack, biting her thumb, her brow puckered.

Lara turned in her chair. 'You know, Beatrix, you don' have to leave,' she said. 'I love having you here. You ca stay for as long as you want.'

Beatrix smiled, her face lighting up briefly. 'That's kin of you, but after spending Grandmother's money, I feel ought to get back and help her win this particular battle

'Then you can come back,' Kelsey suggested hopefully

Beatrix shook her head. 'I can't desert her.'

'But surely there must be someone else who could kee her company?'

Beatrix gave a hollow laugh. 'Maybe, if she made a effort to be pleasant to people. But I'm afraid the onl person who will put up with her is our dear Reveren Beardsley.' Beatrix smiled fondly, remembering that ta stooping frame, the kindly eyes and the folds of ski hanging down from his face like a Bassett hound.

'So, who's living with her now?'

'Daphne, a girl from the village – but they can onl suffer each other if I'm there to referee.'

Lara sighed. 'It doesn't seem fair that after this wonderf transformation you should hide yourself in the country.'

'Oh, don't worry about that. I'm not going to be hidin I'm going to get out there – have fun!' She didn't admi that the only fun to be had was at the local barn danc

Lara leant forward. 'But since you're to marry Mr X surely you'll be deserting her then?'

'I'm not *marrying* him.' Beatrix shuddered.

Lara gazed at her. 'Are you sure about that?'

'Definitely. Why?'

'Well, Grandmother just happened to mention that she was collecting Bliss Bridal coupons.'

'What?' Beatrix sat up in alarm.

Kelsey hugged her knees, her brow crumpled. 'This is getting worse by the minute.' Suddenly her face cleared. 'How about if she thinks you're already engaged to someone else? That you've already got a fiancé?'

Lara took up on this, her pale cheeks touched with colour. 'Yeah!' she exclaimed. 'She's a miser, right? She's doing all this for free meat. So, say this new fiancé is also a butcher?'

'Or a baker,' Kelsey chipped in enthusiastically. 'I don't know about England, but back home the old folk go crazy for cream cakes. Does she like pastries?'

'Yes, actually she does.'

Eager now, Lara sat on the edge of her seat. 'OK, let's say you introduce her to your fiancé, who happens to be a baker and who is also prepared to send her a weekly supply of cakes? This would put her ahead of her rival, right?'

Beatrix nodded. 'But even if I do invent a fiancé, I will still be abandoning her.'

'But it won't upset her,' Lara insisted, 'because it will be to her advantage to see you off her hands. In fact, when she realises she's going to need a companion, she will more than likely start to behave herself.'

'That's true. But I don't know any bakers.'

'Oh yes you do.' Kelsey dug into her handbag, brought out her cellphone and began to dial whilst talking back at Beatrix. 'If this plan works, it will get her off your back long enough for you – and her – to sort out your lives.' She spoke quickly into the receiver. 'Oliver? Hi, it's me. I need your help. What, today?' She sounded dismayed. 'When? OK, but you've got plenty of time before you leave. It's to help Beatrix. You will? Great! All you've got to do is to pretend that you're madly in love with her. Can you do that? *You can?* Great!' She grinned over at Beatrix, giving a thumbs-up sign.

'Just be here before two. Ooh, and there's something else, Olly. I want you to pretend to be a baker who specialises in cream cakes . . . I know, I know, it's crazy – but I'll explain later. Just get here and act like her fiancé.' She slammed down the phone, grinning. 'He's coming straight over. Now all we need is an engagement ring.'

Lara hurried into her bedroom and came back with a diamond band. 'Which finger does it go on?'

Kelsey pointed. 'That one.'

'But what if she doesn't believe me?' Beatrix asked. She

was feeling helpless again, almost back to her old, timid self.

'Why shouldn't she believe you? If she's as mean as you say she is, this will work.'

Beatrix gazed down at the ring on her finger then looked up, appalled to see the expression on Lara's face. She, too, was looking at the ring, a fat tear falling silently down her cheek. 'Oh, Lara!'

Her cousin put out her hands, warding off this show of concern. 'I'm all right.' She brushed the tear aside with her sleeve. 'It's just . . . it's just . . .' She stood up abruptly. 'I'm going for a walk.'

Kelsey bounded in front of her. 'No, you don't!'

'It's only for a few minutes.' She tried to dodge Kelsey, but the American girl stood resolutely in her path.

They were still at it when a tap came at the door. Beatrix glanced towards the sound, assuming it was just another packing case hitting the door, but Kelsey was there like a shot, flinging it wide open. 'Hi!' she exclaimed.

Suddenly, to Beatrix's astonishment, a little boy of about six years old stepped in and looked around with big searching eyes. When he saw Lara, he beamed.

Lara stood immobile. 'Sam!' He rushed towards her, and now she was down on her knees, arms wide. 'What are you doing here?' she asked, hugging him.

'Are you going to be our new mummy?' he pleaded.

Now another boy appeared, darker and older, and he too raced towards her. As she hugged them both to her, she gazed towards the door, as if waiting for a third person. And there stood a tall, broad-shouldered man, his brown eyes coming to rest on Lara.

The little boy repeated his question. 'Are you? Are you going to be our mummy?'

Lara continued to gaze at the man. 'I don't know, darling. We'll have to ask your daddy.'

Two heads shot round beseechingly towards the big man. Without taking his eyes off Lara, the man nodded firmly. Then a huge grin split his face and he strode towards her. Suddenly, there were in each other's arms. They didn't kiss, they just clung on to each other, as if at any moment, they would be dragged apart.

'Yippee!' The boys began to jump about, whooping and grinning in delight.

In that moment, Beatrix forgot her own problems as she gazed at this show of love. Her Cousin Lara had found her man. And she was glad.

'Alrightee,' Kelsey muttered to herself. 'One down, one to go.'

Lara

Pressing her cheek to his strong, wide chest, Lara let the tears of joy well up in her eyes. *Jack, I love you. I love you so much.*

'Now we can have sweeties every day,' Sam chirruped.

She looked down, sniffing and laughing. 'No, you don't.' She moved out of Jack's arms and bent towards the boys. 'From now on, you're going to be doing homework as soon—'

'Oh, no!' they groaned in unison.

She laughed, then, interrupted by the sound of the intercom, she reached over to pick it up. 'Oliver?' she called.

A brisk, imperial voice answered. 'No, it's your grandmother.'

'Grandmother!'

'I do wish you wouldn't greet me as if I were the devil incarnate!'

'Oh, sorry. Please, do come up.' She pressed the entry button and swung round. 'It's Grandmother!' she cried.

Kelsey threw her hands to her head. 'Oh, shit!'

'Kelsey,' Lara admonished. 'No swearing in front of the boys.'

Kelsey made a face. 'Sorry, guys.'

'That's OK,' they chorused.

'So, where's Oliver got to?' Lara wailed. Now that she had found happiness, she was determined that Beatrix would have it too.

'I don't know,' Kelsey replied frantically. 'He promised to be right over. Maybe he's had an accident.'

Lara glanced at Beatrix. She stood there, ashen-faced and trembling. How could they help her? This was an emergency. They needed a fiancé. A man, any man. Jack! Immediately, she grabbed his arm. 'Sweetheart, listen, this might sound crazy but could you do me a favour?'

He grinned. 'You just name it.'

'We've got this plan. My cousin here, Beatrix, is in a bit of a jam. All I want you to do is to pretend to be her fiancé.' Lara smiled at his puzzled face. 'Also, I want you to make out that you're a successful baker and you make cream cakes. Can you do that?'

He nodded slowly, obviously absorbing the bizarre instructions that he had been given.

'I'll explain later,' she told him, standing on tiptoe to

kiss his cheek. She felt the rough texture of his stubbled skin and felt a stab of desire. However, there would be time enough for all that later.

Kelsey stood at the open door, ready with her all-American smile. The old lady ignored this and walked straight past, followed by a tall, freckle-faced young woman with a long plait and a wide, inquisitive gaze.

'Hello, Grandmother,' Lara said, coming forward to give the old lady a peck on the cheek.

'You're looking a bit ropey,' the old lady answered, squinting up at her with pale, milky eyes.

Stifling a grin, Lara turned to nod a welcome at the freckle-faced girl. 'Hi, I'm Lara,' she said. 'You must be Daphne.'

The girl smiled. 'That's right.'

Beatrix had stepped towards her grandmother and now made to kiss her but the old lady backed off sharply, obviously unaware of her identity.

Beatrix blushed. 'It's me, Grandmother. Beatrix.'

'Good heavens!' Those pale eyes nearly shot from the shrunken skull. Now she was looking her up and down. 'Goodness gracious! I don't believe it. Is it really . . . *you?*'

'Hi, Daphne.' Beatrix gave the girl a tender smile before hugging her, but Daphne stood stiff with shock. 'Beatrix?' she breathed. 'Are you sure it's you?'

Kelsey coughed loudly. 'OK, Grandmother. Take a good look at Beatrix and tell me if you're pleased with the result.'

The old lady was looking! She nodded dumbly, too astonished to speak.

Kelsey beamed in triumph. 'So, would you say that Lara's completed her side of the bargain?'

The old lady continued to nod.

'Good. Now, there's been a slight change in plan. Do you like cream cakes?'

Those pale rheumy eyes searched the room hopefully. 'Yes, as a matter of fact I do.'

'Good.' Kelsey turned to Jack. 'Well, let me introduce you to Jack Havers. He owns bakery stores all over the country,' she said impressively. 'And, you might be interested to know, he specialises in cream cakes.'

Mrs Bayley was studying him with interest now. 'Really? Excellent.'

Kelsey finished off with a flourish. 'What is more, he wishes to marry Beatrix. With your consent, naturally.'

With a nudge from Lara, Jack clumsily put an arm on Beatrix's shoulder, causing Lara to roll her eyes to heaven. Darling Jack couldn't act to save his life! The boys looked on, appalled.

Grandmother stood stiff. 'Well . . .'

Lara pushed their advantage. 'I bet your friends will be

so jealous when they hear you're getting *hundreds* of cream puffs – free!'

As Jack knelt to tie Sam's shoelace, he was unaware of the hard, suspicious eyes moving over his back and onto his little family. But Sam had seen it and now stood rooted to the spot in fear.

Suddenly, there was the sound of footsteps bounding up the stairs, and in the next moment the door swung wide.

'Hi, everyone!'

It was Oliver. He swept the room with a dazzling smile, strode towards Beatrix and, before Lara could stop him, folded his arms around her and gazed deeply into her eyes. Slowly, his smile faded to a look of love. Then, gently, his lips came down on hers. Immediately, Beatrix responded, her arms entwining around his neck. The next moment, they were locked in a passionate kiss.

Wow! Lara thought, impressed. You'd think they really meant it. Now, *this* was acting. In fact, it was Oscar-winning!

The silence was broken by a grunt as Grandmother poked Oliver in the back with her walking stick. 'I beg your pardon, young man.'

Oliver instantly broke free, turning sharply to see who was prodding him. The old lady lowered her stick. 'And who are you, may I ask?'

'I'm Oliver Marchant.'

Lara coughed loudly, trying to catch his eye to stop him but it was too late.

'I'm a baker,' he said pleasantly, extending a hand. 'In fact, I specialise in cream cakes.' He ignored the old woman's scowl. 'And I'm engaged to Beatrix.'

As Grandmother opened her mouth to protest, she was interrupted by a voice from the doorway.

'Trix! Darling!' It was Justin. Lara frowned in utter bewilderment; this wasn't part of the plan . . . was it?

Justin gave a perfunctory nod to the room as he headed towards Beatrix. 'Kelsey left me a message,' he said archly, taking her hands. 'I understand now and I forgive you.'

This was too much for the old woman. 'What is *happening*?' she screeched. Justin turned towards her in alarm. She poked him in the thigh. 'So, young feller, I suppose you'll be telling me next that *you* also make cream cakes?'

He gazed at her in confusion, and then quickly looked over his shoulder as if suspecting that she was talking to someone behind him.

She prodded him again, 'And, I suppose, you're going to tell me that you are engaged to Beatrix?'

With a grin he produced a velvet-covered box. 'Well, I'm just about to,' he snickered, opening the lid to reveal a diamond ring.

Oliver glowered. 'You can't!' he protested fiercely. 'She's already engaged – Kelsey told me.'

Justin patiently shook his head. 'No, dear chap. That was all nonsense.'

Wild-eyed, Oliver spun round to Beatrix. 'So you've never been engaged?'

She shook her head, her eyes wide and luminous. Now she looked down at the ring and then up at Justin. 'I'm sorry,' she faltered. 'I don't know what Kelsey has told you, but I do not wish to marry you.'

He looked thunderstruck. 'What?'

As Beatrix's gaze returned to Oliver, Lara frowned, puzzled by the soppy way that Olly and her cousin were staring at one another – as if they were in love.

Justin snapped the box shut and spun on his heels. 'Well, thanks a lot, Beatrix,' he sulked, stamping to the door. 'I've had to postpone my New York meeting for this!' Then he was gone.

'Daphne,' the old woman muttered faintly. 'Fetch me a chair.' She sat down and turned to Beatrix, her eyes glaring. 'I would like an explanation, young woman! I did not send you to London to learn how to behave like *this*! It's scandalous! Three fiancés, indeed. Where are your bags? We're leaving. Fetch them immediately.'

Beatrix moved obediently towards her suitcases by the door. This was too much for Lara. Someone had to do something. 'But she doesn't want to go back to Castlemaine,' she cried.

Grandmother looked at her. 'We are not going back to Castlemaine, Lara. We are going to St Lucia.'

There was a moment's stunned silence.

'St Lucia?' Beatrix echoed.

'That's correct.' The old lady's face softened. 'I'm sorry, dear, but I've got some bad news for you. I did not want to tell you immediately, but now I can see I must. John Chadwick was married to Susan Dobbs last Thursday and they are planning to move to Scarborough with Edith. I knew you would be upset, so Daphne and I – with all our Air Miles – have arranged for you to come with us to the Caribbean.'

Beatrix gaped at her. 'I'm not upset,' she confessed, overjoyed to hear the news. 'I never loved John. He was just a friend, a companion.'

The old lady seemed taken aback. 'Oh well, that's fortunate, isn't it?'

Lara stepped forward. 'Grandmother, Beatrix wants to remain in London but after all your kindness to her she feels duty-bound to stay with you.'

'No need,' the woman replied off-handedly. 'I'm moving into the bungalow soon. Won't be room for her. Save on electricity bills – especially at Christmas! *And* I can keep an eye on Reverend Beardsley's delphiniums.' As far as she was concerned, the matter was firmly closed. Now she frowned at Jack and Oliver in turn. 'I would like to know,

Beatrix – which of these two young men is your actual fiancé?'

Beatrix turned to Oliver, her smile radiant. 'Darling?' she prompted.

He came towards her. 'Why didn't you tell me?' he said fondly. 'All this time I thought you were engaged.' He took her hand and kissed it.

Grandmother gestured to Jack, who now sat on the sofa with the boys. 'And this fellow – who's he?'

Lara sank to the floor by Jack's knee. 'This one's mine,' she said proudly.

'That's right,' Jamie said firmly, as if daring anyone to dispute it. 'She's our new mummy.'

The old lady stared at Lara with incredulity. '*You!*'

Lara laughed. 'That's right. In fact, I could use those Bliss Bridal vouchers you mentioned.' In that instant, she pictured her father proudly walking her up the aisle and her smile vanished. 'What about Daddy?' she wailed. 'What if he can't afford to come over for the wedding?'

Silence.

Daphne cleared her throat and levelled a stern look at her employer. Seeing this, Mrs Constance Bayley glowered back, the thin lips set in a stubborn line. Lara realised that she was witnessing a battle of wills.

'All right!' the old woman exploded at last. 'I will help him.'

Lara stepped forward and planted a kiss on that wrinkled cheek. 'You won't regret it,' she said kindly.

Suddenly, Oliver gripped Beatrix by the arm. 'Come away with me. Now!'

'To Nepal?' She stared at him in wonder. 'Oh yes, Oliver. Yes, please!'

He grinned. 'The ferry leaves from Harwich at nine, so we need to get a move on. We can get your innoculations in Holland.'

Beatrix put a hand to her mouth. 'But I don't have my passport.'

There was a moment of silence. Then Grandmother patted her handbag. 'Yes, you do,' she gloated, obviously pleased with herself and making the most of playing centre stage.

Beatrix eyed the bag hungrily, relief flooding her face as the thin hand lifted out her passport. 'Oh, thank you, Grandmother. Thank you so much!'

But the old woman obviously wanted her pound of flesh. 'I trust you will marry my granddaughter?' she stated imperiously, frowning up at Oliver.

He nodded, but Beatrix shook her head. 'I don't want to get married.' She saw his dismay and smiled. 'Why tie ourselves down?' she said gently. 'Let's just have fun.'

As the old woman began to protest, Beatrix picked up her suitcases and made for her bedroom.

'What are you doing?' Lara demanded, rushing after her.

'Unpacking. I can't take Armani and Betty Barclay to Nepal, now can I?' She had thrown a case onto the bed, snapped it open and began to take out her clothes. 'I'll have to travel light.'

Kelsey had joined them. 'Are you kidding? What about this?' She held up a pink Versace dress. 'I chose this specially for you.'

'I'll be white-water rafting in Nepal,' Beatrix told her. 'I can't wear stuff like that.'

'You'll have to take something decent,' Lara warned her. 'Don't forget, Oliver is also going to be organising parties for multi-billionaires, so you'll need to look good on his arm.'

Beatrix paused. 'Yes, of course, I'd forgotten.' She saw Daphne, still hovering by the door and immediately ran to her and gave her a hug. 'Thank you so much for making me come to London,' she whispered. 'I haven't got time to explain everything now, but I will, as soon as I get back.'

Daphne smiled bashfully. 'I want all the gory details, mind.' Then she went back to the sitting room.

Kelsey had dived into the mound of expensive outfits, holding each one up in turn and frowning in indecision. Suddenly her arms dropped as she gazed into space. 'Do you realise something,' she said slowly.

Distracted, Beatrix and Lara looked up. 'What?'

'You two!' A grin broke through on Kelsey's face. 'You've *traded places.*'

Beatrix frowned, mystified.

'Think about it,' Kelsey exclaimed. She pointed to Lara. 'When this whole thing started, you were irresponsible, going from party to party, not a thought in your head. You were *arm candy*! Now you've taken on the responsibility of a family.' She swung round to Beatrix. 'While *you,* my young friend from the country, you were a Sunday School teacher with endless responsibilities. But now you've changed, you've become *irr*esponsible, flitting from party to party like a butterfly. And what are you? *Arm candy!*'

Beatrix stood absorbing this revelation. 'My God, you're right. How amazing!'

Lara raised an eyebrow at Kelsey's headscarf and apron. We're not the only ones who have changed, she thought dryly. Knowing there was no time to chat, she said, 'Come on, let's hurry, or Beatrix is going to miss that boat.'

'One glass of champagne for the road,' Kelsey ordered, rushing from the room.

Beatrix grabbed a handful of condoms and threw them into her case.

'Wow!' Lara gazed at her cousin in awe. 'Wild child, or what?'

'I've never used them before,' Beatrix said boldly.

'Oh.'

'You see, I've never made love before.'

'*What*? You've never had sex?' Lara sat down on the bed in shock. Then she sighed luxuriously, floating off into a daydream. 'Oh Beatrix, think of it. Your first time, ever. Making love under an Indian moon, with the fragrance of frangipani and . . .'

'I'm not going to wait *that* long,' Beatrix retorted. 'I'm afraid to say that it will all happen in Harwich. In the back of Olly's overland truck!'

Jack

With Sam on his lap and Jamie beside him on the sofa, Jack gazed around in bewilderment. Everything was happening so fast! Lara and her cousin had rushed into another room chattering excitedly. Then the American girl had followed, returning almost immediately and crying: 'Champagne! Champagne!' Now he watched her wiggle across the room in ridiculously high-heeled shoes, waving so wildly that the bangles around her wrists jangled. The man, Oliver, had pulled up a chair and was now talking in a low, soothing voice to the old woman, who seemed quite irate, frowning dangerously and protesting loudly, while the freckle-faced girl stood gazing around in wonder.

Jack too was totally confused. Within the space of five minutes, three men – including himself – had declared their wish to marry Beatrix. Good Lord. She must be one

of those wild London girls, who took drugs and partied a
night. The old lady must have a job keeping her unde
control.

Kelsey reappeared carrying a tray of glasses and a bottle
'There you go, guys,' she declared, putting two small glasse
in front of the boys. After she had handed everyone a drink
her vivid red lips parted in a grin. 'Cheers, everyone!' She
winked at the boys as she moved towards the sofa.

'So, Jack,' she said, inspecting him with keen eyes
'You're the artist guy?'

They were interrupted by a sudden commotion. Lara's
cousin was hobbling into the room with a suitcase. The
man, Oliver, quickly took them from her and headed for
the door. With waves and goodbyes and promises to keep
in touch, they were gone. Now there was silence.

He saw Lara come towards him with a soft smile, her
eyes full of love. 'Thanks, darling,' she whispered, snuggling beside him on the sofa. 'Remind me never to put you
in for an Oscar nomination.'

'Well, I just don't know. These goings on!' muttered the
old woman, shaking her head in astonishment. 'I've never
seen anything like it.'

Kelsey laughed. 'But your granddaughter is so happy!
What did you think of her appearance? She looked great,
didn't she? What a transformation!'

The old lady nodded her agreement. Then she turned

her attention to Lara. 'Even though my plans went awry, I did make a bargain with you, Lara.' She lifted a hand. 'Daphne, you may give it to her now.'

Daphne put her hand in a shopping bag and brought out a brown-paper-wrapped parcel and handed it to Lara.

'This is a gift to show my appreciation,' the old lady declared in ringing tones.

Lara sat straight, obviously puzzled as she tore off the wrapping paper. There emerged an ugly china dog with a gold chain around its neck and a moustache. She stared at it in astonishment, then turned to look at Jack. Their eyes met. 'Are you thinking what I'm thinking?' she asked. He nodded.

'It's lovely, isn't it?' her grandmother enthused.

Lara gurgled with laughter, held the dog's snout to her lips and kissed it. 'Grandmother, it's the prettiest dog in the world.'

'Talking about dogs,' her grandmother remarked, looking around, 'where's this Rottweiler animal of yours?'

Lara smiled serenely. 'He's gone, Grandmother.' With a look of love, Lara's gaze lingered on Jamie and Sam. 'Gone for good.'

The old woman bustled to her feet. 'We have an aeroplane to catch. Come on, Daphne. Goodbye, Lara. Goodbye . . . whatever your name is. I hope you two will be happy.'

Lara walked them to the door. 'We will, Grandmother. And thank you.'

As the door closed behind them, the American girl put down her glass and began swiftly to gather her sketches into her portfolio. 'Got to run,' she said.

Lara settled back on the sofa, putting her arms around Sam as he climbed onto her lap, a grin spreading across his face as he gazed up at her. 'Now you can wear Santa Claus earrings that flash on and off in the dark,' he said.

Kelsey snorted. '*I don't think so, honey!*'

Lara ignored this. 'I can do better than that, Sam. How about snowmen that sing?'

The American girl raised her eyes to heaven. 'Oh, Lordy, Lordy, spare me!' With her portfolio under one arm, she strode to the door. 'Well, folks, I guess . . .' She stopped at the door and looked back at Lara and her little family. 'We've got closure.'

And with that, she smiled her all-American smile and was gone.